Dear Reader,

Autumn is nearly upon us and with it the start of those longer evenings when you can curl up with the latest *Scarlet* novels. What a perfect way to spend an evening!

There are three fabulous titles this month for you to enjoy, including our second hardback *Finding Gold* by Golden Heart Award winner, Tammy Hilz: Jackson Dermont is on the trail of a thief and the mysterious Rachel Gold is high on his list of suspects. Is she guilty or innocent? In Kathryn Bellamy's novel, *A Woman Scorned*, we have a secret baby plot spiced up for the nineties, and in Vickie Moore's third Scarlet novel *Seared Satin*, security firm boss Tess Reynolds doesn't need any man's help until gorgeous Ethan Booker joins her to solve a deadly mystery.

By the way, is your collection of *Scarlet* novels complete, or are you longing for a certain title that sold out before you had chance to get hold of it? If so, feel free to drop me a line and I will ensure that your letter is passed on to the relevant department.

Till next month,

Sally Cooper

SALLY COOPER,
Editor-in-Chief – *Scarlet*

About the Author

Tammy Hilz has been married to her real-life hero, Steve, for ten years, has three children, John, Christi and Trevor and lives in McKinney, Texas.

After selling the computer resale business she'd shared with her husband, Tammy left the corporate world to answer the creative voice that had nagged her for years. Thus began her new career in writing, a challenge she hasn't regretted.

She's the author of *Dared To Dream*, which won the prestigious Golden Heart award and was a December 1997 release. Her second book for *Scarlet*, is *Finding Gold*.

Other *Scarlet* titles available this month:

A WOMAN SCORNED – Kathryn Bellamy
SEARED SATIN – Vickie Moore

TAMMY HILZ

FINDING GOLD

Enquiries to:
Robinson Publishing Ltd
7 Kensington Church Court
London W8 4SP

First published in the UK by Scarlet, 1998

Copyright © Tammy Hilz 1998
Cover photography by J. Cat

A copy of the British Library Cataloguing in
Publication data is available from the British Library

ISBN 1–85487–548–5

Printed and bound in the EC

10 9 8 7 6 5 4 3 2 1

To my children – John, Christi and Trevor – who are each characters in their own right, and think it is 'cool' to have a Mom who writes romance.

And to Leanna Wilson Ellis and Betty Seaman, the best of friends who encourage me to be better. And for always asking the dreaded question, 'what if . . . ?'

CHAPTER 1

'Are we getting divorced?'

Rachel Gold kept her gaze focused on the tarot cards spread across the mahogany table in the traditional Celtic pattern, and considered the woman's frantic question. There had been rare times over the past years that Rachel had regretted her decision to become a tarot reader, but when faced with having to give an unwanted answer she wondered if there wasn't an easier way to make a living.

Passing her hand over the Death card without touching it, Rachel felt tendrils of energy vibrate against her fingers. She lifted her gaze from the picture of an armored skeleton mounted on horseback to study her long-time, and troubled, customer. Anxiety pooled in Sandra Roberts' blue eyes, deepening the faint crow's feet fanning out from their corners.

Drawing hard on her filtered cigarette, Sandra blew a thin stream of smoke through her trembling lips. Her complexion paled, sinking to gray in a room bright with festive light. In an urgent whisper so the other guests wouldn't overhear, she

1

demanded, 'Well? Does Edmond want out of our marriage?'

A warning growl halted Rachel's response. Sitting in her usual position beside Rachel's elbow, Miss Bastet's remaining healthy eye narrowed to a scolding slit. The feline might have lost one eye to age and glaucoma, but her intuition still worked as well, if not better. And she always let Rachel know when she'd upset a customer. Running her palm over the cat's raised black coat, Rachel chose her words carefully. 'The cards indicate a new beginning . . .'

'Cut the bull, Rachel,' Sandra snapped as she leaned forward to douse her cigarette in a flute of champagne. 'You've always given me good advice in the past. Three years ago you told me to end my engagement with my fiancé and business partner because something better would come along.'

'That isn't what I told you, Sandra,' Rachel interrupted. She'd advised her customer to weigh her decision to marry carefully because Rachel had seen there wasn't enough love in Sandra's previous relationship to make it last.

The other woman waved her hand impatiently. 'Obviously you were right then because I did find something better. But you never mentioned that I might lose it.' Rachel didn't doubt that the tears pooling in the woman's eyes were sincere. 'Now, does Edmond want out? Yes or no?'

'The cards don't have the answer.' Knowing that wouldn't suffice, she added, 'They *do* tell me, however, that a part of your life will end, and a new one will begin. It doesn't necessarily mean

2

divorce, but perhaps a change in the way you approach your marriage.'

'I see.' Sandra's gaze drifted to the guests who kept a discreet distance from their table. 'Well, I'll give this some thought.'

Pushing out of her chair, the woman's frost-blue eyes cooled with determination. She managed a grim smile. 'Thank you, Rachel. I'm not always happy about what you have to say, but talking to you always helps. After all, I might not be where I am if not for you.' She skimmed her hands down her beaded gown. 'At least I know what I need to do if I want to keep my husband.'

As her client walked away, disappearing into the crowd of Dallas's elite, Rachel leaned back in her chair and closed her eyes as tension pinched her shoulderblades. Without having to think about the steps involved, she directed the rising buzz of conversation and the delicate clink of crystal into the background of her mind. The six-piece orchestra playing a Strauss waltz began to mellow and fade. The cloying scent of perfume dulled as her thoughts drifted into a meditative state. She searched for the calming space inside her, almost reaching it, but a persistent tingle at the base of her skull kept the traces of her last, difficult reading from dissipating completely.

Rachel frowned, puzzled by the unexpected tightening in her arms and chest. The coiling sensation spread to her stomach, making it flutter and twist in warning. Was it because of Sandra's reading? Rachel didn't think so. Long ago she'd learned to shield herself from her clients' problems, otherwise she'd be emotionally drained, and of no use to anyone. Although she valued Sandra as a customer, Rachel knew better than to worry about the woman.

Sandra's marriage didn't have to end in divorce, not if she took steps to save it. And Rachel knew Sandra had the stubborn wherewithal to get what she wanted. Three years ago, she'd been in a healthy relationship with a thriving business, only to decide she wanted more. And she'd obtained it by marrying Edmond Roberts, one of the wealthiest men in Dallas – a perfect example of how anything could happen once a person set a goal and reached for it.

Rachel's own history was further proof of how taking control, making choices and accepting responsibility could change a person's life.

'Goals are a wonderful thing, aren't they, Miss Bastet?' Rachel whispered. As if understanding perfectly and agreeing with her, the cat's purring escalated to an embarrassingly loud sawing.

Rubbing the cat's neck, Rachel took advantage of her few moments alone to scan the guests attending the Donaldsons' yearly pre-opera gala. She recognized several of her customers as well as a few she'd love to add to her list. Expanding her respected client base was the only reason she continued to give readings at parties.

Her customers hired her to provide amusement for their guests, as if she were a magician performing sleight-of-hand. But so much more was at stake. Each booking Rachel accepted meant new clients for her store, The Golden Pyramid, her metaphysical boutique that intrigued her wealthy clientele. And kept them coming back.

She didn't fool herself into believing that her customers respected her gift. Yet. But with time and patience – and she had both – she knew that would change. Each day, each reading, each time her predictions proved true they would believe a little more, look at her a little differently.

A satisfied grin lifted Rachel's lips. So much had changed in the last few years, not only for her, but for her mother and sister as well. Rachel had only been seven years old when her father had died, leaving them without the benefit of life insurance. With no family to turn to, her mother, who'd never worked outside the home, had done her best to support them. Each year had been a struggle to simply survive. The effort had cost them all, her mother especially, who had grayed and aged before her time. That was when Rachel's dreams had begun, gradually shaping into a vow to escape the hopelessness their lives had sunk into. Along with her vow, a need had been born, a driving, over-whelming need that burned like fire in her blood. She'd wanted more. No, not more. Better. A better life for her and her family.

With the turn of a card, she'd found that new life . . . and success. A success that guaranteed inde-pendence.

Something she would never give up.

Another prickling against her neck jarred her from her thoughts. Tilting her head, she listened, not to the music, but to the energy pulsing in the room, beneath it, through it. A vibrant hum sizzled over the flowing conversation. It shifted, tightened, changed direction. Then it dawned on her: *she* was being watched, studied actually.

From the corner table she'd been given to conduct her readings, she surveyed the marble and gilt ballroom. Twin chandeliers of Irish cut glass with crystal droplets drizzled soft light over a hundred or so guests, all wearing designer gowns or custom tuxedos. No one glanced at her; they mingled among themselves as if she weren't there. Not that she took offense. She wasn't a part of their world, nor did she want to be. Though she needed money to establish a secure future for her family, she'd seen how *too* much of it could destroy a life.

This glitzy, often pretentious world wasn't for her. She'd carved out a special place of her own. A place that was safe and real, and all hers.

Rachel tensed when the nerves along her spine began to hum. Miss Bastet ceased her purring, glanced at her, then emitted a small meow. 'Do you feel it, too?' Rachel asked, scratching the feline's neck. 'Someone must be very interested in us.'

But who? Rachel knew most of the guests, just as she knew most of their secrets and dreams, though she'd never divulge them to anyone. Reputable tarot readers lived by a self-imposed code of ethics. Rachel religiously adhered to those moral principles. They were, she believed, the one reason people with the most to hide trusted her enough to seek her out.

'Mind if I join you?'

Rachel's heart hitched in surprise at the deep-timbred voice from directly beside her. She glanced up, immediately noticing the man's mouth. Firm and full, his lips were tilted with an amused grin. Instead of softening his eyes, the effort hardened them to flecks of stone. His eyes, she noted, were the same honey-brown as the liquor filling the gold-rimmed snifter he cradled in his palm. Thick, wheat-colored hair was swept back from his fore-head and curled over his starched white collar.

There was a bored set to his features, a lazy insolence, which had to be an act, she mused, because she had the impression of . . . of . . . anger? . . . swirling like liquid heat beneath his cool surface. His hard jaw flexed, the movement subtle but telling. He was anxious, edgy. She could feel the roughness in him as surely as she could feel her own heartbeat.

Never having seen him before, her curiosity became as precarious as Miss Bastet's. Inquisitive-ness was her one true fault: her need to delve into a puzzle until she found the answer. Her mother, Emily, repeatedly warned that Rachel's nosing into other people's lives would be the ruin of her. Rachel knew better. She'd turned a liability into an asset. Her curiosity, her ability to tune into people's emotions, made her one of the best in her profession.

Realizing she was staring, she cleared her throat and indicated the empty chair with her hand. 'Please, have a seat.'

In a graceful move that bordered on the preda-tory, and which she found fascinating to watch, he settled in the upholstered high-back across from her. Her gaze swept over his impeccable double-breasted tux that failed to conceal the intensity she sensed honing his trim, unquestionably male body. Miss Bastet rose and crossed the table to him, carefully avoiding the cards. She stepped on the chair's arm, then put her nose up to the strange man's face and sniffed.

Rachel suppressed a grin as he flinched back in surprise. He glanced at her, his brow raised in question. Rachel sensed he wouldn't understand or appreciate Miss Bastet's habit of inspecting each new customer, but she had to say something. 'It's her way of saying hello.'

'I see.' With a grin that did little to ease the hard planes of his face, he gave the cat a scratch beneath the chin. Miss Bastet scooted back out of his reach and turned away. Meowing testily, she settled her ample weight beside Rachel's arm as if she were the one to conduct the reading.

Rachel didn't have time to wonder about the cat's strange response. The fine hairs on her neck lifted as the man's gaze slid over her, examining her. The same wary tingle she'd experienced before rushed down her spine. So, he'd been the one watching her. Why? Perhaps he wanted a reading but was too embarrassed to seem interested? He wouldn't be the first man to feel uncomfortable with her line of work. 'Would you care for a reading, Mr . . .?'

'Dermont. Jackson Dermont.' His intense stare never flickered, unsettling her. 'You tell me. Do I want a reading?'

'I'm a tarot reader, not a psychic.' Her attempt to smile, lighten the suddenly strained mood, failed. She realized he might be dressed as elegantly as any other millionaire in the room, but the similarities ended there. It wasn't just the deep, rasping texture of his voice that separated him, but the uncut ruggedness beneath his smooth edges. He was an enigma; one she felt compelled to explore.

She picked up the oversized deck and, following her instincts, searched for a specific card. Finding it, she laid it in the center of the table, then handed the remainder to him. 'If you will shuffle these, Mr Dermont . . .'

'Jackson,' he interrupted as he set down his drink and took the cards. Pointing to the one on the table, he asked, 'What's that one for?'

Rachel didn't glance at the King of Swords. The formidable card represented a man capable of command, yet remained guarded, suspicious of those around him. All the qualities she sensed in Jackson Dermont. 'It's you.'

'I should warn you, I don't believe in these things.'

Undaunted, she gave him an understanding smile. 'Most people don't . . . at first.'

'You think you can change my mind?' A wicked challenge flared behind his steady brown eyes.

She tilted her chin, more than ready to accept his challenge and open his mind. 'While you're mixing them, think of a question you'd like to ask.'

Her new, disbelieving customer split the deck into

two stacks, bowed them with his fingers and began shuffling them like a regular deck.

'Not like that.' Afraid he might damage them, Rachel reached across the table and put her hand over his. An invisible jolt made her breath hitched to a stop. Her gaze snapped to his, which narrowed, burrowing into hers until she felt her skin burn.

Straightening slowly, trying to discern her response, and his, she pulled her hand back. Tingling energy passed through her fingers, like tiny aftershocks, spiraling upward through her veins. Clenching her hand into a fist, she pressed it into her lap.

He held so still, his eyes hot and vibrant, that she wanted to squirm. She couldn't tell if he was displeased that she'd touched him or if he'd experienced the same . . . whatever it had been. Her glimpse of his emotion ended as quickly as it had begun. His eyes turned cool, unreadable, allowing her to sense nothing but a cold, impenetrable wall, which puzzled her. While she couldn't read people's minds, their emotions were usually an open book to her. All she had to do was look.

Studying him, she realized Jackson Dermont's emotions were like the reflection in a mirror. The images were there; she could see them, but she couldn't feel him, interpret his mood into something real and tangible. Or explicable.

Then it dawned on her. Her inability to sense him had nothing to do with him, but with her. Somehow she'd let a customer affect her in a way she'd never allowed before. She didn't understand the reason for this change, but she'd think about it. Later.

She had to swallow to continue. 'Tarot cards are like an expensive Bordeaux, Mr Dermont. Both must be treated gently or their value will be ruined.'

He laughed softly, a low, seductive sound that made her cheeks flush with warmth. 'You don't say.'

'Separate the cards into three stacks, then choose one.' After he'd finished, she gathered the cards. 'Have you thought of a question you want answered?'

'What's your name?' His fleeting smile was beguiling, and completely false – she was sure of it.

She sighed, annoyed that he could affect her so easily. She'd dealt with non-believers before, and had repeatedly proved her skills weren't a hoax. But Jackson Dermont was flirting with her, or at least, in her limited experience, she thought he might be. For no other reason than to amuse himself, she thought, aggravated. She didn't entertain the idea of teasing him back.

She couldn't interpret the cards correctly with that kind of distraction . . . or annoyance breaking her concentration. And at present, she felt a little of both. Drawing one deep breath after another, she searched for her quiet place. She waited for the tension to ease from her shoulders, the knotted muscles in her back to loosen. A slight fluttering worked its way up her fingers, but any semblance of calm remained just beyond her grasp. Giving up the effort, she pressed her lips together, then said, 'My name is Rachel Gold.'

'Rachel.' He repeated her name as if he'd heard it before but had forgotten. 'You don't really believe in this nonsense, do you?'

She couldn't stop her chin from jutting out. 'I wouldn't be here if I didn't, Mr Dermont.'

'Jackson.'

'Do you have another question you'd like to ask?'

'The woman you were talking to earlier, what did you tell her?'

Frowning, Rachel glanced at the surrounding crowd, but didn't see Sandra Roberts. Why would he want to know about her? 'I don't discuss my clients.'

He gave her a maddening grin. 'Customer confidentiality? I can appreciate that.'

His smooth tone set her teeth on edge. 'Do you have another question?'

He leaned back, laced his fingers at his waist and crossed his outstretched legs at the ankle. On him, the relaxed pose seemed threatening. 'Yes, I do.'

'And would you care to share it with me?'

'No, I wouldn't.'

Feeling the return of her exasperation, she explained, 'Your reading will be more complete if you tell me what you'd like to know.'

His doubting smirk made her more determined than ever to give him a reading he wouldn't forget.

'Very well.' Though it took greater effort than she'd have ever believed, she channeled her thoughts off his presence and turned her attention to the task ahead. She laid one card over the King of Swords. The Moon. Resisting the urge to frown, she laid out the rest of the cards, ten in all, then set the deck down to study the layout.

After a few moments of heavy silence, Jackson drawled, 'I take it they spell bad news.'

She met his teasing gaze. 'Not at all. They're interesting, but not bad. The overall atmosphere is one of unforeseen . . .' *deception*, she almost said, then changed it at the last second to '. . . complications.'

Having reached for his drink, he paused. Rachel noticed his hand – large, fairly smooth, with strong tendons beneath tanned skin. Working hands . . . not pampered.

'You don't think complications can be bad, Rachel?'

She realized his voice held the same qualities as his hand: a hint of refinement on the surface, yet underneath lay a force she wouldn't want to challenge. 'The other cards indicate you must prepare for what lies ahead. You lost someone, or perhaps something, in the past that meant a great deal to you. The event changed your life.'

Catching his slight tensing, she indicated the Four of Swords where a knight lay in repose in his tomb. 'The incident made you retreat, to do some soul-searching, if you will. Which has led you to your current state.'

'Let me guess. My soul is in sorry shape, and if I want to live happily ever after I'd better get my act together?'

Though his statement was derogatory, he sat forward to lean his arms on the table and study the layout with her. He might not believe her yet, but she'd definitely captured his attention. Rachel's small grin faltered when she caught his scent. Not cologne, she realized, but something deeper, wilder. Something . . . male.

'I don't know about your soul, Jackson,' she said, uncomfortable with using his first name. Which made little sense. She was on a first-name basis with most of her customers. Jackson shouldn't be any different. But even in a crowded room, using his name seemed too intimate, and a little dangerous.

Intimacy was something she'd managed to avoid for twenty-eight years. Using the word in connection with the unsettling man across from her, it held a connotation of things raw and violent and passionate . . . things she could give advice on, but wasn't equipped to deal with on a personal level. Something inside the man blared the warning: don't touch or you'll be burned.

Rachel mentally shook herself. What was she thinking? He was a client. And she had a strict rule: she never, *ever* became involved with a customer. There wouldn't be intimacy between her and Jackson – passionate or otherwise.

She picked up the Seven of Pentacles, struggling to interpret it. She sensed a dilemma clouding his life, but she couldn't quite grasp it. The clue to his persona hovered just out of her reach, like a shadow, vague and distorted. 'You have the opportunity to find happiness, but it won't come easily. You'll have to fight for it.'

'Who doesn't have to fight for a little happiness in life?'

'The battle will be within yourself,' she said softly, to which she received no reply.

He pointed to the High Priestess. 'What about this one?'

Rachel bit the inside of her cheek as she thought about the card's meaning. 'Are you married?'

'No.'

His clipped response caused Rachel to lift a brow. 'There is a woman in your future, or perhaps you already know her, who'll help you through the ordeal you'll be facing.'

'A woman?' He grunted. 'Not likely.'

He reached out and caught the runic amulet hanging from Rachel's neck, startling her. Miss Bastet huffed a breath, her gaze darting between the two of them.

Jackson rubbed his thumb over the carved pewter in a way that Rachel had done a thousand times before. The amulet represented unconditional love, something Rachel wanted to believe in, but knew didn't happen without sacrifice, and sometimes blind faith. A quality, in her experience, that most people didn't possess.

He lifted his gaze, capturing hers. 'This *ordeal* you see in my future – it sounds ominous.'

The silver chain against her skin warmed, as if his heat had bled through the metal. The nerves along her back rippled, and she shuddered slightly. His eyes deepened to bronze as emotions filtered to the surface. The fine creases fanning out from his eyes conveyed his doubt, but a subtle stirring revealed his interest. In her, or in what the cards held?

He tugged on the chain, thankfully breaking her contemplation. 'Rachel, what do you see?'

'Do you want the truth?' When giving a reading, she always focused on any good the cards divulged so she could prepare the Seeker for any adversity. Somehow, she didn't think Jackson Dermont would appreciate being sheltered. If she gave him a general reading, he'd think she was coddling him, or, worse, making everything up.

'The truth is the only thing I'll accept.'

Sensing a warning behind his statement, she said, 'Lies. I see lies and deception, both in your past and in your future. Someone hurt you, and though you think you've recovered, you haven't. You trust no one, except yourself.'

Abruptly, he released the amulet, letting it drop against her chest with a thump.

She moistened her lips and continued. 'The mistrust you feel gave you the strength to move on. But if you continue clinging to your cynicism about others, you could lose the most valuable part of yourself.'

He sat back, studying her from behind his protective shield once again. 'That's quite a statement, and a rather general one. You can't get through life without being hurt in some way. And trust, well, that's a quality reserved for fools.'

She wondered if he realized just how much he'd revealed about himself. Yes, everyone had to live through loss and pain. Some overcame them. She certainly had. Some never quite recovered, while others never tried. She wondered which category Jackson fell into. 'Shall I continue?'

'By all means.' His easy grin held an uncomfortable edge.

Settling back in her chair as if to square off with him, she ran her hand down Miss Bastet's warm coat. She didn't pet the cat out of habit, but rather to gather her resolve before telling Jackson what he *thought* he wanted to know. She didn't bother looking at the cards, already knowing what they revealed and what they didn't.

It was what they concealed that piqued her interest in the man. She'd never seen a layout like his before, hinting at both promises and destruction. She knew better than to delve deeper, search for answers, but she felt compelled. There were secrets hidden within the cards, just as surely as there were multiple layers to the man. Like a waking dragon, Rachel could feel her curiosity raising its meddle-some head, looking for answers. A risk, she knew, but the temptation was too great to resist. And she'd never been one to turn away from a challenge.

'You were betrayed.'

Expecting a response, she let the statement hover between them. His jaw clenched, but otherwise he didn't move.

She sighed inwardly. He wasn't going to make this easy for her. 'Was it someone close to you?'

'You tell me.'

'Mr Dermont, the cards haven't given me the specifics of your past, but I do know that history has a tendency to repeat itself. It's called karma.' Using her most patient tone, she continued, 'If you don't learn life's lessons the first time, life will give you another test until you get it right. From what I can tell, you're in for another round.'

Jackson laughed, a coarse rumbling that sounded cynical to his own ears. If he was to believe this sloe-eyed gypsy, and he sure as hell didn't, he'd spent the past three years recovering from the most devious 'test' life could throw at him, only to discover he'd failed in the eyes of some universal power. Well, he didn't buy it.

He'd not only survived, he'd forced his way to the top once more.

Somehow, though, this mysterious, intriguing woman had come close to nailing him. She was right that he didn't trust anyone. Not any more. He'd been blind-sided by that particular lesson, but he'd learned it well. He wouldn't need a repeat test, because if he knew nothing else in life, he knew that trust was a lie. A bold, smiling lie that stroked your ego with one hand while stabbing you in the back with the other.

Familiar anger swelled up his chest, heating his throat, turning his sight hazy with rekindled rage. Shaking his head slightly, he drew in air to halt a trip down that useless path. He'd put his life back together. Nothing, *and no one*, would ever get close enough to threaten him again. That was why he'd sat at Rachel's table. He had to know what she'd told Sandra Roberts.

'Lady,' he said, lifting Rachel's hand from the cat's back and bringing her warm fingers to within an inch of his mouth. He trailed his thumb over velvety skin that smelled sultry, like something forbidden in a man's dream. She resisted his pull, but he tightened his hold. 'Even if such a thing as

18

karma existed, there isn't much it could do to me that I haven't already been through.'

Her gaze flickered between his eyes and his mouth before settling on his lips. She tugged against his grip again, then gave up. 'That's an arrogant presumption, Mr Dermont, one you might want to reconsider.'

'What I'd like to consider, Ms Gold,' Jackson pressed his lips to her fingers – yes, velvet . . . and sweet, 'is dinner, with you.'

He didn't know what possessed him to ask her out, except that his search for information over the past few weeks had led him down one dead-end after another. Lord knew he wasn't interested in her, and she definitely wasn't his type, though his fingers itched to feel her sin-black hair, and her almond-shaped silver eyes could become hypnotic if he held her gaze much longer. He wasn't sure what to make of the gauzy lavender gown that absorbed light, giving the illusion of exposing her slender body when, in fact, it concealed almost every inch. Despite her silky allure, she was nothing more than a con-artist, playing on people's vanities and weaknesses.

Recognizing her for what she was, he cursed himself for ever having sat down. Only an idiot would have failed to realize his mistake. And he didn't like the brewing implications that thought created. Was he becoming careless, or, worse, complacent? Becoming distracted by an intriguing face would guarantee him one thing – deceit. He'd had enough of that trait to last a lifetime. Besides, there were more urgent matters to resolve before the evening ended.

Like finding a thief.

She snatched her hand from his. 'I have a rule . . .'

Rubbing his palm across his mouth, inhaling her faint scent of musk and woman, he muttered, 'I thought you might.'

'I don't date my clients.'

'Since I'm not your client, that rule doesn't apply,' he argued, but only because Ms Gold, sham tarot reader though she might be, intrigued the hell out of him.

'If you aren't interested in hearing the rest of your reading, Mr Dermont, perhaps you could leave so another guest might have an opportunity.'

The woman had grit, he'd give her that much. She was merely hired help, but she'd risked offending him by politely kicking him out. But then, he mentally added, recalling his reasons for attending the party, he was on the payroll as well. Sort of. 'I'll leave when you agree to have dinner with me. It doesn't have to be anything formal.'

'The answer is no.'

'I should warn you, Rachel, I don't give up easily.' Though why he didn't leave now, he couldn't fathom. His job was to observe everyone at the party, not ask one of the employees out on a date, even if it was as a means to gather information.

His company's reputation was at stake. Hell, every scrap of success he'd fought and sweated for could easily slip through his fingers if he didn't find answers . . . and soon.

Someone had discovered a way to breach his state-of-the-art security system. And unless he wanted to lose Dermont Technology he had to find out who was behind it, and how they'd managed the impossible.

Fidgeting with the odd necklace dangling between her breasts, she said. 'I should warn you, Mr Dermont, I rarely change my mind once I've set it.'

'Why am I not surprised?' While studying the stubborn tilt of Rachel's chin, the subtle caution in her gray eyes, Jackson took a drink of the lung-burning liquor, hardly tasting it as a suspicious thought occurred to him.

What if the thefts weren't a random act, but were specifically targeted to ruin him? Could it be that rich, spoiled Sandra was trying to finish what she'd started three years before? As he recalled, she had followed the advice of a tarot reader before delivering the final blow that had caught him off guard and left him spinning, not only in his own humiliated anger, but neck-deep in debt, as well.

Had Rachel Gold been the woman who had given Sandra the idea of ruining him? Or had Rachel and Sandra conspired together to take over the company he and Sandra had built together? The theory was plausible, but how would that tie into the thefts now threatening Dermont Technology's reputation? It was common knowledge that Sandra had run their computer security company into the ground only two years after they'd split. Maybe Sandra resented that he'd made a comeback.

But how would Rachel fit into the picture? If she did at all. What would she get out of hurting him? Money, of course. Sandra had enough to air-condition hell.

Granted, Rachel's composed demeanor hardly fit the profile of a thief. With her wavy black hair pinned haphazardly on top of her head, revealing silver hieroglyphic earrings that brushed her shoulders when she moved, she appeared more exotic than crooked. The air around her seemed to pulse in a slow erotic beat. He wanted to believe the illusion was caused by the Grand Marnier slowly insulating his veins, and the spicy incense burning in a pewter cup on the table, and not the woman, but he knew better. His pulse began a thrumming push through his body as he became occupied by thoughts of how her full lips would taste compared to her hand. Musky and addictive, he surmised.

Christ, what was he doing?

He knew better than to be lured by someone's looks. Especially a woman's! That had been another of life's lessons he'd learned well. Hadn't he etched the results into his soul so he wouldn't forget?

Seeing her business card in a crystal holder, he took one and slipped it into his pocket.

'Well, Rachel, this has been interesting.' For some reason he couldn't shake the sudden urge to take her hand and kiss it again. The need had nothing to do with being gentlemanly, but was caused by another conflicting reason he refused to delve into. Since her hands were clasped around her necklace, and out of his reach, he let the impulse pass. *It's just as well.* 'To appease my curiosity,' he said, pointing to the cards on the table, 'do I get a happy ending?'

She tilted her head back to watch him as he stood. The annoyance in her eyes shifted, gentling them to a misty silver, turning them almost transparent. She hesitated as if contemplating how to respond.

'A happy ending,' she said in a voice so soft and smooth, he felt as if she'd brushed her hand across the back of his neck, 'depends on how badly you want one. You'll never be completely happy until you learn how to trust.'

'Then I guess I'm out of luck.'

Happy endings were as much an illusion as trust. If he couldn't have one without the other, then he'd do without both.

CHAPTER 2

Beneath the laughter and whirl of conversation, the faint chime of a clock striking twelve echoed through the marbled halls. The muscles in Rachel's back twisted with strain, but she ignored the ache, remaining poised as she finished Mrs Phillips' reading. It would be at least another two hours before Rachel could leave the Donaldsons' party. Two tedious hours of forcing serene smiles when all she wanted to do was escape to her own home where she could close off the unsettling vibrations dragging her down.

She blinked her dry, stinging eyes against the thick cloud of cigarette smoke hovering above the sea of perfectly coiffed heads. The scents of cigars, perfume and food battled to dominate the air. She tried to focus on the cards, but they repeatedly made a mockery of her ability to interpret them. Little of what she dealt made sense, and what she did understand was too severe for her to relate without upsetting her customers.

As she nodded her goodbye to Mrs Phillips, Rachel reminded herself that one day soon the

Golden Pyramid wouldn't need the income she earned by hiring herself out. According to her business plan she was almost there, and the promise of such security was enough to keep her going.

In the beginning she'd enjoyed the parties, the elegance so foreign to her, the excitement of meeting new people. But tonight, for the first time ever, she wanted it to end.

Knowing her restlessness was influenced by the eerie certainty that she was being watched only annoyed her more. She knew Jackson Dermont was somewhere in the room with his disconcerting brown eyes focused on her. She felt his gaze as surly as she'd felt the brief, disturbing impact of his lips on her fingers. Annoyed with herself for not being able to block his presence, she pressed her shaking hands into her lap.

'If you keep scowling like that, no one will dare come over for a reading.' Penny, Rachel's younger sister by five years, plopped down in the overstuffed chair with the grace of a tired puppy. Wearing a loosely woven dress of cobalt-blue cotton trimmed with colorful beads, Penny had completed her outfit by adding half a dozen earrings in each ear and enough bracelets and rings to start her own jewelry store.

Rachel sighed, conceding the fact that, though her baby sister was twenty-three, and had missed the '70s hippie era, she would always be the ultimate flower child. Rachel had long since given up trying to convince Penny of the importance of dressing more conservatively for their bookings. Fortunately,

25

their customers were usually charmed by Penny's free spirit instead of appalled.

'Where have you been?' Rachel asked, gathering the cards into a neat stack before putting them in a mahogany box where they could rest. 'You're supposed to be helping me, and I haven't seen you for the past three hours.'

Penny rolled her eyes and flicked her short nails that were always in need of polishing against the table's surface. 'Geez, Rachel, everyone here knows you. If they want a reading, they'll get one. My working the room to remind everyone to come see you will only aggravate them.'

'Not if you do it the way I've taught you. We need the business . . .'

'We *don't* need the business. The Golden Pyramid is doing fine.' Penny narrowed her eyes with the derision of an adolescent teen. 'The way you talk makes it sound like we're in the poor house or something.'

Rachel gripped the arms of her chair. She wouldn't have the repeated argument with her sister, especially with customers within hearing range. It both infuriated and troubled Rachel that Penny could shut the past from her mind, wipe out the countless days they'd gone without food so they could pay the rent on their dingy one-room apartment.

But a part of Rachel envied her sister's selective memory. There were days she longed to forget the past that festered inside her. But she'd lived too many years watching life carve lines into her

26

mother's once smooth, soft skin. Working as a maid at a downtown hotel had weathered her hands to leather. Scrubbing floors and strangers' commodes had caused her knuckles to swell and arthritis to set in.

As hard as Emily worked, sometimes there hadn't been enough money to buy all they'd needed. Fortunately, their school had provided free lunches for Rachel and Penny, but Rachel had had to clean the lunch-room in return. She'd never minded, because she'd known that, as a child, that small chore was all she could do to help her mother. But she'd wanted to do more . . . so much more.

The memories were buried deep, but they were so much a part of Rachel that she'd never be able to forget what it was like to fall asleep in their cramped apartment, listening through sheet-thin walls as neighbors shouted over crying babies. Police were a regular presence in their neighborhood, but they never seemed to be around when gunshots rang out during the night, or when gangs swarmed the alley-ways. But, as bad as it was, she'd prayed each night that they would still have their small home the next day, and not be forced on to the streets. Being homeless had been her greatest fear. If they'd lost the tiny apartment, where could they possibly have gone?

Rachel shook herself from the past. Her family had forgotten those years. They'd moved on. Why couldn't she? She knew she annoyed everyone with her obsessive need to protect them, all of them, but Rachel couldn't change because she couldn't escape the fear buried in her heart.

The fear was what made her who and what she was. If that meant she was flawed, then she and everyone else would simply have to learn how to live with it. Because she wouldn't go back to the horror, the nothingness, that their lives had turned into after her father's death.

'I need a break.' Rachel pushed to her feet, feeling the sudden need for clean air and open space. 'I'll be outside. If anyone comes looking for me, I'll be back in twenty minutes.'

As she passed her sister, Penny reached up and caught her hand. 'Look, Rachel, life is good. Try to relax and enjoy it.'

Rachel stared down into her sister's trusting, innocent eyes. In so many ways her sister was still a child, and somewhere along the way Rachel had turned into her mother. She didn't resent the role, but at times she wished she could do as Penny suggested and just relax. It sounded so easy.

Sighing, she managed a strained smile and kissed Penny on the forehead. 'I'll try.'

Moments later, Rachel stepped out on to an empty patio of white Italian tile. Tiki torches along the marble railing threw light and shadow on to the cultured grounds below. The pungent scent of smoke nearly cloaked the sweet smell of cut grass and blooming gardenias. The heartbreaking cry of violins and flutes drifted through the closed French doors.

Stopping at the stone baluster, Rachel slowly drew in a much-needed breath. Crisp evening air filled her lungs, sending a spiraling sense of awakening through her limbs. She shouldn't have let her sister's remarks upset her; normally they didn't. They wouldn't have, she reasoned, if she hadn't been off center to begin with.

She knew the cause of her agitation, but she didn't care to ponder it at the moment. Only the haunting image of Jackson Dermont's too handsome, too intriguing face lingered perilously close to the edge of her mind, making him impossible to forget.

She'd never had trouble shielding herself from her customers before. So why did he affect her? Of all people, why him?

Mr Dermont. Jackson. She trailed a hand over the smooth carved railing. What were his secrets? The cards had hinted that he had several, but they'd told her nothing more. The reading hadn't revealed as much as she'd have liked, but she'd gathered a few clues to his personality without their help.

Outwardly, he possessed the type of looks and charm that most people would find impressive. Behind the devilish smile and compelling eyes she'd glimpsed a man who could be as hard and unforgiving as the stone pressed against her palm. But why?

Rachel shook her head and grinned at her own foolishness. The 'why' didn't matter. When it came to Jackson Dermont, she knew she'd be wise to keep a tight rein on her curiosity.

Hearing voices, she glanced to her right and saw two couples strolling toward her. She recognized Edmond and Sandra Roberts; the second man was Senator David Hastings, whom Rachel knew. But she didn't know the woman with him.

29

Sandra had her hand wrapped around her husband's arm as she leaned into him. She laughed at something he said, then she ran her palm over his chest. Rachel touched the love amulet that hung from her neck. Sandra had obviously decided to save her marriage. Rachel wished her luck, and wondered if she would ever find a man worth fighting for.

'Oh, Rachel.' Sandra released her hold on her husband and reached for the other woman, a tall brunette wearing a black, floor-length silk slip that cupped and hugged every descending curve. Drawing her away from the men, Sandra murmured, 'Monica darling, this is the fortune-teller I mentioned earlier.'

Rachel stifled a groan. *Fortune-teller*? She hated the shabby term, but if it made her client happy, then she would hold her tongue. For now.

'Monica Beaumont, this is Rachel Gold.'

Rachel automatically extended her hand and took the other woman's cold, stiff fingers into her own. Sandra continued to chat about Rachel's talents, but Rachel barely heard her. Something about Monica's prim, cultured features seemed familiar, but the memory hovered just out of reach.

Sandra glanced over her shoulder, presumably to ensure the men weren't listening. 'I guarantee your life will never be the same once she reads your cards, Monica.'

Rachel noted Ms Beaumont's smooth creamy skin, drawn tight by a shaky smile. Something about the woman's eyes, or nose . . . no, it was something . . . else. But what?

'It's a pleasure to meet you, Ms Gold,' Monica said in an uneasy voice.

It wasn't until the woman spoke that Rachel's memory came into focus. *Linda Monroe*. Her childhood friend had certainly changed during the past ten years. The beauty that rags and grime had hidden during their adolescence was now as polished as a cut diamond. But there was no denying that the slender, elegant woman before her was the same dirt-poor, struggling girl Rachel had grown up with in South Dallas.

She wanted to ask how she had managed to escape the projects, and why had she changed her name, but the panic in Linda's eyes stopped her. Rachel released her faint grip and turned to Sandra. 'I'll be attending Senator Hastings' barbecue fundraiser next week. Will you be there?'

Sandra laughed, and Rachel had the distinct impression that Linda wanted to sink through the floor. 'Of course we'll be there,' her client said. 'Senator Hastings is none other than Monica's fiancé.'

Rachel's gaze snapped back to her long-ago friend, who glanced away as if she wanted to flee. 'It should be quite an event.'

'Yes.' Chaffing her arms, Linda turned to Mrs Roberts. 'Sandra, it's chilly out here. I think I'll go in now. It was nice to meet you, Ms Gold.'

Rachel bit down on her bottom lip as Linda slipped through the French doors and disappeared among the noisy crowd. Once Sandra excused herself, Rachel slowly followed her friend's hurried path inside.

Standing on the edge of the ballroom, an outsider looking in, Rachel observed the rhythmic sway of dancers on the inlaid parquet floor, the servants carrying endless trays of champagne and hors-d'œuvres, the indescribable whirl of electricity that accompanied wealth and prestige. Glitz and glamour. She'd seen it all before.

Only, tonight, nothing was proving to be as it seemed.

She spotted Jackson standing near the fireplace, as separate from the crowd as she. He cupped the same glass of liquor in his large hand as if it were a prop to help him blend in. He scanned the guests, his long body relaxed. He smiled, saying something she couldn't hear as he shook hands with a passing couple. If she hadn't read his cards earlier, she would have thought he was enjoying the party, the people. But the crease between his brows, the emptiness of his smile ruined the illusion.

He didn't want to be here, or, if he did, he wasn't here for merely social reasons. His guarded stance gave her the impression that he was searching – or hunting – for something. But what?

Whatever his agenda, be it a woman or business associate, Rachel mentally reminded herself, it didn't concern her.

As if he'd heard her, Jackson turned, his gaze linking with hers. Rachel felt the blood rush to her head, where it pounded out a warning. Her mouth turned dry, and shivers peppered her skin. She wrapped her fingers around her amulet, needing the cool metal to keep her grounded. She didn't want to admit it, but she was beginning to agree with Jackson and question her own skills.

She was a tarot card reader who could foretell the future, yet she had no idea what was going on.

CHAPTER 3

The Imperial Dragon's eyes flashed, pooling blood-red in the dim light. Rachel ran her fingers over his verdant green scales and imagined his nostrils flaring in pleasure. His sculptured head was tilted back, his mouth parted as if he wanted to roar . . . or purr. Gripped in his paw, the crystal ball refracted color and purpose, and the heart of the dragon's soul. He was dark beauty and regal strength rolled into one.

He was perfection.

And he was all hers . . . that was, until someone bought him.

Having tagged the mythical beast, Rachel entered his eighteenth-century history, along with his extravagant sales price, into the computer. Unable to help herself, she ran her fingers over the cool surface of his gypsum stone body again, hoping that if he truly possessed supernatural powers, some of it would rub off on her. For the past week, ever since the Donaldsons' party, she'd been off-center, unable to focus on and interpret other people's actions. Specifically those involving Jackson . . . and Linda who was now Monica.

How she'd love to delve deeper into both their lives, learn about their pasts. She'd been tempted to ask the cards, but she knew better than to pry. As a tarot reader, she could give advice when asked, but nothing more. Besides, she couldn't shed the disturbing certainty that if she probed into Jackson's life, she might not like what she found. There was something guarded in him, secrets that could affect her if she ventured too close. But she was tempted. *So very tempted.*

'I can't imagine why anyone would buy something so ugly.'

Rachel flinched, barely suppressing a yelp of surprise. 'Mom, don't sneak up on me like that. I could have dropped him. And he isn't ugly.' Scratching the dragon under his gilded chin, she added, 'Are you, darling?'

Cradling her newest treasure, she left her cramped office and wandered through the store without looking. She didn't need to watch her step. She knew where every vase, every Turkish rug and bronze statue was located. She knew their names and histories, if they promised healing powers or were simply meant for the eye to enjoy.

She had chosen each and every item in her store with a specific purpose in mind – to celebrate the beauty of life. Fortunately, her choices had proven to be sound when predicting the tastes of her clientele. They loved the unusual and unique – craved to own a piece of the mystical world she loved. Her customers might want to possess the tools of her trade, but, to Rachel, each Celtic cross

35

and Indian spirit rattle had a gift to give, a lesson to share. One only had to look.

Lounging on top of a hand-painted chinoiserie hall table, Miss Bastet sat up to watch as Rachel gave the dragon an honorary spot on the top shelf of a glass display case in the center of the store. Rachel asked her mother, 'Has Mrs Wier's order gone out yet?'

'Yes,' Emily sighed, sounding overworked, though Rachel knew it was a build-up for what was coming. Her mother had become predictable, if not a bit lighthearted over the years, a change that couldn't have made Rachel happier.

Emily adjusted a polished crystal wand on its black velvet tray so the overhead light glinted off its surface. Picking up the cat, she gave Miss Bastet a healthy scratch behind her ears. 'And I've dusted everything I dare touch, leaving the rest for you.'

Used to her mother's set ways, Rachel turned and gave her a reassuring smile. Emily, with her hard-earned wrinkles and blue eyes that still held an echo of sadness, wasn't afraid she'd break something valuable. Nothing so minor would keep the efficient, hard-working woman from doing her part to ensure The Golden Pyramid's success.

But, being a God-fearing Christian woman, she refused to handle the more bizarre items in their collection – specifically, the horned gargoyles with their devilish grins and the black-robed Shaman statues. Regardless of Rachel's assurances that none of the merchandise possessed evil spirits, Emily refused to have anything to do with it.

Rachel still held out the slim hope that that would change. Her mother had once frowned on the use of tarot cards, but she now had hers read every six months without fail.

'What about the flyers announcing our anniversary sale? Have they gone out?'

'Of course,' Emily returned with annoyance, then burrowed her face in Miss Bastet's thick coat.

Rachel hid a grin, very aware that it was Wednesday, and on Wednesdays the Women's Auxiliary of her mother's church gathered for bingo. All in the name of fund-raising, of course. It was her mother's one vice: meeting her friends to have lunch and gossip for an afternoon. A vice her mother deserved.

For the past several months, Rachel had changed the schedule, giving her mother the special day off, but Emily always came in, insisting that Rachel couldn't sell a paperweight without her. Which was close to the truth. Hard times had turned Emily into an amazing and sometimes merciless saleswoman.

'Your sister, though, God forgive her flightiness, didn't bother to come in this morning to help me fill out the addresses *or* lick the stamps.'

'She's not here?' Rachel shut the door to the display case and glanced around the store, surprised she hadn't noticed her sister's absence earlier. She'd been so caught up in logging new merchandise that she'd barely given anything else much thought. 'Where is she?'

Emily shrugged and studied the room, as if she, too, expected to see her youngest daughter pop up from behind a bookshelf. 'She phoned earlier and said she had things to take care of, but that she'd be in this afternoon.'

A recurring worry surfaced in Rachel's mind as she moved behind the counter to check the previous day's receipts. Her sister, who'd once haunted the store even on her days off, now usually had to be called and reminded when it was her turn to work. Something had changed in Penny's life, which didn't bother Rachel outright; her sister deserved her privacy. It was the secrecy that troubled her, and reminded her of another frightening time when Penny had nearly been ripped from their lives.

Her sister's run-in with the law wasn't something Rachel cared to remember. Or relive. Praying to the one and only God her mother believed in, Rachel asked that He watch over Penny. In the meantime, Rachel planned to read her sister's cards. Where she wouldn't consider prying into a customer's life, her sister was a whole other matter. Especially if it might prevent a disaster.

Feeling her mother linger nearby, Rachel said, 'It's pretty quiet, Mom. Why don't you take the rest of the afternoon off?'

'Are you sure?' Her mother dumped the cat on to the counter to pat the teased curls of her prematurely gray hair, a testament to her years of enduring hardship and stress. Years that Rachel swore her mother would never experience again.

Meowing her displeasure, Miss Bastet began cleaning her paw with delicate little licks.

'Of course. You've earned it.' Collecting Emily's purse from beneath the counter, Rachel kissed her mother's soft cheek. 'I'll speak with Penny when she comes in. See if we can't find out what's distracting her.'

Fishing out her car keys, Emily warned on her way out the door, 'Go easy on her, dear. She really is a child at heart.'

Rachel managed a disparaging grin before turning back to her work. *Yeah, a twenty-three-year-old child with a police record.* Rachel prayed that the sick spinning in her stomach didn't mean her sister was tempting fate again, especially since Penny still had another year of probation to serve. They didn't need trouble in their lives. Not now, when everything was going so well.

The bell above the door signaled her mother's departure. When it rang again seconds later, Rachel glanced up from her stack of receipts, sure her mother had forgotten something. Like a charitable donation to the church, which Rachel would gladly give if it would earn points with Him and help keep Penny safe.

To Rachel's utter shock, Jackson Dermont stood in her entryway, looking imposing and reckless, as if his mere presence could shatter the valuable artifacts. Not spotting her yet, he shifted his weight on to one leg and moved a panel of his navy blue sports coat aside, revealing a white T-shirt. He rested one hand on his trim, jeans-covered hip.

A rushing buzz filled Rachel's mind, deafening her to everything except the sound of her startled heart tripping over itself. God, the man was breath-taking – off limits, but breathtaking. If she didn't breathe soon, she just might faint. She swayed and almost laughed at herself for having such a peculiar, and uniquely feminine, reaction to a man she'd met only once. A man, she reminded herself, who annoyed her.

She ran her damp palms down the embroidered skirt of her teal cotton dress. His appearance may have surprised her, but she'd learned at an early age that surprises came in all shapes and sizes. Some were good and some were bad, and the best way to react to them was not to. Especially when they involved a man like Jackson. She had little experi-ence with men like him. Her clients were mostly female, and the men she knew were older, married and easy to keep at arm's length.

Jackson, on the other hand, had the ability to slip through her control. Even now she felt tense energy pulsing from him, but she couldn't interpret its cause, which both frustrated and troubled her. Evidently, the Imperial Dragon hadn't shared his magic with her.

But what was he doing here? For the life of her, she couldn't think of a reason.

While she struggled to regain her composure, Jackson's gaze casually moved over the room. His face indicated none of his thoughts. He could have been looking at a garbage dump for all he revealed. The hard line of his jaw didn't budge his unsmiling mouth. The creases flaring from the corners of his eyes seemed to have deepened since the night she'd met him, as if he'd added to the weight already burdening him.

Miss Bastet's growling cry brought his attention to her. The instant he saw her, Rachel swore she felt the air snap like a whip. With a simple smile, the guarded expression vanished, transforming him into a dangerous and, she admitted, tempting, playboy. Which she suspected described him perfectly.

He ran a hand through his wheat-darkened hair, sweeping it off his forehead. 'It's quite a place you have here.'

'Thank you.' Embarrassed by the sudden heat burning her cheeks, she forced a deep breath and silently berated herself for overreacting. There wasn't any reason for her to be so jittery, despite the fact that she hadn't been able to stop thinking about him. 'I have to admit, Mr Dermont, I'm surprised to see you here.'

'Yeah?' He quirked a brow. 'Me too.'

Rachel stepped from behind the safety of the counter. To fill the simple need to have something in her hands, she picked up a dustcloth as she crossed to him. 'Is there something I can help you with?'

From his hesitation, she imagined several answers flickered through his mind before he answered. 'I was curious.'

'About . . .?'

In a casual move, he picked up a bound copy of the *Kama Sutra*. As he flipped through the ancient Hindu manual, filled with pictures and advice on sexual pleasure, his mouth twitched with a teasing grin. Her heart did a slow turn in her chest. His smiles, when they were honest, could be both devastating and addictive. Her pulse drummed through her veins, heating her blood. A vulnerable shudder started low in her body.

He glanced up, his smile faltering. Suddenly, she *knew* he'd sensed her reaction to him and wished she could dissolve into a pile of nothing.

With his gaze boring into hers, he said, 'I was curious about you.'

His answer so startled her, she snatched the book from his hands and returned it to the shelf. The sensual roughness of his voice, the unnerving vibrations she picked up in him stole her ability to reason. She could only feel, and what she felt was too much, too deep and too foreign for her to handle. Why couldn't she lock him out! Shield her emotions from him?

Turning her back on him, she began dusting a statue her mother had neglected. She ran her hand over a pair of entwined, polished brass lovers, and realized her mistake as heat worked a flaming path up her neck. Her palms cupped the slender bodies, the metal warming against her skin. She'd never had a lover, not because she prized her virginity but because of an instinct for self-preservation. The one lesson she'd learned well while growing up in the projects.

As dismal as her childhood had been, she'd always believed she'd meet a man she would share her life with. Not someone to take care of her, the way her father had her mother until he'd died, but someone to turn to in the night, share her fears with. Have a child with. She touched the love amulet around her neck. As perfect as her life was, that one piece was still missing.

Though he caused her system to spin off kilter with a simple look, she didn't believe Jackson Dermont would be the man to complete her. But still . . .

She could hear Penny's urging voice, '*Life is good. Try to relax and enjoy it.*'

Closing her eyes, Rachel drew another, deeper breath and willed her heart to stop its chaotic jumping. But it raced out of control as if she had no will of her own.

The soft chuckle from behind her was enough to send her shoulders back and her increasing irritation at herself soaring. She was acting like a fool. Jackson Dermont was a customer. If she wanted his business, she'd better start treating him like one. 'I'll let you browse. If you have any questions . . .'

To her annoyance, he followed her to the counter and leaned his forearms on the antique marble surface. Miss Bastet hurried out of his reach before he could pet her. Rachel frowned. She couldn't recall a time when the cat had acted so antagonistic.

'Actually, I came by to ask you to dinner.' A stray lock of hair draped over Jackson's forehead, daring her to touch it.

Shoving the previous day's receipts into an accordion folder, she said in a surprisingly strong voice, 'I thought we covered that already. I told you, I don't date clients.'

The slight purse of his lips lent him an almost boyish charm. Almost. She doubted anything could completely smooth his jagged edges. Being this close to him, she didn't need her cards to know he'd earned his rough corners the hard way, and possibly kept them close, harboring them as a reminder of . . . of what?

Perhaps that puzzling question was the reason she found him so appealing? So unsettling. He presented a contrast between light and dark, good and bad. Blue-blooded manners and obstinate rake.

'I don't much care for rules, Rachel.'

'Now, why am *I* not surprised?'

He took her hand as he'd done once before and brought it to his lips, whispered, 'Have dinner with me.'

She held her breath as his warmed her chilled fingers. Heat spiraled up her arms and into her chest where her racing heart pumped liquid warmth throughout her body. She didn't want him to kiss her hand again. The first time had been enough to alert her to what could happen. One kiss could lead to another and . . . She tugged on her hand, but the slow, hypnotic circles his thumb made over her skin, made it impossible to break free.

His touch became a seduction, an unspoken invitation, urging her to step over the invisible line he'd drawn and join him. To her disbelief, she wondered what it would be like to be with a man as vibrant, as off-limits, as Jackson. Forbidden – yes. Sensual – certainly. Shattering – she didn't doubt it. She'd spent so many years obsessed with her single

44

goal to achieve independence, she'd never had time to wander off the rigid path she'd set for herself. But she'd never met a man who fascinated her the way Jackson did.

What would happen if she stopped being so driven and tried to be just Rachel? What kind of person would she discover? It frightened her a little to think that she was tempted to find out. Too much was at stake for such careless thoughts.

'Will you?'

She couldn't manage to pull her gaze from his mouth. His lips were full, hard, with an arrogant tilt at the corners. She wondered if he would taste as dark and mysterious as he smelled. 'Wh . . . what?' she stammered.

'Dinner?'

Blinking, she twisted her hand free. 'I . . . I told you, no.'

'Lunch, then.'

'Thanks, but I've already eaten.' Which was a lie, and her stomach grumbled on cue to let him know it. Snatching up her dust-towel, she scooted around him and headed for the display of jeweled Tibetan offering-bowls. Her hands shook as she removed several and cleaned the already spotless glass shelf.

'Rachel?' he asked from directly behind her.

'Yes, Mr Dermont?'

'Jackson.'

She ignored his correction.

'Do I make you nervous?'

She threw what she hoped was an exasperated look over her shoulder. Instead of lying again, she poured her attention on to the sparkling glass, rubbing so hard that the entire case vibrated. 'Did you come here to buy something, or simply to distract me from my work?'

'Hmmm.'

Feeling his eyes roam down her back, she polished harder until her shoulder muscles began to bunch.

'Now that you mention it, my sister's birthday is in a couple of weeks.'

Thankful for the shift in subject-matter, Rachel faced him and cleared her throat. 'What is she like?'

He tucked a loose strand of Rachel's hair behind her ear. The act had been so casually accomplished, as if he'd touched her hair a hundred times before, that she couldn't move. 'Like a sister.'

She swallowed, hard. 'Is she conservative or flashy?'

He lifted a brow in thought. 'Somewhere in the middle.'

'Does she like jewelry?'

He gave a disbelieving smirk that said, Is there a woman who doesn't?

Laughing uneasily, she brushed past him. 'I have something that might work.' At the glass and gold-trimmed jewelry case, she raised the lid and lifted out a black velvet tray that held two items. 'This is a sacred Egyptian scarabaeus.'

'It looks like a necklace.'

Removing her amulet, she unclasped the necklace and slipped it around her neck. 'It's a talisman, symbolizing immortality.'

'Something every woman should have. Think of all the plastic surgeons that would be out of business.'

She removed her own earrings and replaced them with the matching set. 'It's set in fourteen carat gold, and the stones are precious gems, each of them flawless.'

'It's beautiful.'

Studying the jewelry draped between her breasts, a provocative glint flashed in his eyes. Her breath hitched. 'The filigree design set between each stone is hand-carved and dates the piece to the fifteenth century.'

He lifted the necklace, his knuckles brushing her blouse, and rubbed his finger over an oval sapphire. 'I'll take it.'

Rachel bit down on her lip. The touch had been slight, almost nothing at all, but the shock of it jolted her body. Unfamiliar, curling sensations wrapped around her limbs. Her knees wanted to buckle. 'D . . . don't you want to know how much it is?'

He stepped closer, tightening his hold before she could back away. She felt like a cornered rabbit, and didn't care for the analogy at all. She might not be used to men like Jackson, but that didn't mean she couldn't control her own responses.

'Is it expensive?' he asked.

'Very.' Her voice regained an ounce of cool distance, though how she managed it, she didn't know. 'Twenty thousand just for the necklace.'

He hesitated, but only slightly. 'I'll take it on one condition. That you have lunch with me.'

'Mr Dermont . . .'

'Jackson,' he insisted once again with another one of his knee-weakening smiles.

'You may pick out anything in the store you like, but I'm not for sale.'

The bell over the door jingled, but he ignored it. 'How about coffee, then?'

Seeing her sister rush inside saved Rachel from spitting out an answer. Spotting her, Penny slid to a halt with a clattering of bangle bracelets and an annoyed roll of her eyes. A young man with a blond ponytail and serious five o'clock shadow eased into the store. With an insolent gait, he strolled to her sister's side. Hooking his thumbs into his baggy denim jeans, he rolled his slim shoulders inside his black leather jacket decorated with silver studs and fringe. On first glance Rachel pegged him as either a gang member or drug dealer. Or both. Her protective instincts snapped to attention.

Gaining much-needed space from Jackson, Rachel said, 'Penny, I was beginning to worry.'

Her sister's rounded chin tilted. 'I told Mother I had things to do.'

Rachel's gaze flickered between her sister and the strange man who now had a territorial hand perched on Penny's shoulder.

'Who's your friend?' From the glint in Penny's eyes, Rachel knew she'd made a mistake by questioning her, but good sense had given way to outright concern. Though she tried not to judge people by their appearance, she'd known too many men who fitted this guy's rebellious bearing. From

48

experience, she knew they brought nothing but trouble.

'This is Mark.'

'Hey, Rachel,' Mark responded with a brazen grin. 'It's good to meet you.'

Before she could respond, her sister added, 'We met at the Blind Lemon a couple of weeks ago. He's in the band.'

Rachel did her best to pretend Jackson wasn't standing behind her, watching the entire scene, but it wasn't easy. She was familiar with the eclectic bar in Deep Ellum, *and* its reputation for attracting the young and wild.

Excusing herself from Jackson, she followed the couple as they made their way to the back office. What was Penny doing with a guy who fitted the role of a gang leader? The answer was all too obvious and frightening in Rachel's mind. Forcing her voice to sound calm, she asked, 'What did you do this morning?'

Penny stopped, whirled around, and said in a harsh whisper loud enough for everyone in the entire store to hear, 'It's none of your business.'

Holding on to her temper, which felt like the ends of a frayed rope, Rachel said, 'It is when you don't come in to work as scheduled.'

Penny pursed her mouth, and had the good sense to look contrite. 'It was only for a couple of hours.'

Rachel decided retreat was the best course for the moment. 'We'll talk about this later.'

'Excuse us, Mark,' Penny said suddenly, taking hold of Rachel's arm. Guiding her into the office, her sister closed the door behind them.

'Penny, I have a customer waiting out there.'

'The way he's looking at you, he'll wait.' Releasing her, Penny tucked her short dark hair behind her ears then heaved a breath. 'I'm going to tell you something, Rachel, and I want you to listen. I'm sorry for being late, but I had something important and *private* to take care of. I'm not a child any more, and I don't need you mothering me.'

'I'm not sure I agree.'

Waving a jeweled hand in the air, Penny argued, '*You* need a life, outside of this store, away from your tarot cards. You're twenty-eight years old and I bet you haven't had sex in five years.'

'Penny!'

'Or has it been ten?' Her brows shot up, but her voice softened. 'Or ever?'

A blush stung Rachel's cheeks. Her sister had hit so close to the truth that Rachel turned away with embarrassment. Though she had nothing to be ashamed of. The young men she'd known while growing up had all resembled Mark, with rebellious eyes that revealed their hatred of the system. He was the kind of man she'd been determined to avoid. He wasn't the kind of man she wanted Penny involved with.

She crossed her arms over her waist. 'My life is not the issue here. You've probably been out all night with that man, haven't you? He looks like a Hell's Angel, Penny!'

'You don't know Mark.'

'And you do?' Rachel demanded, spinning around.

Penny bit down on her lip and placed her hands on Rachel's arms. 'Look, I know what I'm doing. I love you, Rachel. But I need you to get off my back. I'm not the little girl you need to protect any longer.'

Rachel ran her hands over her face, then paced the small room. Was she that overbearing? Had she taken her obsession to safeguard her family too far?

Tremors shot through Rachel in sharp little jolts.

'Now,' Penny said, her tone light and teasing, 'I heard that seriously gorgeous man out there ask you out for coffee.' Penny opened the door a crack and glanced out. Shutting the door again, she said, 'He's still out there.' Grinning, she added with a sigh, 'And he's talking to Mark. Anyway, I want you to accept.'

'No.'

'Yes.'

'I have too much to do.'

'And I'll take care of it.' Penny imitated Rachel's stance by crossing her arms and giving Rachel a challenging look. 'Or don't you trust me any more?'

'Of course I do.' Vaguely, Rachel wondered when she'd lost control of their relationship. Groaning inwardly, she realized she'd lost control over a good many things, period. She couldn't deal with Jackson any better than she could her sister. Just what kind of tarot card reader/fortune-teller was she, anyway? A pitiful one. Maybe the Imperial Dragon had zapped her abilities to understand people instead of augmenting them?

'Well?' Penny asked, tapping her foot with impatience.

To keep the peace, Rachel said, 'Oh, all right.' If she didn't go, her sister would think she didn't trust her, and Rachel didn't want to add to the tension hovering alive and well between them.

Following Penny into the store, she saw that Jackson and Mark were indeed having an in-depth conversation, though about what, she couldn't imagine.

'Mr Der . . .' Rachel cleared her throat when he cocked a brow in either warning or amusement, she couldn't be sure which. 'Jackson,' she amended with a tight smile. 'Coffee would be lovely.'

Jackson fingered the satin bow Rachel had tied with shaking hands, and suppressed a shudder. They were at a café across the street from her shop, he assumed so she could keep an eye on the hot-tempered sales clerk and her delinquent friend. The silver foil-wrapped box containing the necklace and earrings sat between them like a gauntlet thrown on the white tablecloth.

What was he going to do with them? He sure as hell couldn't give the jewelry to his sister. Being an only child, he didn't have one. Having lost both his parents in his senior year of college, he didn't have any family left, unless he counted a couple of distant cousins he hardly remembered.

By trying to continue his ruse as a member of the elite, he'd set his company back thirty grand. It wouldn't bankrupt him, but it did put a dent in his operating cash. Christ, he'd expected the stuff to be pricey, but not enough to drain the blood from his veins.

He'd have to sell them. That was the only solution. Maybe one of his customers would take them off his hands. Protecting his clients had been the only reason he hadn't choked on the price in the first place. If he had, Rachel might have become suspicious.

And he didn't want to tip her off, not after what his research had uncovered that morning. After weeks of investigating on his own, and coming up empty-handed, a suspect was finally beginning to click into place. To his disbelief, it was none other than Rachel Gold. After examining the guest list of each function where thefts had occurred, only the beautiful, elusive fortune-teller had been at the scene of each crime, giving her the opportunity. Now all he needed was a motive to pin the thefts on her. And had she acted alone?

If his earlier theory panned out and she had teamed up with Sandra, ruining his company would undoubtedly be Sandra's motive. Only the theory had one enormous flaw. Would Sandra risk her position by stealing from her friends merely to take another stab at him? The woman could afford to drop a million on lunch; why would she bother? The few times he'd seen her, she'd made it clear that she didn't care about him enough to give him the time of day. So he doubted she'd exude any energy to ruin him.

So that left Rachel Gold.

Her poor attempt to cover her earlier nervousness with him only strengthened his suspicions. Briefly, his ego had run rampant with the possibilities that his presence, and not her guilty conscience, had caused her anxiety. He certainly found her attractive in a unique, hands-off sort of way. But reality had stepped in with a quick kick in the rear. He couldn't imagine a mere man upsetting Rachel Gold.

Wearing another of her unusual outfits, she seemed as elusive as the first time he'd seen her. Frosty blue fabric, threaded with silver and as insubstantial as air, draped her body. Pearl beads were suspended across her bodice like falling stars.

Watching her now, with her head bent and her hands clasped around her cup of herbal tea, he wondered if she remembered he was even in the restaurant. Or, now that she'd cleaned him out, was she trying to think of a way to get rid of him?

'You look like a woman with a problem.'

Her head snapped up, and she blinked, but the tension keeping her shoulders rigid didn't ease. 'Sorry.'

The frown pulling the corners of her mouth deepened. Jackson lifted his hand, intent on rubbing his thumb over her lips until they softened. He picked up his cup of coffee instead and took a sip of the cooling brew. 'Can I ask a question?'

'Sure.'

'Why do you keep an employee who doesn't respect you?'

She smiled ruefully. 'She's not just an employee. She's my sister. And I apologize for what happened.'

He shrugged it off. 'Sibling rivalry?'

'No, I don't think so.' Emotions churned behind her gray eyes, making them uneasy, restless. 'Penny's been acting strange lately. She won't talk to me. And she . . .'

'She?' Jackson prompted when Rachel stopped to stare off into space for a moment.

She looked at him as if just realizing who she was with, and to whom she was confiding. 'Nothing,' she said, straightening her posture. 'I'm sure I'm making more of her behavior than I should. Penny says I baby her.'

'Do you?'

Looking puzzled, a frown marred the smooth skin of her brow. 'My sister might be an adult, but in many ways she's still a teenager with the occasional hormonal swing. I just need to remember that.'

As she repeated the nervous gesture of tucking her long, mink-black hair behind her ears, he wondered whom she was trying to convince. 'Maybe you should read her cards?'

Rachel opened her mouth, but caught her response, her eyes narrowing as she realized he was teasing. 'Laugh now, Jackson, but I think you'll soon discover your cards didn't lie.'

Hearing the soft, throaty sound of his name, Jackson felt as if a gush of hot air had whipped over his bare skin. He ran a hand over his mouth and suppressed the tightening response in his body. *Remember why you're here, Dermont.* It wasn't to become physically wrapped up in a woman who was too sultry, too fascinating, and possibly too guilty for his own good. He was here to find answers to the questions that pointed accusing fingers at Ms Rachel Gold.

And he needed those answers. His reputation was at stake. In his opinion, and those of his clients, the police weren't doing enough to find the thief. So he'd taken it upon himself to find the person responsible.

'Yes, you warned that my life would take a turn for the worse.'

'Not worse, challenging.'

'You're splitting hairs.'

'Well, whatever happens, I'm sure you'll pull through just fine. Even if you don't follow my advice.'

'Do *you*?'

She raked her hand impatiently through her hair, bringing the loose, wavy length over her shoulder. The overhead light deepened the rich color to black glass. 'I'm sorry, I don't understand.'

'Follow your own advice?'

Sighing, a reverent smile tugged her lips. 'It's what brought me here.'

'Sounds like mumbo-jumbo. Come on, Rachel.' He leaned closer, wanting to touch her, but not daring. 'You can tell me the truth. The cards, the exotic gypsy get-up – its all a farce, isn't it?'

Her calm surface didn't crack as he'd intended. 'Sometimes you have to believe in things you can't see, Jackson.'

'Now what is that supposed to mean?'

Her eyes shimmered like smoky diamonds. She grinned, and to his surprise he wanted to kiss her tolerant smile right off her face. 'Not everything is black or white, right or wrong.'

'Good or bad?' He settled back in his chair and blew out a breath. He was handling this all wrong. His questions were supposed to give him some insight into her character, not send him into a tailspin of confusing nonsense. 'This is starting to sound like a sermon. Are you trying to save my soul?'

She grinned and smoothly changed the subject. 'If you ever want me to delve deeper into your life, just let me know.'

'Not likely,' he said, managing to keep the sarcasm at a minimum. He flicked his fingers off his brow in a mock salute. 'But thanks just the same.'

She relaxed against her chair, and her shoulders lost some of their rigidity. He took it as a sign that he could move forward with the reason that had brought him to her store in the first place. Signaling the waitress for more coffee for him and hot water for Rachel's tea, he asked, 'How long have you been reading cards, anyway?'

'About fifteen years.' She tilted her head back and studied the tiled ceiling. A grin softened her mouth, turning it pouty, kissable. Imagining she would taste like honey, warm and smooth, Jackson stifled a curse.

'When I was thirteen, I had a free ticket to the State Fair and went with a group of friends. The other girls spent what little money they had on rides and arcade games. I only had enough for one ride,' she said softly, her eyes meeting his. For an instant he saw remorse in their gray depths, then it vanished as she smiled. 'So I waited for the perfect one. That's when I heard the carnival barker. In a burly Scottish brogue, he promised that Madame Rousseau would see into my future and answer all my questions.'

'And did she?' Jackson had a difficult time imagining Rachel as an impressionable teenager being lured by a hustler. She seemed too self-assured, too cool and confident. But then, what was the old saying? Looks could be deceiving?

'Oh, yes,' she said, struggling not to laugh. 'Madame Rousseau told me the future was in my hands; all I had to do was guide it where I wanted it to go.'

'Sounds pretty general.'

'Not to a thirteen-year-old. I believed what she said. The experience stayed with me. I couldn't forget her, or the impression I had of how incredible it must be to look at the cards and see people's lives and know how to help them. So,' she added with a shrug, drawing his attention to the curve of her neck. Her skin looked soft, smooth. He wondered if she'd shiver if he kissed her there first. 'I saved my money for six months and bought my own tarot deck. They changed my life. And Madame Rousseau was right, I guided my future. I wouldn't be where I am, or have what I do, without them.'

Thoughts of kissing her dissolved as the hairs on his nape stood on end. Careful to keep his voice neutral, he asked, 'And what do you have?'

'Security.' Her eyes glittered like a bottomless well of satisfaction. 'Financial security. Independence. When I was still too young to help my mother, I swore I'd find a way to pull us out of the hell we lived in.'

'Tough childhood?'

Her mouth hardened as if she'd tasted something bitter. 'Tough doesn't begin to describe what we went through.'

'And so you decided you'd have a better life.'

'Yes,' she said, a little too defensively. 'For all three of us.'

'What did you do after that?'

'Whatever it took.'

A chill rippled down his spin. 'I'm impressed.' And it would have been the truth, if not for the sick downward spiral of his stomach. Suspicions dogged him from every angle. Why her? Why did the few leads he had have to point to a woman he found himself wanting to touch, and kiss, and a whole hell of a lot more?

'You've accomplished quite a bit. Your store, it's rather unique.' He lifted the foiled box and shook it lightly, feeling his smile turn gritty. 'And expensive. You must have some client list.'

She smiled deliberately, and kept irritatingly close-mouthed.

'Do you have a partner?'

Her gaze narrowed as she studied his face. She crossed her arms over her chest. 'You certainly are full of questions this afternoon, Jackson.'

'Just curious. I was wondering how you manage to

stock such expensive merchandise without a backer. Unless you borrowed the money?'

She shook her head as a cat and cream smile transformed her face. 'Simple logic. I reinvested every spare dime I made. As my reputation grew, so did the store. My customers want one-of-a-kind items. Originals, hand-made, and, for some of them, the more expensive, the better. So that's what I give them. They gain a valuable antique; I work with things I love, make a handsome profit, and everyone's happy.'

'You're quite the entrepreneur,' he said, barely managing to make the words sound like a compliment.

'I also help a lot of people, despite your doubts.'

Yes, the cards, the lure. His nerves began to vibrate along his spine. 'Have you booked any more parties?' He found himself wanting her to say 'no', that she'd given them up. Then, if the thefts continued, he'd know she wasn't the one he was after.

'Senator Hastings' fund-raiser is this weekend. I'll be doing readings there.' She glanced at her watch. 'It's getting late. I really have to get back to the store.'

He reached across the table and took her hand before she could bolt from her chair. 'I was wondering . . .' He couldn't let her leave yet, and knew he had to tread carefully. Watching for any reaction, however slight, he said, 'Have you heard about the theft after the Donaldsons' party?'

She frowned, her hand tensing in his. 'No, what happened?'

He tried not to interpret the darkening of her eyes. It could just as easily be concern as alarm. 'Don't know for sure.'

'Well, that's unbelievable. They're such a nice couple, and do so much for the community.' She turned to stare at her shop through the window. Her brow furrowed as she bit down on her lip. 'I'll have to call them, see if I can do anything.'

'Think you can find a thief hiding in the cards?'

He hadn't meant to sound sarcastic, but the derogatory tone slipped out. She glanced at him, her eyes as calm as a lake in the eye of a storm, and just as capable of wreaking unexpected havoc on his system. Damn, but he didn't know if he should shake her or kiss her. Both he imagined, and in that order.

'Thank you for the tea, Jackson.' With an offended tilt of her head, she placed her napkin on the table and rose. He couldn't stop his gaze from sliding over the swell of her breasts to the curve of her hips. His loins clenched, surprising him with the intensity of the abrupt, throbbing beat beneath his skin. He stifled a curse. The woman, with her subtle sensuality, made it impossible for him to focus on his case, much less keep his thoughts straight. And right now he was thinking he didn't want her to leave.

Rising, he moved so close her dress brushed his slacks. Before he could stop himself, he ran his knuckles down her cheek. 'I'm still not giving up on dinner.'

Color flooded her face, making her eyes glitter like mist. 'I hope your sister likes her gift.'

Jackson watched Rachel walk away, her shoulders straight, her steps casual, her hands clenched into fists at her sides, and wondered if she wanted to run. Everything pointed to her as the thief, from her motive of craving success to her being placed at the scene of each crime.

Only one thing stopped him from going to the police right now and sharing his only lead with them. And the reason annoyed the hell out of him.

He didn't want her to be guilty.

CHAPTER 4

Sunlight washed the screened-in porch with hazy, luminous light. Dust motes clung to the air, drifting with the rose-scented breeze that brushed Rachel's face like a soothing whisper. Stretched out on her rattan sofa, heat prickled through her jeans, warming her skin and numbing her body. Her eyelids drooped closed as she slipped closer to sleep.

The couch's green and yellow stripes had long since faded, but the cushions were still plump, cradling her in a cocoon of softness. She turned her face into the sun and breathed in the scents of budding trees, fresh-cut grass and the crisp smell of morning burning into afternoon.

She shouldn't be wasting time lounging when she had so much to do. If she started dressing now, she'd just make it in time for Senator Hastings' fundraiser. But her life allowed so few quiet moments, she hated to give this one up.

A shift in the cushions and the telltale sound of purring caused her to open her eyes. Miss Bastet pawed the couch. With her round, golden eye, she glanced at the space available then stepped on to

Rachel's stomach. Turning in a circle, she curled herself into a black puffy ball and settled down for a nap. Rachel ran her hand over the cat's thick coat, wishing she could indulge the feline with a few hours of laziness, but she couldn't.

Sighing, she cradled Miss Bastet in her arms and sat up, scratching the cat's neck when she meowed in protest. 'I know, maybe tomorrow.' But Rachel knew she wouldn't have any time to waste the following day. She was expecting a new shipment on Monday, which meant inspecting, cataloging and pricing as well as going over the weekend's receipts. There would be customers to deal with, and possibly a number of small crises. Some might consider the lack of free time a drawback to owning her own business, but Rachel welcomed the demands. They gave her a sense of belonging and accomplishment.

Giving up her one day off had been her own doing. Normally, she didn't care for political events, but after meeting Senator Hastings at several parties she'd sensed he was a good man, and had decided to help his campaign. She only hoped it didn't turn out to be as tense and trying as the Donaldsons' party.

As long as a certain whisky-eyed playboy who had more questions than answers didn't show up, her day just might wind up being pleasant. It was, after all, a beautiful April day.

Making her way from the porch to the spacious, sun-filled living room, Jackson's face formed in her mind. Dark, shielded eyes, an angled jaw, a hard mouth that had softened like heated metal when he'd kissed her fingers. She shook her head to shatter the vision, but it hovered close, drawing an annoyed sigh from her.

She hadn't seen or heard from him since his visit to her store three days before; not that she'd expected him to call, but she had yet to determine why he'd shown up in the first place. She didn't believe he was really interested in taking her to dinner. There had to be another reason. Men like Jackson Dermont didn't date women like her – a tarot reader without family connections and a hefty trust fund. She managed a comfortable living, but nothing compared to that of her customers.

No, they were in entirely different social classes. If Jackson was interested in her, it would only be for a brief, amusing fling. If she allowed herself to become involved with him, she didn't think there would be anything *brief* or *amusing* about how it would affect her. Just looking at him was enough to weaken her control over her emotions. Combine that with his graveled voice, his musky, woodsmoke scent, the hot, vibrating feel of his skin, and she'd become a notch on his belt without putting up a fight.

Lifting the cat to eye-level, Rachel asked, 'Miss Bastet, why am I even thinking about that man? I'll probably never see him again.'

The feline's answering purr sent tiny tremors up Rachel's arms. Heading for her bedroom, she paused when the doorbell chimed. Her heart caught, and for one foolish second she thought it might be Jackson. Annoyed with herself, she drew in a breath and opened the door.

Her mouth dropped open.

'Hello, Rachel.'

Linda Monroe stood on her front patio wearing a pantsuit of tangerine linen. She clutched a brown Chanel handbag to her waist, her manicured nails digging into the suede. With an awkward smile, she said, 'I know this must be a surprise.'

Recovering from her shock, Rachel stepped back, opening the door wider. 'It's a pleasant one. Please, come in.'

Setting Miss Bastet on the hardwood floor, Rachel shut the door and led Linda into the living room.

'Oh, Rachel, this is lovely,' Linda said, her gaze circling the room. A genuine, if somewhat nervous smile curved her lips. 'So different from what I'd expected.'

Rachel glanced at her white deep-seated couch that had a patchwork quilt carelessly draped over one corner. An overstuffed chair upholstered in a blue cotton print sat cattycorner to the fireplace. Mahogany Chippendale tables and throw rugs complemented the furniture she'd carefully selected. Unlike her store, there were few knick-knacks cluttering any surface. After living so long in cramped corners, she preferred her home to be open, spacious, one room flowing into the next.

'Thank you. Can I get you something to drink?'

'No. I can't stay long.' Crossing to the sofa, Linda sat on the edge, her handbag perched on her silk covered knees. 'You must be wondering why I'm here.'

Taking a seat in the adjacent chair, Rachel slipped one leg beneath her, trying to seem relaxed, and hopefully putting Linda at ease. 'I assume it has something to do with your being Monica Beaumont.'

'I knew you'd recognize me. It was such a surprise, seeing you. I can imagine the thoughts that went through your head.'

'I admit, I was taken back.'

Linda stood to pace the room. Rubbing her brow with her manicured fingers, she crossed to the bank of windows that overlooked the wooded backyard and the creek that ran beyond Rachel's property. Holding her body as stiff as a live oak, her voice trembled as she said, 'I can't thank you enough for your discretion.'

Rachel rose from her seat and went to stand beside the other woman. The sunlight, which had seemed so comforting before, dug harsh lines around Linda's mouth. Her eyes were glassy, tear-filled and desperate, as they focused on everything except Rachel. Her complexion paled, turning pasty against the soft waves of her brown hair. 'What's wrong, Linda?'

'Nothing.' She dropped her head forward. Rachel followed her line of vision to the enormous diamond solitaire on Linda's finger. 'Well, yes, actually, there is a problem. But there doesn't have to be, not if you keep my secret.'

'Does the senator know you changed your name?'

'No!' Linda turned away only to abruptly face Rachel again. With her shoulders back, searing determination flooded her eyes. 'He can't know. No one can. If the press discover his fiancée has a background as disgusting as mine, he'll lose the election before it's even begun.'

'You don't know that . . .'

'You don't understand! He'd lose the election because of me! Then I'd lose him.' Tears spilled from her eyes, streaking her cheeks with black, watery mascara. Linda stepped forward and grasped Rachel's hands. 'Please, Rachel, we used to be friends. Please, don't tell anyone.'

Rachel offered a grim smile. She didn't agree with what Linda was doing, but it wasn't her place to interfere. She could feel the fear in Linda's grip, the shudders that trembled though her body. Rachel's heart went out to the other woman. She wanted to hug her, but refrained, sensing that Linda was fighting to keep her composure from shattering altogether.

'Of course I won't. You have my word.' Giving Linda's hands a gentle squeeze, she said, 'I want to hear about what's happened to you, though. You've obviously done well.'

'Yes, ah . . .' Taking a linen handkerchief from her purse, she dabbed at her eyes, but didn't offer anything more.

Leaning back against the window frame, Rachel asked, 'Where are your parents?'

'In hell, I suppose.' She bit down on her lower lip, her eyes welling again. 'I suppose that wasn't very kind of me. They've been dead for nearly eight years, and I'm still mad as hell at them.'

Rachel tentatively touched Linda's sleeve. 'They weren't easy people to live with.' Which was such an understatement, they both smiled cynically.

'I used to envy you your mother. What I wouldn't have given to have my mom hug me the way yours always did you and Penny.' Linda laughed, a sharp sarcastic sound. 'But then old mom would have had to sober up long enough to remember she even had a daughter.'

'But you got out.'

'Yes, I did.' Linda held her arms out to her side as if to present proof that she'd survived. 'And I'm clean. No drinking, no drugs. I live a good life now, going from social teas to charity galas and now on to the campaign trail.'

Grinning in return, Rachel asked, 'How did you meet the senator?'

'Quite by accident. I guess you'd call it fate.' Folding her handkerchief, she sighed. 'Look at me, all watery-eyed and red-nosed. I'll have to go home before the barbecue or I'll cost David a few votes.'

'You look fine.'

'Can we visit another time? I'm already late, and well, I just had to stop here first to see you again.'

Glancing at her watch, Rachel grimaced. 'I'm late myself. I need to hurry and change.'

What little color Linda had regained drained from her cheeks and her mouth went slack. 'I thought – well, considering the circumstances, I thought you could cancel.'

Rachel felt a dull stab of rejection in her chest. She understood that Linda, a person she had once known so well, felt threatened. With an alcoholic father and an abusive mother, and her own run-ins with the law, Linda had never trusted easily. Since they hadn't seen each other in almost ten years, she realized Linda had no reason to trust her now. Rachel only had her word to give, and she'd already given it. 'The senator's expecting me. It's too late to back out now.' Taking Linda by the arm, she guided her to the front door. 'Besides, everything I make will be donated to his campaign.'

'But still . . .'

'You've found a wonderful man, Linda. I'm not going to do anything that would take him away from you.'

Linda bit down on her bottom lip, chewing off her glossy orange lipstick. 'Thank you.' Her eyes pooling with tears again, she tilted her head back and whispered, 'I never should have started this. I thought I could handle it.'

Feeling the need to reach out, Rachel hugged her friend. The contact was brief, but Linda's shivers bled into Rachel until she felt every erratic beat of Linda's heart, the cold numbness seeping through her veins. Though taller than Rachel, the other woman seemed to shrink within her skin. Desperate to say something that would help, Rachel offered, 'If he loves you, he'll stand by you.'

Pulling back, Linda blinked her green eyes clear of all signs of tears. Her mouth settled into a grim line, aging her beyond her years. 'I'm afraid it's too late for confessions.'

'It's never too late,' Rachel assured her, unnerved by the conviction she heard in Linda's voice.

'It is for me.'

With his plate loaded with ribs, brisket and baked beans, Jackson took his plastic cup of draft beer and dodged his way through the crowd. A dozen picnic tables were packed with jeans-clad campaign contributors, as was the temporary dance floor. Laughter and the whirl of conversation deepened with the pulse of the music. The country and western band, with their harmonicas and violins and boot-stomping beat, had stirred the atmosphere into a Texas frenzy.

The air was redolent with beef-flavored smoke, cloying perfume, tangy barbecue sauce and lots and lots of money. From all appearances, the senator wouldn't have to worry about reclaiming his seat in Washington.

Though Jackson recognized the same faces, the senator's fund-raiser was a far cry from the Donaldsons' black-tie event. But that didn't mean he could relax. With the picnic being held on Senator Hastings' vast lawn, the potential for another theft was just as threatening. The two-story colonial house had been roped off, but that didn't mean someone couldn't manage to find their way inside unnoticed.

In addition to Hastings' men, Jackson had placed a few of his own around the property while he kept a thumb on the crowd. On one person in particular.

Rachel had chosen a quiet spot beneath a gnarled oak, its green leafy branches creating a veiled backdrop. She'd covered her small table with white gauzy cloth that billowed to the ground like a sinking cloud. The overall effect was of a Thomas Kinard painting: elusive, untouchable, secretive.

The ever-present cat sat at Rachel's side watching the cards unfold for their customer. Rachel's sister, Penny, and her boyfriend, Mark, were at a smaller table a few feet away. Penny wrote in a notebook while Mark counted a handful of greenbacks.

Jackson observed the scene with a mixture of concern and suspicion. Why were Rachel's sister and boyfriend at the picnic? Because Penny was her accomplice? Perhaps she scoured the scene and reported back to Rachel. The idea seemed so probable that Jackson had to scowl. Though Mark had seemed decent despite his punk clothes and degenerate appearance, he could be the one who fenced the stolen items. Jackson wanted to reject the thoughts as quickly as they formed. The scenario was too easy. Too obvious. Would Rachel be that naïve? That careless?

He'd know soon enough, as soon as the background check he'd initiated came through.

But who would suspect her? She was the epitome of the elusive female, the kind of woman a man wanted to touch but was afraid to for fear of losing himself. As he had nearly done each time he'd seen her.

'You have the look of a hungry man.'

Tensing at the sound of the familiar voice, Jackson tilted his head around. 'Sandra, what a . . . surprise.'

72

'Is it, darling?' she purred. Though the barbecue was supposed to be a casual affair, Sandra managed to smell like money in her designer jeans, ostrich boots and plum-colored silk shirt. But then, she'd always been the type to wear a Chanel suit to the grocery store, though he doubted she did anything so menial these days.

'I'd say the *surprise* is seeing you here.' She rubbed the backs of her pearl-tipped nails against her collarbone. 'I've heard about the trouble you've been having. Evidently no one's safe any more, regardless of how much we spend on gadgets to keep the undesirables out. Just this morning, Edmond and I were discussing changing our security company. Perhaps you could work for us.'

Jackson refused to let her bait him into a retort, because he honestly didn't care what the woman said. It amazed him that he'd thought himself once in love with her.

When she failed to receive a response, she added, 'But you have several customers here, don't you? I can imagine how embarrassed you are, having to explain why your ingenious system isn't working. Any other man would be off hiding with his tail tucked between his legs.'

Stepping into her space, welcoming the startled widening of her eyes, he asked with chilling calm, 'You wouldn't happen to know anything about the thefts, would you?'

She gave him an insulted once-over, then took a step back. 'Me? Why on earth would I know about them?'

'Because you're so proficient at stealing from other people, of course.'

'I only took what belonged to me.' She tucked a strand of highlighted curls behind her ear. 'I can't help it if you couldn't make your half succeed after I left.'

The 'half' she'd left him had been the debt and unemployed employees. 'And you'd know about failure, seeing as it only took you two years to completely destroy what we built.'

'The company may have failed, but I didn't lose.' She angled her head back, dropping her eyelids as if a beggar had stepped into her path. 'You of all people should know I don't give up without a fight.'

'You must be referring to Edmond.'

'Have you met my husband?' She grinned with bitchy pleasure.

Maybe losing a company had been a small price to pay, he reflected – it had, after all, saved him from a marriage from hell. 'I've heard running a company is a piece of cake compared to creating a successful marriage.'

'Oh, don't worry about me, Jackson. My marriage is solid. But let's talk about you.' Glancing to where Rachel sat, Sandra's eyes took on a shrewd gleam. 'I see you're interested in our little tarot card reader. I'd be careful of her, Jackson. She's gifted. After all, she warned me about marrying you.'

Backing away, she gave him a final, cunning smile and said, 'You won't be able to stop her from seeing all your secrets.'

Jackson waited the few minutes it took for his temper to settle back where it belonged. So, Rachel *had* been the tarot reader Sandra had mentioned when she'd given a reason for breaking their engagement. He'd have to remember to thank Rachel later.

Still holding his food, he hesitated another moment for her to complete her reading. As her customer left, he broke from the circle of people and approached her table. Though her focus had been on gathering her cards, he saw her tense and her head came up, her gaze locking with his. Her gray eyes didn't register surprise, but resignation. Her full mouth even quirked with irritation.

'You've been sitting here for hours. I thought you could use a break.' Jackson took the empty chair and set the plate of barbecue between them.

'That's very thoughtful of you, but . . .'

'I didn't know what you liked, so I brought some of everything.' He handed her a set of napkin-wrapped utensils before she could voice another objection. 'You don't look like the beer type, but I ran out of hands.'

She cocked her head to the side. Her eyes narrowed behind thick, sooty lashes. 'Just what "type" do I look like?'

The question provoked an answer he didn't dare utter. Candlelight and satin, smoke and flame. Clearing his throat, he managed, 'Sparkling water.'

The cat snorted at him. She scooted closer to Rachel's side, where she watched him with her one narrowed eye.

'Why doesn't Fluffy like me?'

'She's very particular, and has excellent taste.'

'So do I.'

75

Smiling, Rachel picked up the cup of beer and took a drink of the gold liquid. Her gaze never wavering, her eyes deepened from silver to pewter. Was it a challenge he saw, or an invitation? He didn't need either, but, God help him, after his encounter with Sandra he was tempted to accept both. A breeze stirred the shadows of her black hair about her face and shoulders, making her seem more fantasy than reality. What was this woman doing to him, and why couldn't he stop it? She was his only suspect in a string of thefts that could be the ruin of him. No matter what he felt, or what he wanted, he had to focus on clearing the stain on his business and his name.

He picked up a buttery roll and tore off a piece. 'Penny,' he said, leaning his elbows on the table in a struggle to seem relaxed. 'Why don't you and Mark grab a plate and join us.'

'Thanks.' Penny closed her notebook. 'But I'm sure you'd prefer to have Rachel all to yourself. You don't mind if we head out, do you, Sis?'

Rachel's mouth compressed briefly, then she said, 'Sure, go ahead.'

With Penny giggling, the young couple linked arms, turned as one and headed toward the far side of the house. Jackson's skin prickled with apprehension. He wanted to follow, but refrained. He had a man stationed near the side entrance. If Penny and Mark tried to enter the house, his man would send a coded message to Jackson's pager.

When Jackson turned back to Rachel, he found her quietly studying him. Her features were set, as if every part of her was focused solely on him. His body reacted instantly, warming with his increasing pulse. He didn't like the way she could unbalance him, send his thoughts off-track, while she remained unaffected. It gave her too much of an advantage. And that was something he couldn't allow. Even if it killed him, he had to be the one who controlled their relationship, such as it was.

'You seem tense, Jackson.' Her voice was sultry, like sin. 'Is something bothering you?'

'You aren't trying to read me again, are you?'

'Not at all.' She reached out and unfurled his fist, removing the remainder of his bread. She set the smashed roll aside. Her dark brow arched, and her mouth quirked with an amused, mischievous grin. 'I'm surprised to see you here.'

'Why is that?'

'You don't seem the "type" to enjoy this kind of gathering.'

Going along with her play on words, he asked, 'Just what kind of gathering do you think I'd prefer?'

She took a bite of brisket, chewing slowly as her gaze moved from his hands to his shoulders and finally to his face. She swallowed, her impossibly slender throat working with the effort. 'You don't care for crowds.'

'Lucky guess.'

'There's nothing wrong with that. I don't care for being lost among the herd myself.' She leaned back in her chair and ran her hand through her hair. The movement stirred her sleeveless blouse, a confection of air and sun. Starburst yellow, yet so weightless it

77

seemed to be made of nothing. Where the hell did she buy her clothes? He'd never seen anything like them before.

The ever-present silver necklace lay between her breasts, defining the full mounds. He threaded his fingers together and pressed them against his mouth. She'd be soft, he thought, stifling a moan. As soft and milky pale as a handful of mist. Her nipples would be dark, though, as dark a rose as her generous mouth. Another groan forced its way up his throat, but he ruthlessly held it back. It took effort, but he looked away. *Business, Dermont. Keep your mind focused on the job.* 'How's your sister doing?'

Rachel laughed, but he thought he heard caution underlying the throaty sound. 'She's in love.'

'Sounds like trouble.'

'You have no idea.' Smiling openly, she reached for another bite of meat. He held his breath as she washed the food down with a sip of beer then handed the cup to him. A trace of pale pink lipstick clung to the plastic. Without thinking, Jackson put his mouth where hers had been and drank.

'Mark is nice enough,' she said, her breath catching. 'Th . . . though his wardrobe seems comprised mainly of leather, fringed leather and studded leather. But I suppose the suited type wouldn't fit Penny. She's happy, and that's enough for now.'

A tangible silence shifted between them as he took small bites from the plate without tasting any of the food. Rachel abandoned eating altogether. Because it was too easy to focus on her as a woman instead of his case, he threw out a question guaranteed to keep him on an appropriate path. 'Does your sister always accompany you at these functions?'

'Yes, she makes the appointments and collects the money.'

'What about Mark? How long has he been working with you?'

Rachel's eyes took on a knowing, glassy sheen. The mood shifted. Jackson imagined he could see the air cool between them, circling, turning to icy fog. He didn't think she'd answer, then she said quietly, 'This is Mark's first time.'

When she crossed her arms, Jackson knew he'd tipped her to his suspicions. But damn if she didn't make it impossible for him to think straight. It had been years since he'd met a woman who interested him, and none as much as Rachel did. To put it simply, he didn't know how to be around her *and* keep her at arm's length. 'How long are you staying?'

'Questions again, Jackson? Either you're a very curious man or you're taking the long road to asking me something specific.' Her unwavering gaze made the hairs at the base of his neck stand on end. 'Which is it? And don't give me that garbage about wanting to have dinner with me.'

'That's not garbage.' In fact, her refusals had become a challenge, one he was determined to win if only to have the opportunity to gather more information about her. Blood pounded in his middle, spreading upward to his chest and involving every part of his body. His ears filled with the sound, his temples pulsed hard and slow. He wanted to take her away from the picnic at that moment, take her someplace where they could be alone. And not to ask her more questions.

He had to find out if she was as elusive as she appeared, or if the heat of a passionate woman hid behind the façade. He wouldn't know until he held her, filled his hands and mouth with her. Maybe then he could get her out of his system. He shuddered at the dangerous thought.

'I don't intend to become your next flavor of the month.'

Snapped back to the present, he demanded, 'What the hell is that supposed to mean?'

She tossed her black mane of hair over her shoulder like a feisty colt. 'Don't take it personally, Jackson. But wealthy men like you don't become seriously involved with women like me.'

It took him a moment to read between the words. 'You mean because you're a tarot reader?'

The dismissive shrug of her bare shoulder made him want to bite her smooth skin, then kiss it until she purred as loudly as her annoying cat. 'Don't attempt to categorize me with other men you've known.'

'I couldn't pigeonhole you even if I tried. I've never met another man like you.' The widening of her eyes told him she hadn't meant for that bit of information to slip out.

Jackson caught his grin before it spread across his face. Did her statement mean she found him attractive, or merely puzzling? He took a deep drink of his beer, wishing it were something stronger. This obsession had to stop. At this rate he'd never learn who was responsible for breaking through his security systems.

Briefly, he considered the option of handing over the investigation to the police. They wouldn't let a woman's sensual voice and scent as potent as lightning sway their judgement. No, once they learned she was connected they'd haul her in for questioning, possibly even arrest her and charge her for the crimes. Unless they came up with another suspect, which he knew wasn't likely.

His gut tightened and a denial pushed up his throat. Christ, he didn't want her to be guilty. No matter how hard he tried to fool himself, he couldn't stand the thought of Rachel being a petty thief.

'Let's get out of here.' Jackson pushed out of his chair and rounded the table.

Startled, she straightened then glanced around as if looking for help. 'I can't just leave.'

'Sure you can.' Taking her arm, he hauled her to her feet. 'It's almost over. The crowd is already thinning out.'

She jerked free. 'I'm not going anywhere.'

'Look, Rachel . . .'

'I don't even know you.'

'I'm trying to change that.'

She went still, not even drawing a breath. 'Why?'

'Hell if I know,' he fired back.

Slowly, she expelled a pent-up breath.

Jackson reached out, took a handful of her long hair and wrapped it around his fist. But he didn't make the mistake of drawing her closer. Regardless of the two hundred guests milling about, he'd be unable to resist burying his face in the thick softness. Then he wouldn't be content until he kissed her, and God knew what would come after that. Damnation.

'There's something going on here. I want to find out what it is.' He knew she'd think he referred to the volatile emotions sizzling between them and not his case, but the line he'd drawn separating the two seemed to become more abstract each time he saw her. Since Penny and Mark had left, he felt confident that another theft wouldn't occur if he stayed with Rachel. The three of them had been under surveillance the entire day. He knew they'd never had a chance to check out the house or the security system. 'Come on, let me drive you home.'

She bit down on her lip. Indecision clouded her eyes. 'I brought my car.'

'Then I'll follow you.'

The air crackled with expectancy in the moment it took her to answer. 'All right.'

With her two simple words, Jackson knew he'd stepped into trouble with both feet. Going home with her would most likely end up being the most foolish thing he'd ever done. But he needed to learn more about her. Perhaps her house would reveal a clue, where her store had held none.

Whatever he discovered, he prayed to God that he didn't live to regret it.

CHAPTER 5

Not only had curiosity killed the cat, Rachel thought as she turned her Acura into her neighborhood, but this cat had purposefully stepped into a wild bull's pasture without a tree to hide behind. What was she thinking, inviting Jackson to her house? She glanced at her rearview mirror and saw his silver Jaguar make a sleek turn right behind her.

She flexed her fingers on the steering wheel. He thought there was something between them. Attraction, yes, she would have had to be dull-witted not to have sensed that, but she didn't delude herself into thinking there was something more. There were too many unanswered questions regarding Jackson Dermont. Too many shadows and hidden corners that she couldn't see around. Which was exactly why she'd agreed to spend more time with him. The chance to discover his secrets was too tempting to ignore.

Maybe her mother was right: her curiosity would be the ruin of her one day.

But something was brewing beneath his shielded surface. Something that caused him to seek her out time and again. That was what bothered her. And intrigued her. Each time she saw him, she learned a little more of what the cards had failed to reveal. Regardless that he was more handsome than any man had a right to be, she'd sensed he was lonely. His habit of reaching out to touch her hinted at his need for physical contact.

She'd labeled him a playboy when she'd first met him, falling from one woman's bed to another without a second thought. She still didn't think him capable of a deep relationship, but he wouldn't want just any woman. He'd be very selective, she reasoned, the women he chose having to meet his strict requirements. He guarded himself closely, carefully asking questions the way a lion circled his prey, waiting, watching for the right time to pounce. But pounce on what? Or whom?

Perhaps she was about to learn the answer to that question.

Pulling into her driveway, she decided it was her turn to ask the prying questions. Who was he? What did he do for a living? What did he really want from her? And why was he so interested in her?

She didn't want him delving into her family's past. There were things better left buried, things Rachel was afraid might come back to tear her family apart. Penny had sworn five years ago that she'd never steal again. And Rachel believed her. But with her sister's odd behavior of late, Rachel couldn't ignore the possibility that Penny might be involved. Rachel shuddered inwardly. She prayed her suspicions were wrong. If her sister was robbing their clients, there would be no keeping Penny out of jail. Probation didn't allow for relapses. Once a judge reviewed Penny's past with gangs, drug dealers and auto theft, Rachel wouldn't stand a chance of helping her sister this time.

She turned off the engine and gathered her purse. In the passenger seat, Miss Bastet uncurled her plump body and stretched, yawning widely. 'Let's go,' Rachel said, lifting the reluctant animal.

As she fumbled with her keys to unlock the front door, Jackson reached her side. She hefted the cat into his arms, and hid a grin at his startled look. Miss Bastet propped her paws against his chest, leaned back and dug in with her claws.

'Ouch! Dammit, Garfield, you did that on purpose.' He jerked back, holding Miss Bastet at arm's length. Man and cat glared at each other, then, with a hiss, Miss Bastet twisted and leapt from his hands.

'Well, that's strange. She usually likes everyone. Maybe if you called her by her real name she might not be so contrary with you.' In answer, Jackson shifted his glare to her as he rubbed his chest with the flat of his palm. The dead bolt clicked, and she swung the door open. A flash of black fur darted inside. Rachel frowned, not liking Miss Bastet's reaction. Perhaps the cat sensed something Rachel had missed. Perhaps she'd made a huge mistake inviting Jackson to her home. But he was a member of the elite, one of society's privileged. He might not be the happiest man she'd ever met, but she didn't believe him to be threatening.

Rachel stepped into the house and turned, expecting Jackson to follow, but he hung back, his gaze roaming over the front porch and green lawn. She could imagine how he saw her home. The grass was freshly cut, but weeds were beginning to sprout in the flowerbeds, crowding the newly planted begonias. Her renovated clapboard house was more than thirty years old. The wood-plank floors groaned, the plumbing rattled temperamentally, but the gabled roof no longer leaked. She'd replaced the red shingles two years before at a cost that had shriveled her savings.

But she loved the old place with its gingerbread design; the smell of aged wood, the sturdy, timeless structure, the neighbors who were as solid and steady as the ground their homes were built on. She didn't have to worry about drugs or gangs or drive-by shootings. Not any more.

She wondered if Jackson saw the quaint setting, felt the peaceful lull, or did he merely picture an old house in a middle-class neighborhood? Her insides twisted with resentment. He probably regretted his insistence to follow her home. In a surly tone, she asked, 'Are you coming?'

His gaze swiveled to her. A dark brow raised in question, but he said nothing. He stepped past her, cloaking her senses with the smell of sun-warmed man. In the living room, Miss Bastet leapt on to the couch. Snorting in her delicate, cat-like manner, she turned away and began laving her front paw.

'Can I get you something to drink?' Rachel faced him and caught her breath.

Hands braced on his lean hips, he stood in the center of the room, consuming what she had once considered a spacious area. He wore pressed jeans, a white button-up shirt and polished gray cowboy boots. A simple outfit, yet on him the look was powerful, seductive. And much more appealing than any tuxedo. Waves of whisky-brown hair brushed the top of his collar. His shuttered gaze circled the room and finally came back to her. 'Scotch on the rocks.'

Not liking the way her nerves jittered beneath her skin, she ran both hands through her hair then folded her arms across her waist. 'Would a glass of Chardonnay do?'

Receiving a nod and a wistful grin in answer, she turned and headed for the kitchen. His booted step echoed behind her. Taking a bottle of chilled wine from the refrigerator and two antique wineglasses from the cabinet, she set everything down on the counter. She reached for the corkscrew in a wicker basket, but Jackson beat her to it, opening the bottle himself. She watched the tendons in his hands flex as he worked the cork free. They were strong hands, capable of hurting if he chose. But, as she recalled the times he'd touched her, he could be gentle as well, which gave her a strange sense of security.

The thought bothered her. She was used to doing things herself; having a man assume the dominant role made her feel delicate . . . and annoyed.

'Your house,' he said, watching her with an intensity that set her nerves on edge. 'It's not what I expected.'

He was doing it again, she realized, putting her on the defensive. She tried to close him off, block his presence from invading hers, but she couldn't. 'What's wrong with it?'

'Nothing.' He poured the pale gold wine into the glasses, handed her one. His brown eyes darkened, shifting to rings of copper as they focused on her. 'But considering the woman who lives here, I suppose that shouldn't surprise me.'

She didn't know how to respond, and decided she'd be better off not bothering. Clutching her wineglass, she skirted past him and made her way to the enclosed rear patio, knowing he'd follow. She settled on the rattan couch, expecting him to take the opposite chair. She should have known that he wouldn't do what she'd expected. He sat beside her, facing her so his bent knee touched hers. Tiny fissions of electricity shot up her thigh. Discreetly, she moved away.

He glanced through the bay windows overlooking her back yard, wild with trees, rose bushes and a pebbled path leading to the creek. 'This place is great.'

Sudden unexpected relief fluttered inside her. 'Did you think I'd live in a hovel?'

The devilish twist of his mouth made her breath lodge in her throat. He ran the tip of his finger down her bare arm. 'To be honest, I thought I might find a crystal ball on your coffee table. I imagined black-painted walls and beaded drapes, maybe some eerie music.'

'Oh, God!' She couldn't help laughing. 'Is that how you see me?'

'Well, your store is a little . . .' he grimaced '. . . unusual.'

'The shop is special. If I started bringing home the pieces I loved, I'd have nothing to sell.'

He twirled a strand of her hair around his finger. 'This place suits you.'

Feeling unsteady, she pulled her hair free and stood, crossing to the opposite window. Facing him, she asked, 'And what about you? What do you do for a living?'

Outwardly, nothing changed in Jackson's posture or expression. But she felt the spike in tension, as if she'd opened a door to the forbidden. 'I have my own business.'

'Which is?' she prompted, annoyed that he wasn't more forthcoming.

He rose and leisurely strolled towards her. He leaned his shoulder against the windowpane. When his eyes settled on her they were restless, edgy. 'Nothing as interesting as yours.'

What was he hiding? She delved beneath the protective layers that he'd wrapped around himself and found nothing. It frustrated her, not being able to catch a glimmer, a hint of what motivated him. Was it money, power, politics? Women? What made Jackson Dermont pry into her life while he kept his own safely concealed?

More determined than ever to find out, she said, 'Despite my profession, I do understand business.'

'I never thought you wouldn't.'

'So why the secret?'

He leaned closer, consuming the space between them. 'It's no secret.'

'Then bore me.' Resisting the overwhelming need to move away, she straightened her back and crossed her arms over her waist. He was trying to intimidate her, cause her to change the subject. She refused. If playing with fire gained her the answers she wanted, then she'd play.

'I'd rather talk about you.' He shifted, placing her between his body and the window. His free hand came up to rest against the pane beside her head, partially trapping her in his own little prison. He was too close, swallowing her space with his size and smell and force. She could escape if she took one step to the side, but sheer stubbornness forced her to remain still.

She hardly recognized her voice as she asked, 'Are you involved with something illegal?'

A roguish light flared in his eyes, eyes that saw too much and revealed nothing. She drew in a breath that filled her lungs with scents of Jackson, of exertion and man and something more primal. Something new and different. 'What would make you ask such a question?'

'Because you're hiding something.'

'I just don't like talking about myself.' The lines around his eyes softened. And she thought that, for once, he might be telling the truth.

'Neither do I.'

'Fair enough.' He took her drink and set both glasses on the window seal. Facing her, he clasped her waist between his hands, startling a gasp from her.

She slapped her hands against his chest to keep him from pulling her close. 'What do you think you're doing?'

'I'm going to tell you what you want to know.' Heat soaked her thin dress, passing to her skin, spreading into the fire she'd so arrogantly toyed with. 'I'm in the security business.'

Aware of his soft cotton shirt and the muscles beneath, she snatched her hands back and crossed her arms again. 'Was that so hard?'

He straightened, inching her closer. He towered above her, forcing her head back. 'You'd be surprised how often people try to get me to divulge inside information.'

A deep-seated flicker in his eyes warned her that he held something back, or perhaps had even lied. She couldn't be sure which. Exasperation boiled up inside her.

'I promise not to ask any unethical . . .'

'I want to kiss you.'

The soft statement slammed into her mind. Her heart pounded against her chest, her temples, the base of her throat. If he moved any closer, she knew he'd feel her frantic pulse. Logic screamed for her to pull away. But the feel of his hands on her hips, the hypnotic lure of his eyes, the brush of his clothes against hers kept her from moving.

She'd risked playing with fire, and this was what she got, an inferno spreading inside her with no way to put it out.

'Jackson, I don't think this is a good idea.'

'Don't you want me to kiss you?'

'I don't even know you.'

'Yes, you do.' He bent his head, his mouth so close she imagined she could taste him – rich, dark, mysteriously carnal. 'You want me to kiss you.'

Somehow she managed to whisper, 'No, I don't.'

The corner of his mouth lifted with a smile. 'Now who's the one hiding something?'

'I've nothing to hide.' Her gaze lowered, stayed on the curve of his lips. It amazed her, how something so simple could change his face from handsome to devastating. *Breathe, Rachel, breathe.* 'Kissing you wouldn't be simple.'

'And you like things simple?'

She liked to be in control of a situation, and at the moment, she lacked even the pretense of control.

'I . . .' His mouth closed over hers, cutting her off. His hands slid up her back and into her hair, cupping her head. Too stunned to move, she let him tilt her head. Slowly, as if the world had fallen away, he deepened the kiss. A small, helpless sound escaped her. She gripped his shirt in her fists to push him away, but the act only drew him closer.

His tongue broke past her lips, startling her with his texture and taste. He felt like raw silk, cool and uncut. A hint of wine, of man and a passion she'd barely glimpsed heightened her senses. She heard Miss Bastet's distant cry over the pounding of her heart. She thought to pull away, but she couldn't. She held on.

And kissed him back.

An anguished growl rose from him, rumbling against her hands. Something spiraled down her center, tightening into a knot in her belly. She sucked in a breath and closed her eyes so she could feel. His arm tightened around her waist, solid, secure, holding her flush against him. Her body molded to his, angles linking to curves. Her softness cupped his hardness.

The back of her knees weakened. She shouldn't be doing this; she shouldn't want him so much. She was curious about him, but she knew better than to become involved. He was still a stranger, secretive, elusive, like a shadow without a beginning or an end.

'Jackson,' she said, though she wasn't sure if it was a whisper to stop or a plea for more.

His palm skimmed up her side, brushed the outer curve of her breast. She shivered, her head dropping back. He buried his face in the bend of her neck, biting, kissing. His thumb grazed over silk, teasing her center, making her breasts feel full and flushed. She arched into his palm without thought, trembled when his fingers closed around her, kneading and caressing and taking.

His mouth covered hers, their kiss turning wild and hot, frightening her with its intensity. She felt herself sliding away and into him. Part of her didn't care. She wanted to feel the intangible cravings he ignited, the desperate need that until now had never existed. Another part of her fought it, terrified of losing herself to a stranger.

'Jackson, please . . .'

He pulled back slightly. His breath as labored as hers, he rested his forehead against her brow. She clutched his upper arms, his muscles flexing against her palms.

'Rachel?' a female voice called out, echoing though the halls.

In unison, they looked toward the doorway leading to the house. The voice called out again. 'Rachel? Where are you, honey?'

'Who is that?' Jackson demanded in a rough whisper.

'My mother.' Stumbling over Miss Bastet, who'd wrapped herself around Rachel's leg without her realizing it, Rachel managed to put a step between her and Jackson before Emily appeared in the threshold.

'You couldn't have locked the front door?' Jackson growled under his breath.

'There you are.' Wearing a white sundress imprinted with tiny red apples and a sleeveless denim jacket, her mother breezed in. Without breaking stride, she crossed to Jackson, her hand outstretched. 'That gorgeous Jaguar in the driveway must belong to you. I'm Emily Gold, Rachel's mother.'

'It's a pleasure, ma'am, and yes, the car's mine.' Taking her hand, Jackson introduced himself.

'I hope I haven't interrupted anything.' Emily's gaze flicked between Rachel, Jackson and the abandoned wineglasses. Rachel couldn't gather her wits fast enough to reply before Emily asked, 'Have you known my daughter long?'

'We met at the Donaldsons' gala last week.'

Heat bled into Rachel's cheeks as her mother studied the twin set of wrinkles creasing Jackson's

94

shirt where Rachel had gripped the fabric in her fists. 'Mr Dermont was just leaving, Mom.'

'Oh, what a shame.'

'Yes, it is,' Jackson stated, his gaze boring into Rachel.

She held her weak smile in place, but she couldn't meet his eyes for fear her blush would burst into flames. 'I'll see you out.'

On the front porch, Rachel hesitated, knowing her mother would try to eavesdrop. Since Emily would make more of Jackson's presence than she should, Rachel closed the door behind her.

With his hands in his pockets, he stepped off the porch and onto the sidewalk. 'I learned something about you today,' he said, his steady gaze as disturbing as a physical touch. 'You're not as calm as you appear.'

Calm? That emotion didn't begin to fit into her state of being. She felt like a ball of unstrung yarn and her emotions were scattered across the floor. 'I learned something about you, as well.'

'Oh, really?' His mouth lifted with a cryptic grin.

'You're not as indifferent as you try to act.' From the husky rhythm of his breathing to the feral glint in his eyes, she could tell he wanted to kiss her again, and, irrational as it seemed, she wished he would. She gripped the porch's support beam to steady herself.

'No, Rachel, indifferent wouldn't describe how I feel about you.'

'How do you feel about me?' she asked, then wished she could bite off her tongue.

He shook his head, his jaw clenching as he looked away. 'Hell if I know.'

On his way out of his small, barren kitchen, Jackson picked up the manila folder labeled 'Confidential: Insurance Reports.' With a cold can of beer in one hand and the thick file in the other, he stretched out on his leather sofa. Jimmy Buffet's graveled voice broke through the stereo speakers, the familiar words and melody filling Jackson's townhouse, making it seem not quite so empty. He'd never bothered decorating his new home after splitting with Sandra, acquiring only the essentials. He hadn't neglected to add novelties like pictures and plants because of a lack of time, but because of a lack of interest. The townhouse was merely a place to shower, sleep and store his clothes.

When Sandra had ended their engagement, she'd moved out, taking the furniture, pots and pans, linens – everything down to the salt and pepper shakers, before he'd realized she'd also helped herself to his business. She'd been one hell of a saleswoman, he thought with a askew twist of his mouth. Because she'd sure pulled one over on him.

In reflection, he'd had no one to blame except himself. He'd handed over everything to her from accounting to sales so he could concentrate on developing upgrades for his software, a necessity to keep their business ahead of the competition. While he'd had his nose buried in code, she'd assumed control of the checking accounts, sales people and client lists.

Because she'd helped start the company, and because they'd planned to marry, he'd put the business in both their names, giving Sandra equal rights to the software license. It was supposed to have been the beginning of their future.

The thought forced a cynical laugh past his tight throat.

SafeBank had been his baby, and it would have become a goldmine within two years. His and Sandra's lottery ticket. There hadn't been a security software program like it on the market. There still wasn't. His system had encrypted data for the banking industry, ensuring safe transfer over the Internet. He doubted there ever would be anything comparable, especially now that he wasn't involved. Sandra had hired a staff of college grads who'd tried to improve his baby. He'd told her it wouldn't work, and it hadn't. It had only taken her two years to lose everything. But the woman had enough drive and grit to outmaneuver most men. Though she'd lost the business, she'd still come out on top by marrying money. Her single-minded determination was what had attracted him to her. Until she'd turned on him and he'd learned that she'd never wanted him, but what he could give her.

His attorney had called him a fool for not suing. Jackson hadn't wanted to endure the years of dragging her deceit and his own foolishness through the court system. He'd wanted to forget. He'd tried to move on by developing a new software program, but he'd found he didn't have the enthusiasm for it any more. So he'd chosen another field – home security.

Developing his system had taken time, but he was proud of what he'd accomplished. He might not ever make the kind of money he could have made with SafeBank, but he didn't care. He gave his living room a cursory glance. It wasn't as if he spent what he did make, anyway.

But he had a new dilemma to overcome. This time the situation might be different, but his company was no less at risk of being stripped bare. It wouldn't happen again, he swore. This time, he knew better than to trust anyone.

Dusky sunlight flowed through parted drapes, spreading orange slashes over white, pictureless walls. Shadows gathered in the corners of the room, adding a sense of gloomy security. Reaching behind him, Jackson switched on the table lamp.

He propped the report on his lap. He'd read it several times already, and had failed to come up with any clues. Each list was a detailed description of the stolen items. In some cases, his customers had included pictures. Gathering the information had proved as difficult as finding any leads. As slow as his clients had been in getting the insurance papers to him, they'd been just as insistent that he find the person responsible. The police hadn't done much to investigate the robberies, having more important cases to handle – like murders, and drugs dealers peddling their wares in schools.

His clients hadn't wanted to publicize the thefts in the media, which Jackson understood and respected. His customers demanded privacy, and it was, after all, the reason for his business. But with the majority of them being egocentric, even obtaining a complete guest list had taken more time and patience than he possessed.

Jackson swore under his breath, deciding the rich expected the world to spin both ways at once. With the threat of suing him for misrepresenting the impenetrability of his systems, they demanded that he find the thief, but they didn't want to help him do it.

He ran his finger over the edge of the file, reluctant to open it. Part of him wanted to stop the investigation, suggest his customers had lost the items, or someone on their staff, a maid or gardener, had stolen from them. It was a possibility. Though unlikely, considering the pattern that was forming. Each theft had happened a day or two following some type of charitable function, which meant someone, a common denominator, had to be present at each party, scouting the area and devising a way to penetrate his system.

Even if his customers didn't sue him for everything he was worth, he'd lose their business. If that were to happen, he could move to another town, he supposed, start over, but he'd fought too hard to climb this particular hill; he wasn't about to backslide now.

But how did losing business compare to the possibility that Rachel might be the one responsible? He was committed to nailing the thief, but could he turn Rachel in if he discovered she was the one he was after? He'd have to.

'How do you feel about me?'

Her direct, startling question had shaken him. Caring about her would mean risking everything – something he'd sworn he'd never do again. The first time he'd loved someone he'd been betrayed, but he'd recovered. He didn't think he'd be so lucky a second time. He wanted to believe Rachel was as innocent as she seemed, as caring, as strong, but deep down he was afraid he was deluding himself.

He took a drink of his beer, the icy liquid sliding down his throat to his stomach, then he rested his head against the couch. Murky light crept across the ceiling, producing angles and shapes that formed nothing in particular, yet managed to remind him of Rachel. The first time he'd met her, she'd seemed as elusive as a shadow, unreal, as if his subconscious had created her for his own pleasure . . . or torment.

Today had cured him of any such illusion.

Her reserved, secretive image had shattered the instant he'd touched her. She'd fallen apart in his hands, clinging to him as if she'd been unable to stand on her own. Jackson ran a hand over his face as the renewed memory churned desire through his veins. He took another drink, but this time the beer burned a path down his throat.

He muttered a curse. Kissing her had been a mistake. She'd tasted as erotic as she looked; sultry and sweet, like a humid summer evening. But the feel of her had been his undoing. He'd thought her slender arms and delicate body fragile, breakable. She was neither. She was firm and soft, and fitted him so well, he'd lost sight of everything except making love to her.

Which scared the hell out of him. The few women he'd dated since Sandra had known up front that they were getting a brief, non-committal relationship based on sex. The dates had been emotionally empty, which had been fine with him. Except, recently, he'd quit pursuing even that type of connection.

Of everything Sandra had taken from him, he hated her most for stealing his ability to trust. He'd thought himself incapable of caring about anyone ever again. He certainly never thought he'd feel the slightest glimmer of . . . He stopped himself, not wanting to name the deep churning inside his chest.

Rachel had been right when she'd said kissing her wouldn't be simple. It was damn complicated. For the first time since Sandra, he wanted more than a few hours of gratuitous sex. He wanted the impossible – he wanted to know Rachel every way possible, which meant allowing her to become a part of his life.

Expelling a breath, he pressed his fingers to his closed eyelids. He'd wanted to throttle Rachel's mother for interrupting them. On hindsight, he knew her arrival had been a blessing.

Rachel might not have called a halt to their kiss, and he'd been so driven he wouldn't have stopped until he'd made love to her. And that was a dilemma he didn't need.

Pushing thoughts of Rachel aside, he forced his attention on the folder in his lap. A report he'd expected weeks ago from a furious customer had finally arrived. He didn't think the information would shed any more light than the rest had, but it had to be reviewed. Opening the file, he skimmed the new material. Suddenly, his heart lurched against his chest. His body numbed, prickling with disbelief. The beer slipped from his hand and landed on the floor, spilling on to the tan carpet. A dark stain spread in a lop-sided circle.

Jackson swung his legs off the couch and sat up, staring at the photograph. He blinked, but the picture didn't change. Questions spun around his mind, blurring his vision. 'No! Christ, this can't be happening.'

Anger pooled in his gut then shot through his veins like hot iron. Sweat dripped from his temples. Jerking the report out, he crumpled it in his fist. In a voice that shook, he whispered, 'Damn you, Rachel.'

CHAPTER 6

'Mom says you have a boyfriend.'

The antique, Austrian crystal angel slipped through Rachel's fingers. She watched, horrified, as the iridescent body hit the tile floor and shattered. Pieces slid in all directions, scattering tiny bits of broken light over tile. 'Penny, look what you made me do.'

'Me?' Quirking her mouth with dismay, she returned, 'All I did was ask a question.'

Shaking, Rachel pressed a hand to her pounding heart as she retrieved a hand-broom and dustpan from the storage closet. Back in the showroom, she knelt and swept up a pan full of fallen stars. Despite her anger at herself, she snapped, 'Look at this.'

'Was she expensive?' Penny asked, sounding contrite as she leaned over the counter to watch. The front door opened, jingling the bell.

'No. But she was old, and one of my favorites.'

'What's this?'

Rachel glanced up to find Emily hovering above her, a stern, motherly frown pinching her brow.

Rachel stifled a groan. The store had just opened and her mother wasn't due to work until three that afternoon. This did not bode well for her. She wasn't up to fending off questions from both her mother and sister about why Jackson had been at her house.

'Rachel dropped an angel,' Penny volunteered, as if the fact weren't obvious enough.

'It isn't like you to be so careless, Rachel.' Emily set her purse on the counter and took the broom and pan from her eldest daughter.

'I think I upset her.' All innocence, Penny turned her attention to adhering price tags to a new shipment of Celtic pentagrams.

Dumping the angel's remains into the trashcan, Emily asked in a warning tone, 'What have you done now?'

Sitting back on her heels, Rachel considered getting up and walking out the door before the conversation went any farther.

'All I did was ask about her boyfriend.'

'I don't have a boyfriend,' Rachel said, annoyance pushing her to her feet.

'Oh.' Emily brushed past Rachel. Returning the broom to the closet, she quickly rejoined them. 'Penny, I told you not to mention that.'

'It slipped out.'

'I *don't* have a boyfriend.' Rachel looked at the two women and wondered if she'd suddenly become invisible.

'She still hasn't told me anything.' With a sulking pout, Penny glanced at her sister.

'Yes, I have.' Unaccustomed to dealing with the kind of anger fuming inside her, Rachel crossed her arms and paced in a tight line. 'Jackson Dermont is nothing more than a . . . an acquaintance.'

Penny rolled her eyes. 'Well, if that's the case, you're an idiot.'

'I don't want to discuss this.'

As if she were blind to Rachel's presence as well as deaf, Penny continued, 'The man is gorgeous.'

'I have to agree with you,' Emily said.

'Mother! I told you . . .'

'And from the looks of him, I'd also say he's mad enough to eat the devil with the horns on.'

Following the direction of Emily's gaze, Rachel spun around. Having parked on the far side of the parking lot, Jackson stood beside his car, waiting for a break in the traffic. She'd never seen him in worn jeans and a faded T-shirt. He had a wild, jagged look to him, as if he'd fought a battle and lost. With long, stalking strides he crossed the short distance to her store. Wind tossed his wheat-colored hair into his eyes, but he pushed it back with a sharp swipe of his hand.

His shoulders were rigid, his face a tight mask as if he were braced for a fight. Something had obviously happened since he'd left her house the night before, but what? And why was he bringing it to her store? Whatever had him upset, she didn't want her mother exposed to it.

Collecting Emily's purse, Rachel took Penny by the hand and pulled her around the counter. 'I'd appreciate it if the two of you would go into the office.'

105

'And do what?' Penny protested.

'Do some filing, relax. I don't care. Just go.'

Pursing her lips, Emily took her purse from Rachel. 'There's no need for us to hide.'

'You're not hiding, you're just . . . I want to . . . Oh, Mother, please just let me talk to him alone for a few minutes.'

'All right.' Emily frowned and glanced out the window again. 'I don't know what you did to get him so riled, but try to straighten it out. It's time you settled down. He's handsome and obviously well-to-do. You could do worse.' Reaching the office, she added, 'I'll be right here if you need me.'

Rachel faced the front of the store just as Jackson barreled inside as if he intended to blow the building down. He spotted her instantly. He said nothing, just walked the perimeter of the store, circling the shelves, his hostile gaze moving over the merchandise.

At a loss for something to say, she resorted to her usual sales line. 'Can I help you find something?'

'Yes, you can.' He didn't say more, but continued up one aisle then down another. He examined a jewelry case, then a small Egyptian urn she'd been thrilled to discover at a garage sale. He moved from one item to the next, studying them as if he expected to find something dire.

'Jackson, what are . . .?'

'Where do you get all this stuff, Rachel?'

Picking up the lethal tone of his voice, she frowned. Cautiously, she answered, 'No one place. They come from auctions, estate sales, and brokers. Sometimes people contract me if they're remodeling and want to sell their things. Why do you ask?'

'Where are they?'

'Where are what?' She took a step forward, then caught herself when he spun to face her.

'Have you hidden them?' he asked, his voice so deceptively calm she barely heard him. 'Or are they sitting out in plain view?'

'Have I hidden what?' Feeling her pulse begin to throb in her neck, she demanded, 'What are you talking about?'

'The vase from the Donaldsons' party. The diamond choker from the Rodmans'.' He shook a folder at her, moving closer in a dangerous, predatory manner. 'How about the Fabergé egg the Downeys had carelessly displayed on their fireplace mantel?'

'What are you accusing me of?' His fury struck her full force, like an inferno exploding before her eyes. Heat boiled up around him, consuming her, sucking the air from her lungs. The closer he came, the more her skin prickled, burned as if she'd been struck by lightning. Time and again she'd cursed the inability to feel his emotions; now all she wanted was to shut him off, escape while she could.

'Jackson . . .' She couldn't finish her thought. He reached her, swallowing her in a whirlpool of trembling rage. She held her breath, afraid to move, afraid of what he might do. She'd never imagined he'd hurt her physically; now she wasn't so sure.

'Is that how you acquired your inventory?' he demanded. 'By stealing it?'

'Stealing?' The word barely rasped from her throat, the sound so low she didn't think he'd heard her.

'I almost believed that bullshit story about your saving every dime to build this store. God, I wanted it to be true! But then I guess everyone believes you, don't they, Rachel?' he said in a voice so menacing the hairs on her nape stood on end. 'With your wide, innocent eyes and your pious air, everyone buys into the garbage you feed them while you rob them blind. But I know the truth. You're nothing but a goddamn thief.'

The blood drained from Rachel's head, making her sway slightly. *Thief*? She glanced at the office door where her mother and Penny were undoubtedly listening to every word. Her heart struck against her ribs. *God, no. Please don't let this happen again.* 'I . . .' She swallowed hard. Calm, she had to remain calm. 'I think you'd better leave.'

'You're not even going to deny it?'

'I don't know what you're talking about.' And she didn't want to know. The past was buried, over, it couldn't hurt them again. *I won't let it*! But even as she silently repeated the litany, she knew it was a lie. With frightening certainty, she feared the past was now hidden in the manila folder Jackson clutched in his fist. 'I don't know why you'd accuse me of stealing, but I want you to leave, now, or I'll call the police and charge you with harassment.'

'There's no need to call the cops, sweetheart.' He delivered the statement as a cold, unnerving threat. He stepped back, his squared shoulders creating a wall between them. His chest heaved with each breath, firing the room with added tension. Silence dragged out, and for an instant she imagined she saw regret dim the hot glare of his anger. 'I'm on my way to the police station now. I'm sure they'll be interested in what I have to show them.' He slapped the folder against his thigh. 'Say goodbye to your business, Rachel. You're about to lose it.'

Jackson clenched his jaw until it ached as emotions fell across Rachel's face with the pounding force of an iron gavel. She sucked in a breath and her dark pewter eyes faded, turning stark and glassy. She swayed, staggering backward. Jackson strangled the reflex to reach out and steady her.

He waited for her to deny his accusations, say anything that would take away the suffocating pressure in his chest. Long, endless seconds passed in charged silence. A surge of cold air pushed through the vents overhead, cooling the sweat on his brow. A ticking clock marked time from some-where behind him. The erratic beat of his heart pounded in the veins of his throat, echoing in his ears. Why wouldn't she defend herself? Give him a reason to stay so she could explain? But what had he expected? Surely not a confession?

She merely watched him with those deceptively calm eyes, the same eyes that made him want to sink into her, kiss her, force her to convince him he was wrong.

Something brushed against his leg, breaking the moment. Jackson glanced down. Miss Bastet was wrapped around his calf, her black face tilted up to his. She meowed, the sound sharp and scolding. He imagined her one golden eye filling with disapproval.

'You're always one to give advice, Rachel. Now I have some for you.' He clenched his jaw, regretting that he'd ever laid eyes on her. Turning away, he said over his shoulder, 'Get a lawyer.'

'Jackson, wait.'

He heard her plea but he kept going. He never should have stopped here in the first place. Only anger at himself for wanting to believe in her, hope that she might be different, had brought him to her doorstep, not with the intent to warn her, but to see the truth for himself. He'd imagined her shock at being discovered, and he hadn't been disappointed. What he hadn't counted on was how sick it made him feel, how it left him shaking with fury. Even now he wanted to smash something, rip something apart the way she'd slashed the first hint of caring he'd felt in years.

His only consolation was that he'd discovered her true character before it had gone too far.

Some consolation, he thought, as empty dread reached up though his body, jarring him from the inside out.

With his hand on the door he felt her touch on his arm, but he couldn't bring himself to shrug it off.

'Jackson, please wait.'

'I'm afraid it's too late to start the denials now.'

'Honestly, I don't know what you're talking about,' she said quietly, though he heard the soft tremor in her voice.

She knows, he thought with sinking acceptance. Which means she's guilty. She'll be arrested and go to prison and I'll never see her again. Case closed.

She stepped around to face him. Her eyes were liquid with fear. She really ought to learn how to shield her emotions, he thought. He could teach her; he'd become an expert.

'You charged in here and accused me of being a criminal. How did you expect me to react? Maybe you thought I'd run for the back door to escape now that you've *found* me out?' Her voice hitched with a thread of anger. 'I'm stunned and appalled that you'd accuse me of something this horrible, Jackson, but I'm not guilty of anything.'

She took a steadying breath. 'Could we start over, please?'

'Why? So you can try to change my mind about turning you in?'

Blanching, she snapped her gaping mouth shut, then said through clenched teeth, 'I deserve an explanation.'

'Fine, I'll humor you, then. You've built yourself a nice little empire here.' He swept his arm around in a wide arc to encompass the store. 'Only you didn't accomplish it by *saving* money, you did it by stealing from your clients.'

Her eyes widened with disbelief. 'No . . .'

'You worked each party. Had access to everyone's house.' He stepped toward her, stalking her, forcing her backward through the store. 'What I want to know is how you managed to get by their security systems? Have you studied them the way you've studied your cards?'

'I haven't stolen anything.' She halted her retreat and straightened her back, and still the top of her head barely reached his chin. She was so small and compact, so deceptively vulnerable. Yet determination lit a fire in her eyes. 'What kind of proof do you think you have against me?'

Crossing to the counter, he slapped the folder on its polished surface. He reached into his coat pocket and pulled out a necklace, letting it dangle from his fingers – the same necklace he'd bought from her the week before.

She started at it, her eyes narrowing in confusion. 'I don't understand.'

Jackson opened the file. The photo he'd crumpled in a blaze of anger lay on top, wrinkled but recognizable.

Rachel's gaze moved from the string of gems he held to the paper and back again. Finally, her gaze lifted, meeting his. 'You're saying this necklace was stolen?'

Her unguarded tone made his skin go cold. 'I suppose you're going to tell me you didn't take it.'

She stepped back, clenched her hands at her waist as if she were afraid the jewelry would come alive and bite her. 'I didn't.' She swallowed. 'Who does it belong to?'

'Martha Richardson. I checked with her; you worked her charity dinner for Alzheimer's five months ago. The necklace was reported stolen two days later.'

'That doesn't prove anything.'

'Admit that you were there!'

'Yes, dammit, I was there.' She took quick little breaths, her chest rising and lowering in the same staccato rhythm as his. 'But that doesn't mean I'm a thief.'

He picked up the stack of detailed reports and photos he'd gathered. 'This is information I've collected over the past seven months, listing the items stolen from various people. You're the only common denominator, Rachel. You were at the scene of each crime.' She shook her head in denial, but he didn't stop. 'You had access to their security systems, time to plan a return trip.'

'That's not true.'

'And you had a motive.'

She gaped at him, her hands propped on her hips. 'You seemed to have figured everything out. What kind of motive have you decided I have? And why are you involved with this anyway?'

He ignored that last question. 'You said yourself that you'd do anything to keep this store, take care of your family, be a success.'

'I didn't mean I'd steal to get it.'

His smirk made her eyes narrow with anger, sparking with shards of white lightning. The cat from hell leapt on to the counter and hissed at him.

'Then how did you come by it?' Jackson demanded.

'I don't remember offhand. I've had it for months.' She raked her fingers through her hair, pulling the curling, shining length over her shoulders.

'Could you be more specific?' The anger pounding though his veins slowed to an incessant throb. Last night, when he'd felt the stab of betrayal slice into him, he'd steeled himself against feeling anything at all. He'd been intrigued by this woman, but not enough to allow her to hurt him. It had taken half the night and a fifth of Jack Daniel's for the conviction to sink in and stick.

Rachel opened her mouth, then closed it as if her announcement refused to come. Jackson gripped the counter's edge and braced himself for her confession. 'Where did you get the necklace, Rachel?'

'I don't know!' She pivoted on her heel to pace about. 'I'll have to look at my records. But I don't have files that far back here.'

'I want the invoice.'

Slowly, her head came up and she turned to face him. Shadows clouded her eyes like thoughts, dark and untouchable. 'Has something been stolen from you?'

'No.'

Her shoulders sagged slightly with relief. 'Then why are you involved in this?'

Jackson suppressed a sigh and looked away. The cat blinked an accusing eye at him. 'I'm investigating the thefts.'

From the fine line creasing her brow, he could tell she was trying to make the connection. 'Because they're friends of yours? Why wouldn't . . .?'

'They're clients.'

She straightened, and, though she didn't move, he felt her withdrawal as if all the warmth and light had been sucked out of the room. 'What kind of clients?'

'Dermont Technology is a state-of-the-art security company. Everyone who's been hit has my system installed. Since the design is supposed to be foolproof, I've spearheaded my own investigation.'

The little color left in her cheeks, drained away. Her eyes lost their fighting sheen and dimmed as if a switch had been turned off. 'So, you've had me under surveillance all this time?'

He clenched his jaw. 'Yes.'

She nodded. Her gaze held his and refused to let go. 'The offer to buy me dinner, the pretense of wanting to get to know me, that's all it was – pretense. Every bit of it a lie.'

Afraid to utter a word, afraid a denial might slip out, Jackson let the silence speak for itself.

'And when you weren't getting anywhere, you decided to move things along by kissing me.' Her voice was blunt, as if a piece of her had broken off. 'Did you think I'd be so overcome by your appeal that I'd confess?'

He refused to let the angry, wounded look in her eyes affect him. Damn if he didn't want to say something that would undo everything that had just happened. But there was no going back to that moment on her patio, that sweet, stunning moment that had changed something inside him. Something he didn't want changed.

Gathering the necklace, he slipped it into his pocket. An apology hovered on the tip of his tongue. He didn't know what he wanted to apologize for: kissing her maybe, or blowing her cover, which would result in the ruin of her life. It didn't make sense, this need to tell her everything would be all right. Because it wouldn't be. And he knew it.

He reached for the folder, but she slammed her hand down on it. 'What are you going to do?'

'I told you, turn this over to the police.'

'You'll list me as a suspect regardless that the evidence you *think* you have is circumstantial? I told you I didn't do it?'

'Then give me the invoice that will prove you bought it.'

She hesitated, her chin jutting out. 'I told you I don't have it here.'

'That's because there isn't one, is there, Rachel?'

'Of course there is!' A tremor vibrated her body.

He made the mistake of meeting her gaze, and for an instant he almost believed her. He could become lost in her eyes, so clear and deep they were, like flawless diamonds perfectly cut. But were they the eyes of a liar? He couldn't tell. 'I'd like to believe you, but doing so would make me either foolish or stupid. And I try not to be either.'

Shifting from one foot to another, she studied the folder as if she wanted to grab it and run. 'I'm innocent, Jackson. But that won't matter. If my

116

customers learn I'm a suspect in the burglaries, I'll be ruined all the same.'

He'd considered the possibility that he might be wrong, that she could lose everything if he made a mistake. He didn't like the stab of guilt that brought. 'That's a chance you'll have to take. Unless you can prove you're not guilty.'

'You can't prove I am.'

'I've only just started digging.'

Her breath turned sharp, and her eyes widened. He could feel the panic rising up inside her. The air trembled with it, sizzled as if the space around her had been set on fire. He wondered if she felt cornered, locked in with no way out, and he hated the fact that he'd been the one to trap her. If only things could have been different. If only he could believe she was innocent; if only she could prove she was. If only . . .

'I'll make a deal with you,' she said, her eyes glowing as if a desperate fever burned inside her.

'Like look the other way? Forget what I know?' His voice lowered to a suggestive tone without his meaning it to. 'In exchange for what?'

'I ought to slap you for that.'

She ought to, he realized, regretting his comment the instant it had left his mouth. But he hardly recognized himself or his actions. He shouldn't have come to her first, but gone to the police. He shouldn't be standing here now, drowning in the liquid pools of her eyes, breathing in her whispering scent – yet he couldn't move. 'What do you have in mind?'

'Give me a chance to clear myself. Wait until you have all the facts before you go to the police.'

'You mean give you a chance to run.'

'I won't leave.'

No, she wouldn't run, he decided. She might appear fragile, as delicately made as stardust, and just as elusive, but she was a fighter. The evidence lay in her tilted chin, the pressed line of her full mouth. A mouth he wanted to kiss again and again, despite the evidence, despite his good sense.

He wanted to kiss her and hold her and finish what they'd started. A shudder erupted beneath his skin. He curled his hands into fists to keep from acting on the insane urge. He'd been raked through burning coals once. He couldn't allow it to happen again, no matter how great the temptation. Yet he couldn't seem to deny the quiet pleading in her eyes.

It dawned on him then that she wouldn't beg, and that small bit of courage on her part decided the moment. That, and the fact that his evidence wasn't foolproof. If she could produce an invoice that proved legitimate, she would be cleared of stealing the necklace. Unfortunately, it wouldn't absolve her altogether. She was the only person present at the scene of each crime – too many burglaries for the connection to be a coincidence.

'You have one day to produce the invoice, Rachel. After that I go to the police.'

She nodded her acceptance.

'I'll be watching you.'

'I know.'

Gathering the folder, he turned, crossed to the door.

'Jackson?' Her soft voice reached out and stopped him with the force of firm hand, but he couldn't face her again. 'I'm going to prove you wrong. And when I do, you're going to have to trust me.'

He'd told her once before that trust was for fools. He'd believed it then, believed it now more than ever. Because only a fool would dare risk his heart, his life, his existence . . . for the trust of a woman.

CHAPTER 7

The bell above the door jingled, announcing Jackson's departure, the sound light and gay, like the chirping of a sparrow, when it should have vibrated with the finality of a death-toll – slow and brooding. The pressure in Rachel's chest increased, as if stone after stone were being placed there. Her lungs burned, and her skin turned hot and prickly.

She was innocent, dammit! Why wouldn't he believe her?

She drew in a searing breath, her body filling, expanding, trembling as it drew in much needed air. She could still imagine seeing Jackson standing at the door, his lean body braced against anything she had to say, his eyes averted, unwilling even to look at her.

I'm innocent, she'd wanted to scream again and again until he believed her. But to do so would cast his suspicions elsewhere, and that she couldn't risk. Not until she knew the truth herself. She hadn't been the only one at each of the parties. Penny had been there as well, mingling with the guests, walking through the houses. She'd had the opportunity to slip a necklace into her pocket. But what about the other things Jackson had mentioned? A diamond choker, a Fabergé egg, the vase. What had happened to them?

Miss Bastet nudged Rachel's hand so she would pet her. Rachel did one better, gathering the cat in her arms and burying her face in the thick black fur. She stayed where she was, wrapping her arms around the cat's body, afraid to look up, terrified she'd see cracks in the protective walls she'd so painstakingly built. It wouldn't take much to tear those walls down. Only a few choice words to her customers and it would all be gone. Her home, her business, her ability to protect her family.

She shivered as if someone had dragged his nail down her spin, leaving a trail of foreboding. She dropped Miss Bastet to the floor and received an angry cry. Rachel headed for the office door, reaching it just as it opened.

Her mother poked her head out. 'Is he gone?'

'Yes.' Rachel pushed the door open and entered the cramped office. Penny sat in the one chair at the cluttered desk, surveying the chipped remains of her black nail polish.

'Did you straighten everything out?' Emily asked, her pale blue eyes assessing Rachel.

'Not exactly.'

'I suppose he didn't ask you out, then. I'd hoped he would. Penny's right, you need to get out more. I heard there's a wonderful new restaurant in Addison.'

'He won't be asking me to dinner, Mother.'

'Well, what did he want, then?'

Rachel glanced from her mother's curious gaze to her sister's bored pout. Evidently Emily hadn't overheard her conversation with Jackson. Relieved, Rachel counted it as a blessing. Her mother would only worry, and that was something Emily had done enough of after suffering the abrupt loss of their father, then nearly losing Penny to prison after she'd been arrested for automobile theft. It had taken a miracle, a crafty lawyer and every dime they'd had to keep her sister out of jail. It would have destroyed her mother to lose her child. She couldn't put Emily through that again. No, for as long as Rachel could hide the truth, she would.

But she'd have to confront her sister.

When the bell jingled, announcing the arrival of a customer, Penny sighed and heaved herself out of the chair. 'I'll go.'

'Penny?'

'Yeah?' Her sister paused in the threshold.

Rachel's palms turned sweaty. She felt deceitful, and more than a little sick to her stomach. 'Do you remember the Egyptian scarabaeus necklace Mr Dermont purchased?'

'Sure. What about it?'

'You bought it, didn't you?'

Penny tilted her head back, her mouth puckering a little, as she thought about the question. 'I'm not sure, but I think it came from Weatherby's Estate Sale. Yeah, it did. Remember, that's the first sale you let me go to on my own. Why, is something wrong with it?'

'No, of course not.' Rachel faced the filing cabinet tucked into the corner of the room, preventing her mother and sister from seeing the worry and fear filling her up inside. Opening the top drawer, she said, 'Mr Dermont is curious about its history. I told him I'd see what I could find out.'

After Penny left, Rachel didn't need to smell her mother's powdery perfume to know Emily stood behind her, she could feel her mother's eyes on her back. 'Are you sure everything's all right?'

Forcing a smile, Rachel glanced over her shoulder and caught a glimpse of skepticism in her mother's eyes. 'What are you doing here, anyway, Mom? You're not scheduled to work for hours.'

'Rachel Marie, I may not have your talent for reading people, but I know when something isn't right with my own daughter.'

'Mom . . .'

'The man didn't look "curious" to me. He was upset, and I doubt it was due to a piece of jewelry.'

'Please, I'd rather not go into it.'

Something old and tired entered Emily's eyes, making them dark and heavy, a look Rachel hadn't seen in years. 'Rachel, honey, ever since your father died you've tried to carry the burden for our family. You always were such a serious child, but our troubles only seemed to make you more determined.' Smoothing the hair from Rachel's brow, Emily added, 'You can't always be the strong one.'

'I know, Mom.'

'I can handle whatever you have to tell me.'

Rachel's throat closed, trapping a gamut of emotions inside her. Years ago she'd promised to take care of her family, and she'd thought she'd succeeded, only to discover she'd failed. They were still at risk of being thrown into the street, penniless, with nowhere to turn. Well, she wouldn't let it happen.

'Mom, you're the strongest woman I know. Now,' she took her mother by the shoulders and guided her out of the office, 'go have lunch with your friends and let me work. I'll see you later.'

Emily hesitated as if she wanted to say something more, but Rachel didn't give her a chance. She turned her attention to the files. Though packed with letters, receipts and bills, everything was organized by vendor, date of purchase and date of sale. She'd entered every bit of information into the computer as well, but always kept a hard copy, preferring the feel – or evidence, as it had now become – of the original invoice.

Going back five months to when the necklace was purchased, she laid the file on top of the drawer and opened it. She flipped through the papers, her heart pounding harder in her ears as she drew closer to the end without finding anything. What if she didn't have a receipt? That wouldn't prove she'd stolen the necklace, but it wouldn't clear her, either. No, there had to be a bill-of-sale. Once she waved that bit of proof in Jackson's face, he would take his investigation elsewhere and leave her alone.

That he'd even suspected her, though . . . An angry tremor rolled through her. She'd been attracted to him from the first moment she'd seen him. But the attraction was obviously one-sided if he could believe the worst of her.

That must have been the distrust she'd sensed in him, she realized. She shook her head and closed her eyes, drawing a deep breath. She didn't care about Jackson Dermont. He'd set her up, toyed with her while he laid his trap. Now, she only wanted him out of her life before he learned anything more. But first she had to prove him wrong – before anyone learned that she, or, God forbid, Penny, might be involved.

Her hand hovered over a piece of notebook paper with the name 'Weatherby's Estate Sale' handwritten at the top in a script she didn't recognize. Pulling it out, she read the brief description and price for the necklace and earrings. She saw Penny's signature at the bottom. Someone else had signed as well, though Rachel couldn't read the scribble.

Then she noticed what the paper failed to record. There was no address or phone number where the purchase had taken place. No payment method or invoice number. Not even a date. The paper rattled as Rachel's hand began to shake. Anyone could have written this.

Sitting at her desk, she opened her check register to the same month. She ran her finger down the column for a check made out to Weatherby's. She didn't find that name, but she did find Penny's, written in her sister's messy print. The amount was for nine thousand dollars, the same as the invoice.

Rachel sat back in the chair and stared at the opposite wall, not seeing the thumbtacked messages, the family snapshots or the calendar crowded with penciled-in appointments. Numbness started in her toes and worked its way up her legs. Dark suspicions crowded her mind, and as hard as she tried to deny them, hold them back, they pushed in.

Why had Penny made the check out in her name instead of Weatherby's? And why had her sister entered the check in the register instead of Rachel?

Yanking the calendar off the wall hook, Rachel flipped back to November. Finding the same date, she read her own neat print. Her memory came flooding back. She'd been in Houston that week, picking up a shipment of valuable tapestries that had arrived from France. She'd decided to give Penny the responsibility of attending the estate sale by herself. She'd even given her sister a signed check to make the purchases.

Rachel looked out the doorway. She couldn't see her sister, but she could hear Penny's chattering voice as she finished ringing up a sale. With the receipt clutched in her hand, Rachel left the office, but hesitated out of sight behind a Tiffany floor lamp. As the customer signed her credit card slip, Penny wrapped a Greek urn in tissue paper then carefully placed it in a marbleized bag with 'The Golden Pyramid' written in gold script.

Waiting until the customer left, Rachel then crossed the room. 'Penny?'

Cleaning off the counter, she said, 'I can't believe what some people will buy. That woman paid eight hundred dollars for that urn, and I saw something just like it at the mall for thirty bucks last week.'

'The one you just sold is over two hundred years old.'

Penny laughed. 'I'm not complaining. It just amazes me, is all.' Tucking her cropped black hair behind her pierced ears, she added, 'I can't imagine what it would be like to have that much money to blow.'

'I want to ask . . .'

'And by the way . . .' her sister gave her a superior grin '. . . I'm ahead of you in sales.'

Rachel managed to smile at the ongoing competition between the three of them. 'You're *always* ahead of me.'

'Don't I know it!'

'And Mom's always ahead of you.'

Penny's playful smirk loosened some of the tension in Rachel's stomach. Her suspicions had to be wrong. And so off base she wouldn't be questioning her sister's actions now if not for Jackson Dermont's devious mind.

'I want to ask you about this.' Rachel set the receipt on the counter and watched Penny's face while she read it.

Folding her arms together, she leaned on the marble surface. 'What about it?'

'I . . . it's unusual, that it's handwritten.'

Her sister shrugged, but her face remained calm. 'That's what they gave me.'

Shielding her doubts from her own features, Rachel said in as neutral a voice as she could, 'I checked the bank register. The check was made out to you instead of Weatherby's.'

Without tilting her head, her sister's eyes flitted up, meeting Rachel's. Questions passed through Penny's blue eyes, turning them dark and alert. A stillness gathered around her. 'Is that a problem?'

'No – well, yes, it is. It's not usual business procedure.' Rachel said with a quick laugh, trying not to read too much into her sister's response. It didn't take much to make Penny defensive, Rachel reminded herself. The building tension she sensed could be nothing more than Penny's usual resentment of being questioned. It *didn't* mean her sister had stolen from their customers or had forged a receipt. 'I just thought it strange.'

'They wouldn't take a check for an amount that large.' Penny turned her back to Rachel and pulled a tray of necklaces off the shelf along the back wall. 'Cash or credit cards only. So I went to the bank and withdrew the money.'

'Well, that explains it.' Rachel picked up the invoice, but hesitated.

'Is there something else?'

'I've never known Weatherby's to be so sloppy with their receipts. They normally have preprinted forms.'

'Their computer was on the fritz,' Penny said without glancing up from the tray of jewelry.

'I knew it had to be something like that.' Leaving her sister to finish tagging merchandise, Rachel returned to her office and closed the door behind her. She leaned against the hard surface and stared at the ceiling. Her heart pumped hard and fast, but she was cold, so cold inside. Her legs began to tremble, almost buckling beneath her. She reached for her chair, collapsing into it.

This couldn't be happening. Weatherby's had never refused a check from her before. And as for their supposed computer problems, she knew they used manual preprinted forms on occasion. Not notebook paper.

After all they'd been through, she couldn't believe Penny would risk everything they had, and for what? A few thousand dollars? If she needed money Penny knew she had only to ask. Or was something more going on? Jackson said he had a list of items stolen over the past seven months. And she had been at the scene of each crime. Which meant Penny had been there as well. Her sister accompanied her to every event. She handled the scheduling, collected the money.

Most of the time, Rachel never saw her sister. She'd always believed Penny was visiting with the guests, letting them know Rachel was available for readings. What if she hadn't been mingling, but casing their homes? Searching for items that could be easily taken, even carried out the door undetected that night?

Like a necklace.

The diamond choker and a Fabergé egg weren't things she would sell in her store. *If* Penny had taken the pieces, what had she done with them?

A moan rose up Rachel's throat as a vision of black-fringed leather, a blond ponytail and defiant eyes appeared in her mind. It didn't take much for her to believe Mark could be capable of fencing the pieces. After coming to know him, she'd thought his looks had been deceiving. He'd been friendly, and seemed to care about Penny. But she'd grown up surrounded by men who'd wormed their way through life flashing their 'trust me' smiles.

Why would Mark be any different? Rachel surged to her feet. Somehow, he'd convinced her sister to steal for *him*.

Rachel pressed her clammy palm to her brow and forced herself to calm down. Penny wasn't stealing. This was just more circumstantial nonsense. What she needed was information. Facts. Hard evidence.

What she needed was to look at the folder Jackson Dermont had so arrogantly waved in her face.

'Well, are you going to give me the details, or are you going to keep me in suspense?'

Considering the question, Jackson stood in a flood of heated afternoon sunlight and stared out the window of his Galleria high-rise office. A silver flash snagged his attention as an airplane entered his line of view. It banked its big, lumbering body and turned toward DFW airport some twenty miles away. Each day, plane after plane lined up in neat little rows as they made their ascent. So organized, so skilled.

Two qualities Jackson had always prided in himself, yet lacked in abundance at the moment. Fortunately for the people in those planes, he thought as a grim smile twisted his mouth, he wasn't the flight controller responsible for seeing them safely to the ground.

'I've screwed things up, Derrick.' Jackson slipped his hands into the pockets of his Alfani slacks and faced his sales manager.

'God, Jackson, and here I thought you walked on water.' Uncrossing his feet and taking them off the desktop, Derrick sat forward with his elbows braced on his thighs. 'So spill. What's going on with the investigation?'

Rubbing his palm over the back of his neck, Jackson circled the confines of his office. 'Remember that necklace I bought from Rachel Gold?'

'Yeah, brilliant move.' Derrick shook his head without disturbing a single strand of precision-combed brown hair. 'But don't sweat it. I think I've found a buyer.'

'Don't bother.' Jackson selected a photo from the creased manila folder lying on his cluttered desk. Leaving Rachel that morning, her pleading gaze stabbing him in the back, he'd crushed the file in his hand to keep from going to her. The temptation to hold her, then strangle her had been overwhelming. Handing the picture to his manager, he said, 'I found the real owner.'

'Shit!'

'Exactly.'

Derrick stared at the photograph, his eyes nearly as wide as his gaping mouth. 'You think the tarot reader stole it?'

Jackson shrugged in answer, not wanting to voice

the words that made him feel as if he'd been sucker-punched.

'She'd have to be crazy to steal something this valuable, then turn around and display it in her store.'

'I know. That's the one part I don't understand.' Jackson pressed his mouth into a thin line. 'Has Andy come up with anything?'

'Our computer whiz hasn't found so much as a parking ticket on the little lady.'

The news didn't surprise Jackson. He couldn't imagine a cop giving Rachel a citation once he'd glanced into the well of her eyes. 'What about her mother and sister?'

'They're clean, but he's still looking. So,' Derrick blew out a breath, 'are you ready to go to the police?'

'No.'

'No?' Derrick's incredulous gaze followed Jackson around the room. 'Care to explain why not? Discovering the missing necklace in Rachel Gold's possession is the break we've been waiting for. The Whitneys canceled their contract this morning. A few more and we'll be closing our doors for good.'

Jackson swore. What he wouldn't give to lash out and hit something.

'You've got to clear your name with our clients, pronto, boss, so we can get back to business.'

Sighing, dreading what was coming, Jackson said, 'I'm aware of that.'

'So why the glum face?'

He returned to the window as another plane glinted like a shiny new dime in the sun. Weightless, the craft crossed a perfect blue sky. Though he knew it to be impossible, it seemed as if he could reach out and hold the plane on the tip of his finger. But that was an illusion, like so many other things in his life. 'She says she didn't take it.'

'What else would she say?' Silence stretched taut between them, but Jackson couldn't bring himself to add anything more. 'Why do I get the feeling there's another shoe that's about to drop?'

Sucking in a breath, wanting Derrick to leave so he could be alone to straighten out his thoughts, Jackson relented. 'I gave her one day to prove she's innocent.'

'You're kidding.'

Facing the other man, he said, 'I wish I were.'

'Jackson,' Derrick said, throwing his hands wide, 'I'm good at my job, but there's a limit to how much I can sweet-talk our customers.'

'It's only one day.'

Pushing up from his chair, Derrick dropped the photo on the desk then crossed to the door. 'Man, she must be something, because I never thought of you as a chump.'

Jackson scowled. 'Shut up, Derrick.'

'Are you sleeping with her?'

'No,' he growled. But he wanted to. God help him, regardless that she might be guilty, he wanted her. Even the thought of making love to Rachel had his body hardening in response. 'I gave her the time because there isn't enough evidence against her yet. If she can produce an invoice proving she bought the necklace, she'll be cleared of this theft. The invoice might even give us a lead to the real criminal.'

The phone on Jackson's desk buzzed, thankfully interrupting any response his sales manager might have felt inclined to make. Pressing the intercom button, he asked, 'What's up, Linda?'

'There's someone here to see you. A Miss Rachel Gold.'

Jackson started at the phone, certain he hadn't heard his secretary right.

'Mr Dermont?'

'I'll be right with her.' He released the button, but continued staring at the phone, trying to sort out this turn of events.

Derrick beat him to it. 'How much you want to bet that she wants more than her one day?'

Rachel settled into the plush leather chair in Jackson's reception area. She didn't want to sit, feeling swallowed up in the overstuffed padding, and at a disadvantage. She'd prefer meeting Jackson on even ground, face to face. Even if his was a good seven inches above hers. She mentally shook his image from her head and smoothed a faint wrinkle from her cotton skirt. That morning, she'd decided the pale peach skirt and matching sleeveless blouse would be a calming color. She'd lost sight of the tranquil place inside her, as if tension had moved in, absorbing everything, leaving nothing but empty, groping space.

Being in Jackson's streamlined, utilitarian office, she realized her mistake in her choice of wardrobe.

134

She should have worn black, or red. Harsh, vibrant red that would give her the strong front she needed. In a matter of days, Jackson had managed to uncover the one vulnerability she'd thought she'd mastered. No man had ever affected her so intensely before. It would be disastrous if he ever learned how she felt. If he should ever realize . . . She snapped that thought closed. Her feelings didn't matter to him. Finding a thief did. He'd used her, tempted her to care even when she knew better.

She folded her hands in her lap and forced herself to remain still. She could imagine the thoughts spinning through his mind as he kept her waiting. He probably suspected her of any number of things, attempting to coerce the enemy, begging for mercy. Maybe he hoped she'd come to confess. Her spine straightened painfully at the thought.

She wasn't guilty of theft, and she couldn't believe Penny was either. Whatever it took to clear them, she'd do it – even if it meant putting herself in Jackson's line of fire. It would be worth it if she could stop him snooping into her family's past.

The polished oak door opened and a man wearing a pinstriped suit emerged from what she assumed was Jackson's office. The man's gaze swept over her, his eyes narrowing with disapproval.

His emotions were open, easily read. She sensed his suspicion in the subtle tightening of his slender shoulders, the slight pinch of his mouth. Then she sensed a shift in him. The cool vibrations warmed as his doubts turned to surprise, then interest.

He hesitated beside the secretary's desk and ran his palm down the front of his perfectly knotted Paisley tie. His mouth quirked as if he was about to launch into a well-rehearsed line.

'That will be all, Derrick.'

The man stiffened. The secretary glanced up from her computer. Rachel's attention shifted to the doorway where Jackson stood glaring at her. Any emotion or surprise he might have felt at her arrival he'd locked behind guarded brown eyes. He stepped back and waved his arm, allowing her entrance to his domain. 'Miss Gold.'

Clutching her purse, Rachel stepped around the suited man and passed Jackson, noting his wrinkled charcoal slacks. The starch in his white collared shirt seemed to have prematurely wilted, and his loosely knotted tie was askew. One glimpse at his mussed chestnut-colored hair told her he'd had a difficult time since he'd left her shop. The thought gave strength to her shaky limbs.

The door clicked shut behind her. 'Have a seat, Miss Gold.'

She remained standing and lifted a brow at the formal address. He'd never bothered with civilities before. She didn't need her well-honed instincts to know it was an attempt to keep her at arm's length. But why? He held all the power, controlled the strings to the game. With one tug, he could unravel her entire world.

So why did his hair look as if he'd run his hands through it time and again? What had caused the shadows beneath his eyes, the stern set of his mouth?

He watched her from behind narrowed lids, as if to prevent her from seeing inside him.

He settled into his swivel, high-backed chair. Tilting it back, he braced his fingers together over his waist. 'It's my turn to say I'm surprised to see you.'

During the twenty-minute drive to his office, she'd rehearsed her speech. Now that she faced him, every word vanished from her head, leaving her feeling tongue-tied and defenseless. But then, the man always seemed to have that effect on her.

'That's quite a view,' she said, looking past him at the hazy outline of downtown Dallas in the distance.

'You didn't come all the way over here to check out my office.'

'No, I didn't.' Swallowing, she glanced down and spotted the folder on his desk. Feeling his curious gaze on her, she straightened and gripped her purse with both hands.

'Then why are you here?' The remoteness of his voice sent panic over her skin, making it feel cold and tight against her body.

She wasn't handling this right. She couldn't dance around the issue with Jackson and expect him to open up with her. He was black and white, hard edges and blunt points. She had to be direct with him, no matter how difficult that might be.

'I've decided to accept your offer to dinner.'

A single dusky brow arched, and a skeptical glint entered his eyes. 'You don't say.'

The impulse to slap the dubious look off his face made her turn away. Perhaps she'd been *too* direct.

Heaven help her, she'd never had to deal with a situation like this before, or a man as impossible as Jackson Dermont. She stared down at her hand as she ran her palm over the back of the upholstered chair. 'Why are you making this harder for me than it already is?'

He laughed, a harsh, edgy sound. 'I'm just trying to decide what it is you want, besides dinner, that is.'

'Answers,' she said before she could stop herself. 'You lied to me, pretended to be someone you weren't.'

'And you're exactly who and what you appear to be?' His face closed off, as if he'd shut down and felt nothing, nothing at all.

'I'm not a criminal.'

He threaded his fingers together, gripping his hands until his knuckles turned white. 'What would you have me say, Rachel?'

She took his use of her first name as a positive sign. 'Yes – to dinner.'

'Why?'

She glanced at the folder, and he must have interpreted her thoughts, because he said, 'You want the evidence.'

Setting her purse down, she pressed her palms flat on the desktop and leaned forward. 'I want to know what I'm up against.'

Jackson surged out of his chair. Mimicking her stance, he pushed his face inches from hers. 'Me, Rachel. You're up against me.'

Her breath caught, more from his musky scent than because of his words. Energy pulsed off of him in provoking waves. If she leaned forward her lips would be on his. She would be able to taste the potency of his anger instead of just feel it.

She'd been surprised when he'd given her one day to prove her innocence, but on the drive to his office his reasons had become clear – he didn't have enough evidence to convict her.

But why was he so angry with *her*? *Because he thinks I'm guilty*? Why should he care? She tried to push the questions aside, but they persisted, circling her mind. Did he want to believe her? Did he regret accusing her? And what about his kiss? If he'd been faking it, she thought, feeling a flush spread beneath her skin, he should leave the security business and become an actor. She recalled the way he'd held her, tight and possessive. His touch had been urgent, demanding.

He hadn't been pretending his response. He'd wanted her as much as she'd wanted him.

She almost smiled at the thought. If he wanted her still, that could be the reason for his warring emotions. She was tempted to run her hand down his lean, angled face, soothe the taut lines bracketing his mouth, but she refrained, afraid she might be wrong and he'd jerk away from her touch. 'Have dinner with me, Jackson. My house, tonight. At eight o'clock.'

'You don't know what you're asking for.' He pushed away from her, the darkening of his eyes exposing the refusal she saw coming.

'A chance to clear my name. You gave me the time, but I can't do it alone. I need your help.'

His temper faded to reluctance, then he turned away, leaving her with the cold broadness of his back. His answer. Briefly closing her eyes, she released a pent-up breath. She gathered her purse, knowing she'd lost the first battle. But she wouldn't quit. She didn't know what her next step would be, but she wouldn't give up so easily.

Reaching the door, she turned the knob.

'Rachel.'

Breath held, she glanced at his stiff shoulders, his rigid torso, and found herself wishing they'd met under different circumstances. Maybe introduced by a mutual friend, or they could have bumped into each other at a grocery store. Even a blind date would have been preferable. What would their lives have been like then? He said something she didn't quite hear.

'Excuse me?'

He turned his head, but his eyes didn't come close to meeting hers. 'I said I'll be there.'

Afraid to risk saying anything more, she nodded. Outside his office, she pulled the door closed and left the reception area. She maneuvered through the hallways by instinct, not seeing the glassed-in offices or the other occupants she passed. Every thought, her entire vision was centered on one frightening fact: her future lay in the hands of a man who didn't believe in trust. Somehow, she had to change his mind.

CHAPTER 8

Rachel took a sip of red wine, letting the dark, velvety taste pool on her tongue before it eased down her throat. She rarely drank more than one glass of wine, not liking the way it dulled her senses, but tonight she thought she might have a second. She could use a bit of numbing to take off the edge.

Since leaving Jackson's office, her nerves had become twisted ropes of energy, amplifying every thought and emotion she possessed as well as those she picked up from others. The trip to the grocery store had become unbearable. The frustration of women trying to balance work and family, a stressed check-out clerk, a manager who was furious over receiving a shipment of milk that had already expired had all somehow woven into her own frantic state. She'd felt them all in a way she'd never experienced before. It had been over-whelming, even painful, leaving her nerves raw and exposed.

Taking a fortifying drink of wine, she vowed to regain control of the safe environment she'd created for herself and her family. Jackson and his suspicions had to be put to rest, tonight, if she wanted her life to return to normal. Which she most certainly did.

The first thing on her list was to gain access to his 'evidence'. She suspected her hand-written invoice would only deepen his suspicions about her. She'd already telephoned Weatherby's office, but Mr Weatherby was out of town on a buying trip and not expected to return for another week. No one else could explain why the invoice had been written on plain paper instead of a pre-printed form.

In the meantime, she intended to learn as much as possible about the thefts, and hopefully steer Jackson in another direction. He'd seemed so set on accusing her, she felt there had to be another clue he'd missed.

She made a quick inventory of her kitchen. The steaks were seasoned and ready for the grill. The asparagus only needed to be steamed, and the potatoes *au gratin* were already baking in the oven. A salad was chilling in the refrigerator and the table was set for two. She'd even added a mélange of candles as a centerpiece. Not to induce a romantic ambience, but to give the breakfast room a . . . a comfortable, homey feel. Everything was ready to go . . . as soon as Jackson arrived.

She glanced at the teakettle clock hanging on the wall above her phone. Five to eight. Her stomach turned over and her hands began to tremble. Carefully, she set down the wine then ran her palms over her black ramie twill dress. The fitted bodice carried its smooth lines over her hips, the straight hem with mahogany embroidery ending a few inches above her sandaled feet.

Skimming her hands over the fabric, she debated the wisdom in her choice of dress. While she wouldn't call the outfit seductive, it wasn't barbecue attire, either.

Thoughts of changing clothes fizzled when the doorbell chimed. Drawing a steadying breath, she glanced down as Miss Bastet appeared from wherever she'd been sleeping. The cat meowed and wrapped herself around Rachel's leg in a practised request for a treat. 'Later, sweetheart,' Rachel said. 'We have company. Since neither of us is faring very well with him, I suggest you behave.'

Rachel passed through the hallway, smiling when Miss Bastet trotted along beside her. At the entryway, she hesitated for a brief, fortifying second, then opened the door.

Jackson stood in fading sunlight, his features caught in angled shadows. The world behind him had softened with a dusky glow, that hazy instant before night settled in and put the world to sleep.

He towered above her, broad and threatening, though she didn't detect a hint of the anger she'd felt in him before. She puzzled over that for an instant. Strangers had bombarded her with their emotions all afternoon, yet she couldn't glimpse what Jackson was feeling now. He could be bored, or furious; it was impossible to tell. Obviously, she thought with resentment, he could control his emotions far better than she could.

He watched her, his stance casual, with his thumbs hooked in the front pockets of his jeans. The forest green polo shirt left most of his arms bare, the V offering a glimpse of his chest and a patch of dark curls.

She knew she was staring, but couldn't stop herself. The moment seemed to demand she note every fact, every subtle nuance, if she wanted the evening to proceed as planned.

Evidently Jackson thought so as well. His gaze left no part of her untouched as it skimmed down her body, then up again, lingering on her breasts. Tingles erupted beneath her skin, making her feel too warm and sensitive. A fullness centered inside her, and to her horror she felt her nipples harden and strain against the silky fabric.

In a panicked move, she reached down and lifted Miss Bastet into her arms. Stepping back, she said, 'Please, come in.'

She caught the quirk of his mouth as he passed, as if he knew what she was feeling. A definite turn of the tables for her. Then she was left in the wake of his scent, a subtle spice that lingered like smoke.

Closing her eyes with a sigh, she shut the door then followed him into the living room where a piano solo by Jim Brickman played softly in the background. Without a word, Jackson crossed to the window to stare at her backyard as if he were a caged animal who wanted out.

Well, this won't do, she thought. She'd never convince him of anything if she couldn't even get him to face her. 'Would you like some wine?'

'Sure.'

She went to the kitchen, hoping he would follow as he had before. She listened for his footsteps, but heard nothing except Miss Bastet's purring and the mellow piano tones from the CD. Setting the cat on the floor, Rachel poured a glass of Cabernet for Jackson. Collecting her own, she returned to the front room. Since he hadn't moved, she crossed to him, handed him his wine. She almost tipped her crystal glass to his in a silent toast, but caught herself. They had no warm words for each other, no comforting smiles. And probably never would, she thought, and felt a dragging weight settle in her chest.

For a brief, delusional moment after leaving his office, she'd believed Jackson might care for her, at least a little. She'd thought he might even desire her. But the useless thoughts had quickly passed. His only concern was finding enough evidence to convict a criminal – namely her.

They had one thing in common, though. They were both determined to protect their businesses. She wondered if she'd ever find a man who would care about her as passionately as Jackson did his company? How would it feel to have a man love her enough to stand up and fight for her? Be there when she needed support or simply listen when she needed to talk about her day? She wondered if Jackson could ever be that man.

'Thank you for coming.' She took a sip of her drink when he said nothing. 'I was afraid you might change your mind.'

'And miss whatever you have planned for to-night?' He turned to her, a cynical light flickering in his eyes.

'Steaks,' she said, willing her teeth not to clench. 'I've planned steaks and potatoes.'

He smiled at her comeback, his gaze lingering on her face. The tingles returned, spreading into a warming blush that heated her cheeks. This one-way attraction had to end, she thought with disgust. Either she had to learn how to ignore him, or she had to make him as uncomfortable as she was. She almost laughed at the improbable odds of that happening.

'I thought we could sit outside on the deck while I cook.' Without waiting for a reply she hurried to the kitchen, retrieved the plate of marinated steaks and went out the back door. She didn't care if he followed or not, she thought as she jabbed a T-bone with a fork and dropped it on the grill. The meat hissed and spat in response. He could stay in the house and sulk or sneer or whatever it was he was doing.

'You're nervous.'

His rough voice, so close to her ear, made her gasp. The plate with its one remaining steak careened to the side, but Jackson caught it, deftly taking it and the two-pronged fork from her hands.

Snapping up her wine from the shelf attached to the grill, she took a deep drink and watched him master the barbecue pit. Men.

With only the sizzling steak breaking the silence, she watched him stab the slabs of beef as if he were trying to kill them. Smiling behind the rim of her glass, she said, 'You seem a little uptight yourself.'

Pausing as if realizing what he was doing, he set the fork down and faced her. 'Not at all.'

She retreated to the deck railing and leaned her arms on the rough board, her wine dangling between her hands. She glanced over her shoulder at him. 'I've been curious, Jackson, about your business.'

'I bet you have.'

She ignored the sarcasm and asked, 'What kind of security systems do you sell?'

'Surely you know all about them.'

'Humor me.'

He retrieved his wine from the table and crossed to her with slow, predatory steps. She had the sense of being hunted, cautiously, with the patience of someone determined to win. 'The systems are my own design.'

'Really?'

'Really. The cameras, both internal and external, are wireless, sending the image to a central transmitter, which is connected to a satellite dish. The image is then sent to a receiver in my office, where we monitor the activity. But you already know all this.'

She resisted the urge to tell him otherwise, knowing nothing would come of it. 'I've never seen any cameras.'

'They're hidden in pictures, on lamps, smoke detectors.'

'That's very ingenious, but it doesn't sound very complicated, or unique. I image there are a lot of people who could get past your system.'

'Not unless they know how to block the signal, then transmit a false image, giving my monitors the illusion that everything is status quo. Each house is equipped with motion detectors, all of which were bypassed during the burglaries. No system is completely the same.'

'If that's the case then you must have picked up something unusual.'

He studied her for a moment, his gaze dark and intense, but she refused to back down and look away. 'Perhaps we did.'

She didn't let his baiting tone unnerve her. *She* had nothing to hide. But her sister was another matter entirely. 'No, you didn't,' she responded thoughtfully.

'How do you know?'

'You had no qualms about accusing me of stealing. If you had something suspicious on tape, I'd be in jail right now.'

The corner of his mouth lifted with a rueful grin. 'As I said, the monitors have been circumvented.'

'So, is that it? Motion detectors and hidden cameras?'

Moving within a foot of her, he rested his forearms on the railing and looked out over the shadow-draped lawn. 'There are also the usual devices: window sensors, spectrum analyzers . . .'

'Which do what?'

He gave her a tolerant look, then said, 'I guess you wouldn't have any use for those. It's a system that sweeps a selected area, detecting bugs, hot mics, that sort of thing.'

'No,' she said, shaking her head. 'I wouldn't have any use for something like that. And I can't imagine the kind of life where I'd need one.'

'Can't you? Most of your customers have some type of scanner installed in their homes and offices. Surely if you've done any readings for them, you'd know what kind of business they're in.'

'Well, yes. They're CEOs, bank presidents, entrepreneurs or old money. They're upstanding citizens, Jackson. Why would someone want to bug their homes?'

'God, you can't be that naïve.' He returned to the grill and flipped the steaks.

Following him, she said, 'I suppose I am, because I thought things like that happened to, I don't know –' she waved her free hand '– drug lords or the Mafia.'

'Or people who want to be alerted to corporate takeovers, or billion-dollar mergers, or to use them for industry theft. Imagine,' he said, coming so close that she was forced to take a step in retreat, 'if you had prior warning that Microsoft was going to buy, let's say, AT&T, what would you do? You'd buy a few thousand shares of AT&T stock and make a bloody fortune overnight.'

He caught a strand on hair that blew against her cheek and tucked it behind her ear. 'Those people are my clients, and since my systems have failed, I'm in danger of losing them. It will cost my employees their jobs. I'd lose everything. I won't let that happen again.'

'Again? Is that what I saw in your cards? You lost another business?'

His jaw clenched, and she knew he wouldn't reveal anything more. She also knew she'd hit close to the truth. He'd lost something he'd cared about, a business most likely. Whatever had happened had hurt him, deeply. She could imagine his despair at seeing something he'd worked for slip away. She mentally shook herself. She didn't need to imagine it, because she knew how he felt. *She* was in jeopardy of losing hers. But she'd fight tooth and nail before she let it happen.

'I'd hate living like that, worrying if someone was listening to every word I said.'

He moved closer, invading her space again. She tilted her head back, keeping eye contact with him. She refused to let his he-man approach, or his intimidating stare, get the better of her. Did he expect this kind of behavior would cause her to break down and confess?

Rachel straightened and looked through the windows into her living room, a place of refuge with soft colors and a welcoming pull, a place she'd worked hard to create for herself. She'd left him alone in there with more than enough time . . . Her gaze swung back to his. 'You haven't put one of those listening devices in my house, have you?'

He blinked once as if taken back, then his mouth quirked with an unscrupulous smile. 'No.'

From the tone of his answer, she thought he'd left off the words, *not yet*. 'Promise me you'll never put one in my home.'

150

His jaw clenched, and she thought the words might be trapped inside his mouth.

'Promise me!'

'I won't bug your house, Rachel,' he growled with annoyance.

'I'm not that well versed in the law, Jackson, but I'm sure bugging someone's home is illegal.'

'And you wouldn't hesitate to sue the pants off me if I did.'

The statement had been a dare, one she couldn't resist. 'I won't even leave you with the ones you have on if you try something like that.'

'As threats go, that's a rather interesting one.'

The flash of desire in his eyes sent unexpected warmth pooling in her stomach. Spinning on her heel and heading for the house, she said, 'I'm going to steam the asparagus.'

'How do you like your steak?' he called after her.

Was that amusement she heard in his voice? Impossible, she decided, the man was as sour as a teased rattlesnake. She jerked open the patio door. 'Well done.'

He grumbled something. Sticking her head back outside, she asked, 'Did you say something?'

'I said it figures.'

A flip rejoinder about Neanderthal men liking their beef raw sprang to mind, but never left Rachel's mouth. Seeing Jackson with a glass of wine in one hand and a fork in the other, smoke wisping up from the grill as he turned the steaks, made her throat constrict. She'd never had a man in her home before. Never cooked one dinner.

151

Growing up in a housing project, she'd learned early about the consequences of dating the wrong man. Unwanted pregnancies had just been the beginning. She'd known several girls who'd been raped and abused by their boyfriends. Linda Monroe had been one of those girls. She'd become pregnant at fourteen, but she hadn't had to worry about making the choice of keeping the baby or not. Her father, drunk on a week-long binge, had beaten Linda so severely when he'd learned she was pregnant that she'd miscarried.

That lesson, and dozens of others like it, had fueled Rachel's determination to escape their life. She'd learned to recognize the smooth talkers, men who could lie as easily as they breathed, but improving the caliber of men she associated with hadn't changed her opinion much. In her experience, men, whether rich or poor, only wanted what she could give them in bed.

That hadn't kept her from dreaming, though. She knew there was a man for her; she just hadn't found him yet. One day she'd know what a physical relationship would be like, but she also wanted something deeper. Whoever she eventually married would have to understand her, share her dreams, be there to build a future with her, and love her unconditionally.

She didn't want to think it, knew it would be futile and useless and lead her nowhere, but Jackson looked as if he belonged in her home. She could picture him stretched out with her on her sofa watching TV, or using her shower, or lying in her bed with his arms wrapped around her. The visions seemed so real, so effortless that they could have already happened and were now a part of her memory.

The pressure in her throat spread to her chest, squeezing until she couldn't breathe. Rachel hurried into the kitchen where she leaned against the counter, eyes closed, and searched inside herself for some sort of calm. She didn't expect to find any because she'd lost any pretense of calm the day she'd met Jackson. How had she reached this level?

If this had happened to anyone else, she'd have offered to read their cards. But she knew from experience that she couldn't read her own. She'd see only what she wanted to see, and in this case she'd search for the impossible. A relationship with Jackson wouldn't happen. He didn't care about her. He'd made that plain enough at his office. Besides, if he did feel something for her, surely she'd be able to pick up some glimmer, however small? But anger seemed to be the only emotion she could sense in him, and the few times she'd felt it, it had been hot and direct before he'd regained control.

'Are you all right?'

Jumping, she suppressed a yelp with her hand and spun around. Seeing Jackson frowning in the doorway, she faced the stove again and turned on the gas burner beneath the vegetables. 'I'm fine.'

He came to her and, reaching around her for the bottle of wine, his arm brushing hers, he refilled his glass then topped hers up. 'Steaks'll be done in a few minutes.'

'Great.' She stepped around him to the refrigerator. Retrieving the salads, she put them on the table, then added the potatoes. *Take control of the situation, Rachel!* But for the life of her she didn't know how to bring up the thefts without straining the evening and herself even more.

Jackson gave her a moment's reprieve by asking, 'How did you come up with a ridiculous name like Miss Bastet? It's no wonder the cat has an attitude problem.'

Striking a match, Rachel tried to focus on lighting the cluster of candles on the table instead of Jackson as he knelt to return the cat's stare. With his forearms braced on his thighs, he didn't try to pet Miss Bastet.

As the fur raised on the cat's back, and a growl rumbled from her throat, Rachel decided it was just as well that Jackson didn't attempt to win the cat over. But she still didn't understand the feline's dislike of him. 'Bastet is an Egyptian goddess. She's the mother of all cats.'

'I take it you don't mean size-wise. I recall Fluffy here weighs about a ton.'

Returning his faint smile, Rachel said, 'In ancient Egypt, all cats were sacred, but physicians used the symbol of the black cat in their healing.'

'You're really into all this mystical stuff, aren't you?'

Surprised that he sounded interested and wasn't condemning her beliefs when he could have, she said, 'I suppose I am. And thank you for not saying mystical *nonsense*. A lot of people have no qualms about belittling my profession.'

154

He straightened to his full six-foot-two height. 'Does it bother you when someone says something petty?'

'It depends on who it is.'

He studied her for a moment as if he would say something more. 'I'd better go get those steaks.'

Scooping Miss Bastet into her arms, Rachel watched him leave. What had he been about to say? That he was sorry, he'd made a mistake in accusing her? He wanted to start over? She didn't think it was anything as important as that, but he'd been tempted to reveal something. Maybe he was beginning to doubt his own stubborn convictions. Maybe she had a chance of convincing him he was after the wrong person, after all.

Rachel drew a deep breath, but the pressure in her chest didn't ease. Or she was deluding herself and she would end up in prison for a crime she hadn't committed. A crime her sister might have done.

'Have you ever been married?'

Having just taken a sip of wine, Jackson nearly spat it across the table. Pressing his napkin to his lips, he met Rachel's curious gaze across the dancing glow of candles. 'No. Have you?'

She shook her head. 'Where I grew up there weren't any men I considered the marrying kind. Or even the dating kind for that matter.'

'Why's that?'

She fidgeted with her place mat, and he could tell she didn't want to continue, but then she said, 'I grew up in the projects in South Dallas.'

155

As her statement took meaning, he found himself curling his hands into fists. He wanted to reject the image of her living in such a poor part of town, but he realized that must be where a part of Rachel's strength came from. 'That's a rough area.'

'And as far removed from the people I deal with now as one can get. I lived among the poorest, most desperate people in the city. Drug abuse, alcoholism, gangs; they were all a part of daily life. Did you know that nationwide, one out of every five women will be raped by the time they're thirty? In my neighborhood, the statistics are that four out of every five will be raped, and usually by a relative.'

'Yet you escaped all that.' His insides clenched as he imagined her a young woman dodging bullets and needles and men with shit for morals.

'Yes, we got out.'

'And you didn't date then?'

She grinned. 'In my opinion, men were a disaster better avoided. So I poured all my time and energy into the store.'

'Are you saying you've never dated?'

She straightened, bristling. 'Of course I have.'

But not much. He'd bet his last dollar on it. The idea of Rachel's being innocent, perhaps even a virgin, had his blood racing to his groin, hardening it to stone.

She pushed food around on her plate with her fork. She hadn't eaten enough to fill a bird, and she hadn't touched her steak at all, even though he'd ruined it by cooking it the way she liked. Reaching for the bottle of wine, she refilled both their glasses.

Her third since he'd arrived, though he wasn't counting, but her eyes were a little glassy. He doubted she would have revealed as much about her past as she had if she hadn't had any wine. Perhaps she would slip up and tell him about the thefts. His jaw tightened with disgust at himself at the thought of taking advantage of her.

'I only asked if you were married because when I read your cards, I couldn't tell much about your past.' Her gaze locked with the circle of candles, her eyes widening as if she could see inside the flames. 'So many secrets, Jackson. What are you hiding from? What happened to you?'

'You're the mind reader; you tell me.'

She blinked several times, then leaned back in her chair, her expression candid. She heaved a disgruntled sigh. 'I'm not clairvoyant. I can't read people's minds, thank God. It would probably drive me crazy.' She frowned. 'But I do have some empathic skills.'

'What's the difference?' His internal defense system kicked in, sending prickling chills over his skin. He didn't like discussing this psychic nonsense. And he *did* believe it to be nonsense, regardless of what he'd said earlier. There were too many variables, no simple equation. Proof and belief depended on how gullible you were. People might be fascinated by sleight-of-hand, but it was only a trick of the eye. The world was made up of facts and solutions. Two key pieces missing from Rachel's mystical world.

'Empathy is feeling another person's emotions.'

'Which would be pretty convenient in your line of work.'

She leaned her head back against the top rail of her chair, giving him a clear view of her long, slender neck, the creamy slope of her chest. He rubbed his hand over his mouth, but couldn't look away. 'Sometimes, yes; other times it's draining. Delving into people's lives, their hardships, it's impossible not to absorb their emotions. It's taken years, but I've learned to block them most of the time.'

'What are you saying – that you can turn it off?'

'Something like that.' She made a breathy sound, part sigh and part laugh. Light glowed from her eyes, as if the candles burned from inside her. Jackson knew he should get up and turn on the kitchen light, shatter the cozy atmosphere. When he'd agreed to have dinner with her, his sole reason had been to learn more about her, question her, push her, see if he could find another piece to the puzzle. So far, he'd only confirmed what he already knew: he was at risk of becoming obsessed with Rachel Gold.

'So tell me, what am I feeling now?'

She caught her bottom lip between her teeth and shook her head. 'That's just it. I never know, except when you're mad at me, of course. Then a part of you slips free, escapes.' She waved her hands and made a noise simulating a bomb blowing up.

The action was so out of character that he had to stifle a laugh. 'You don't drink much, do you?'

Blushing, a timid smile curving her mouth, she said, 'No, I don't.' She touched the tip of her nose with her finger. 'It's numb.'

158

'Come on.' He reached across the table and took her hand, pulling her to her feet. 'Let's go outside. Maybe some air will help.' He'd never seen her so relaxed and unguarded. A part of him wanted to explore this side of her more, but his rational side knew he might never have another opportunity like this to question her. It might not be entirely honorable, but he was determined to conclude his investigation soon. Then he could focus on his business. He'd never see her again, and life would return to normal.

Linking her hand around his arm, she said, 'But your accusations – well, they've made me nervous.'

He held the door open for her to pass. 'I'm sure they have.'

She paused, leaned her shoulder against the doorjamb. With her gaze averted, she whispered, '*You* make me nervous, Jackson.'

He stepped closer without intending to. She smelled as seductive, as stirring as the warm breeze that rustled through the trees. Wind filtered through her hair, lifting it from her face, her neck, tempting him to catch the black length in his hand and tangle his fingers in shadows. 'Why is that?'

'I don't know,' she answered, sounding bewildered. 'I've never met anyone like you before. If I had any sense at all, I'd stay as far away from you as I could.'

He'd had the same thought himself. But common sense didn't seem to be a strong point for either of them.

Smiling, she tilted her head to look at him. 'My mother always swore my curiosity would get the better of me one day. I'm afraid she might be right.'

'Mothers usually are.' He stepped out on to the porch and turned, waiting for her to follow him.

'Would you kiss me?' she asked in a whispery voice. Her lids were half lowered, her eyes focused on his mouth.

'Excuse me?'

'I know you don't really like me, but . . .'

'Whatever gave you that idea?' The woman was an enigma. A tempting, beautiful problem he didn't feel capable of handling at the moment. Or was that her plan? Had her claim to having little experience with men been a lie to throw him off guard? Was she trying to seduce him now so he'd stop his investigation? Christ, he never knew what to think where Rachel was concerned.

Her eyes narrowed, honing in with silent accusations. 'My thinking you dislike me might have something to do with the fact that you constantly scowl at me. I wish I had a mirror so you could see the look on your face right now. It bothered me at first, but I think I'm getting used to it.'

He knew he was glaring at her; he'd felt his entire body tense, wind into a knot of pulsing need when she'd asked him to kiss her. She stood so close, all he had to do was reach out and pull her to him. She wouldn't fight or even try to stop him. She wanted him, and dammit, like it or not, he wanted her. The thought was alarming because he didn't know how much longer he could maintain the line he'd drawn to keep them apart.

'There's also the issue of your believing I'm

capable of robbing my clients. Do you really think I'd do such a thing?'

He didn't know what to think or what his next move should be because he couldn't see past her full mouth. The memory of her taste still lingered in his mind. He wanted more than a memory; he wanted the real thing. But he couldn't have it, not without risking his business. 'I can't ignore the evidence.'

'Yes, the evidence,' she said, raising her index finger into the air as she pushed away from the doorjamb and passed him.

Jackson followed her down the deck stairs and into the yard, grateful for the space between them. He shoved his hands into his pockets to still the urge to wrap his arm around her waist in a move that would seem as natural as it would be foreign. In silence they followed a pebbled trail through clipped bushes and flowering plants. The ground crunched beneath their feet. A honey-sweetness cloaked the air. He drew a deeper breath and realized it was gardenias. He couldn't recall the last time he'd paused long enough to taste the scents of spring. Rachel's home had that effect on him, though, tempting him to close his eyes and enjoy it.

Rachel stopped suddenly and turned to face him. Losing her balance, she teetered to the side. Jackson reached for her, caught her by the hips and pulled her closer. Her breath hitched as she gripped his arms. 'I'm not usually so clumsy.'

She felt too good in his hands, smelled too erotic for him to think straight. Releasing her, he stepped back.

'I'm not going about this right.' Sighing, she ran her fingers through her hair. 'Probably because I don't know how to handle you,' she added in a mutter.

'What are you trying to *handle*, Rachel?'

Frowning, she blurted, 'I want to talk to you about the evidence you've collected.'

'What about it?'

'Could I have your file?'

Jackson took another step back and crossed his arms, his suspicious mind grasping for motives. Had the entire dinner been a set-up for this one moment? His mouth set in such a grim line, his face ached. She might have had better luck if she'd waited for him to kiss her. 'Why do you want it?'

Her brow dipped with a frown. 'You don't have to snap at me.'

'Why, Rachel?' He tried to repeat the question in a gentler tone, but it still had the effect of a barked order.

She sighed, a deep, soulful sound. 'You're mad again.'

'Rachel . . .' he warned.

'I want to see if I recognize anything else on your list.'

'You could have asked to see it in my office. You didn't have to play games and invite me to dinner.'

She propped her hands on her hips. The soft lines of her face vanished as she drew her shoulders back. 'Games? You think I'd play games when you're hell-bent on ruining my life?'

'If you're not trying to convince me to look for another suspect, then what is all this about?'

'I told you earlier today, I need your help.' She ran her palms down her dress, drawing his attentions to the sleek curve of her hips, the line of her thighs.

Jackson stifled the urge, the painful urge, to jerk her body against his. His need for her bordered on the insane. So insane, he was nearly blind with it. She possessed a quality of innocent sensuality that he wanted to explore. The longer he knew her, the more certain he became that she'd never been loved by a man. To his disbelief, he found himself wanting to be the one to teach her how incredible it could be between a man and woman. He doubted he'd ever have the chance to make her his, and the thought of not having her ripped at his gut.

'Help from you makes absolutely no sense, since you believe I'm the one who's behind the thefts.' She ran her hands through her hair again, arching her back and tilting her head to the stars.

He clenched his shaking hands, willing himself not to touch the pale skin straining above the bodice of her dress. She was a temptress. A witch, luring him into her trap. Centuries ago, she would have been burned at the stake for seducing him. The hell of it was, he wanted to burn. With her.

A surge of adrenalin whipped through him. Grinding out a curse, he gripped the back of her neck, his fingers sliding into her hair as he hauled her to him. He swallowed her gasp with his mouth.

'Wait.'

He couldn't wait. His other hand circled her waist, skimmed up her side then down to cup her bottom, fitting her to him. A moan vibrated from his throat as the craving in his body exploded. He couldn't think, could only feel as he pushed past her lips with his tongue, swept the velvety interior. Heaven laced with sin. She tasted forbidden, like a dream out of reach.

A groan vibrated his chest. He finally understood the meaning of addiction. He wanted, hungered for more of her softness. He had to feel her bare skin against his, fill his palm with her breast. He longed to taste the musky heat of her belly, brush the silky place between her thighs. God, he wanted her, all of her. Whether on the rough, pebbled ground or inside the house on a bed, he didn't care which. Only it had to be now.

His blood had simmered with need from the first moment he'd seen her. Now his veins boiled with life, scorching him from the inside out. Only burying himself deep inside her would put an end to the fierce ache.

He pulled away, intent on carrying her inside. Her startled, wide-eyed expression stopped him. She had a death-grip on his shirt. 'Why did you . . . ?' She drew a shuddering breath and swayed in his arms. 'I thought . . .' She swallowed and tried again. 'Why?'

'Why did I kiss you?'

Nodding, she managed, 'I know I asked you to, but you didn't seem thrilled with the idea.'

He had to smile at that. Despite her mysterious, knowing eyes, her aloof manner, she really was naïve. Shifting his hips so she'd know exactly how much she affected him, he said, 'I want to make love to you, Rachel.'

Though he hadn't thought it possible, her eyes widened even more. Then she dropped her head back and laughed, laughed until tears spilled from her eyes. It didn't last long. He gritted his teeth, feeling his desire dissolve to annoyance. She wiped tears from her cheeks, sobering as if she hadn't been laughing but crying. When her eyes focused on his, they were dark and troubled and, he thought, wounded.

'I wonder what kind of game karma is playing with us? I'm attracted to a man who wants to make love to me today and put me in jail tomorrow. A man who doesn't give a second thought about doing either.'

The declaration jolted home just how foolish, how careless he'd become. She was right on both counts. If he could prove without any doubt that she was involved, he'd have no choice but to turn her over to the police.

He released her, stepping back, though the pitiful space didn't begin to diminish the lust staggering his mind and body. Unable to stop the shuddering tremors in his loins, he swiped a hand though his hair. Resorting to the scowl she'd accused him of favoring, he said, 'I'm going to be at your store tomorrow morning. I want the invoice proving you bought the necklace and earrings.'

Her chin jutted out the tiniest degree. 'And if I don't give it to you?'

'You will, Rachel. Because I'm your only hope.'

CHAPTER 9

Stopping at a red light, Rachel closed her tired, burning eyes and took a sip of herbal tea from a travel mug. Though she'd brushed her teeth several times, she could still taste the bitter residue of wine from the night before. A dull thudding had taken up residence in her temples, behind her eyes and at the base of her skull.

No more drinking, she swore. And no more dinners with Jackson. Though she doubted she'd have to worry much about that. Not after the way he'd left her. Cold anger had deadened his eyes. He'd pulled away, both mentally and physically. She'd imagined layer after layer of polished steel settling over him, molding to his features, turning him hard and unbending. His order to hand over the invoice had been a blatant threat—one she didn't dare challenge for fear he'd turn her in to the police before she could prove Penny wasn't involved. How she would manage that without tipping Jackson off, she didn't know.

'The light's green, Rachel. Do you intend to go or sit here for the rest of the morning?' Emily chimed much too loudly.

Rachel cracked open her eyelids and saw the light was indeed green. Easing the accelerator down, she turned on to Preston Road, her stomach turning as well. Oh, God. Slowly, she made her way to the store.

'Thanks for picking me up this morning, honey. Miss Bastet, I don't want you sleeping on my lap. You'll get hair all over my new suit.' Urging the cat on to the floorboard, Emily sighed. 'I can't believe my car battery died on me. It's hardly a year old.'

'No problem, Mom. We'll get you a new one this afternoon,' Rachel whispered. Just how long did it take for aspirin to kick in?

'You know, we could do something crazy today.' Emily flipped down the visor and checked her lipstick in the mirror. 'Why don't we leave the store closed and go to Dallas Market Hall and do some shopping, then have lunch? Just the two of us. It would be fun.'

Normally, Rachel would never consider *not* opening the store, but, knowing Jackson would be there, intent on making her day more miserable than it already was, the idea was tempting. Very tempting, Becoming tipsy had been had enough, but asking him to kiss her . . . Humiliation heated her clammy skin. She'd give anything to be able to live last night again. Knowing that was impossible, she considered going back home to spend the day, or perhaps the next week, in bed. She glanced in the side mirror and debated making a U-turn. But hiding out for a day would only delay the inevitable. And her one-day reprieve was coming to an end. Pressing the warm travel mug to her forehead, she said, 'Maybe another time, Mom.'

'What's the matter, honey? You don't look like you feel well.'

'Just a little headache.' That felt like a continuous explosion pounding against her skull. Absolutely, positively no more wine!

Pulling into the Prestonwood Shopping Center, she parked her car in front of her store and gathered her purse in her lap. 'Come on, Miss Bastet. Time to work.'

Used to the routine, the cat scurried beneath Rachel's legs and gracefully exited the car as Rachel opened her door.

'Look, honey, we already have a customer waiting for us to open. And look who it is.'

Glancing through the windshield, a tired moan escaped her. Her headache escalated, crashing in rolling waves against her forehead. Casually dressed in a loose, collarless white shirt tucked into jeans, and a pair of hiking boots, Jackson leaned against a brick pier, his hooded gaze fastened on her. Imagining she could see tension humming around his athletic body only enhanced the impact of his presence. Her senses reeled, making her insides shake in a way that had nothing to do with how much wine she'd had.

His brooding frown hadn't eased since last night, she realized, wanting to scream in frustration, though she didn't dare, knowing the resulting pain would probably kill her.

'He must really be interested in you, honey.'

Rachel grunted. 'Hardly.'

'Oh, don't let his frown fool you,' Emily said. 'I've seen that look in a man's eyes before. He's definitely attracted to you. Mad, but attracted. I take it the two of you didn't solve his problem.'

'No, we didn't.' Could her mother be right about Jackson? There *was* a certain . . . something in his eyes that could be interpreted as interest.

'Just what has him so upset, anyway?' Emily settled her purse strap on her shoulder and opened her door. 'Maybe I should help him this time. He would look wonderful in one of the new tapestry silk ties we received from France.'

'No!' Rachel snapped, and regretted it immediately. She rubbed her temple and got out of the car, saying over her shoulder, 'I'll take care of this. He's just here to pick up something.'

Slamming her door shut, Rachel winced, then hurried to Jackson's side. Before her mother reached them, she uttered under her breath, 'Don't say a word as to why you're here.'

Receiving an indiscernible nod, she unlocked the door. Miss Bastet trotted inside first. She leapt on to the counter and settled on her haunches as if she knew something was about to happen and intended to play referee.

'Mr Dermont, it's a pleasure to see you again.' Emily took Jackson's arm and guided him inside, while Rachel flicked on the overhead lights.

'Mrs Gold.' Jackson's mouth eased into a rakish grin. 'You're looking lovely this morning.'

Rachel dropped her purse on the counter, startling Miss Bastet. Where had this charming side of Jackson been hiding? She'd certainly never seen it. She'd received nothing but glares, accusations and dire threats. And, of course, the memory of two kisses that continued to keep her off-balance. 'Mom, would you mind putting the coffee on?'

'Why, of course,' Emily said, disengaging herself from Jackson. 'Would you care for a cup, Mr Dermont? It'll only take a few minutes.'

'Thank you, ma'am.'

The silence turned thick and expectant as Rachel waited for her mother to enter the office and close the door behind her. Resisting the need to squeeze her eyes shut and massage her temples, she faced Jackson. Her heart hitched in surprise. The charming smile lingered. He looked at her, their gazes locking.

'You don't look as if you slept well, Rachel. Is something wrong?' The teasing light in his eyes made her stomach flutter.

'I'm fine.'

'If you say so.' His cocky grin told her he enjoyed seeing her in pain. 'I like your mother.'

'She's a character. The customers love her.' Rachel shifted, suddenly uneasy with his attention focused solely on her. She didn't have to ask to know he was thinking about their kiss. She might have been tipsy, but she couldn't forget the way he'd crushed her to him, taking her mouth as if she belonged to him. She'd bet her deck of tarot cards that he hadn't forgotten, either. It was obvious in the

170

way he studied her face, lingering on her lips. They began to tingle as her memory strengthened.

She pressed a hand to her forehead. She'd get the invoice and give it to him so he would leave. With Mr Weatherby out of town, she wasn't worried that he'd learn anything. Though she dreaded the idea, she'd already decided she'd have to stay close to Jackson while he continued his investigation. If by some chance he did learn something, she'd be there to defend her sister. She'd considered refusing to give him the receipt, but had decided against it. The police would learn of Penny's record and make an instant connection. Jackson, on the other hand, might never discover her sister's history, since it was sealed in juvenile records. She hoped it stayed that way, because if he found out she'd kept such damaging information from him, she was certain he'd make her regret it.

Without a word, Jackson turned away and milled about the store. His steps were casual, but the way his eyes narrowed as he scanned the shelves sent a chill down her spine. Alert to the warning, she made a frantic sweep of the room. Was he looking for something? She shook her head. He was simply behaving like any other customer.

'I'll get the invoice for you.'

He paused, glancing up at her. 'You do that.'

Inside her office, Rachel smiled as her mother looked up from arranging her prized collection of Haviland china cups on a serving tray.

'He hasn't left yet, has he?' Emily added silver spoons beside the sugar bowl and creamer.

Rachel couldn't imagine Jackson's large, rough hand holding one of the delicate cups without crushing it. 'No, he's still here, but I don't think he has time for coffee.'

Her mother's eyes narrowed with a shrewd look. 'Try to delay him, honey. I haven't had much of a chance to talk to him – get to know him, if you know what I mean. But I think the Balinese humor mask is what he needs. The man has a beautiful smile, though I don't think he uses it very often.'

Rachel knew it would take more than a carved wooden mask to soften up Jackson, but she didn't bother saying so. 'I'll see what I can do.'

Opening the file drawer, she pulled the hand-written invoice from the folder. Making a copy using her small copier, she returned the original to the drawer and pushed it shut. Before leaving the office, she said, 'Give me a few minutes, Mom, before you come out.'

'You want the first sale yourself, don't you?' she teased with a wink. Making a shooing motion with her hands, she said, 'You go ahead, and good luck. I'll keep myself busy in here for a while.'

Shutting the door behind her, Rachel took a deep breath. Her head swam dizzily, causing her to sway. She pressed her palm to her temple, and waited for her vision to clear. Maybe she should have tried eating something before coming to work. Her stomach heaved at the thought of food, and her throat closed with a sickening squeeze. Bad idea. No food, she thought weakly.

Realizing there wasn't a sound in the store, her

nerves skittered with awareness. She moved past the back wall and a row of bookshelves and saw Jackson standing in the center of the room, his head tilted down as he looked at something in his hands. She eased forward, not wanting to break the daunting silence. She could feel the quiet, strained and shaking, as it reached across the room to her.

She expected him to lift his head, maybe even smile again, say something, but he remained still, as if moving would shatter something inside of him.

Stopping a few feet away, she held up the invoice. 'Here's the bill-of-sale you wanted. But I need to explain . . .'

His head came up slowly; his eyes were twin disks of stunned disbelief. She saw questions – no, not questions, she realized, but resignation. She wanted to whimper. *Oh, Lord, what now?*

He moved toward her, and she instinctively took a step back, bumping into a glass display case. When he came within a yard of her she saw he held something in his hand, but she couldn't look away from his eyes to discern what it was.

Halting an arm's length away, he took one labored breath after another. His jaw clenched and his skin darkened. He started to say something, but stopped and shook his head.

'Jackson,' she said, not wanting to ask, but she had to. 'What's happened now? Why are you looking at me like that?'

He raised his hand, making her flinch, but then she saw that he held a vase. She frowned, her gaze going back to his. 'How long have you had this, Rachel?'

She glanced at the vase again, this time noting that it wasn't a vase at all, but a scent bottle. Eight inches in height, with a curved handle on one side, the enclosed top was a lion's head, its fanged, gaping mouth the spout. From the carvings of battles on the sides and the condition of the pottery, Rachel assumed the bottle to be Greek, and ancient. Hundreds and hundreds of years old. 'Oh, dear God.'

'How long have you had it?' he demanded again.

Her brain shut down, making her go numb all over. She gripped the display case when she swayed, afraid her legs would buckle and she'd hit the floor. With her heart pounding in her ears, she said, 'I've never seen it before. Did you bring it with you?' Though she knew he hadn't. His arms had been crossed, his hands empty when she'd arrived.

'Where did you get it?' he asked pointedly, his voice deceptively calm. She could feel the anger trembling inside him, the sense of betrayal that threatened his control.

'I told you, I've never seen it before.'

'But it's in your store.' He hadn't shouted, but she flinched as if he had.

She shook her head and took a step sideways along the case. He moved closer. Rachel backed up. She needed space, room to think. She kept retreating; Jackson kept advancing, slowly, methodically, like a hunter who'd discovered a scent.

Impossible thoughts ricocheted around her mind, unable to find a place to land and make sense. Every

time she saw Jackson, her life became more en-
tangled, insanely bizarre. Her gaze fastened on
the vase, the molded body, the intricate markings.
She searched her memory for any recognition, but
found nothing. Which meant . . . She pressed her
hand to her throat, felt her pulse thud hard and fast
against her palm. Which meant what? *Nothing*! She
screamed mentally. She couldn't believe Penny was
involved. But how had it got into her store? She
knew where Jackson was going with his line of
questioning – he thought the vase might be stolen
and she was the one who'd taken it.

'Answer me, Rachel! You said you've never seen
this before, so how did it get here?'

'I . . . it could have . . .' She cursed herself for not
being able to think of an excuse fast enough that
would detract attention from her sister. Then the
solution came to her, and with it a laugh of relief.
'Obviously it's a new purchase.'

'That you know nothing about?' He rejected the
idea with a quick shake of his head. 'I may not know
you all that well, sweetheart, but I'll bet the price of
this vase that you know the location of every last
dust-ball in this store.'

She couldn't argue with the truth. She knew her
inventory so well, she could describe every piece and
its placement with her eyes closed. Everything
except the vase in Jackson's hands. 'My guess
would be that a customer brought it in yesterday
afternoon after I left. It's not uncommon for us to
buy items back from clients.'

'Then you'll have a receipt.'

175

Panic surged up her body. She licked her lips and willed herself to breathe normally. Cool air dried her lungs, prickled her skin. She couldn't shake the sense of foreboding, the fear that there wouldn't be any receipt, that somehow the vase had come to be in her possession by some other, more sinister means.

'Of course we'd have a bill-of-sale, only it isn't . . .'

Jackson reached out with one hand, gripped her upper arm and pulled her to him. 'Don't try to lie and tell me it isn't here.'

'I . . . I wasn't.' Though that was exactly what she'd intended to do. She needed to buy some time so she could question Emily and Penny without Jackson listening. 'Why are you assuming it's stolen? Are you preprogrammed to always think the worst of me?'

'The vase is hot, Rachel.'

'How do I know that? Because you say so?' She drew a shuddering breath. 'You come into my store throwing accusations without backing them up. How do I know you didn't plant it yourself? I don't know you that well, either, Jackson. Maybe you're so desperate to save your business you'll sabotage mine, offer me up as a sacrificial lamb.'

He pushed closer, trapped her between the wall and his body. She thought about struggling, but knew the effort would be futile. Besides, she wasn't afraid of him – what he could do to her business, yes – but not of him physically. In a strange, illogical way she welcomed his towering height, his heated musky scent, the immobile shield of his body. If

176

they could ever move past the thefts, she knew she would be safe with Jackson. But at the moment, safety with him was an illusion. He intended to ruin her, she thought with a helpless, silent scream.

'You damn well know I'd never set you up.' He cupped the side of her head, the pressure of his fingers firm, but not painful. His thumb grazed over her mouth, up to her cheek. He sighed and rested his forehead against hers. 'Are the records in your office?'

They were, but her mother was in there as well, and Rachel didn't want Jackson alerting Emily to the real reason for his visit.

'Oh, dear,' Emily said from behind Jackson as if on cue. 'I think I should have waited a little longer.' Her mother breezed by in a powdery whiff of Chanel, a silver tray loaded with cups and a teapot in her hands. 'But now that I'm here, I'm sure we'd all love a cup of coffee. It's a special blend, from Hawaii.'

Jackson pulled away, his rough palm sliding down Rachel's bare arm. Her entire body shivered in response. His eyes darkened, his pupils expanding with awareness, but his mouth hardened into a grim line. A muscle twitched in his cheek. Though he didn't say a word, she knew he wouldn't keep quiet about his suspicions for long. Regardless of what it took, she had to keep him from telling Emily about the thefts. The accusations had to be false, and she refused to have her mother worried over nothing.

'Why don't you have some coffee?' Rachel suggested. 'I'll be right back.' Before he could object, she darted into the office and shut the door. The previous day's receipts were on her desk as usual for her to review and enter into the computer.

Not taking time to sit, she flipped through the small stack of papers and found nothing relating to the vase. Pressing her palms flat on the desktop, she dropped her head between her shoulders, but that only increased the pounding inside her skull, and made thinking impossible.

Dropping into the chair, she pulled the check register from the bottom drawer and opened it. She skimmed her finger down the last few entries. Her skin tightened with each line she read. The closer she came to the bottom, the harder it became to breathe. At the last line, she pressed both hands to her mouth, afraid she might be sick. Not one check had been written that she hadn't written herself. And none of them was for the purchase of an antique scent bottle. 'No,' she whispered. 'No, no, no!'

She glanced at the door and knew she couldn't hide in the office. She'd left Jackson with her mother, and she didn't trust him not to interrogate Emily the way he had her. Hurrying into the showroom, she came to a stumbling halt when she spotted the pair standing at the counter, the dull beige vase in Emily's hands.

Her mother had donned her reading glasses and was studying the intricate carvings on the curved body, oohing and ahhing over the details. Rachel clenched her sweaty hands and closed the distance between them. Jackson glanced at her. The lean angles of his jaw, the tight brackets around his full mouth told her he'd discovered what she had just learned – Emily hadn't seen the vase before today, either. Which meant . . . Penny. Rachel blinked as hot tears pushed against the back of her eyes. *Oh, Penny. Why?*

'Rachel, this scent bottle is marvelous!' her mother said after noticing the direction of Jackson's gaze. 'Why didn't you tell me you bought it? And where did you get it?'

'That's what I'd like to know,' Jackson said in a quiet stone-cold voice.

Over the rim of her glasses, Emily glanced from Rachel to Jackson, then back to her daughter. 'What's going on here?'

'Nothing, Mom, it's just that I . . . well . . .' She wanted to cry and rant all at the same time. She couldn't answer the question without alerting Jackson to her own suspicions about her sister. But she couldn't stand there and mutter nonsense, either. Rachel took a steadying breath and decided Jackson would dig until he learned the truth. If he had to learn it, or what he thought was the truth, she'd prefer the information came from her when she could somewhat control the situation. 'I didn't buy it.'

'No? Well, then, who did? I don't recall Penny mentioning anything about it.'

'No!' Rachel reached for the vase, but Jackson beat her to it and cradled it protectively in the crook of his arm. Biting down on her lip, she said, 'I'm sure Penny doesn't know anything about the vase, either.'

179

'Honey, that makes no sense.' Emily removed her glasses, and Rachel could feel her questioning stare as intensely as if Emily were looking at her though a magnifying glass. 'If none of us bought it, how did it get here?'

Rachel hesitated, unable to answer. Her heart pounded in her throat, making it impossible to breathe, let alone speak.

Emily reached out and took Rachel's hand, cradling it in her soft, wrinkled fingers. 'You don't look well at all. I think I'd better take you home.'

'Mom, I'm fine.'

'Well, you don't look fine.'

'Where did you get the vase, Rachel?' Jackson asked, pulling her gaze to his with the restrained sound of his voice.

Feeling helpless and trapped and unable to think of a viable excuse, she whispered, 'I don't know.'

He sighed, a deep reluctant sound that lifted his chest, stretching his shirt across a plane of muscle. 'That's unfortunate.'

'Why is that, Mr Dermont?' Emily asked as she came around the counter to press a hand to Rachel's forehead. 'It's certainly a puzzle, but one I'm sure we'll clear up.'

'It's unfortunate, Mrs Gold, because I have no other choice now, except to go to the police.'

'Police?' Emily echoed and faced him in a startled move.

'You can't!' Rachel cried.

'Rachel, what is going on?'

'Nothing, Mother.' Rachel moved to shield Emily with her body. 'Jackson, you can't go to the police.'

'Don't *nothing* me, young lady,' her mother snapped from behind her. With a hand on her shoulder, Emily forced Rachel to turn around. 'I want to know what this is about.'

'The vase is stolen,' Jackson announced.

Emily gasped.

Rachel whipped around, glaring at Jackson. With teeth clenched, she said, 'You don't know that.'

His wheat-colored brow lifted in silent objection.

'You haven't shown me any proof that it *is* stolen. Until you do, I won't discuss this any further.' Rachel felt her life, her control, the safety net she'd fashioned for her family come unwound, and she now dangled by a weak thread. 'I won't have you barging in here, making accusations and upsetting my mother.'

'I haven't accused you of anything.'

'Yet,' Rachel finished for him. 'But I'm sure you're getting around to it.'

Emily tried to step between them, 'Why on earth would you accuse my daughter of stealing? I told you there had to be an explanation for the vase's appearance.'

Rachel gripped her mother's shoulders and urged her back. 'Mom, I'll take care of this.'

Emily crossed her hands at her waist and sighed. Her expression took on a scolding glare that normally would have had Rachel backing down. But not this time. The continuation of their very existence depended on Rachel convincing Jackson that he was mistaken.

'Rachel Marie,' her mother said in a stern tone. 'I'll not be treated like a child. I demand you tell me what is happening here. What does this stolen vase have to do with you?'

'Nothing!' Rachel shouted, then squeezed her palms to her head to contain the pounding surge of pain. In a quieter voice, she added, 'That's what I'm trying to tell Jack . . . Mr Dermont. If he would give me some time to research it, I'm sure I can explain everything.'

'I gave you a break with the necklace . . .'

'What necklace?' Emily interrupted.

'But I can't ignore this,' Jackson continued, his severe tone forcing Rachel to meet his gaze. She felt the abrupt halt of his anger, as if his impenetrable wall had slammed into place, shutting her out.

The result made her sigh in relief. She couldn't take the onslaught of his emotions when they were as charged with tension and anxiety as his were. She trembled, feeling weak-kneed and vulnerable. But she wasn't foolish enough to think this confrontation was over; he'd merely gained control of his emotions.

She didn't know what to do or who to turn to. How the hell had the vase gotten into her store? She needed answers, and quickly, before she lost everything. Right now, she'd do almost anything, say almost anything if only Jackson would believe her, tell her he'd made a mistake, and then hold her until the shaking stopped.

His next statement proved that would never happen. 'If you didn't steal this yourself,' he said, lifting the scent-bottle, 'then you must be fencing for whoever is. Either way, I have to hand this over to the police.'

He turned away, his towering body stalking toward the door. Rachel went after him. If he thought he was going to drop a bomb and leave before it exploded, he had another think coming. She gripped his bicep with both hands to stop him. She registered iron muscle and heated skin, and knew nothing she could do would cause him to stop unless he wanted to.

'Wait!' He kept going. 'Jackson, dammit, wait.' When that received no response, she added, 'Please.'

He opened the door, and without looking back, walked out. Rachel turned helplessly to her mother.

'Well, just don't stand there,' Emily ordered.

Rachel reached for the door just as it was silently gliding shut, and wrenched it open. Hurrying on to the sidewalk, she halted with a gasp as rays of fiery light stabbed her eyes. Using her hand as a shield, she squinted, cursing her eyes to hurry up and adjust to the sunlight. She spotted Jackson just as he reached his car, parked a few spaces from the store. She hurried after him, skirting around the Jaguar to the passenger side. Before she could stop and think she opened the door as the motor roared to life, and flung herself into the seat.

'What the hell do you think you're doing?' Jackson asked.

Panting, she gathered her skirts out of the door-jamb, and pulled the door closed. For an instant, she closed her eyes and leaned her head against the headrest to catch her breath. In the tight confines, the scents of sun-heated leather and Jackson's unique, spicy odor of pure male, the tangy bite of her own fear nearly overwhelmed her. She couldn't let this continue. Somehow, she had to convince him to believe her, if only for a little while longer. One more day, she thought, nearing hysterics, she only needed one more day. Long enough to find Penny.

'Unless you intend to come to the police station with me to turn yourself in, I suggest you get out.'

She turned her head and opened her eyes. Stress had carved stark lines into his face, obliterating any pretense of the softness she'd glimpsed on rare occasions. She wanted to reach out and run her hand down his beard-roughened cheek, smooth her fingers over his cold eyes, caress her thumb across the curve of his mouth. Force him to soften. She'd rub the full, tight line, and keep on rubbing it until the corners lifted, easing into the smile that could devastate her with its rare beauty.

What was *wrong* with her? The man was hell-bent on ruining her and destroying her business. He didn't care if he ground her family into the dirt while he was at it, either. Yet she couldn't stop the helpless yearning she felt when she was with him – or even when she thought of him, for that matter.

'Stop looking at me like that,' he growled.

Rachel blinked and curled her hand into a fist to stop the building need to touch him, see if his skin still burned with rage, or if he had cooled and merely simmered with his anger. He would be burning, she thought, a harnessed fire that he would take extra care to control. 'We weren't through talking about this.'

'Is there something you'd like to add?'

'Yes, there is.' She swiveled in her seat to face him, then crossed her arms beneath her chest. 'I didn't steal that vase,' she said, nodding to the object in question lying in the back seat. 'And I'm going to keep saying it until you believe me.'

He grunted in disbelief, but his gaze flickered down to her breasts, where a series of electric tingles ignited.

Her skin felt singed, as if he'd marked her with a branding iron. Her blood pulsed, pooling in her breasts, making them full and tight. Her nipples hardened against her will, pressing into the confines of her lace bra. In a voice that warbled with her distress, she asked, 'How can you be so certain that I took it?'

'It was in your store.'

She rolled her eyes heavenward. 'Do I look foolish enough to steal something, then display it for the world to see? Especially after a "security specialist" has accused me of having stolen a necklace?'

He rubbed his hands over his face, then raked his fingers through his hair, mussing it just enough to make him look dangerous. 'It doesn't make sense, Rachel, but I have to go with the facts.'

'That's just it. We don't have them all yet.'

'What are you saying?' With one arm draped over the steering wheel, he leaned closer, so close she could taste his heat as well as feel it. Potent and rich, like a swirl of brandy left lingering on her tongue. 'Do you know something you aren't telling me?'

'No,' she all but screamed. 'But I want to know why you're so determined to pin this on me. You know what I think?'

'Tell me.'

'I think you're afraid.'

'Bullshit.'

'You're afraid your company might be at fault. And,' she added, 'I think for some crazy reason you're afraid of me.'

'That's absurd.'

'Maybe. But why else would you be unwilling to look at anyone else? Why do you want me locked away? To put me out of your life?'

'Rachel . . .'

'Well, too bad, Jackson.' Her body trembled as her temper erupted. 'I'm here. And you're going to have to deal with me.'

'Rachel,' he said as if the fight had drained out of him. 'I don't want you to be guilty. God knows I don't. But look at it from my viewpoint. You had the necklace, and now the vase. Two out of the seven items stolen have turned up in your possession within the past week.'

'But I didn't take them,' she whispered.

'I want to believe you.' He reached out to touch her face, but pulled back at the last second.

Tingles leapt across her skin regardless. She could see the struggle in his eyes. He wanted to believe her. Despite the facts, he wanted to. 'You never said where the vase came from.'

186

'Senator Hastings.'

'The senator?' Rachel sat as upright as she could in the confines of the sports car. 'We . . . I mean, I wasn't even in the house. You were there. We were in the back yard.'

'During the party, but what about afterward?'

She raised her hands in a helpless shrug, her eyes widening incredulously. 'You went home with me.'

'Maybe you went back, bypassed the security system and stole the vase.'

'You make it sound so simple.'

'There's nothing *simple* about it.' This time when he reached for her he picked up the amulet dangling between her breasts and used it to draw her to him. The chain bit into her skin, forcing her to move. When their faces were inches apart, he said, 'That's why you had to have help. Your family, perhaps?'

'You leave my family out of this!' She pulled back, but his grip on the necklace held her in place.

'You're very protective of your mother and sister.'

She gripped his wrist and thought her fingers would blister from his heat. She was tempted to hit him over the head until he listened to her. Instead she softened her voice, and met his scornful gaze with an imploring one. 'I didn't take the vase, Jackson. Let me prove to you that I didn't.'

'How do you intend to accomplish that?'

His pulse hammered against her fingers where she gripped him. His gaze narrowed, boring into hers. The brown orbs turned dark, fierce with a primal hunger. A hunger she recognized and felt down to her soul.

He wanted to kiss her, she realized as her pulse thrummed through her veins. Only his stubborn will kept him from acting on his urge. She didn't think his kiss would be like any she'd ever experienced before. No, this time he would take, ravish her with his harsh taste and texture, expose her layer by layer until her heart was at his mercy. If she gave him her heart, what would he do with it?

She was afraid she knew the answer to that question. He wouldn't care for her, return her feelings, any more than he'd risk his business to save The Golden Pyramid.

Yet, he hadn't reported her to the police. She decided it was time to find out how far she could push him before he turned away from her for good.

'I have an idea, Jackson, though I'm sure you won't like it.'

'You're probably right.' He dropped her necklace and tried to pull away. She tightened her hold on him, sliding her hand down to take his. His fingers were warm, strong and rough as they closed around her hand like a human vise. In a graveled voice, he asked, 'What did you have in mind?'

Knowing she was literally putting her life at his mercy, she said, 'I want you to set me up.'

CHAPTER 10

'Excuse me?' Jackson tugged on his hand, but the cunning little witch refused to loose her grip on him. He wasn't going to fall for the pleading look in her eyes or the smoky seductiveness of her voice. She was up to something, and she was right when she'd said he wouldn't like it. He didn't. Not one damn bit. 'Just what kind of game are you playing?'

Her silky lashes flickered as if she was taken back by his challenging tone. 'It's not a game. What I have in mind makes perfect sense.'

Cold air pumped through the vents, but sweat beaded on his forehead. Whether it was from the morning heat, finding the vase in Rachel's store or because of her hold on him, he couldn't decide. 'Then spell it out for me, quick, because I'm leaving in two minutes.'

'All right, let's look at the facts. Rare, expensive items are being stolen. I didn't take them, but somehow two of them have ended up in my store.'

'There are only two because I haven't searched your house yet, which I intend to rectify,' he informed her, and watched her gray eyes widen, then narrow with a flash of temper.

'You aren't setting one foot in my house –'

'You wanna bet?'

'– because what I have in mind will clear me of any wrongdoing.'

Easing back into his seat, he willed the tension pinching his shoulderblades to relax. The woman constantly amazed him. He could come after her spewing fire, and though she might be shaken, she never backed down. Regardless of what happened from that moment forward, he respected her for her tenacity.

He grazed his thumb over the back of her hand, aware of the velvety texture of her skin, the cool smoothness. It didn't take much to imagine that the rest of her would be just as soft, just as yielding. The intensity of his irritation shifted, flaring like a well-tended fire in his gut. Jerking his hand free, he rubbed the tense muscles in his neck. Christ, the woman affected him on every level. Staying focused was all but impossible when a part of him wanted to believe her, even comfort her. *Hell, Dermont, admit it: you want her.*

'I'm listening,' he said, his voice strained. 'How are you going to clear yourself?'

'You said the only common denominator for each event was my presence.'

'That's right.'

'Which can't be possible. These parties involve the same group of people – all rich, all connected, all attending the same functions. Why am I the only suspect? Is it because I'm not one of the affluent? A wealthy person can't be a criminal?'

'Rachel, I've compared the guest lists, as well as the hired staff. In every case, someone missed one event or another. Everyone except you, that is.'

She sat back against the seat with a sigh, her gaze narrowing as she stared through the windshield. 'You must have missed something. I can't believe I'm the only one.'

'Believe it.'

She clenched her jaw and tilted her head. He could see the thoughts spinning through her mind. 'In a few days there's a Women's Fair for charity at Mrs Gibbons' estate in North Richland Hills. I'll be working there. You can watch me, attach some wires or something, do your security thing and keep me under surveillance while I do the Fair.'

'That'll only work if something is stolen. If nothing happens, it won't clear you.'

'It's worth a try.' The determination sharpening her gray eyes made him want to growl with annoyance.

Something had to be done about her, and the overwhelming need to protect her that kept rising up inside him. The feelings jarred him, continually throwing him off balance. Even when he'd thought himself in love with Sandra, he'd never felt the need to shelter her from the outside world. It wasn't that he didn't think Rachel could take care of herself, he just wanted to make sure she wasn't hurt. Which was a laughable contradiction, since he'd probably be the one to cause her downfall.

191

Either he had to clear her of the crimes or have her convicted so she'd be out of his reach once and for all. Perhaps she'd been right. Perhaps he was afraid of her, of the emotion that ran so deep, he couldn't begin to name it. He thought about her shut away in a dingy gray cell, away from him, separated from her family, the life she loved. His stomach clenched ruthlessly.

A violent denial sprang into his mind, and he let it come. He knew the risks in letting his emotions rule his thoughts. He'd tried to stop them, deny them, but he admitted the effort had been futile. He cared about what happened to her. It was as simple as that. He cared.

She was tough, and she'd built a life for herself, but he suspected the horror of prison life might break her. And how would he cope, knowing she was suffering? His mind backed away from the ugly picture and the unsettled feelings it brought.

No matter how he felt about her, he had a case to solve. If he proved she was guilty, he wouldn't have any choice but to turn her in. It would rip him apart to do it, but he would. 'What's to keep you from going back after the Fair and stealing something to make it look as if you're innocent?'

She watched him, her eyes flickering over his face as if she were trying to read him. He wished her luck. 'According to you, I research the layout while I do my readings. If you're watching me, you'll know if I'm up to something.'

'Which is only my theory, and not good enough to clear you.' Though he wished to hell it was.

Unfortunately, she was his only lead, and he had to follow it. 'Besides, if you know you're being watched, you aren't likely to keep to your routine, now, are you?'

'Good grief, Jackson! What do you want? To move in with me so you can watch me around the clock?'

'I think that's exactly what I need to do.' The idea would never have occurred to him if she hadn't brought it up, but now that she had, it was the perfect solution – provided he could keep his hands off her and survive it.

'You're kidding!' Her voice dropped with disbelief.

'I wish I were.'

'Think again. You aren't setting foot in my house.'

'It's that or I go to the police.' He hated threatening her, but in order to solve the case he needed her cooperation.

She hesitated. He could see the grasp for options in her eyes as she considered then discarded one idea after another. Her chin tilted. 'Go to the police, then.'

'Think about it, sweetheart. Once I show them what I have, they'll arrive with a search warrant, then they'll arrest you, lock you in a cell. Then you wouldn't be able to stop your customers from finding out.' He felt like the biggest bastard for pushing her, but he wanted her agreement so he could prevent those very things from happening to her.

She grunted, her mouth curving with a challenging grin. 'There's no smoking gun or dead body, Jackson. The Dallas police will drag their feet on a mere theft. They might show up at my store . . .'

'And your home.'

'. . . but it will take them at least a week. Until then, perhaps I'll start my own investigation into the burglaries.'

'I wouldn't advise it. If you think you like your privacy, you haven't seen anything until you've dealt with your clients' idiosyncrasies. They don't appreciate people snooping into their affairs.'

'Neither do I.'

Jackson signed. 'It's the only way, Rachel. Either I move in with you or I go to the police.'

A calculating glint entered her eyes, but he wasn't entirely fooled by her brave front. She was clutching her amulet with both hands so hard, her knuckles showed white. 'If you thought you had enough to convict me, you'd be at the police station now.'

She didn't know how close to the truth she was. The necklace could turn out to be circumstantial. The vase gave his case more credibility, but it might not be enough to convict her. 'I have the scent bottle. That's all I need.'

'That's right. *You* have the vase. Not me. It would be your word against mine as to where you found it.'

'Your mother knows.'

She released the necklace and crossed her arms. 'For all I know you planted the vase yourself. You specialize in security systems. Which means you can probably get *into* a room as easily as you can keep someone else out.'

'What are you saying?'

'You could have broken into the store and left the vase to set me up.'

Jackson rubbed his hand over his mouth. Christ, the woman was like a rat-terrier – she wouldn't let go. Didn't she understand he wanted to help her, but in order to do so he had to learn all the facts? No, she didn't, he realized, because all he'd done since meeting her was accuse and badger her for answers. 'Nice try, but it didn't happen.'

'Well, there we go again. Your word against mine.' Her chin tilted with defiance.

'You're right, Rachel,' he said in a conceding tone. 'I don't have enough evidence to go to the police yet. But everything points to you. Eventually, they'll piece it together. When they do, I won't be able to help you.'

'I didn't do it,' she said, her voice softer, but still determined.

'Then let me prove it by setting up a surveillance in your house.'

Her entire body stiffened as if she were bolstering herself to continue the fight. 'No.'

'Rachel . . .'

'No, Jackson. I don't know you, or anything about you except for the fact that you're trying to convict me of a crime I didn't commit. Why on earth would I allow you to move into my home?'

'Because you need me.'

'My knight.' She rolled her eyes heavenward and shifted to stare out the windshield. She ran a hand through her thick, black hair, then wrapped her fingers around the silver amulet again.

He'd never asked what the carvings meant, and now wasn't the time, but the necklace obviously meant something to her. He wondered if she was even aware of the telltale sign that she held the amulet whenever she was agitated.

'You're not coming inside my home, but if you feel this macho need to guard me from myself you can do it the old-fashioned way by sitting outside in a car.'

Not the solution he'd prefer, but he decided not to push her any further. 'All right.'

Silence expanded in the car, gaining a thrumming beat that matched his pulse. He couldn't take his eyes from her classical profile, so porcelain-clear and elegant, it staggered him. He'd thought her attractive when he'd first met her, but each time he saw her, he discovered something new, something that made her more beautiful, more tempting, more dangerous to his carefully planned life.

Why couldn't he have met her under normal conditions? They could have dated, gradually coming to know each other while learning each other's likes and quirks. Nothing would have stopped him from having her in his bed long before now. Instead he sat in his car, determined not to touch her, which meant suffering from an ache that threatened to blind him.

'One more thing. I don't want you telling my mother about any of this.'

'You can't keep this from her. Besides, she already knows the vase is stolen.'

'I'll handle my mother. She's been through enough.' Her voice softened, hitching with emotion. 'She'll worry. I don't want that for her.'

'She seems pretty tough to me.' Like mother, like daughter, he surmised.

Rachel managed a tolerant smile. 'Just promise me you won't announce our . . . situation to anyone.'

'I'll be so discreet *you* won't even know I'm there.'

'If only.' Sobering, she tilted her head around to look at him. Strands of black hair fell from her shoulder, falling into her lap, creating a backdrop of mink against her face. Her angled cheekbones seemed carved from marble, polished to a satin finish that couldn't be real. Her eyes glowed, but he couldn't see inside her. The gray orbs were tangled silk, finely woven like a spider's web.

Gut instinct told him she kept secrets hidden there; he imagined them locked between layers and shades. He wanted to learn what made her so strong, so incredibly fascinating. Why had she survived her difficult childhood, when others had failed? That element of strength was what drew him to her, tempted him to believe in her when he'd sworn he'd never believe in another woman again.

He looked past her straight nose to her mouth, a mouth he could taste in his dreams. He lifted his hand to touch her face, but she straightened, her eyes flashing a warning. He gripped the steering wheel instead and stared out the side window at her store where a pair of blue-haired ladies were entering. He was tempted to call the entire thing off. He'd learned of the stolen vase just after midnight last night when the Senator had called, furious and demanding results. Jackson had clung to the slim hope that Rachel wouldn't have the antique vase. He'd been doused with cold shock when he'd spotted the scent bottle prominently displayed in the center of the store on a marble pillar.

Her surprised expression flashed in his mind. She'd seemed genuinely confused, then panicked. He might eventually regret not going to the police now, but a few days wouldn't matter. Rachel wasn't going anywhere. And, if nothing else, whatever he learned about her in the meantime would either strengthen his position or clear her.

'Jackson?' she asked, breaking the long silence.

'You can tell your mother whatever you like about why I'm hanging around.'

Though she nodded in acceptance, she didn't look entirely pleased with his response. 'I'd better get back inside. Mom's undoubtedly beside herself, wondering what's going on out here.'

'I'm coming with you.'

'W . . . what?' she sputtered, pausing in opening her door. 'Why?'

'I plan on going through your books.'

'No, you're not.'

'Rachel, let's not argue about it. You can help me if you like.'

Facing him, she leaned close and poked her finger in his chest. 'Let's get one thing straight, Jackson.

You can sit outside my home until it snows, you can browse through my store looking at the inventory until you're blurry-eyed, but you aren't, I repeat, you are *not* going through my files. I haven't a clue as to how that vase got into my store. For all I know you put it there. If you did, you might decide to alter a few things so you can close your precious case that much sooner.'

'I wouldn't do that.'

'Well, I'm not going to take that chance. If you want to see my files,' she said, sliding out of the car and bending down so she could keep eye contact, 'go get that search warrant you keep threatening me with.'

'You're making a mistake, Rachel.'

'You know, Jackson,' she said, shuddering as she drew a breath, 'I ought to hate you for putting me through this.'

With that she slammed the door. Skirting the front of the Jaguar she hurried for the store without looking back.

Jackson watched her go. She'd said she 'ought to' hate him, not that she 'did'. He caught the distinction and unwillingly filed it in the back of his mind. He *ought* to walk away from her, too, yet he couldn't bring himself to do it. Instead he was invading her business, tailing her every move, burrowing himself deeper into her life.

He already wanted her more than he'd ever wanted another woman. How in God's name would he be able to live through the next few days of smelling her addictive, feminine scent, of hearing her sultry voice that filled him with the incessant need to touch and taste her? But he had to, he thought, driving the reality of their situation into his heart. He'd built walls to protect himself from falling into another trap. No matter how much he wanted her, how desperately he needed to protect her, he couldn't.

Rachel didn't need to hate him, he thought with a bitter inner laugh, because if he accomplished his goal and proved her guilty, stripped her of everything she owned, he'd hate himself enough for the both of them.

CHAPTER 11

Arriving with the destructive force of a flash flood, Jackson's dark eyes took on the appearance of bruised clouds whipped with icy rain. The air around him sizzled with trapped electricity. The hair on Rachel's arms stood on end, tracking a path up to her nape where tingles crept across her scalp. She thought it odd for the sky to be clear and crisp and softening with the approaching dusk. Heated wind should be beating against the wooden slats of her house, while stinging rain slashed her windows. But the storm had come inside – with her. Somehow she had to get rid of it.

She tilted her head back and held her ground as Jackson stepped into her entryway. Her grip on the doorknob tightened and she planted her other hand on the wooden trim, blocking his path. 'You're not coming inside.'

He hesitated, backed up a step. His eyes narrowed a calculating degree. 'Aren't you acting a little childish?'

'About letting a virtual stranger into my home? A man who has done nothing but harass me and might be trying to frame me? I don't think so.' Miss Bastet wrapped around her leg and emitted a sharp meow. Rachel glanced down at the cat and made an unfeminine snort in agreement.

He sighed with exaggerated patience. 'You've didn't seem to mind having me in your home last night when you invited me to dinner.'

'Things were different then.' She flattened her hand against his chest and pushed. He didn't budge. 'Go back to your car, Jackson. You can watch me to your heart's content, but you're going to do it from the curb.'

She shoved again. He caught her wrist and lifted her hand from his chest as easily as if he were removing a piece of lint. 'All right, Rachel. We'll do this your way.' He rubbed his thumb down the curve of her palm. 'But I *will* be watching.'

It nearly killed her to do it, but she closed the door in his face instead of slamming it the way she wanted to. 'Come on, Miss Bastet. Let's pretend he isn't here and go make dinner.'

In the kitchen, her hands shook as she chopped vegetables for a salad. Watch her, indeed. Just who did he think he was, dogging her every step as if he expected her to grab *all* the jewels she'd stolen and leave the country? Dropping the knife on the cutting board, she picked up the phone and punched in her sister's number.

Penny hadn't called in all day, which wasn't like her sister. She might occasionally arrive late for work, but she always phoned to let them know. A thorough search of the office had revealed Mark's home number, and though Rachel had called his apartment a dozen times, no one had answered.

On the fourth ring, Rachel closed her eyes and fought down the wave of panic pushing up her throat as Penny's recording came on, telling the caller to leave a message. Rachel complied, not attempting to disguise the irritated snap in her voice. 'This is the tenth time today I've left a message, Penny. You've got to call me. Something's happened and I have to talk to you about it.'

Hanging up the phone, Rachel rubbed her hand over her brow then dragged her fingers through her hair. 'Where is she?'

Not wanting to go to Penny's apartment with Jackson following her, Rachel had sent Emily, but only after she'd told her mother as much as she dared about the stolen necklace. But she hadn't fooled Emily. Rachel had seen the quiet worry enter her mother's eyes, the unspoken disappointment and fear.

Where could Penny be? What had happened to her? Was she off joy-riding with Mark, or was she in trouble? Were they fencing more stolen pieces? Maybe they suspected she was on to them and they were hiding out? Rachel couldn't rest until she knew the reason behind her sister's sudden disappearance. If her sister was caught, and found guilty, she'd go to jail. The Golden Pyramid would be forced out of business after the facts were made public, snatching away the security Rachel had promised her family.

Rachel shook off the burdening thoughts. She had to talk to her sister first, look into her eyes when she asked if Penny knew about the scent bottle. Then she'd know the truth.

She hadn't heard from her mother yet, which meant Emily hadn't found Penny. Rachel doubted her sister would resurface until she was ready. But how dire would their situation be then? The necklace had been circumstantial. But until she spoke with Mr Weatherby and verified that Penny had legitimately purchased the jewelry from him, she wouldn't be completely cleared of that theft.

But the vase. Rachel picked up a knife and began slicing carrots, more than she'd need for a dozen salads, but she couldn't stop. Her nerves were twisted like bands of steel. She didn't want to admit it, but the appearance of the stolen items, and now Penny's mysterious absence . . . How could she not suspect her sister's possible involvement with the burglaries?

Sprinkling a few of the carrots on the shredded lettuce, she dumped the rest into the trash. Slicing part of an onion, she put it in a pan to sauté then took a package of hamburger meat out of the refrigerator. Both she would add to the spaghetti sauce she'd put on earlier to simmer.

Something thumped against the front of the house. Tensing, cocking her head, she listened, but couldn't detect anything over the ticking of her teakettle clock, the sizzling onions and the thunder of her heart pounding in her ears. 'Jackson, you had better not be snooping around outside,' she muttered.

But the possibility had her hurrying to the living room. She peeked through the front blinds. Night had completely closed in, but light from a street lamp reflected white streaks off the Jaguar's polished body. Through the windshield, she glimpsed the broad outline of Jackson's shoulders. A shiver tore up her spine. Though she was hidden from view, she imagined he could see *her* watching *him*. She could feel the pull of his intense gaze reach across her yard and through the walls of her house to touch her. Another shiver followed the first. She dropped the blinds and backed away.

'You're over-reacting,' she whispered to herself. 'He might be intimidating, and as canny as Miss Bastet, but he can't see through walls.'

A high-piercing shriek blasted through her house. Flinching, she turned. *The smoke alarm*! Miss Bastet screeched and ran from the kitchen, disappearing down the hall into Rachel's bedroom in a flash of black fur. Running, Rachel reached the kitchen just as a cloud of white, steamy smoke billowed through the door. The onions!

Grabbing the coated handle, she removed the pan from the fire while simultaneously turning off the burner. A large hand closed over hers, shocking a gasp from her. Jackson took the pan from her grip and nudged her aside. She moved away as he scraped the charred black bits into the sink.

'Open the back door,' he yelled above the alarm.

'I thought I told you not to come into my home?' she stammered, crossing her arms over her waist to contain her nerves, which were jumping with adrenalin.

'Yeah,' he said, replacing the pan on the stove. 'I know what you told me, but I thought you were in trouble.'

Had he rushed in to save her? Obviously, he had, she thought, and felt her heart race a little faster. She spun around and opened the back door. When she turned back, the thunderous look on his face stopped her where she stood.

With both hands placed flat on the counter and his arms stretched taut, he seemed to be holding himself erect, as if he didn't trust himself to come too close to her. His rigid stance consumed the space around him, making the room seem tiny and too crowded to hold them both. He wore the same white shirt from that morning, though now it looked as haggard as she felt. His heavy-lidded gaze focused on her, his expression revealing turbulent emotions as his brown eyes scanned the length of her body. Then he looked away.

The familiar prickling excitement that plagued her whenever she was near him worked through her exhausted limbs, making her want to scream at her own foolishness for responding to him.

You're a fool, Rachel. An absolute fool.

At that instant, the smoke detector stopped its shrill siren. Deafening silence slammed into the room with a vibrating quiver. Rubbing her hands down the front of her skirt, she straightened her shoulders and walked past him.

Chopping more onions and adding them to the pan, she said, 'Thank you for your help, Jackson, but as you can see, everything's fine.'

She felt his eyes on her for the full minute it took him to respond. 'I always loved the way onions smell when they're cooking.'

She glanced at him as he rubbed his palm over his stomach in a male, feed-me-I'm-hungry manner.

'It's only spaghetti. And I only made enough for one.' Which was a lie. She'd made enough to feed an entire family of five. The manners her mother had taught her revolted against being rude, but Rachel couldn't give in to the temptation to ask him to stay. The man could unravel her control and better sense without trying. The sad truth of the matter was that she couldn't trust herself where Jackson was concerned.

'Need any help?' he asked. He fished a carrot out of her salad and popped it into his mouth.

'You're not eating here,' she said, inwardly cringing at her surly tone. 'If you're hungry, there's a Dairy King down the street.'

'Why are you so nervous around me?'

She slanted him a 'get real' look, then retrieved a glass because she needed a drink of water to ease her dry throat. 'If I appear nervous, which I'm not, it could be because I don't want you in my house.'

'Is it really just me you don't want here, or would any man cause you to be so uptight?'

'I'm not uptight.' Avoiding the first part of his question, she went to the sink, filled her water glass and downed half of it. It unnerved her, having to admit, even to herself, how much Jackson affected her. No man had ever made her question herself, her own femininity. Watching him from the corner of her eye, his broad-shouldered height dominated the room. The fixture overhead angled light over his face, casting shadows beneath his thick lashes. His cheekbones could have been carved from stone, so perfect were they, so skilfully defined. Her hand began to tremble as longing curled up inside her.

Perhaps Jackson didn't think her pretty enough or smart enough to attract a man's attention. Or that her profession made her a cut below the acceptable female? She had little experience with dating, but she'd never met a man worth the trouble it would take to add him to her schedule. Until now. Only her timing with Jackson couldn't have been worse.

'If you're through bothering me, would you please close the door on your way out?'

The corner of his mouth cocked with a grin that said he saw through her facade. In a gentling tone, he said, 'We only have to tolerate each other for a few days.'

'I shouldn't have to be tolerating any of this at all.'

He eased her aside and added the hamburger meat to the onions. Picking up her wooden spoon, he chopped the meat into small clumps. She grabbed the spoon and elbowed him out of her way. It was bad enough having him dog her every step at work, keeping watch on her in her own home, but she'd be damned if she'd let him take over her kitchen. It didn't matter that he looked as if he belonged in the bright nook of a room in his worn, tight-fitting jeans and comfortably rumpled shirt. This was her space, and she didn't want his musky, masculine body crowding it. Honestly, she didn't!

'You know, it's not safe to leave your doors unlocked.'

'Thanks for the warning,' she said, sounding so flippant, she wanted to bit her tongue. 'I'll make sure to lock it as soon as you use it to leave.'

Turning her back to him, she continued cooking in silence, and, after a moment, she heard his footsteps in the hall. Sighing, she wiped the back of her hand over her brow, then straightened to look at the back door, which still stood open. Since he seemed so particular about her locking herself inside her house, why hadn't he shut the door? Then it dawned on her. He hadn't left yet. She leaned over the counter to look down the hallway, but she didn't see him. Frowning, she uttered a curse as it occurred to her that he might be snooping though her things.

Slapping the spoon into the ceramic holder, she wiped her hands on a towel and marched down the hall. Reaching the living room, she paused in midstep, a heated demand on the tip of her tongue.

Jackson sat on her sofa, his bare forearms braced on his thighs, his hands clasps lightly together. He leaned forward, his attention focused on Miss Bastet, who sat upright on the coffee table, her attention fixed solely on him. Cat and man seemed to be in the midst of a Mexican standoff, neither looking away, or even blinking for that matter.

Rachel had thought Miss Bastet's dislike of Jackson odd, because the cat normally liked everyone. She had an uncanny knack of picking up people's emotions. Rachel had assumed the cat had sensed Rachel's unease around Jackson. Now, she wondered if the cat wasn't sensing something in Jackson that Rachel had missed. Did Miss Bastet not trust Jackson? Or did having him near unsettle her as much as it did Rachel? Miss Bastet wasn't used to having a man around any more than Rachel was. It could even be that the cat was jealous of Jackson. The possibility almost made her grin.

'You're going to have to give me a break here, Felix,' Jackson said in all seriousness.

The feline didn't flinch in response. Rachel pressed her lips together when an unexpected smile sprang free.

'There's enough tension in house to sink it. I don't need your grumpy attitude adding to it.'

The cat huffed a breath.

Jackson lifted his hand so Miss Bastet could sniff it, which she did with a delicate move of her head. In a surprisingly gentle touch, he rubbed the cat beneath her chin with his large, rough knuckles, drawing a sawing rumble from her thick, furry chest. 'Now, if I could just get your owner to purr.'

Rachel's shoulders jerked back, and her mouth dropped open. Did he think he could give her a nice scratch and she'd fall into his arms? She glanced from his gently kneading fingers, burrowing deep into Miss Bastet's rich black coat, to the easy smile on his lips and knew she wouldn't fall, she'd crumble and cling to him in a way that made her want to growl at her own weakness.

She needed time to put her feelings for him into perspective. Everything had happened so fast, she couldn't make sense of anything.

Jackson's head tilted back and he sniffed the air. He turned, finding her instantly. 'Rachel . . .'

'Damn!' She spun around and ran for the kitchen. She didn't hear Jackson come up behind her – the man moved like a ghost – but she felt him. All six feet, one hundred and eighty pounds of him loomed over her like the grim reaper.

'Tell me,' he said, his breath warm against her ear as she scraped the meat into the strainer. 'Do you usually have this much trouble cooking?'

Glaring at him, she said, 'You can go now, Jackson.'

'Because if this is a sample, I can learn to like my meat well done, or even shrivelled.'

'That won't be necessary, because you're never going to be invited to my table again.'

He ignored her hint and goaded her instead. 'We could take turns. I don't cook much myself, but I know my way around a kitchen.'

'Not mine.'

A faint smile touched his mouth. The look he gave her sent her blood humming through her veins. His eyes told her he wanted her, and though she understood perfectly, she didn't know what to do about it.

'All right, Rachel. You win,' he said, then left through the back door, closing it behind him.

Her stomach twisted, coiling into a knot. Finally she had her house to herself again. She drew several breaths before coherent thought resurfaced. She glanced at the phone and considered calling Penny, but discarded the idea. In a few minutes, maybe.

She needed time to recover from the last encounter with Jackson and the vibrant, turbulent emotions still building inside her. What she felt for him, the things she wanted from him despite the fact that he threatened her safe existence, astounded her.

Going to the kitchen table, she sat in a chair and cradled her head in her hands. Whenever she was with him, she didn't simply experience a physical reaction, though heaven knew she couldn't stop thinking about how his arms felt around her, or how his kiss sent her mind swimming with dizzying pleasure. Who would have ever thought a man could taste so rich and warm and spicy? What she wouldn't give to remove the barriers and make love to him. Her body pulsed with possibilities she could only imagine. Shaking her head, she ran her fingers through her hair.

She'd never even been tempted by promiscuity, but now she realized her lack of knowledge left her at a disadvantage when dealing with Jackson. What would he think if he knew how inexperienced she was? That for all her talent at giving advice about life, she'd hadn't lived much of one. Would he be intrigued, or would he run for the hills?

But there were other feelings besides the sexual ones that confused her. She wanted to know Jackson, learn what drove him, what made him smile, something she didn't think he'd done much of lately. Had he ever been married, did he want kids? There were so many unanswered questions. Yet the more she learned about him, the more layers and questions she discovered.

Rachel slumped back in her chair as she realized what was happening. She was falling for a domineering, obstinate, mule-headed man whose rare smiles made her insides curl and her brain empty of all common sense. Her response to him had nothing to do with her original curiosity about wanting to know what made him tick, though it would help tremendously if she could figure out that key element. No, her feelings for Jackson were born of something far deeper and wholly feminine.

A dangerous combination, she realized, especially when it involved her heart, because Jackson would most likely trample it on his way out the door when he was through ruining her life.

Suddenly feeling bone-weary, she pushed up from her chair and turned off the stove on her way to her bedroom. Trying to force down food would be impossible when he was sitting in his car, hungry. And cold, she added, well aware of how frosty April nights could be in Dallas. Maybe she should take him a blanket and a pillow? Good grief, what was she thinking? That would be like surrendering, or, worse, admitting that she was worried about him. Telling herself he deserved to suffer didn't help, though, as she entered her bathroom and turned on the water as hot as she could stand it for a bath.

Miss Bastet slipped into the room just as Rachel shut the door.

'And I suppose you've gotten over your dislike of Jackson,' Rachel said as she stripped off her blouse. She froze and glanced at her reflection of bare skin covered by a nearly transparent lace bra. She pressed a hand to her throat and looked at the surrounding blue and white tiled walls. There were no windows in the room, but Rachel could *feel* Jackson as if he were standing next to her, watching her undress. She turned the lock in the doorknob, wishing it were a deadbolt. Miss Bastet curled into a fluffy ball at the base of the door as if to create another barrier. Rachel grinned, feeling better, but only slightly.

She didn't think Jackson would try to break down the door to get to her, but then she didn't know him as well as she wanted to. She doubted she'd ever get the chance, either.

Removing the rest of her clothes, she eased into the tub. Heat bit into her skin, bleeding into her tight muscles, loosening them as she lowered herself all the way in. Gritting her teeth at the pleasure-pain, she closed her eyes and leaned back with her arms braced on the cool porcelain sides.

It was her usual routine to take a few minutes to soak away the worst of the day, believing all would be right with the world afterwards. Rachel choked on a tired laugh. 'Now, what are the odds of that happening?'

I want her. The thought struck out from the night so loud and clear that Jackson glanced around to see if someone else had said the words. The street where Rachel lived was lined with middle-class brick and wood-frame houses, lit with warm yellow light that pooled on well-tended lawns. Cars were parked in driveways or tucked into garages. No one roamed the streets, but then who would want to take a walk in forty-degree weather? Jackson thought as he hugged his arms tighter against his chest in an effort to ward off the cold.

Since no one else could have uttered the words, Jackson had to admit they'd come from him. *I want her.* The phrase came so easily, so unmistakably clearly. But she might be guilty, he mentally argued. *I don't care. I want her.*

He leaned back against the headrest and blew out a fogged breath. He had to be out of his mind. Rachel was right when she accused him of wanting to make love to her, but she'd been way off base when she'd said he wouldn't give a second thought to sending her to jail. If that happened, he thought some vital part of him might be torn out of his chest and ripped in half.

His gaze lingered on her small house, the porch that ran across the entire front, the wood pillars that supported the sloped gabled roof. Everything from the flower-lined walkway to the faint light coming from within urged him to leave his car, find Rachel and shake her until he either had the truth or had her in bed.

Clenching his teeth, he drew a breath through his nostrils, thinking he could use a shot of whisky to stem the flow of blood pulsing to his groin.

He wanted her, which didn't make a damn bit of sense. But neither did watching her house. Except that by keeping an eye on her he'd know she wasn't trying anything foolish. She was planning something, though. The woman was as nervous as a fly around a glue pot. He couldn't escape the suspicion that she was keeping information from him. If so, he had to find out what *it* was. A queer sensation in his gut told him that once he learned her secret, the pieces to the puzzle would fall into place.

Until then, he'd wait and watch.

The light in her bedroom flashed on. He held his breath, expecting her silhouette to appear against the drawn blinds. Seconds ticked by with the veins in his neck throbbing with anticipation. Drawing in air, he propped his arm on the door and rubbed his hand across his mouth. Maybe watching, and the strain it caused on his system, wasn't such a good idea after all.

Jackson reached for the keys in the ignition, ready to head to the nearby hamburger joint Rachel had mentioned for a cup of coffee. Had he really thought he could fight the temptation of going into her house to see her? The smoke alarm had been a godsend, giving him an excuse to check on her. He wasn't going to make the mistake of trying again, though. She'd made it clear. She wanted nothing to do with him.

And he couldn't blame her. Not with the way he'd disrupted her life.

Just as he gunned the engine to life, he saw her front door open, emitting a hazy strip of amber that outlined Rachel's body as she emerged on to the porch. He turned off the car and relaxed against the seat, curious as to what she intended to do.

After a brief pause, she hurried down the steps and crossed the yard. Bathed in moonlight, her black hair draped her shoulders like a satin cape, rich and impossibly thick. Her robe swirled like a silver cloud against her legs, and looked too flimsy to protect her from the cold. In her arms she held a bulky object.

At the front of his car, she halted and looked back at her house as if she were perplexed as to how she'd come to be outside. But when she faced him again, her features were set with determination. Reaching the passenger door, she opened it and tossed her bundle inside. Blankets, he thought with a grin. And a pillow.

Leaning down to see him, she said, 'I thought you might be cold.'

Before he could respond, she slammed the door shut and hurried back to her house, closing herself inside. Jackson gathered the covers to him. Without thinking, he brought the soft fabric to his face and inhaled the scent of spice. Rachel. He leaned his head back and closed his eyes, thinking he would have been better off if he'd gone for coffee.

CHAPTER 12

Rachel dabbed concealer beneath her eyes in a hopeless attempt to disguise the purple shadows – evidence of her sleepless night. Blending in the tinted cream with the tip of her finger, she straightened and studied herself in the mirror. With a sulky frown, she admitted the make-up wouldn't be enough. Nothing short of wearing sunglasses all day would camouflage the tired circles under her eyes. Glasses were tempting. She didn't want Jackson to know how much his spending the night freezing in a cramped car had disturbed her. Admitting that she cared annoyed her enough.

She'd berated herself endlessly for tossing and turning during the wee hours, frustrated because her imagination kept conjuring up a different kind of Jackson – one who would stand up for her, believe in her without question. If only he'd open his mind, risk having faith in her, he'd know she could never have stolen anything from anyone.

The mere thought of him drew her gaze to her bedroom window. As was her habit, she'd opened the blinds to admit morning light. A sheen of dew on

218

the glass blurred her view, but she could still make out the Jaguar's sleek shape. The whorling confusion she'd suffered all night returned, rushing beneath her skin, making her feel flushed and winded. She wasn't sure how she would act when she saw him next. Keeping him at arm's length took entirely too much effort. And as persistent as he was, she didn't know how much longer she could force him to remain outside, when she was so tempted to invite him in. Only her pride, her fear of the consequences and her determination to prove him wrong kept her from acting on that impulse.

She thought back to the afternoon when he'd first kissed her. She hadn't been aware that he'd suspected her of the thefts then. If only she'd known! Instead, she'd returned his kiss, losing herself in the hot probing of his tongue, the spinning mixture of his taste and heat. The shocking length of his body pressed against hers, nestling her, fitting her to him as if she'd belonged there. Was she crazy for wanting to experience those feelings again? With Jackson?

Yes. Resolutely and undoubtedly, yes.

Not having the patience to do more than run a brush through her hair until it was free of tangles, she decided to wear it hanging loose down her back. She slipped into a black ankle-length broomstick skirt and a black lace camisole. Over it, she added a colorful Victorian patchwork vest in soft velvet. Sheer black hose and ankle-strap pumps completed the outfit.

Clothes were the one vice she couldn't break, not having had many while growing up. Her tastes didn't lean toward the traditional, but rather the unique. She preferred flowing skirts with embroidered designs, vintage attire that had character and style. Several times she'd noticed Jackson examining her outfits. He'd never said anything about what she wore, therefore she had no idea whether he liked them or not.

And it doesn't matter, she mentally snapped, adding the final touch to her outfit – her silver amulet. She stared at the necklace in the mirror's reflection. While on a buying trip two years before, she'd found the necklace in a cramped, dust-filled antique store outside Cape Cod. She'd recognized the symbols and had bought the piece for a fraction of its value. She'd intended to add it to her collection in her own store, but some time during the drive from the east coast to Dallas she'd become attached to it. Now, she wore it every day as a reminder of the one attribute missing from her life.

Tracing her fingers over the magical runic letters M, X, C and P, she whispered their meaning. 'Trust, love, passion and joy.' She and Jackson had passion, but they lacked the other three vital parts that made a relationship.

Though she could see into other people's lives, she couldn't see into her own to know if they would ever trust each other completely. And without trust they would never find joy or love. She thought back to his parting words the first night she'd met him. In a controlled, smoky tone, he'd informed her that trust was for fools. If that was the case, then she was the fool for even giving him a second thought.

Sighing, she left her room to make a much-needed cup of hot Earl Grey tea. Perhaps she'd take a cup to Jackson, though she imagined he would prefer coffee, black and as strong as tar.

In the kitchen she came to a stop as she caught a trace of his unique scent in the air. Had he been in the house again? Or did the scent linger from the night before? Disregarding her desperate need for a cup of tea, she went into the living room. Empty. She released a pent-up breath. He couldn't have come inside without breaking in. The thought made her clench her teeth. How difficult would it be for a security specialist to slip a lock? She'd known plenty of men who'd lacked education but could jimmy a dead bolt within seconds. Certainly hers wouldn't have been much of a challenge. Jackson wouldn't do it, she told herself, not after she'd made it clear that she hadn't wanted him in her home.

Miss Bastet's echoing meow drew Rachel to the front door. The cat sat patiently in the entryway as if wanting to be let out, though Rachel knew that wasn't the case. Miss Bastet's rotund weight made it impossible for her to climb trees and there were too many kitty-hungry dogs in the neighborhood for her to outrun.

'What are you doing in here, sweetheart?'

Blinking her one eye, the cat purred then looked at the door.

'What is it? Are you trying to tell me something?' Rachel asked as she unlocked the door, then opened it, half expecting to see Jackson standing there, waiting to be allowed in. She stepped outside and felt two different emotions tug through her. One being relief at not coming face to face with him. The second, and most disconcerting one, was astonishment that his gray Jaguar was nowhere in sight.

He's gone.

She stared at the empty spot where the car had been parked as her mind absorbed the fact. Instead of welcoming the respite, she experienced an absurd form of resentment that he'd left without telling her. Back inside, she shut the door, her thoughts narrowing on the man who was quickly becoming an obsession. He'd been so adamant about following her everywhere, why would he leave without talking to her first? Was he up to something, or had he simply gone for a cup of sludge coffee and a restroom break, which he must definitely need after nearly ten hours of surveillance work?

Returning to the kitchen, she switched on the gas under the kettle filled with water. She reached for a cup but hesitated when she spotted a piece of her stationery on the counter. Her heart missed a beat as she picked it up.

So he had been inside. She glanced around, expecting him to appear. She remembered unlocking the front door. Then how . . . ? The back door. Had she locked it after he'd left? She couldn't recall. Maybe she should be more careful and do as Jackson said from now on. Her stomach churned with irritation, at herself and at a certain whisky-eyed man. She'd definitely have to set some ground rules for Jackson Dermont.

She unfolded the note and studied his handwriting. The style was bold, angled, with definite sweeps that were as sharp and to the point as the man. While his penmanship possessed a certain elegance, he sorely lacked communication skills.

Rachel,
I'm at my office. I'll be at your store when you open.
Jackson.

She set the paper down and stared at it. As far as letters went, it didn't reveal much. Except that he'd made a conscious decision to leave her on her own. Maybe, just maybe, he was beginning to trust her – if only a little.

Fingers of purplish light stretched across the Dallas skyline, fading to amber at the tips. Fourteen stories below, Loop 635 was already gridlocked with morning rush hour, but Jackson barely noticed. He cradled a ceramic mug in his hand and sipped hot black coffee that tasted as if it had been brewed the day before. He turned away from the view to focus on the detailed proposal for a new client his sales manager, Derrick, had handed to him two days ago, claiming the technical aspects were too intricate and complicated for him to bid accurately. Normally, Jackson preferred delving into the planning stage, finding possible weaknesses, and designing a system that would surpass any previous installation. The more complicated the job, the more he loved it.

But there was nothing 'normal' about this contract. Word had already reached Mr Henderson, an affluent computer parts distributor, of the string of thefts. To keep from being eliminated from the bidding altogether, Derrick had promised Mr Henderson a system designed to outclass anything on the market.

Jackson had been torn between wringing Derrick's neck for making such a rash commitment and giving his manager a raise for his fast thinking. The job would be difficult, but not impossible.

If he won the bid to install the security system in Mr Henderson's estate, it would be their largest job yet. The initial set-up would bring in a hefty sum, but the monthly surveillance involved would take Dermont Technology over the top. He'd be able to expand nationwide sooner than he'd planned.

But as much as he loved devising ways to improve his system, he couldn't focus on the challenge. A pair of troubled gray eyes continually replaced the blueprints and building codes he studied. Nor could the earthy scent of coffee steaming from his mug abolish Rachel's unique fragrance from his mind. Regardless that he held a pencil in his hand, he could imagine the firm curve of her back pressed against his palm, the flawlessness of her cheek as he'd cupped her face the first time he'd kissed her. The woman was a temptress. A fiery, black-haired mystery that made every nerve in his body jerk to attention.

He rubbed his eyes to relieve the burn, the result of a night without sleep. Sitting in his car half-frozen, and numb from the hips down, he hadn't watched her house so much as he'd tried to put his bizarre relationship with Rachel into perspective.

Time and again he'd been tempted to enter her house and crawl into bed with her. Though he couldn't deny his longing to make love to her, the compelling need to simply hold her thrummed just as strongly in his mind. A damn confusing, unbelievable thing to want, he admitted. He'd never needed something so basic from a woman before. To want Rachel made him think he might be in need of psychotherapy.

High on the reasons why was the fact that she might be a criminal. Even if he proved she was innocent, she didn't fit into the rigid path he'd set for himself after Sandra. He'd been content to bury himself in his work, breaking the routine with an occasional date. Until now. Until Rachel. Her combined strength and compassion continually amazed him. Though he had yet to learn the details of her childhood, he'd gleaned enough to know it had been difficult. Since life hadn't given her a break, she'd fought to make her own.

His chest tightened with the need to help her, protect her – a need he hadn't thought existed in him.

His mind circled back to the possibility that she might be convicted for the thefts. Could he watch her go to prison, knowing he'd been the one to send her there? How the hell could he possibly live with himself afterward? Worse, how could he live with himself if he didn't do his job and she was guilty? *Guilty*. The word didn't fit, not with Rachel.

Something else was going on here. Something he'd missed. He'd already ruled out Sandra being involved. There was no love lost between them, but she wasn't stupid enough to break the law merely to hurt him. Only his past dealings with her had made him suspect her in the first place.

Which left Rachel still in question. If she didn't steal the vase, that meant someone else had planted it in her store. But why? To ruin her? Or to throw the trail off the person responsible?

'I'll be damned.' Jackson stared, unseeing, out the window. He drew in a breath and held it. Maybe she was innocent. He wiped his hand over his mouth, set the coffee down and shoved to his feet. He glanced at the photocopied bill-of-sale for the necklace lying on his desk. The handwritten receipt struck him as suspicious. A quick check had confirmed that Weatherby's was a well-established operation. He doubted they made a habit of scribbling receipts on pieces of notebook paper. He'd already contacted the company, only to learn the owner wouldn't be back in Dallas for a few days. The secretary had refused to divulge where and how they'd acquired the necklace. So, he had to wait.

But the vase . . . Jackson frowned. From Rachel's stunned reaction, he believed she'd never seen the bottle before. Despite his badgering, the evidence stacking against her, she held firm to her innocence.

But there were facts that couldn't be disputed. If he went to the police now, they'd arrest her. He doubted they'd bother to investigate any further. Why would they? She'd been caught with the evidence red-handed. Which smelled more and more like a set-up to him. But who would want to frame her? Who could possibly hate her so much? The first name that came to mind was Penny, Rachel's sister. There was obvious sibling rivalry between them, but would Penny bite the hand that fed her? Or did Penny want total control of the store, but knew that was impossible unless Rachel was out of the way for good? Rachel would be furious if he went after her sister, but unfortunately, he had no other choice. Penny was his next best lead.

He swore under his breath as a thought occurred to him. If he understood Rachel as well as he thought he did, he wouldn't be surprised if she confessed to the crimes just to protect her sister.

If that happened, would he be able to poke holes in her confession? If she had stolen the vase and the necklace, she wouldn't have kept them in her store. The woman was too sharp to do something so stupid. But would a jury believe or care about that? They'd only look at the evidence, and as it stood, Rachel still was the one who would go down for the crimes unless he could prove otherwise.

The more he thought about it, the more he realized staying close to her was the best thing he could do. As long as he could keep his hands off her, he amended. He needed to know whom she associated with, who might want to ruin her, or worse, see her in prison. The charity luncheon was three days away. If someone was trying to frame Rachel, odds were they'd try something again.

He dropped his head back, releasing a pent-up breath. Or, her being framed could be wishful thinking on his part. He shook his head and walked a slow path around his office. She wasn't guilty. Gut feeling told him she wasn't, because the evidence didn't make sense. If his failed engagement with Sandra had taught him nothing else, he'd learned to listen to his instincts. Doubts had plagued him all along, only he'd chosen to ignore them. And right now his instincts were telling him to give Rachel a chance.

Her being innocent would put him back at ground zero, but he didn't care. If he proved someone was setting Rachel up, he knew he'd also find the person responsible for the burglaries.

He wouldn't tell Rachel that he was beginning to believe her for fear she'd turn her expressive gray eyes on him, believing the barrier between them had been removed. If she gave him the slightest encouragement, he'd forget the investigation, his business and hers, ignore her demand that he stay out of her house. He'd take her to bed, keeping her there until neither of them could think.

He didn't have her intuitive skills, but he knew desire burned in her as fiercely as it flamed in him. Together, they were a powder keg, waiting to explode. The thought stirred the constant longing in his loins, raising the fire to an unbearable level. He rubbed his hands over his face, then threaded his fingers through his hair. This ordeal had to end. Soon.

When this was over, maybe he'd take Rachel away for a few days. Hell, it'd been years since he'd taken a vacation. The white sandy beaches of St Thomas would be a perfect place to get to know one another.

They would both deserve it.

An abrupt knock on the door preceded Derrick's entrance. 'Hey, boss,' he said, then came to a halt. A cocky grin pulled his mouth up as he scanned Jackson from head to toe. Though he'd showered and changed before coming in to work, Jackson knew fatigue lined his face. Forgoing his usual suit and tie, he wore jeans and a button-up shirt, though beneath the starched cotton, his taut muscles ached with strain.

'Looks like you had a rough night.' Derrick ran his hand down his politically correct blue, white-dotted silk tie. 'And I say it's about time. So, who is she?'

'Unfortunately, it's not what you think.' Jackson rubbed the back of his neck, rotating his head to relieve the kinks. 'I spent the night in my car, watching Rachel's house.'

'I suppose you had a reason.'

'I found the senator's vase at Rachel's shop,' Jackson answered reluctantly.

Derrick moved his jacket aside and propped his hands on his hips. 'And instead of going to the police you stood guard?'

Ignoring the derision in Derrick's voice, he said, 'Something like that.'

'She's not worth it, Jackson. If you keep this up, she'll cost you this business the same as Sandra did last time. I don't understand you . . .'

'You don't have to,' he snapped, not liking to hear his fear thrown out into the open. 'I know what I'm doing.'

'Do you?' Derrick demanded, arching a brow. Pulling his shoulders back in an arrogant stance, he said, 'Then let me share some information we just discovered.' Going to the door, he stuck his head out into the reception area. 'Andy, come on in here.'

Dermont Technology's computer guru entered with the lanky gait of a boy just reaching puberty, though Andy had turned thirty-two last February. The Cowboys baseball cap crammed on his head made the spring-tight curls of his shoulder-length brown hair fan out around his face. Shoving his glasses up the bridge of his blade-thin nose with the tip of his finger, he grinned as if he'd just broken the code to the Fort Knox bank vault.

'Tell him what you found,' Derrick said, as he crossed his arms over his chest and leaned against the wall.

After Jackson nodded his assent, the computer tech said, 'Well, I did a search on Rachel Gold like you asked.' He shook his head, sending wiry hair bouncing around his thin face. 'But you already know that. Didn't find anything. She's as clean as a whistle, same as her mother. I couldn't continue my search after that though because of the Millers. Lightning hit their house and man, what a mess!'

'Andy,' Jackson interrupted as dread curled up inside him. 'Did you find something new on the Golds?'

'Did I ever.' Rocking back on the balls of his feet like a kid, he handed Jackson a computer printout. 'I found something on the sister, Penny. She's got a juvenile record.'

230

'Juvenile?' Jackson repeated. 'Those records would be sealed. How did you get them?'

Andy smirked and made an 'Are you kidding?' grunt.

Jackson didn't like the idea of one of his employees breaking into police records, but since Andy had already done it he asked, 'What did you find?'

'She's got a record that'd cram a hard drive. In the beginning she was picked up for shoplifting, petty theft, mostly small stuff. Then she progressed to jewelry, expensive designer pieces, you know, artsy things. She even stole a car, at least one that the cops know about. She would have served time, except she was a minor *and* she turned state's evidence, testifying against the guy that headed the fencing operation. Turned out it was big-time organized crime. Drugs, the whole bit.'

The blunt weight of Andy's words forced Jackson into his chair. He couldn't breathe for the pressure squeezing his chest.

Rachel wasn't involved. The words kept repeating in his mind, momentarily blocking out everything else.

'. . . she's still on probation,' Andy continued in a delighted voice. 'If she's behind these thefts, she'll go to prison for a long, long time.'

When Jackson didn't respond, Derrick pushed away from the wall and said, 'Thanks, Andy. That'll be all.'

'Sure, Derrick.' Flushing as Derrick patted him on the back, Andy nodded to Jackson. 'Hope this helps, Mr Dermont.'

Jackson held still as the door closed behind his employee, too stunned to move or even think. But the truth blared in his mind regardless of the fact that he didn't want to face it. *Penny had a record . . . for theft.* A record Rachel had kept from him. Did she know her sister was responsible for the burglaries? Was that the cause of Rachel's nervousness? Was protecting her sister the reason she didn't want him to investigate her family or tell her mother the truth? Or was Rachel fencing the merchandise Penny stole? His mind leapt from one ugly possibility to another, making him sick to his stomach.

If Rachel wasn't mixed up in this, he'd bet his last dime that she knew Penny was somehow involved and was covering for her.

Derrick pressed his hands flat on Jackson's desk and leaned forward. '*Now* will you go to the police?'

He had no choice. He'd asked Rachel time and again to be honest with him, but she'd refused, choosing to lie instead. Threading his fingers together, he pressed them to his mouth and dragged air into his tight lungs. In a graveled whisper, Jackson said, 'Yeah, it's time.'

CHAPTER 13

The telephone screeched with the ear-piercing shrill of an angry child. Rachel flinched and resisted the urge to run from the room as memories of another police station on another long-ago night assailed her. Hallways crammed with people, shouted curses, some drunken, others hateful, the sharp tang of ammonia and the underlying stench of unwashed bodies had added to the mayhem when Penny had been arrested for stealing. But 'stealing' was too casual a word for what her sister had been involved in. She'd been drawn into a world of organized crime, and Rachel had been too busy to notice. Once she had, it had almost been too late to save her.

Today, the pale gray hallways were busy, but not overly crowded. A steady hum of conversation layered the room, adding definition to the people milling about. A musty odor coated the building, a collective residue from people who'd previously walked through the doors to report a crime or to search for lost loved ones.

Was she too late now? Or was she overreacting? Perhaps she should have waited a little while longer?

After all, Penny could be willful, even thoughtless at times. Rachel gave herself a mental shake. She had to act. Something was wrong. She felt it in every fiber of her body.

The ear-splitting bell rang again. Rachel stood before the battered desk, praying the sergeant would set his newspaper aside long enough to pick up the receiver and stop the shrill noise before her nerves shattered. She clenched her hands as he leisurely answered the call and directed it to another officer, then, to her dismay, he hung up the phone and went back to his reading.

'Excuse me.' She stepped forward into his peripheral line of sight.

'What can I do for you?' he asked without sparing her a glance.

Tempted to rip the paper from his hands and shred it to pieces, she took a steadying breath. 'I need to file a missing person's report.'

Slowly, the officer folded his paper and placed it on top of a stack of manila folders marred with fingerprints and coffee cup stains. When he focused his brown eyes on her, she saw they were tolerant, weary and bloodshot. 'Is this person a child?' he asked.

'No.'

'Has this adult been missing for over forty-eight hours?' he asked in an automatic tone, as if he'd repeated the same question everyday for a thousand years.

With her nerves jumping inside her skin, she gripped her purse to her stomach with both hands. 'I'm . . . I'm not sure. I know she's been gone for at least twenty-four hours.'

He raised a brow and the corner of his mouth pulled up with annoyance.

Afraid he'd dismiss her, she rushed, 'It's my sister. She was supposed to work yesterday in my store, but she never came in. I've called her repeatedly and gone to her apartment, but she wasn't there. She hasn't shown up today, either.'

'How old is your sister?'

'Twenty-three.'

'Maybe she's off with a friend.'

Rachel had considered the likelihood that Penny was with Mark. However immature her sister might be, she wouldn't have left with him without calling their mother, if not Rachel first. But Penny was gullible, as evidenced by the trouble she'd been in before. She tended to be impressionable and so trusting that at times she'd been incapable of seeing right from wrong. But she'd learned her lesson. Or at least, Rachel had wanted to believe she had.

'She wouldn't have left town without telling someone.' When the sergeant reached for his paper, she gripped his starched shirt, forcing his attention back to her. 'Look, she hasn't been home all night. Can't I at least file a report?' Gentling the panic rising in her voice, she added, 'I have to do something.'

Leaning back in his chair, he studied her for a moment while he scratched the side of his face with his short nails. 'All right. You wait here while I get a detective. But, just so you know, he won't be able to do much until she's been gone for two days.'

Nodding, unable to speak for the tremors in her stomach, she turned to sit in the over-used, rock-hard chairs lining the wall. She collided face first into an immobile chest. Gasping, she backed up as two large hands locked on to her arms.

'What the hell are you doing here?' Jackson growled.

She sagged back and dropped her chin for a second to gain her bearings. She couldn't deal with him right now. The thefts be damned. She had to find her sister before she could handle anything else. Meeting his challenging gaze, she groaned inwardly. From the rising color in his face and the hardening line of his jaw, she knew his temper was about to blow. Pushing against his chest, she tried to break free. He gave her an abrupt shake, jarring her entire body. 'Answer me.'

She stilled, swallowing, forcing her anxiety down to a controllable level. 'It's none of your business.'

'I'm afraid it is.' A dangerous light entered Jackson's eyes, the kind of which she'd never seen before. Lines were carved at their corners, mean grooves were dug into his angular cheeks. He leaned into her, his hard mouth inches from hers. 'Have you come to confess?'

She tugged out of his hold and slapped his hands away. 'Not in your lifetime. Before you start off on another tirade . . .'

'Hey, Dermont, haven't seen you in here for a while,' the desk sergeant said, resuming his seat, the cracked vinyl creaking beneath his beefy weight. His once tired eyes had sharpened to pinpoints, scrutinizing the two of them. 'You know this lady?'

Jackson stepped back and ran a hand through his hair. 'How's it going, Pete?'

Rachel crossed her arms, matching Jackson's angry stare. Why was he so upset, and why was he at the police station? And why was he on a first-name basis with a cop? He might have to interact with the police to install his security systems, but that wouldn't account for his knowing an officer by name. Or was he working with them to solve the thefts? Prickling heat crept up her body as the answer filled her mind with frightening clarity. *He's going to tell them about the vase.* She caught his arm. 'Jackson . . .'

'Miss . . . ah . . . ?' the sergeant interrupted.

'Rachel Gold,' Jackson answered for her.

'Miss Gold, Detective West will take your statement now.'

Jackson took a step closer until he towered above her. 'What are you going to tell him?'

When she didn't respond, Pete filled in. 'She's got a missing person.'

Rachel thought it convenient that the two men seemed content to answer for her. Her voice refused to work.

Jackson's brow furrowed. 'Penny?'

She nodded and sucked in a breath when he caught her around the waist and herded her toward the exit. Over his shoulder, he called, 'Tell West we'll be back later.'

Rachel wasn't sure if Sergeant Pete responded or not because Jackson ushered her outside and down the sidewalk. Knotted clouds had gathered, bringing wind, cool and heavy with the scent of rain. 'Jackson, stop.' She twisted away, but he pinned her to his side. 'What are you doing?'

At his car, he opened the passenger door. She pulled back, her hair blowing in her face. 'I'm not going anywhere with you.'

'Oh, yes, you are,' he answered in that dangerous purr of his.

'I told you Penny's missing.' Hot tears pushed against the backs of her eyes, welling. She blinked rapidly, refusing to let them fall. 'I have to find her. She might be in trouble.'

'She's already been in trouble,' Jackson said in a voice so low, so calm, a shiver ran through her.

She rubbed her arms when the chill penetrated her bones. 'What are you talking about?' she asked softly.

He drew a breath, then leveled a wary look at her. 'You lied.'

It took a moment for his words to sink in, but then she knew. She could see it in his eyes. He knew about her sister's past. Frantically, she tried to think of something to say that could placate him, but her mind had shut down.

'All this time, you've been trying to steer me away from her. Playing a game.'

'No.' She closed her eyes and turned away as the tears fell. She pushed her hand into her stomach until it hurt, drew one quivering breath after another to pull herself back together. But she couldn't. She couldn't. Everything was caving in too fast. She tilted her head back and blinked. White sunlight stabbed her eyes as tears ran down her temples and into her hair.

Jackson took her by the shoulders and turned her to face him. She shook her head, waving him away. She didn't want him to see her like this, crying as if she'd given up. Lost. But everything in her life had been a battle: her father's sudden death, the struggle to escape the hell they'd lived in, saving Penny from herself and the people who'd used her. She'd fought to build a place for them. A future.

Only to lose it all?

The tears came harder, shuddering out of her body. She pressed a hand to her eyes and tried to break free of Jackson's hold. With a stifled curse, he drew her to him. She buried her face in his shirt, letting him support her. She held her breath, refusing to give in to the pressure building in her chest, rising up, expanding, choking her. She couldn't let go and cry the way she wanted to, not now.

But she'd never had anyone hold her, take the weight from her shoulders, even for a little while. Her hands slipped to his waist, an expanse of lean muscle that flexed with her touch. His strength worked its way into her, magically calming the drumming beat of her pulse. For the first time in her life, she knew she had to ask for help. She believed in Penny's innocence, but doubts were crowding in, making her faith in her sister waver.

239

There were elements at work that she didn't understand. A mystery with too few clues, and those she knew about pointed to her family. She *needed* Jackson's help. She couldn't solve this nightmare on her own.

'Penny didn't do it, Jackson,' she cried against his chest. 'I don't know what's going on, but I know she didn't do it.'

He rubbed her back, soothing his palm up her spine and kneading the tense muscles in her neck. He pressed his lips to her hair, making her sigh. 'Why didn't you tell me?'

She pulled back to meet his eyes. They were dark and turbulent with confusion, but lacked his earlier rage. Maybe he'd listen to her, believe her this one time. 'Because I knew you'd jump to the wrong conclusion. And you have, haven't you?'

His jaw clenched and his arms fell away. He rested his hands on his hips and studied her. His silence was all the answer she needed. She wiped the dampness from her face. 'That's why you're here, isn't it?' Her voice shook with reproach. 'You're going to tell the police Penny's the thief.'

'You weren't the only one at each of those parties.' It wasn't a question, but a statement of fact. 'Penny is always with you, isn't she, Rachel? The day of the senator's picnic, you told me she accompanies you to set the schedule and collect the money.'

'That proves nothing.'

He sighed and looked past her toward the police station and the low ceiling of gunmetal gray clouds. Panicking, her heart throbbing in her throat, she

240

gripped his arms to keep him from walking away. 'You were going to give me a few days to prove myself innocent. Jackson, please, can't you do the same for my sister?'

'That was before I knew she had a police record.'

'Dammit, I didn't volunteer the information because I wanted to protect her! If she'd been your sister, you would have done the same.'

He looked down at her, his eyes a mixture of indecision and anger. 'Give me one reason why I shouldn't walk into that station and turn Penny in.'

She moistened her lips and put herself on the line. 'Because I'm asking you not to.'

Seconds ticked past. He lifted a hand and grazed his thumb across her damp cheek. The brown of his eyes deepened with what she thought might be remorse. His mouth thinned into an inflexible line, and for one horrible moment, she was certain she'd lost her one ally. Then he stunned her by saying, 'I'm probably going to regret this.'

'You won't. I promise, you won't.' She ran her hands down his arms, feeling his muscles tense. Inwardly shaking with a combination of relief and dread, she put distance between them, and turned to leave.

He caught her shoulders, swung her around and hauled her back to him. 'Oh, no. Where do you think you're going?'

She glanced to the side as a squad car slowly drove past, the officer watching them though his tinted window. Forcing her expression to relax, she said, 'I'm going to file a missing person's report.'

'No, you're not.'

'Jackson . . .'

'Get in,' he ordered.

'Not until I'm finished here.'

'Rachel, get in.' The controlled demand vibrated as if it had been struck with a gavel. 'There are things we have to discuss, and we probably shouldn't discuss them here.'

'It will have to wait until later, because right now my sister is the only thing that matters to me.'

He planted his hands on either side of her, leaning against the roof of the car, trapping her between two immobile walls. 'If you involve the police in this now, I won't be able to do anything to protect Penny.'

The meaning behind his words slowly sank in. 'Are you saying you'll do more than give me the few days? You'll help me find out who the real thief is?'

'It goes against my better judgement, but yes, I'll help you.'

She hugged her arms to her waist, afraid of the hope lifting inside her. Unable to voice her appreciation, she clamped her mouth shut and got into his car. She held herself rigid in her seat, her purse clamped in her hands as he negotiated the car through morning traffic. He was going to help her. He didn't believe Penny was as much a victim as Rachel, but he wasn't going to turn her sister in yet. It was a small reprieve, but one she'd gladly take.

She recalled that he wanted to talk to her about something. She didn't think she was up to an intense

242

discussion; her emotions were too raw, bubbling too close to the surface. Even being in such close proximity to him, with no immediate means of escape, added another form of tension she felt incapable of handling. He was too big, too overwhelming, too much of everything she wanted and couldn't hope to have.

It took her a moment to find her voice, but finally she broke the tangible silence. 'Where are we going?'

'To my place.' He said the words as if they irritated him.

They certainly shocked her. 'Your house? Why?'

Jackson's gaze locked on her, daring her to protest. 'We need to talk, and for this discussion, Rachel, I don't want any interruptions.'

A tremor rippled through her. 'You make it sound like a warning.'

His attention shifted to the road. 'Let's just say it's time we cleared up some things between us.'

Rachel sat back in her seat as heat trembled through her body, whether it was a result from her roller-coaster emotions or the indescribable look in Jackson's eyes, she didn't want to guess. But if his statement hadn't been a warning, she didn't know what was.

Rachel stood alone in the middle of Jackson's immense living room, absorbing facts about him that he would never have revealed on his own. White mini-blinds on the patio door blended with the off-white walls. He hadn't bothered with pictures or drapes to relieve the bleached color. The couch, set at a haphazard angle in the middle of the room, was a burlap, Rent-to-Own special that no one in their right mind would ever buy. Or at least, no one with any taste. A veneered walnut-brown end table supported a pastel lamp that she guessed dated from the 60s. He didn't own a coffee table. The room seemed a contradiction to the man she thought she was coming to know.

She made a slow turn, noticing the lack of personal mementos, framed photographs, anything that would allude to a hobby or special interest. No books or magazines. A pile of folders and newspapers tossed on the floor was the only evidence that the place was inhabited at all. She couldn't imagine anyone living here. It was as if Jackson had purposely swept away any trace of his past or present, content to live in a place devoid of comfort. She cherished her home with its warm colors, its open space, the sense of solidity that welcomed her each time she walked through the door.

He hadn't bothered with a dinette table in the breakfast nook, but he did have two barstools at the pass-through bar to the kitchen. She didn't dare go upstairs to the bedroom, where Jackson had gone to make a phone call, to check it out, but she imagined it would be just as sparse, just as lacking in warmth as the rest of the townhouse.

The bleak surroundings didn't make sense. This place didn't belong to the passionate, turbulent man she knew. So why did he live here, like this? Then it dawned on her. He didn't *live* here. This was just a place to *exist* when he wasn't at work. He wasn't attached to this space, and he didn't care how it looked. Which didn't fit his character. He drove an expensive car, and dressed to perfection, even if it was jeans and a button-down shirt. He was the type to extend his taste to his home. So why hadn't he? Was this a part of his nature, or had something happened to him that made him resist creating his own place? It was human nature to establish roots, build an environment that suited specific needs and style.

Yet Jackson had shunned all that.

She didn't believe it was due to a lack of money. The man did drive a Jaguar, after all. And he owned a business that catered to the ultra-rich. That didn't guarantee wealth, but she didn't think he was in financial trouble. There had to be another underlying reason at work. Her curiosity piqued, she couldn't help but want to know why he lived as if he were a refugee.

Her analysis ended when she heard his footsteps on the stairs, as imposing as the distant thunder creeping over the city. Tensing, she thought about sitting on the couch or even the barstools, but gave up the idea and stood where she was, in the center of the large, dismal room.

He appeared like a gust of wind, upsetting her senses all over again, and making her question the sanity of agreeing to come to his home. She chastised herself. They were only going to discuss the thefts, and Penny's possible involvement. She should be grateful, not suspicious, that he was willing to help her. She might be attracted to him, which was a mild understatement, but her feelings didn't matter at the moment. Even if they hadn't had the burglaries to contend with, he hadn't made any move to kiss her again, proving he wasn't interested in her. Which should have relieved her. At least one of them would manage to keep focused.

'Want something to drink?' he asked as he entered the kitchen.

She crossed to the bar to watch him study the contents of the refrigerator, which she imagined held next to nothing.

He glanced at her over the top of the door, raising a dark brow. 'Beer or water?'

Bring proven correct in the contents of his refrigerator, she almost smiled. 'Water's fine.'

He handed her a glass of iced water and popped open a beer for himself. He took a deep swig, his eyes focused on her.

Rachel cupped the cool glass between her hands, thankful for something to hold. 'What did you want to talk about?'

Stepping around the bar, he came to lean his elbow on the surface beside her. 'You name it. Me, you. This case. Your sister's being a prime suspect, which means I haven't ruled you out as an accomplice.'

She bristled. 'If you think I'm involved, why are we here and not at the police station, fingerprinting me and issuing a warrant for Penny's arrest?'

He sent her a disreputable grin, then took another drink of his beer. 'You have me there.'

'You know I'm not involved, you just don't want to admit it.'

246

He met her gaze with such directness, she had to look away as a tingling flush crept up her face. Sometimes she thought he could see inside her, hear what she was thinking, feel how much he affected her. The possibility unnerved her.

'What I think, Rachel, is that you love your sister so much, you'll do anything to protect her. Maybe even confess to a crime you didn't commit to keep her out of prison.'

She ran her finger over the water glass, causing the condensation to drip down its sides. How far would she go to keep Penny out of prison? Rachel had asked herself that question time and again, knowing she'd do whatever she thought necessary. But would she confess to something she hadn't done? Rachel didn't know. What would happen to her family with her in jail? How would her being locked away help them? If Penny was stealing again, she would need special counseling, something she wouldn't receive if Rachel were in prison.

'I can't believe she'd do something like this,' she whispered, more to convince herself than Jackson.

'You don't want to believe it, but lying to yourself isn't going to help her. Face it, Rachel, she's done this before.' Setting down his beer, he took her left hand, cradled it between his. 'If she is innocent, then we'll prove it, but first we have to find her. Where do you think she might have gone?'

Rachel pressed her free hand to her brow. 'That's just it, I haven't a clue. I called the Blind Lemon where Mark works, and he hasn't shown up for the past two nights. Mom couldn't tell if anything's missing from Penny's apartment, because she keeps it such a wreck. We've called her friends, and no one's heard from her. She's disappeared.' Her voice broke as frightening possibilities clarified in her mind. 'What if something has happened to her? She could be hurt, or . . .'

Jackson slid a hand around her stomach. Turning her to him, he drew her close. He cupped her sides, his hands large and solid and so warm she could feel his heat through her clothes. She'd never before wanted a man to hold her, she'd certainly never needed their strength, but now she wanted both from Jackson. Perhaps it wasn't logical, this need to rely on him, but instinctively she knew she could. There was something primal about him that made her believe he would protect her, as a man protects his woman.

'Don't worry. We'll find her.'

Hearing the cold calculation in his voice, so different from the possessive feel of his hands, she tilted her head back to meet his gaze. Her chest tightened and she shook her head as confusing doubts crept into her mind. Could she trust him to help her? She wanted desperately to believe she could, but he'd been adamant about pinning the crimes on her, and now he'd made a complete about-face. Why? Suddenly, she knew the answer.

'You don't really want to help me, do you, Jackson?'

His eyes narrowed.

She pressed her hand to her brow as shudders

raced beneath her skin. 'You're only pretending to help so you can find Penny and save your business.'

She shoved against his chest, but his hold on her tightened until his fingers dug into her hips. 'You're setting me up, making me think you really care.'

'Rachel . . .'

'No!' She threw up her hands to stop whatever he might say to try and sway her. Pushing away, stumbling free of him, she grabbed her purse from the couch. She had to get out of there. She'd had so many shocks and disappointments over the past few days, she didn't think she could take another one. 'Take me back to my car. No, never mind. I'll call a cab.' Glancing around the room, she asked, 'Where's the phone?'

'If you'd give me a minute to explain . . .'

'I've listened to enough of your theories, now where's the damn phone?'

With his hands propped on his lean hips, he nodded toward the stairs. 'In my bedroom. First door on the left.'

She gave him a withering glare and headed for the front door. 'Never mind. I'll walk.'

She jerked the door open, but Jackson's palm hit the surface and slammed the door shut again. Refusing to face him, knowing her temper was out of control and she was helpless to rein it back in, she stared at her hand gripping the brass knob. 'Let me go, Jackson.'

He leaned so close that his rich, masculine scent enveloped her senses. Her hair whispered against her face as he said in a voice so low and seductive she couldn't help but listen. 'Not until you hear what I have to say.'

'You'll say anything to save your company. I don't blame you, really, but I'm not going to help you by sacrificing myself or my sister.'

'You're right. I want to find the person responsible for this, but you couldn't be more wrong about my not caring about you.'

She shifted and stared at the opposite wall, too afraid to face him and see that he was lying, or, worse, telling the truth. If by some miracle he truly did care about her, she'd have no defenses to protect herself with. 'Don't do this to me.'

'I didn't want to care about you. And I tried damn hard not to,' he said as if he had to struggle to say the words. 'Hell, I'm still not sure what to make of you or what I want to happen between us, but I do know I don't want you or Penny to be charged with the thefts. But I have to be honest with you – everything points to your sister.'

Her grip on the doorknob slipped. She tightened her hold, afraid to let go. Afraid if she did, she'd give in to the need to turn to him, bury her face against his neck and give in to the doubts hammering down on her. But she couldn't turn to him, trust him completely until she knew for certain that he wouldn't betray her.

'Look at me, Rachel.'

She pressed her lips together and closed her eyes. 'Why should I believe that you're concerned about my family?' She couldn't say the words 'care for' because that would make it too personal.

He stepped in front of her, nudging her stretched out arm with his ribs. 'Your intuition is usually right, isn't it? Listen to it. I know it's telling you to trust me.'

'Trust?' Her eyes snapped open at the unattainable, magical word. She met his gaze in the shadowed entryway. 'You don't believe in the concept, remember? Why should I trust a man I know nothing about? You keep everything a secret, Jackson, asking questions while revealing nothing. Look at your home.' She swung her arm behind her to encompass the barren room. 'There's nothing here except a shell of a building. Who are you? Where do you come from? What happened to make you so guarded and distrusting of everyone around you? Those are the questions I need answers to before I can *trust* you.'

He leaned against the door, his shoulders sagging as he hooked his thumbs in his jeans' pockets. He tilted his head to the side to watch her, his eyes dark with reluctance, as if he dreaded the idea of revealing himself. Or had he played with smoke and mirrors for so long that he didn't know how to answer her? 'I would prefer not to go into this.'

'You don't have to,' she said, her voice clipped. 'Because I'm leaving.'

'Not yet. I'll tell you what you want to know.' He extended his hand to the side. 'Why don't we move into the living room? You look as if you need to sit down.'

Not trusting her legs to support her if she unlocked her knees, she shook her head. 'I'm fine right here.' But she did release her grip on the doorknob so she could fold her arms across her chest.

He blew out a breath and looked down at the floor between their feet. 'Five years ago, I made the biggest mistake of my life.'

After he'd paused for a full minute, making her wonder if he intended to expand on the vague statement, she said, 'I'm listening. What was this mistake?'

When he met her gaze, his eyes were cold and remote, a reflection of the man she'd first met. 'I fell in love.'

Something inside Rachel split open, sucking her into an icy whirlwind. She'd thought she was prepared for whatever he'd had to say. She'd been wrong.

CHAPTER 14

Jackson watched the color drain from Rachel's face. The firm set of her lips relaxed as her mouth dropped open. Her expressive gray eyes grew round and wide. A series of emotions passed through them – surprise, confusion and finally disbelief.

'You think falling in love was a mistake?' she asked in a carefully controlled voice.

'I didn't think so at the time, but in retrospect, yes.'

She nodded, her entire body tensing. 'And loving this woman caused you problems?'

'I won't go into the gritty details,' he said, not because he thought she wouldn't want to hear about Sandra, but because admitting how big a fool he'd been still had the power to strike a raw chord in his ego. 'She had been my business partner as well as my fiancée, and I *trusted* her enough to give her fifty per cent of my company. Because of my bad judgement, I lost everything. Almost had to file for bankruptcy,' he added with a rueful laugh.

'So you decided never to trust anyone again.' She said it as a statement of fact and tilted her chin. 'You lost your business; a lot of hardworking people do. Why didn't you just pick up and move on?'

'I could deal with the financial loss, but . . . Christ, Rachel, I don't know. Sandra betrayed everything I believed in.'

'Sandra?' she repeated, paling slightly.

'As in Roberts,' he finished drily. 'As in one of your customers.'

She touched her fingers to mouth and sucked in a breath. 'So you're the . . . Oh, no . . .'

'Oh, yes. On the advice of a tarot card reader, Sandra decided she didn't need me as her future husband or business partner.'

'But I . . . Oh, Jackson . . .' She pressed the flat of her hand to her chest and shook her head in dismay. 'I never told her to end her engagement with you. That was her interpretation. Had I known . . .'

'What would you have done? Stopped her? Changed her mind?' His shoulders jerked with a shudder as he imagined what his life would now be like if Rachel had convinced Sandra to marry him. A muscle ticked in his jaw, but he managed to smile nevertheless. 'I should be thanking you for saving me from a marriage from hell.'

'What you went through . . .' She turned gray, agonized eyes to him. 'I'm so sorry.'

He swiped a hand through his hair, once again impatient and frustrated with having to reveal a part of himself he hated. But he had to. Meeting her gaze, he saw the force of her inner strength reflected there. He also saw her need to understand. Did any other woman have eyes like hers, he wondered, so clear and liquid he thought he could crawl inside her and find himself?

He realized then that he wanted Rachel to understand why he'd refused to give her the benefit of the doubt; why, even now, it was a struggle to believe in her. Though he did. But as the saying went: old habits died hard. Believing an intimate relationship would only result in another mistake, he had found it easier to keep his distance than risk being hurt again. Until now.

Rachel wasn't like Sandra. Rachel had the compassion of a woman who wanted to better her life and cared for those she loved, while his ex-fiancée had wanted only what she could take. It was like comparing roses to weeds.

'I began doubting my own decisions after that. I'd made choices, bad ones that cost me my company, my employees their jobs, customers thousands of dollars in losses. I began questioning everything and suspecting everyone.'

'You put your faith in her; that wasn't wrong,' she said softly, almost making him believe it.

'Well, right or wrong, it's done, and I swore I wouldn't let it happen again.'

'So you made the manly decision to isolate yourself, emotionally, that is.'

He shrugged, not liking how absurd his behavior sounded coming from her. At the time, it had been necessary to protect himself in order to put the past behind him. He realized now that he hadn't put it behind him, he'd merely tucked it into a corner of his subconscious so he could drag it with him wherever he went. 'Something like that.'

'And your home?' She glanced behind her. 'Why is it so empty?'

For the first time, he saw the room through Rachel's eyes. He had to admit, it looked as if a homeless vagrant had moved in with his scavenged belongings. He hadn't had the energy or the desire to replace the furniture after Sandra had moved out, taking everything with her, except her engagement ring. That she'd left behind with relish.

He'd even become accustomed to his sparse surroundings until he'd seen the warm comfort of Rachel's home. He'd been tempted by the sense of belonging she'd created. He hadn't wanted to reproduce it; he'd wanted to fit into hers. Only he hadn't realized it until now. 'It's just me and I'm rarely here. There didn't seem much point in decorating.'

'I see.' She swallowed then exhaled. 'Thank you for explaining. Now, I'd appreciate it if you'd take me back to my car. I still have to find my sister.'

She reached for the doorknob, but he didn't move out of her way. 'Do you really believe she's in danger?'

She briefly closed her eyes, her black lashes fanning her pale cheeks. 'No.' She shook her head. 'Not physical danger, at least. I can't explain it, but I know she's done something rash.'

'Has she been in trouble since her last run-in with the law?

'No,' she admitted hesitantly.

256

'Then stay for a little longer.' They'd gotten off the original subject of why she should trust him. He needed to circle back to it if he wanted her to stay. Which he definitely did. Partly because of the case, but mostly because each time they were together, lies and suspicions had sparked distrust between them, overshadowing the passion that simmered just below the surface, waiting for a chance to build.

He'd isolated himself for so long, he wanted to know what would happen if the doubts were removed. She wanted him; he saw passion in her eyes each time she looked at him.

Aware of what he risked by opening himself up to her, he prayed she would risk the same and trust him.

He straightened, and she stepped aside, backing up against the wall as if she'd expected him to move into the living room, only he angled himself in front of her.

'What are you doing?' she asked with a new kind of panic.

He lifted her hand, threaded their fingers together and pressed his lips to the back of her cool flesh. Her fingers flexed and a shiver rippled up her arm. Her eyes darkened to pewter, as if the turmoil inside her was caught in a swirl of turbulent shadows. He slipped his other arm around her back, lifted her to him. He sucked in a breath as he absorbed the feel of her lithe thighs pressed against his hard ones, the soft curve of her belly molding to his sex. Her stomach muscles quivered, making his clench with need.

He hadn't brought her to his home with the conscious thought of making love to her, but he now knew the idea had been in the back of his mind all along, waiting for the right moment to make itself known.

'We've talked about your sister,' he said, grazing his teeth over her thumb. 'Now it's time to talk about us.'

She gave a futile tug on her hand, but went still when he drew her thumb into his mouth, sucking lightly. 'I understand why you thought I was behind the thefts. You don't have to do this.'

Oh, yes, he did. Now that he'd started, given life to the need he'd denied, he couldn't back away. 'You want me, Rachel. Every time you look at me, I see the truth in your eyes.' He released her hand to stroke the pad of his thumb over the ridge of her cheek. 'I want to make love to you.'

'You only want to solve your case.' Her voice quivered as she looked to the side, searching for a way to escape.

He wasn't any good at this. How could he convince her? Pressing his forehead against hers, he shook his head. He understood she still didn't believe him completely, and might even be frightened of what was happening between them. Before the day ended, he would change her mind, even if all they did was talk, which he'd settle for, though it just might kill him. 'Have I mentioned how beautiful your eyes are? They're clear, so translucent I can see inside you.'

'Stop that.'

'Don't you want to know what I see?'

'Why are you doing this?' She planted her hands against his chest, but instead of pushing as he'd expected her to, her breath caught and she stared at the open V of his shirt. Her palms cupped the curve of his chest, his nipples caught in their center. Her fingers branched out, tentatively touching him. Hot lightning streaked through him. He gripped her waist but resisted the urge to grind himself against her. But he wanted to, so badly his limbs shook with the need.

'Don't do this, Jackson,' she whispered, but continued watching her hands as if she didn't know who they belonged to.

'Just one kiss, Rachel,' he said, moving closer.

'You know what will happen.' The words sounded torn from her throat.

'One kiss.'

She didn't move, not even to breathe, but he did, inhaling her sweet scent into his body. He filled his lungs with her, almost groaning when he imagined the faint taste of her on his tongue. Drugging warmth washed over his skin, seeping through his pores, blocking every rational thought but one. She would be his. Before she walked out of his house, he would make her his.

He cupped the side of her head in his hand, tilting her back so she was forced to look into his eyes. Desire warred with confusion in her dark gaze. Fear and need and hope all blended in one unique flash of silver. Sweat beaded his brow and he clenched his jaw to keep from crushing his mouth over hers.

Once he kissed her, there'd be no going back, he realized, because one kiss wouldn't be enough for him . . . or her. The rules between them would change . . . irrevocably.

She drew a quivering breath, straightened her back. She shifted again, this time innocently brushing his groin. With a suppressed growl, he closed his mouth over hers. He moved one hand down her back, fitting her to him. The feel of her high, rounded breasts crushed against him set off a riot of sparks that exploded in his brain. She wore too many damn clothes, but he couldn't focus yet on taking them off. She held on to him, her slender hands kneading his shirt. Emitting a small cry, she alternately grasped his chest and stroked the heels of her palms against him.

He shuddered, his body tightening like a length of twisted rope. He pushed his tongue past her lips, delving deep into the cool, wet texture of her mouth. She tasted like morning dew, fresh and untouched, glistening with purity. She was innocent, he realized, kissing him as if she was unsure how to proceed.

Hesitantly, she opened her mouth, taking him deeper, slowly battling his tongue with her own. Though caution told him to move slowly, he thrust into her, heightening the urgency, taking her again and again in a primal imitation of where the kiss would lead. She didn't pull back or ask him to stop, but matched him move for move, taking from him as much as she gave.

He never dreamed anything could be so sweet while simultaneously being so demanding and rough. With a shudder he deepened the kiss, turning it hard and biting, pushing her for more, needing more from her.

The overwhelming, possessive need shocked him, but he couldn't stop it or control it. He could only let it come and feel every raw emotion, every nerve-shattering twist of his heart hammering blood through his veins. He gripped her bottom and lifted her against him, crushing his erection into the indention between her legs. Her breath catching, she stilled. He expected her to pull away, and knew he wouldn't be able to stand it if she did. Her startled gaze met his. Dizzying hunger spiraled down through his body, heating his limbs, centering in his shaft until he was bone-hard and in pain.

He pinned her against the wall, testing her. A gasp tangled in her throat. She arched her back, gasping for air. Jackson kissed her jaw, the tender spot beneath her ear. He caught the soft flesh at the base of her neck between his teeth and sucked lightly. She cried his name, her hands going to his shoulders as she held on.

He moved lower to the curve of her breast. He pushed aside her vest, the silver amulet, and kissed her through her black lace top. 'I want to make love to you, Rachel.'

She moaned, pushing her breasts higher against his mouth. 'Jackson, please . . .'

He didn't know if 'please' meant she wanted more, or wanted him to stop. If she wanted to call a halt, he quickly reasoned, she'd have to be more specific, because he wouldn't be able to stop unless she made it perfectly clear that she didn't want him. But the way she held on to him, her body cupping his groin, moving in a helpless, searching way, he didn't think she was any more capable of saying no than he was. Recalling his suspicion of how innocent she was, he wondered if she knew what she was getting into. While his baser instincts rebelled, his conscience wouldn't ignore the facts.

He straightened, but wrapped his arms around her, keeping her snug against him. Her hands slid to his neck, and she leaned into him, crushing the swell of her breasts against his chest. Jackson clenched his teeth. He had to touch her breasts, soon. He wanted to see them, know if her skin was pale, translucent with faint blue veins. Were her nipples soft rose or dusky brown? They were pebble-hard, that he knew for certain because he could feel their hardened points. But what did they taste like? Decadent, he imagined.

Brushing strands of hair from her face, tucking them behind her ear, he marveled again at how soft she was. Like velvet. Passion unlike any he'd known before pearled like beads of heat in his body.

He trailed his fingers over the curve of her cheek, her wet, kiss-swollen lips, the line of her jaw. The more he touched her, the more he couldn't seem to stop.

'You understand where this is leading, don't you?' he asked roughly.

She opened her mouth, and he would have sworn she was about to say yes, then hesitancy, and a shadow of doubt, crept into her eyes.

Tension coiled inside his gut, making breathing damn near impossible. 'If you want me to stop, you've got to tell me.' Seconds dragged by with him staring down at her. He felt tremors erupt in her body, one after another like tiny aftershocks. 'Tell me what you want.'

'I . . .' She shook her head as if she didn't know what to say, or how to break the news to him that she wasn't interested. Which would be a lie, and he'd know it. Her face was flushed golden pink with desire. Her hips were fastened to his, burrowing his erection in the cocoon of her body. Her thighs were braced against him, the heat of her longing burning through her clothes and his, raising his desire to the boiling point.

With his fingers spread, he skimmed his palm up her side until he grazed the full curve of her breast. She didn't trust him completely. He understood that, and would do whatever it took to change her mind. Because she was the last person he'd ever want to hurt.

In a voice that demanded an answer, he asked, 'Do you want me?'

Her expression softened, and she closed her eyes. 'Yes,' she whispered. Then she met his gaze, and her eyes were bright with appeal. 'But I don't want to be hurt.'

A pent-up breath shuddered out of him. 'That makes two of us. But if you want me to stop and take you to your car, you need to tell me. Now.' He thought he should earn extra points in heaven for asking.

Her fingers slid into his hair and gripped his head. Her eyes glazed, shining as if a light burned inside her. She drew him closer, holding his gaze until his lips touched hers with a sweetness that bordered on devastating. He kissed her again, then again, the urgency building as she told him without words how much she wanted him. Her eyelids fluttered shut. She moaned into his mouth, a sound so sweet and welcoming, Jackson knew he'd been given a precious gift. 'Rachel . . .'

The hoarse growl of her name worked through the sensual fog in Rachel's mind. *Jackson wanted her.* Her! The words circled her mind, over and over, making her chest ache with the struggle to believe them. He'd shielded his emotions from her for so long, she'd never guessed his desire ran so deep, so hot and deep and consuming. Or had she been too afraid to see it and believe?

She felt him now, and that was all that mattered. Burning heat ran through his veins, searing hers with the same luscious need. Her emotions were so intense, so frayed, shifting so quickly, she couldn't make sense of them. Sensations spun inside her, circling up, carrying her to another level that held so much pleasure, it edged toward pain. But she didn't want it to stop. God, no, please don't let him pull away or decide he'd made a mistake. After waiting for so long, to finally meet a man that made her want to risk her heart, she knew she wouldn't be able to bear the loss.

Jackson pulled her vest from her shoulders, dropping it to the floor. His breath coming hard and fast, he skimmed his palms down her sides, grazing the pad of his thumbs over her breasts, brushing her nipples through her clothes. Rachel gasped, tensing, clenching her fingers in his hair as hot lightning ripped down her stomach. She wanted to cry out; the feeling was too intense, agonizing as it burned a path to her core. He did it again, drawing the same wrenching reaction from her.

'I have to touch you,' he breathed, kissing her mouth, her jaw, the base of her throat while he forced her lace top down over her shoulders. She heard the rent of fabric as it gave. The garment hadn't been made to slip down her body, but to be pulled over her head. She didn't care. She just wanted it off, to feel his hands on her skin. Before she knew it, he'd unclasped her bra, and it too joined the growing pile of clothes at her feet.

Cool air grazed her heated flesh, and the cold disk of her amulet against her chest made her shiver. She thought he'd remove the necklace too, but he merely grazed the back of his fingers over it. Instinctively, she wanted to raise her hands and cover herself, but she remained still. She didn't want to hide from him. She held her breath, her eyes closed, waiting for him to touch her. He leaned back, and she immediately missed his warmth, the solid pressure of his body. 'What . . . ?' She blinked her eyes open, afraid that her worst fear had been realized, and that he'd changed his mind.

One look at his face, and she knew that hadn't happened. His dark, intense gaze was focused on his hands as they hovered over her chest without touching her. He moved them around and beneath her breasts, teasing her, leaving tingles behind as if he'd caressed her soft skin with the rough texture of his. She drew in a breath, pushing herself toward him, but he moved back, keeping an inch between them.

'Jackson,' she pleaded.

He moved his thumbs above the space over her nipples, stroking them in imaginary, erotic circles. Her nipples pebbled even further, straining toward him, making her want to scream that he stop. She clenched her fists at her sides and kept her body rigid against the wall. He had a reason for doing this. Torture, perhaps, or some unique form of bonding she wasn't aware of.

'Jackson, please . . .' He had to touch her. Tingles spread out from her breast, forming shivers through her body. She wasn't cold, far from it. She was hot, so frustrated she wanted to rip the rest of her clothes off. But she waited for Jackson to move. He knew what to do. She didn't.

'You're so beautiful,' he murmured.

His eyes were still focused on her breasts, his expression tender with awe. Her mouth trembled. She wasn't built very large, but neither was she small. She'd always thought of herself as average, nothing special, certainly not beautiful.

She placed her hands over his and pushed him to her. Her breath swelled inside her and she arched her back, pushing deeper into his palms. Her nipples contracted, spiking with pleasure. His fingers moved, lifted her weight, caressed, molding her until she cried out, groaning his name.

Then his cool, wet mouth was on her, sucking lightly, his tongue grazing and tasting. Rachel gasped, gripped his head and held him to her. Her knees buckled and she felt herself sliding to the floor. Jackson caught her behind the legs with one arm, around her back with the other and swung her up.

With her arms around his neck, kissing any part of his face she would reach, she registered their climb up the stairs, then they entered a room. She glimpsed a few furnishings and bare walls. He had a bed, she realized with a sigh of relief, and that was all that mattered. He laid her down on a mattress with rumpled sheets, then began unbuttoning his shirt.

Hazy light leaked through partially closed blinds, keeping the room dim, closed off, as if nothing outside the four walls existed. Which was fine with her. She didn't want to think about what came next. She only wanted to live this moment, absorb every nuance Jackson possessed. Lose herself in his touch. She wanted to taste him, learn the shape of his body, let him fill the empty ache spreading between her thighs. She knew what the building pressure meant, and knew what it would take to relieve it – the loss of her virginity.

Her chastity had never been something she'd prized, but having sex with someone she didn't love hadn't been an option for her. But did she love Jackson? she wondered as she watched him loosen the buttons of his cuffs then drag his shirt off, tossing it aside. He crawled up the bed, his big body skimming over hers until their faces were level. He dipped his head to the bend of her neck, kissing and nibbling until she squirmed beneath him.

Do I love him? Do I dare take such a chance? She felt connected to him, bonded on an emotional level that made her feel complete. She reveled in the rich texture of his hair when she wrapped her fingers through it. Whenever he looked at her, her insides clenched with expectancy and longing. The deep timbre of his voice had the ability to stop her breath and make her weak in the knees. And she continually found herself yearning for the next moment she'd see him. But did she love him?

Jackson leaned over her, the crisp brown hair on his chest brushing her nipples, making her flinch and suck in a breath. She ran her hands over lean muscle and tanned flesh, marveling at his hardness, the carved angles of his body. He was the one who was beautiful, not her. He had harsh curves that exuded power, yet hands that were nothing but gentle and giving.

She reached up, cupped his face and pulled him down for a kiss. He took over, kissing her so tenderly, probing so gently that her throat closed. Tears pressed against her eyes. She loved the feel of his lips, the dark hunger in his eyes when he looked at her, the grating feel of his hand against her sensitive skin. What she felt wasn't simply lust, this was something else, something deeper that came from her heart.

Jackson shifted between her legs and pressed his erection against her. Heated light seared her body. She arched against him, shocked, but wanting more. She kneaded his back and moaned. 'I think we have too many clothes on.'

He laughed, the sound stretched with tension. 'I was trying to go slow.'

'That's very sweet of you,' she said, pushing against his shoulders. 'But I want to see all of you.'

His face darkened; he clenched his jaw and made a low, growling noise. He shoved up from the bed, but didn't remove his pants as she'd hoped. Instead he propped her feet on his thigh and unbuckled the ankle straps of both her shoes, then discarded them. A feral glint entered his brown eyes as he slid his hands beneath her skirt, found the top of her pantyhose and stripped her free of them. Her skirt went next, leaving only her white cotton panties. They vanished before her next breath, leaving her completely naked except for the amulet that lay between her breasts. Her cheeks heated with embarrassment, but she didn't cover herself.

Jackson straightened, staring down at her, the dark pupils of his eyes expanding, turning his eyes black and smoky with desire. 'God, you're incredible.' A shudder jarred him, then his eyes flashed to hers. His were turbulent, overflowing with possession and need and hunger. Suddenly, he bent over her and pressed an open-mouthed kiss to her stomach.

He kissed her again and again, making a wet trail to her breasts. Rachel pressed her palms to his chest, stopping him from going any further and distracting them both.

His brows furrowed. 'What?'

'One of us is still dressed.'

Cursing mildly, he loosened his belt, unfastened his pants, carefully sliding the zipper over his bulging erection. He hesitated for an instant before pulling his pants off. He looked at her, the question evident in his face. Did he realize this would be her first time? Was that why he'd wanted to move slow and had paused in stripping? Did he think he would shock her? Embarrass her? If that was the case, she loved him all the more. She might not have ever made love to a man, but she knew how they were built.

Or she'd thought she'd known. Rachel sat up and tried to breathe, but her heart had moved to her throat. Dusky light played over his body, casting shadows against taut lines, making him look carved from stone. Thick muscles corded his stomach. His arms hung loose at his sides, but he wasn't relaxed. Sexual tension furled beneath his skin, rippling down to thighs that were wide and molded with strength.

His sex stood rigid, pulsing with life. She'd known what he would look like – how could she not when she'd grown up in a building where most of the tenants lacked the most basic morals, not caring if they had sex in the hallways? – but she'd never wanted them, never once had she been tempted.

Not like she wanted Jackson. Nothing like Jackson.

She could feel her body responding, reaching out to him in a way she'd never imagined possible. She thought she'd wanted him before, but now she knew that had only been a glimmer of need.

Shifting on to her knees, she ran her palm down his chest, the tight curls grazing her skin, to the flat plane of his stomach. He held still, letting her explore the shape of his broad chest, the slope of his shoulders. She slid her hands around to his back and down to his buttocks that were smooth and tight. Still he didn't move.

His eyes bored into her as she gathered her courage and wrapped her fingers around his shaft, holding him lightly. Jackson's body jerked and he sucked in a breath through his teeth. His eyes closed and his face flushed. Rachel watched, mesmerized as he trembled each time she moved her hand, stroked his length, rubbed the smooth tip. He was iron and silk, and so hot to touch she wondered if it would burn when he entered her.

His breathing turned heavy, and a growl rumbled from his chest. He gripped her wrist and held her hand away from him.

A feral light entered his eyes. 'My turn.'

He eased her back on the mattress and half covered her body with his. A blanket of living heat enveloped her. He cupped her breast, kneading roughly, making her cry out with the stunning pleasure. He took her mouth, kissing her almost savagely, pulling emotions from her that made her head spin and her heart hammer against her ribs. She opened her mouth wider, giving him more, taking every hard, bruising kiss he gave. Her desire spiraled up and away, leaving only primitive need.

God, she wanted this. She wanted him. All of him. On top of her, around her, inside her. She needed him to fill her, break down the last barrier and make her his. 'Now, please . . . !'

'Not yet.'

'Jackson,' she shifted her legs, restless and frustrated all at once, 'now.'

'Shhh.' He slipped his hand between her legs, making her go still.

She focused on his movements, the gentle rhythm and the electric shocks it created. He found her small, sensitive nub and rubbed it with the pad of his thumb. She strained her head back, and rocked her hips, defenseless against the burst of sensation, helpless to stop it or direct it. Her breath hitched time and again, making her dizzy and afraid that she'd faint and miss wherever he was taking her.

'That's it, baby,' he said, kissing her mouth, her eyes. He moved to her breasts, locking on to one nipple. His hand added more pressure.

In an instant, she was swept up, carried off by impulses so strong, so incredibly unreal she thought she *had* passed out until the world exploded, shooting her upward into bright, devastating light.

Gasping, she held still. Her heart drummed with a pulsing rhythm. The sound filled her, then centered, bringing everything down to that one, quivering part of her body.

'That was some orgasm,' Jackson whispered, smiling as he brushed her lips with his.

'Thank you. It was my first.'

His grin broadened to a satisfied, purely male smirk. She considered punching him, but at the moment she was entirely pleased, herself.

She felt his penis flex, then he was between her thighs, pressing against her entrance.

'I want to be inside you.' He nudged her opening, gently testing her. He clenched his teeth and hissed as he pushed. 'God, you're so tight.'

For a moment, Rachel wondered if he was doing it right. She seemed much too small for him; he couldn't possibly fit. She tensed, alarmed when she felt a sharp twinge of pain, diluting the lingering traces of passion. She arched her back, trying to scoot away.

Jackson stilled. He brushed the hair from her face, kissed her eyes. 'Shh, baby. I know it hurts.' He pulled out of her then eased back in, not going any deeper than her body would easily accept. The pain vanished and a gentle pressure took its place as he continued rocking back and forth. She moved with him, gradually urging him to take more. She felt her body stretch to accept him, mold to his length, hug him as if he belonged solely to her.

She lifted her leg to his hip, opening herself, and felt him slip deeper inside her. He *was* hot, she realized, not enough to scorch, but hot enough to make her feel complete for the first time in her life.

He paused, a tremor running through him. A sheen of sweat bathed his body and face as he looked down at her with stunned disbelief in his eyes.

Confused, worried that she'd done something wrong, she asked, 'What?'

'I hadn't been sure.' He kissed her, his mouth hard and fierce.

Sure of what? she wanted to ask.

He pulled almost free of her, then plunged deep, burying himself completely. A cry tore up Rachel's throat. Jackson swallowed the sound, then gathered her in his arms, pressing his face to her neck. She sucked in a breath, fighting the shock of pain that spliced up her middle. She writhed against him.

'Don't move!' he ordered, his voice sounding graveled. 'Whatever you do, don't move.'

'Why do you sound like you're in pain, when I'm the one who's been torn apart?'

He rose on his elbows and cupped her face between his hands. When he saw a tear running down her temple, he wiped the wetness away with his thumb, then kissed her lips, slowly, leisurely, as if they had all day and he wasn't buried deep inside her and she wasn't hurting. Only the hurt had eased to a constant throb, mellowing with the passing minutes.

'Is it better?' he asked after a moment. His voice was steadier, but she could feel the strain shivering in his body. His damp hair clung to his face and neck. Raw hunger flared in his eyes, turning them to pools of black passion in the darkening room.

He eased out of her, and she tensed, but when the pain didn't reoccur, she tightened her leg around his hip, urging him to her. His gaze locked on her, silently pinning her to him. He rocked in and out of her, going deeper each time, taking more, stretching her, filling her until he touched her soul.

She gripped his back, felt his struggle for control in the rigid muscles bunched beneath his skin. He adjusted his position, changing the rhythm, setting a new course. She felt a shift inside her, a remnant of the earlier desire she'd felt. Tightening her muscles around him, she strained toward it, let her body feel and absorb his rhythmic mating. He reached between them, found her sex. She arched against him, lifting herself closer to the building pressure, the hot, liquid swirl that spun through her body, tightening as it twisted hotter and faster.

The force of it grew stronger, until it finally spasmed, exploding over her, shocking her with arrows of pure pleasure. She curved into Jackson, holding on as streams of blessed fire rushed through her veins, spreading out, consuming her, leaving nothing but ashes.

The heady sensations had barely faded when Jackson bucked hard against her again and again, then he tensed, a hoarse, agonized cry becoming her name. He found his release with his head thrown back, the corded veins in his neck bulging.

Rachel ran her palms down his slick chest and watched in awe, her vision blurring with tears.

CHAPTER 15

Thunder rumbled the walls of his bedroom, pulling Jackson from his light doze. He was on his back with Rachel curved into his side, her head tucked against his shoulder. Her steady breathing warmed his neck as she slept. Moments before her eyes had slipped shut with exhaustion, she'd burrowed her fingers into his chest hair, then nestled against him, fitting her body to his as if it were the most natural thing for her to do. Since she'd never had sex before, he knew there was nothing *natural* about the act. But then they hadn't had *sex*; it had been something . . . else. Something that defied description.

He had no idea how long they'd slept, but he thought it hadn't been more than an hour. He didn't want to risk waking Rachel by twisting around to look at the clock on the nightstand to find out. Gray shadows sealed the room. He couldn't tell if the lack of light was due to the approaching dusk or the storm clouds that had gathered over the city during the day. Hearing the soft tapping of rain against the windows, he guessed it might be a combination of both.

They needed to get up, start their search for Penny, but he didn't want to move, not yet. Pressing his lips to Rachel's soft hair, he closed his eyes and ran his fingers through the black satin tangles, then trailed his palm down her side to cup her small waist. She shivered and curled tighter against him. Reaching down, he covered them both with a sheet and blanket. Content to lie still and think of nothing except the feel of her in his arms, he settled back and stared at the ceiling.

Content. That wasn't a word he'd used much lately, if he'd ever used it at all. But that was how he felt now: languid with relief, satisfied to do nothing but hold her and listen to the rain. He regretted that the moment wouldn't last for long. They hadn't solved any of their problems, but confronting reality would wait, he decided, for a little while longer.

Right now, he wanted to inhale the unique scent that was Rachel until nothing else existed. He'd touched every inch of her body, but he hadn't kissed it, and that he wanted to do before the day ended. He felt his body stir, growing warm with the recurring need he always experienced with her. He wanted to make love to her again, but knew she'd be too sore to do it so soon. Somehow he'd wait, maybe love her without entering her. The possibilities made his body tighten, and a groan worked up his throat.

He rubbed his hand over her hip when a thought occurred to him, clarifying in his mind with such force he couldn't breathe. He hadn't used a condom.

He glanced down at her pale face, softened with sleep, relaxed and trusting. He'd never forgotten to use protection before. No matter how aroused he'd been, taking care of practicalities had always come first. Even during his three years with Sandra, not once had he chucked caution to the wind and gone without.

But the thought of protection had never occurred to him with Rachel. He'd wanted her warmth and wetness surrounding him. Driving into her, becoming a part of her had been all that had mattered. He drew in a steadying breath, felt the pounding of his heart against his chest and knew he couldn't be so careless again. She'd never had a partner, and he'd always been careful, so he knew they had nothing to worry about regarding diseases, but he didn't want her to get pregnant. *Not yet.*

He pushed a hand through his hair, shaken by the foreign thought. With his life in constant turmoil, he hadn't considered children – hell, even a wife – as being a part of his future, near or distant. The possibility that he might have just changed all that created a pressure in his chest, not panic but uncertainty.

Shifting on to his elbow, he stared down at her. She blinked her eyes open and smiled, a small, demure smile as she stretched, thrusting her breasts upward. Except for the sleepy satisfaction in her gaze, she didn't look any different, he thought as he ran his palm over one taut mound, his thumb grazing the amulet that neither of them had bothered to remove.

But what did he expect? That her eyes would turn pink for positive like the results of a pregnancy test?

A future with Rachel.

If this had happened with any other woman, he'd be pacing the floor and calling himself an irresponsible fool. Walking away from Rachel wasn't an option. If anything, he wanted to hold her closer, brand her as his. He took her nipple into his mouth, losing himself to the pulsing beat of his body as it filled and hardened, his muscles tightening with possessive heat.

Her arms slipped around his neck, cradling him to her. She shuddered, arching against him. She responded as if the last time hadn't been her first and she knew what he wanted. Wordlessly, she adjusted to him, moved beneath him until he was between her thighs and positioned at her core. He touched her with the tip of his shaft and gritted his teeth. Jagged light flashed behind his closed lids, followed by the ghostly echo of thunder. He didn't want to hurt her, but her willingness was making it impossible to stop.

Sighing, she claimed his mouth in a slow, open-mouthed kiss that stripped the last of his resistance. Her leg moved up his thigh, cupped his buttocks, holding him to her.

'Make love to me, Jackson,' she whispered.

He pushed into her, realizing he still didn't have protection, but he couldn't find the will to object. Skin to skin, buried in soul-burning heat, sheathed inside her as if she had been made for him was the way it *should* be with her. He slipped deeper into her and felt his body convulse as he reached for a new level of contentment.

'What is this?' Jackson asked.

Rachel blinked her sleep-heavy eyes open to find him examining her necklace. After the second time they'd made love, she'd insisted on calling her mother to check in. Emily had been frantic with worry, which had infused Rachel with guilt, but there wasn't much they could do to find Penny that she and her mother hadn't already tried. Since the store was closed and there had been no word from her sister, Rachel promised she'd explain everything to her mother the following morning. Though how she thought she'd justify the past few hours, she wasn't sure.

Yawning and snuggling closer to him – heaven help her, she couldn't get close enough – she answered, 'It's a Runic love amulet.'

He grunted. 'Sounds interesting. What does it do? Cast spells that promise love?'

She tilted her head back to look at him. For all his teasing words, a frown marred his brow. 'Nothing can promise love or force it if the elements aren't there to begin with.'

'Elements?' he asked with a disbelieving smirk.

She pointed to the carved letters. 'M, X, C and P represent trust, love, passion and joy. Trust,' she continued, aware of how important her next words could be, 'and passion are the two elements that make love binding.'

'And joy?'

Puzzled by his cautious tone, she carefully said, 'Joy is the result when you have the other three elements.'

He settled the necklace between her breasts, then hesitantly kissed her forehead. She hadn't a clue what had caused his shift in mood. He sighed, a deep regretful sound that sent a wary chill over her skin. She expected him to tell her that they had a shot at passion, but nothing more.

'I didn't use any protection.'

'Oh, my God.' She clamped a hand over her mouth and tried to sit up. His arms tightened, pinning her to his side. How could she have been so careless? How many friends had she helped through unwanted pregnancies? How many times had she sworn she'd be more responsible?

'I take it you hadn't recalled our . . . um . . . lapse.'

There hadn't been room in her mind for details or consequences, which proved just how powerful his influence over her had become. The realization, the loss of control over her own reasoning, unnerved her.

'Say something, Rachel,' he whispered against her hair.

She pressed her face into his chest and called herself every kind of fool. Her heart thudded against her ribcage, in her ears, at the base of her throat, but against her palm, she felt the steady beat of Jackson's heart. How could he be so calm?

'I suppose I should apologize,' he said, though from his tone she didn't think his apology would be sincere. Did that mean he didn't regret what they'd done?

She bit down on her bottom lip and considered her options. She could get dressed and shove the issue aside or she could confront it. The former was tempting, but since running away had never been an option for her, she said, 'I'm sure I'm not pregnant.'

Tilting her chin up with his finger so she was forced to look at him instead of his chest, he asked, 'What makes you think that?'

'Well, it was my first time . . .' She cut herself off, knowing once was enough.

'And second,' he added with a maddening grin.

'It's probably not the right time for . . . for . . .'

He kissed the tip of her nose. 'Sweetheart, I guess we'll find out soon enough.'

Pregnant. She closed her eyes. She couldn't think about that right now, not with their other problems still unresolved. Meeting his gaze, she said, 'What about the other reason for wearing a condom?'

'You mean AIDS?'

She shuddered at the horrible, frightening word. She obviously didn't have it, but Jackson . . .

'I've never forgotten to wear protection when I've been with . . . well, with . . .' He trailed off, and she silently thanked him for it.

But that didn't mean she didn't finish the thought herself. *When he'd been with other women.* Specifically, Sandra Roberts. Heaven help her, she didn't want to think about *that*, either.

She sat up and threw the covers off, suddenly needing to put space between them. Jackson pulled

282

her back down, rolling on top of her, trapping her on the mattress.

'Where do you think you're going?' He caught her hands and held them above her head.

'I was just . . . I needed . . .' She clenched her jaw and tried again. 'I want to get up.'

'You're not leaving this bed with your eyes all fired up. Now why are you mad?'

'I'm not.' Though she was, she could feel the turbulent emotion expand inside her like a hot air balloon in danger of exploding.

'Is it because you might be pregnant?'

'No!' The possibility might have caught her off guard, but it by no means made her angry. In fact, it gave her a sense of hope. Something that had once seemed unfeasible could be possible. Though she had to admit, her timing was lousy.

'I promise,' he said, rubbing his thumbs across her palms. His eyes softened with genuine honesty. 'I'm healthy.'

She squirmed beneath him, but he had her good and trapped. 'I believe you.' Then before she could stop herself, she said, 'I'm sure you were very careful with all your *other* women.'

The concern in his eyes began to glitter with amusement. 'You're jealous.'

'I am not.' She heaved against him, but only succeeded in wedging his hardening shaft against her. She stilled as he pushed tentatively. To her annoyance, and despite the soreness between her legs, she felt her body quicken to prepare itself for him. 'I'm just feeling at a disadvantage here.'

283

'Because you were a virgin?'

She decided it would be best to ignore his question.

His expression turned thoughtful as his gaze roamed over her face. 'How did you manage to reach the age of . . . How old are you anyway?'

Her cheeks warmed, which annoyed her further. She had no reason to be embarrassed by her virginity. 'Twenty-eight.'

'You're a beautiful woman, Rachel.' He rubbed his thumb over her cheekbone, something he'd done so often now, she'd come to expect it. 'How is it you've never been with a man?'

'It seemed to be the wise choice.'

'Don't get huffy on me.' He kissed her and grinned. 'I'm not complaining.'

'You're a man.' Pulling one hand free, she pushed against his chest. He didn't budge. 'You wouldn't object to being my first.'

He recaptured her hand and pressed her fingers to his mouth. His eyes narrowed on her. 'Tell me why.'

She settled back, realizing that if she ever wanted out of bed, she'd have to answer him. 'Where did you grow up?'

He raised a brow. 'Richardson.'

She nodded, familiar with the expanding middle-class suburb of Dallas. 'We lived not far from there, before Dad died. I remember our house being enormous, with a huge back yard and a swing set. Penny and I had our own rooms with big picture windows and walk-in closets. I had a white four-poster canopy bed.' She laughed softly when the memory made her eyes brim with familiar tears. 'Do you know that every little girl dreams of having a canopy bed? It was a place to dream.

'After all these years, I've never been back there.' She drew in a breath as blurred images and faint, comforting smells of the past came into focus. After a moment, she said, 'I'm sure it was an average house, but to a seven-year-old it was wonderful.'

'Then your father died?' He rubbed her knuckles against his lips, but she felt him tense as he waited for her to continue.

'We lost everything. Mom only knew how to be a mom. We had no family to turn to, so we moved to a housing project in south Dallas.' She shuddered as the happy images turned sharp and vile and much too vivid.

'Only knowing my safe world of Girl Scouts and slumber parties, I thought we'd stepped into a nightmare. Huge families were crammed into tiny apartments. Nothing worked properly. The floors had holes in them; paint could be peeled off the walls in strips. And the noise.'

She closed her eyes but it didn't stop the echoing shouts, the cussing and fighting that never ceased. 'There wasn't any privacy. You could hear what people were saying in the apartment next door, knew if they were dealing drugs or having sex or if some drunken man was beating up his girlfriend.'

'Jesus Christ.' Jackson's face darkened with anger before he rested his forehead against hers. He sucked in a hissing breath and held her tighter as if to stop her from speaking.

But now that she'd started, she had to finish. 'Mom would hug Penny and me to her and tell her how sorry she was that we couldn't leave. She worked so hard, Jackson, and still we had nothing. She never had time to grieve for her husband; she kept everything locked inside. I couldn't stand seeing her so sad and hopeless. And afraid. There was always this quiet fear in her eyes.'

'So you decided to do something about it.' The words snapped with suppressed anger.

Was he mad because of her childhood? She touched the tousled strands of his hair. No one beside her mother had cared how she'd lived or what she'd had to endure. To think that tough, life-can't-hurt-me Jackson might be furious on her behalf sent a flutter up her chest. 'There wasn't much I could do at first. I watched girls I grew up with having abortions or babies . . .' she slanted a look at him '. . . which is why I can't believe I didn't think about protection with you.'

'You're not a helpless girl any longer, Rachel. And you're not alone.'

She didn't know how to respond to that, so she said, 'They would go from one abusive relationship to another. I realized the same could happen to me, that I could be trapped in the projects forever unless I made some decisions. So I avoided men, which wasn't difficult considering what I had to choose from. It wasn't until a few years ago that I had my first date.' She laughed with the memory. 'Mom was so excited, Penny was mumbling that it was about time, and I was terrified.'

286

'I don't think I want to hear about this date,' he growled.

Grinning at the possessive glare in his whisky-brown eyes, she shrugged. 'There isn't much to tell. I had plans to open The Golden Pyramid, and I refused to let anything distract me from that. I didn't have time or the desire to work a man into my schedule.'

'Good.'

Ignoring him, she continued, 'When things settled down, I . . . um . . .' She shrugged again when she couldn't find the words to explain why she'd never entertained the idea of going out with the few men who'd asked. She wasn't sure how Jackson would interpret her response.

'What?'

She sighed. 'Nothing. I just didn't date.'

Clasping both her hands in his, he drew them above her head and settled himself squarely on top of her. This time she felt oddly exposed and vulnerable, but his determined expression made the feelings evaporate. She sensed the caged tension inside him; he controlled it, was careful not to let it show, but she felt his concern as well as his helpless anger over her childhood.

'Tell me, Rachel,' he demanded, his voice as coarse as granite. 'Why didn't you go out with other men?'

His intense gaze held hers for a suspended moment. She thought about shrugging off the question or even lying, but knew he'd see through her. So she gave him the truth. 'I never met the right one.'

Sighing, he rested his forehead against hers. She closed her eyes, certain she'd made an enormous mistake. Would he assume she thought *he* was the only man for her? She might be falling in love with him, but even with her lack of experience, she knew better than to reveal too much too soon.

Certain he was feeling trapped by a newly *ex*-virgin, she half expected him to roll off of her and leave. How could she have been so stupid to all but admit how she felt about him?

His kiss caught her completely off guard. His fingers tightened around hers. Pushing against her, his erection slipped inside. She winced as she stretched to accept him, the soreness turning to pain, but there was pleasure as well. Shocking, building pleasure.

With a curse, Jackson shoved off of her and sat back on his heels. He ran his hand over his mouth, and gave her a look that bordered fierce hostility. She couldn't move, not even to shiver as a chill ran over her skin. Oh, God, she could hear the excuses forming in his mind. He was going to tell her he wasn't the right man for her. He'd hand her clothes to her, tell her he just remembered an appointment and she'd never see him again. It'd be her own, stupid fault for letting herself care so much about him.

'Damn it, woman,' he said, his teeth clenched. His hungry gaze swept over her body. 'If I make love to you again, you won't walk for a week.'

Her mind spun for an instant before his meaning sank in. She blinked, but was still too stunned to speak. He didn't sound like a man who felt trapped. He wasn't angry, she realized, but frustrated.

Gripping her hands, he pulled her up and out of the bed. 'We have things to do.' Planting a kiss on her mouth, he turned her toward the bathroom, then gave her a gentle swat on her bottom. 'I'm starving, so we'll eat first, then go find your sister.'

Rachel watched his tall naked body as he crossed the room in a confident gait, her gaze skimming down his broad back to his firm buttocks to thighs thick with power, unsure of what to make of him. He'd wanted her, and now that he'd had her, were they back to business as usual?

A strange combination of irritation and uncertainty flinched inside her. Had he shut off his desire for her that easily? Or was she overreacting? After all, she hadn't expected him to profess loving her just because he'd slept with her. But to just turn around and leave . . . She didn't know what to think or how to react.

You need to slow down, Rachel, she told herself. Things were moving much too quickly. Despite the warning, she touched the amulet around her neck. They had passion, and the beginning stages of trust, and God knew she was falling helplessly in love with him. But she had to protect herself.

If he proved Penny was guilty, she wasn't certain the elements binding her and Jackson together would be strong enough to hold.

CHAPTER 16

Jackson stood in the doorway to Penny's apartment, frowning as he surveyed the destruction. His first impulse was to locate the maintenance office and request a shovel, but he refrained and instead took mental notes. The place looked ransacked, or perhaps a bomb had gone off, leaving the walls and ceiling intact but destroying everything else. Or maybe someone had left in a big hurry.

Half of the cushions of the yellow and orange striped couch were on the floor; the others were buried beneath layers of clothing, towels and plates stuck with stale, half-eaten food that he estimated were at least a week old. In the dim light, he couldn't see enough of the carpet to determine what color it was supposed to be, but he guessed a murky brown.

The suffocating smell of debris and musty air infused the room. Wads of paper, Styrofoam cups and cereal boxes littered the small kitchen table to his left. Three of the red vinyl chairs were askew; the fourth was turned over. Was it on its side because the person had been careless? Or had there been a struggle?

Rachel stepped past him, carefully avoiding a collection of discarded shoes and a stack of books with titles like *The Tao of Meow* and *The Heart of Yoga*. She crossed to the window and touched the collage of wilting plants on the sill. Shadows bruised her face, deepening her high cheekbones, making her look small and haunted. Not liking the effect, he switched on the light in the breakfast nook. He watched her gaze roam over the room, her eyes narrowed and troubled. It amazed him that the two women were related. They'd lived through the same experiences, suffered the same losses and fears, yet were black and white, as opposite as two people could be. Rachel was the epitome of energy, filled with the drive to succeed, while Penny seemed to live life for the moment and damn the consequences.

But, sister or not, Jackson vowed that Penny would regret the consequences if she was responsible for involving Rachel in the burglaries. Unfortunately, the more he learned, the more he believed Penny was behind the thefts. The questions that remained unanswered were, why would Penny frame Rachel? Or had leaving the items in the store been a careless, overconfident act?

He glanced at the woman he'd spent half the day in bed with, and felt the now familiar, burning need to protect her surge inside his chest. He wanted to hold her, soothe his hands over her hair, and reassure her that everything would be all right. But he kept his mouth shut and his hands to himself, afraid he'd end up hurting her even more when he failed to prove Penny innocent.

That Rachel trusted him at all was a miracle he didn't take lightly. She'd given herself to him, *to him*, avoiding other relationships because she'd never met the right man. That knowledge had seared through him, humbling him, and making him determined to clear Rachel's name at all costs.

'I don't know where to start.' Rachel straightened an overturned lamp and sighed, tension thinning the small sound.

Jackson shoved his hands into his pants pockets when the urge to touch her had him taking a step forward. 'Is this the way she normally keeps house? Or should we call the police?'

She gave him a tempered smile. 'I'm afraid messy is status quo for my sister. It drives Mom and me crazy.'

Jackson made his way to the kitchen and flicked on the switch. Stark fluorescent light bounced off white cabinet doors that stood ajar. After one glance at the sink piled with dirty dishes and counters crowded with a collection of Coke cans, used Tupperware and zip-lock bags, he shut off the switch and backtracked to the living room. Despite the clutter, there had to be a clue to Penny's disappearance, he thought. People didn't just vanish without leaving a trail. All he had to do was dig deep enough, which would be quite an undertaking considering the woman lived in a pigsty.

'Why do you have a key to your sister's place?' he asked to fill the silence as he sorted through a pile of junk mail on the coffee table.

Picking up plates to take to the kitchen, Rachel answered, 'As a precaution. We all have keys to each other's homes.'

'What about her boyfriend, Mark? Does he live here?'

'No. Whether he stays here, though, I can only speculate.'

Not finding anything, Jackson went into the bedroom and turned on the light. Shaking his head, he stepped over rumpled bedding, pillows and clothes strewn across the floor, and opened the closet door. Piles of boxes, empty hangers and an assortment of 'stuff' was jammed into the corners. He ran a hand through his hair in frustration. The bathroom was next, though he dreaded facing the disaster he imagined lurking in there. If any of the stolen items were in Penny's apartment it was going to take considerable time to search through everything.

He stopped himself. He couldn't conduct the search, not after he'd found the necklace and the vase in Rachel's store. She'd made it clear that it could be her word against his, and she was right. If there was any evidence in Penny's apartment, it needed to be found by the police, who would search the premises by the book. For now, he only needed to be concerned with where she might have gone.

'Can you tell if anything's missing?' he called out as tension tightened his spine. After a quick scan of the bathroom, he turned to the dresser. People usually hid things in their dressers, believing it a safe place, when actually, it was the first spot a burglar would hit. He pushed aside perfume bottles, hairbrushes and a vast assortment of costume jewelry, but found nothing that would indicate where or why Penny had vanished. When he realized Rachel hadn't answered him, he started to ask again, but stopped.

She stood in the doorway, her face drained of color, her clear eyes wide with dismay.

He crossed to her and took her by the shoulders. 'What did you find?'

Her gaze dropped to the piece of wrinkled paper she held in her hand. 'It . . .' she took a deep breath '. . . it was on the floor in the kitchen.'

Jackson took the note from her and read the scribbled print.

Depart Sunday, 9:45 p.m. #1375

'She's flown off somewhere.'

'Maybe. But there's no date or airline name. This could be anything.'

Rachel pressed a trembling hand to her brow. Her cheeks flushed, and for a moment Jackson was afraid she would cry. Then, hot color flooded her face. Jackson watched the transformation from shock to fury as her temper boiled to the surface. He suppressed a sigh of relief, better prepared to deal with her anger than her tears.

'She just left.' Rachel stared at the demolished room with growing indignation. 'No phone call, no note, nothing. How could she be so thoughtless?'

'You understand how this looks, don't you, Rachel?'

She faced him, squaring her shoulders as if she expected an incoming blow. 'You think she ran,' she demanded, her eyes glittering with angry tears. 'After supposedly stealing from our clients, you think she got scared and left town.'

'Look at it from my point of view.'

She nodded and pressed her lips together. 'I understand, but the note doesn't prove anything.'

Not yet, Jackson wanted to add, but refrained. He knew this was tearing Rachel apart. She'd made it clear from the first time he'd met her that all she cared about was taking care of her family. But with every new clue they discovered, believing in Penny was becoming more and more impossible. If his suspicions proved to be true, the most they could hope for would be a short prison sentence. As for Rachel's business, she might lose it as well. If that happened, Jackson would make damn sure he was there when the rough times hit.

'It doesn't specify, but I assume this is an airline flight number. I'll have my office check it out.' He walked past her, intending to use the phone in the living room to call Derrick, but seeing her so still, as if she were in danger of caving in on herself, he gathered her in his arms. She gripped the sleeves of his shirt, but didn't relax against him the way he would have liked. Though he regretted having to do it, he had to be honest with her and prepare her for the worst. 'There isn't a return flight listed here. Penny might not be planning on coming back.'

Rachel nodded and dragged in a breath that shook her body. She lifted her gaze to his. Determination darkened her gray eyes to steel, reminding him once again just how deep her strength ran. 'Do what you can, Jackson. I have to know where my sister is.'

He pressed a kiss to her forehead. He'd find Penny. He had to, because until he knew all the answers, he and Rachel wouldn't stand a chance of surviving. And even then, the odds were against them.

Rachel held herself rigid in the soft leather seat as Jackson negotiated his car through the dark streets of Dallas toward her house. She considered telling him to go to the police station first where her car was still parked, but she didn't have the energy to say the words, let alone make the drive herself.

She was so cold. A chill had settled in her body, piercing bone-deep. She welcomed the spreading numbness; it kept her from feeling the emotions waiting to bombard her. She'd caught a glimpse of them before she'd willed herself to shut down. Shock, disbelief, betrayal, they were all lingering in her mind, circling her heart, just waiting for the moment she admitted that Penny had not only stolen from their clients, but had involved Rachel, condemning her as an accomplice.

The note proves nothing! The phrase became a litany in Rachel's mind, playing itself over and over. There had to be another explanation for her sister's disappearance. Until she heard from Jackson's office, she wouldn't give up hope. Penny wouldn't do something so horrible. *But she's stolen before; she has lied to me before*!

Rachel ran her fingers through her hair and squeezed her eyes closed to stop the battling voices in her mind. Jackson took her hand and brought it to his lips where he pressed a kiss to her skin. When she looked at him, his eyes were dark and intense and focused on her.

'We're almost there.' He glanced away as he turned into her neighborhood, then on to her street. 'Andy has to check with each airline to find out who the flight belongs to, but we should hear something within the hour. Until then, try not to worry.'

'Impossible.'

He squeezed her hand. 'I know.'

Pulling into her driveway, he put the car in park then turned off the ignition. He watched her as she gathered her purse and opened her door. When he didn't move to exit the car, she hesitated and asked, 'Aren't you coming?'

Though it was dark, the street lamp caught the softening in his eyes. 'After last night, I wasn't sure you'd want me to.'

Had it only been a few hours before that he'd spent the night in his car, watching her house? It seemed like a lifetime ago; so much had happened between them since then.

'I . . .' Suddenly uneasy, she clenched her purse in her lap and looked away. Was she moving too fast? Had she made the universal mistake of assuming their lovemaking had meant something more than a casual fling? Perhaps he didn't want to stay with her. Her chest clutched with a new kind of anxiety. She might have been a spinster virgin who'd thought with her heart instead of her mind, but she needed him right now. Which was a new experience for her. Until now, she'd never relied on anyone but herself. The change frightened her, but not enough to push him away. 'I want you to stay, but only if you want to.'

The corner of his mouth curved as he said, 'Come on. Let's go.'

On the porch, he took her keys and unlocked the front door. She followed him inside, but halted in the living room and watched as he moved through her house, flicking on lights, locking doors and checking each room. She couldn't imagine what he was looking for, or that she was in need of such precautions, but if it made him feel better she wouldn't argue or question him.

Feeling a small body curl around her leg, she stooped to pick up Miss Bastet. Rachel buried her face in the cat's fur, welcoming the familiar comfort. 'And how was your day, sweetheart? Or did you sleep through all of it?'

At the thought of sleep, Rachel's shoulders drooped with fatigue. Her entire body yearned for a hot bath and a soft mattress. If she didn't count the brief time she'd dozed after making love to Jackson, she'd only had a few hours' sleep since the night before. She could imagine how exhausted Jackson was. Having passed the night in his car, she doubted he'd slept at all.

She smiled and shook her head. Only yesterday she'd been determined to keep him at arm's length;

now she wanted nothing more than to feel the solid strength of him around her.

'Everything looks fine,' Jackson said, joining her.

'Did you think it wouldn't be?'

He shrugged. 'With everything going on, I wouldn't be surprised to find something suspicious. And your back door was unlocked again. You really should be more careful. Hey, Frisky, how's it going?' He rubbed his knuckles beneath Miss Bastet's chin and was rewarded with a snort. Lifting his gaze to her, he said, 'You need a security system. I could install one for you.'

'Thank you, but no, that's not necessary.' She'd always felt safe in her home. She still did, and didn't see any reason to become paranoid and hot-wire her house.

'I'm not talking about bars on the windows.' His eyes were hard, and so dark a brown they were almost black. His stern, don't-argue-with-me tone made her think he'd switched gears from generous lover to dominant male. 'Just some window and door sensors that will alert the police if someone breaks in.'

'No.' She eased the cat to the floor, then ran her hands through her hair to ease the headache starting at the base of her skull. 'I don't have anything worth stealing, anyway.'

'You can't be that naïve.'

'I'm not going to change the way I live because my sister might – *might*, if I may remind you – have stolen something.' Her voice rose to a shrewish pitch. She swallowed and struggled for a calmer tone. 'Can we please not talk about this any more?'

He gave her a stony, determined look that she didn't quite like but was too tired to worry about.

To change the subject, she asked, 'Would you like some coffee or wine?'

He shook his head and took a step back, resting his hands on his hips. 'It's late and you need to sleep.'

Was he leaving? Something inside her chest squeezed. She stared at him, her throat constricting. She thought she'd made it clear that she wanted him to stay. Evidently she hadn't. She crossed her arms and squared her shoulders. 'I'm getting the impression that you want to leave.'

With one hand, he rubbed the base of his neck. 'That all depends.'

'On?'

'Do you let Fifi sleep in your bed?'

The question startled her so much, she had to bite the inside of her cheek to keep from grinning with relief. 'Of course.'

'I was afraid of that.' Though his expression remained immobile, mischief flashed in his eyes. 'You know that rogue cat of yours doesn't like me being around you.'

'Really?' She tightened her arms against her waist to keep from throwing them around Jackson's neck. 'I hadn't noticed.'

'How do you think little Sheba's going to react when she's sitting next to us while we're making love?'

A tingle erupted in her stomach, shooting heat beneath her skin. She drew in a breath, and could taste the sexual tension pooling in the air. 'I . . . I see what you mean.'

300

He took a step closer, so close their clothes brushed. 'Perhaps you could keep Miss Bastet in another room?'

She had to tilt her head back to continue holding his gaze. 'You said her real name.'

'I slipped.'

She had to concentrate on breathing, but it didn't ease the pressure building in her chest or the threat of tears in her eyes. God, she wanted him, so much it hurt. He hadn't touched her yet, but she could feel his heat in the pulsing current that washed over her, sweeping her up. She savored the responding pull in her body, the tightening, the confusing sensations of being full and empty all at once. 'I'm sure something could be worked out.'

Suddenly frustrated with the spinning questions, the waiting and worrying about her sister, Rachel knew only one thing would keep her from going crazy – and that was losing herself in Jackson. Having suppressed her body's needs her entire life, she'd never learned how to be the aggressor, but she decided now was the time to turn the tables. She didn't care about making it to the bedroom, she only wanted to feel Jackson's skin against hers. Smell his musky scent, bury her hands in his hair while he buried himself in her.

He tugged at her vest, but she shoved his hands aside, determined that he would be the first to be undressed this time, and she would be the one to do it. She needed him, all of him, fast and hard. Everything was threatening to fall apart now more

301

than ever, and through it all, he seemed to be the only solid link for her to hold on to.

She fumbled with his belt, and this time when he moved to help, she let him. Within a moment, he removed his shoes and pants and stood before her naked and glorious and hard as stone. She wanted to run her hands over him, grind her palms into the curved muscles of his chest, his lean hips, the powerful length of his thighs. But there wasn't time. She was burning up inside. She had to have him. Now.

'Jackson,' she pleaded as she kissed the line of his jaw, the base of his neck. He reached beneath her skirt and pulled her panties and hose down with one hand. At the same time they both realized they wouldn't come off until she unbuckled her shoes.

She cursed. He cursed and forced her on to the couch. Mumbling something about throwing her shoes away, he had them off her, as well as her hose, then skimmed his hands beneath her skirt again. She expected him to remove her clothes, but he cupped her bottom and pulled her to the edge of the couch, the soft fabric of her skirt grating her bare buttocks, until his body was snug between her thighs. Her breath caught as she watched the intent in his eyes. His mouth drew into an immobile line. He pushed into her, hard and impatient, one deep stroke that touched her soul.

She cried out from the shock, the spiraling pleasure.

'God, you're so tight.' His voice was thick with strain.

She was still sore from that morning, but the pain quickly faded. She closed her eyes and dropped her head back, clinging to his shoulders as he pumped into her, filling the empty ache, stretching her farther, pushing her higher with mind-numbing speed.

Her muscles convulsed, her skin tingled with raw sensations, making every touch sharp and painful. Yet she wanted more, and hated that she hadn't removed her clothes. His hands were on her thighs, firm and commanding, but she wanted to feel her stomach against his, the grating texture of his chest hair against her breasts. She strained against him, seeking more, but only found frustration. Desperate for his taste, she gripped his head and kissed him. Their tongues met and fought, drowning her in a tide of his musky heat.

He wrenched his mouth away and growled, 'I can't wait.'

'Then don't.'

He spread her legs further apart, grinding the nub of her sex with his constant rhythm. A cry tore up her throat and she bucked when he found her with his thumb, adding exquisite, unbearable pressure.

Tension coiled inside her, then sprung free, shivering through her as she held on, gasping for breath, crying his name. Shuddering, he strained against her, finding his release as a harsh, guttural sound vibrated up his chest.

He collapsed on top on her, crushing her into the cushions. She didn't care, she thought, still dazed and feeling liquid with relief.

As their breathing slowed, she became aware of a soft snoring beside her ear. She turned her head the same time Jackson became aware of the noise to find Miss Bastet not a foot away, hunched on her legs, watching them with alarm in her one golden eye.

'Oh, no.' With a flare of guilty embarrassment, Rachel buried her face against Jackson's neck as she choked on a startled laugh. 'We've been caught.'

Jackson's shoulders shook beneath her hands. 'She doesn't look too happy about it, either.'

'Oh, no.'

'At least you're dressed.'

'With my legs wrapped around your naked body.'

'Yeah.' He lifted his head to meet her gaze. She saw hunger in his eyes, a deep, yearning hunger that made her laughter stop and her breath catch. 'Since it's going to happen again,' he said in a gruff voice full of promise, 'Fluffy had better get used to seeing us this way.'

'Remembering her name might help win her over.' She felt him move inside her and couldn't believe that he would be ready again so soon, or that she could be either. But she was. 'Maybe we should move to the bedroom, unless you want an audience.'

'Not for what I have in mind.'

Rachel closed her eyes as he lifted her in his arms. She couldn't imagine anything that could surpass what she'd experienced with him so far. But she was willing to keep an open mind.

CHAPTER 17

The abrupt ringing of the phone stopped Jackson in mid-step. Rachel tensed in his arms as her head came up off his shoulder with a jerk. Without a word, he set her on her feet and grabbed his jeans from the floor as she ran for the kitchen. He heard her soft voice answer, then silence. He zipped up his pants without buttoning them and joined her.

She held the receiver to her chest with both hands, then reluctantly held it out to him. 'It's for you.'

He took the phone. Without bothering to ask who it was, he asked, 'What did you find?'

'It took a while,' Derrick said, 'but we traced them to a charter that took them to Mexico, Puerto Vallarta to be exact.'

'They?'

'Yeah. Penny and her boyfriend, Mark.'

'Have you found where they're staying?'

'Not yet.' Derrick sighed. 'They're not using credit cards, so we haven't been able to trace them.'

Jackson met Rachel's anxious gaze. 'What about a return flight?'

'Nothing. Puerto Vallarta is a hot tourist spot, but there's nothing but mountains and jungle surrounding it. It would be a perfect place to disappear for a while, if that was their plan.'

Jackson clenched his jaw. If he ever got his hands on Penny, he'd wring her neck for running off and leaving Rachel to pick up the pieces. 'Keep looking, and let me know when you find something. I'm staying here at Rachel's if you need me.'

Her eyes widened at his announcement that he wasn't leaving, but concern quickly doused her reaction, making him wonder if she'd been surprised or relieved.

Hanging up the phone, he took her by the hips and pulled her to him. She remained stiff with tension. He wished like hell that he could withhold the news that would only hurt her. 'It doesn't look good.'

She remained silent, her jaw angled in a mutinous line.

'They flew to Puerto Vallarta without scheduling a return.'

She crossed her arms. 'How do you know it's them?'

'My people don't make mistakes.'

Her chin jutted out defiantly, but he could see her struggle to keep it there in the darkening of her eyes. 'It still doesn't prove anything.'

Anger pushed up through Jackson so fast and hard, the emotion nearly choked him. Releasing her, he paced to the doorway. Grinding his jaw, he faced her. 'Christ, Rachel, what's it going to take

306

for you to believe your sister set you up? She has stolen from your clients, planted the items in your store, and when she was afraid she might get caught, she ran!'

'She wouldn't do that to me,' Rachel argued, her voice reed-thin.

Clamping his hands on his hips, he took a deep breath to keep from reaching out and shaking her until she faced the truth. 'Fortunately, I don't have the blind trust you seem to have. In the morning I'm going to the police. They need to search her apartment. I'm sure we missed something.'

'No!'

He arched a brow and held up a hand to keep her from continuing, though it knew the effort would be futile. 'You won't change my mind.'

'You promised you'd wait until after the Women's Fair.'

'That was before I knew about Penny.'

She came to him, her fingers threaded together as she pressed them to her chest. 'Her leaving looks bad, but it's still circumstantial. The fair is the day after tomorrow. Can't you wait until then?'

He stared at her, grinding his hands into fists to keep from letting go of his resolve. He knew what he needed to do, even if she didn't. He was trying to save her from being arrested. Didn't she understand that?

Yes, she did, he admitted, and that was why she was so desperate now. If he proved she was innocent without clearing Penny in the process, the end result would be just as devastating for Rachel.

He met her pleading gaze, felt the anger in him begin to buckle around his knees. He called himself a fool for even considering it, knew this could be the biggest mistake he'd ever made, but he wanted to give her what she asked. God help him, he wanted to take away the fear that drained the light from her eyes.

If there was the slightest chance that Penny might be innocent, he had to investigate it. But knowing how desperate Rachel was, the lengths she'd go to protect her family, stopped him from giving in completely. 'How do I know you won't try to steal something just to prove Penny isn't involved?'

Rachel blinked, her surprise evident. 'I won't have to, because neither of us is responsible for the thefts.'

'And what if nothing's taken?'

She swallowed, and her body visibly trembled. 'Then we'll go to the police station together and tell them what we know.'

It rocked him that, in spite of knowing what Penny was capable of, Rachel still trusted her.

He wasn't accustomed to that kind of devotion, never having felt even a glimmer of it . . . until now. He wasn't sure how it had happened, but somehow he'd let Rachel matter to him. She mattered more than finding the thief, more than saving his damned company. If the possessive, territorial emotions building inside him were any indication, he was well on his way to falling in love with her. What surprised him the most was that he welcomed the feelings, regardless that they scared the hell out of him.

But he did care about her, so much that he would go against his gut instinct and give her the two days she wanted.

But during those two days he would initiate a plan that had been brewing in the back of his mind. Come hell or high water, this time there wouldn't be a trail leading back to Rachel.

CHAPTER 18

The day of reckoning had finally arrived.

Rachel sat at her table in the formal living room of Mrs Gibbons' mansion, her back iron-straight, and a light smile on her lips that hopefully covered the tremors jetting beneath her skin. The turnout for the Women's Fair was as Rachel had expected. Every débutante and headline-hungry socialite had arrived with the solitary goal of outshining the others. In a distracted way, Rachel realized these people were like the seasons: they could be counted on to drift from one event to the next without interruption or fail. And somehow because of them, or in spite of them, her life would never be the same.

A major reason for the change was now roaming the house, mingling as if he were a member of the elite instead of a man who was taking note of every move they made in the hope of finding some clue that would link them to the thefts. Though she couldn't see the men Jackson had stationed around the property, she knew she was being watched. Like watching a buzzard hovering above her, she could feel their building anticipation as the night progressed and nothing happened. Let them watch, she thought. She hoped they never took their eyes off her. Then, when something was stolen, she and Penny would be cleared. A theft had happened at every event she'd attended. She prayed the pattern didn't end now.

For her final show, she'd taken extra care in choosing her outfit, a crimson velvet V-backed gown. Though the life she'd always hungered for, and had finally obtained, might vanish before the night ended, she realized Penny was right. She didn't need to hire herself out any longer.

Even if Jackson proved to be right and Penny went to prison, she'd survive. She loved her business, but losing it wouldn't destroy her. She'd pick up and start over. She cradled the cards in her hands as she recalled giving that same advice to Jackson when he'd told her about losing his business. She drew a deep, cleansing breath and decided it was time she followed her own words of wisdom.

Aware of someone approaching her table, she managed to smile as she set the tarot cards in their box and folded her hands in her lap.

'Hello, Rachel.'

Rachel managed to cover her surprise at seeing Linda seated in the chair across from her. In deference to Linda's wishes, she'd made no effort to speak to her. Seeing her now, Rachel wondered if something had changed.

Her childhood friend looked like perfection, pieced together as if an artist had molded every line and curve into place. Her gold brocade princess-shaped gown undoubtedly cost more than

Rachel's monthly mortgage, and she didn't want to attempt to guess the expense of the string of pearl-sized diamonds draped around her throat.

'Linda . . . Monica,' she corrected when the other woman tensed. 'It's good to see you.'

Linda braced her forearm on the table and swirled her engagement ring so that light from the chandelier reflected off the three-carat marquee. 'I wouldn't have missed this. Evelyn – Mrs Gibbons, that is – is going to host a wedding shower for me next month.'

To which Rachel doubted she'd receive an invitation, but she didn't begrudge Linda's new life. On impulse, she reached out and squeezed the other woman's hand. 'I'm happy for you.'

Linda's smile froze, and she pulled her hand free. Her gaze dropped as she covertly checked to see if anyone had noticed Rachel's gesture.

Annoyance gathered inside Rachel, but she succeeded in pushing it back down to where it belonged. Reaching out to a customer, or anyone in need of reassurance, was something she'd always done. Obviously, Linda didn't deem it necessary or appropriate.

Lifting the tarot deck from the mahogany box, she gently shuffled them. 'So, how do you think life as a senator's wife will suit you?'

Flashing a smile that defined the molded curve of her cheek and jaw, she laughed. 'It's everything I've always dreamed of having, Rachel. I was born to be a part of this.' She sat upright, arching her neck as she surveyed the elegant room. Turning back, Linda's stone-green eyes hardened for such a brief instant that Rachel wondered if she'd imagined it. For that moment, she thought she'd glimpsed the determined and sometimes rebellious teenager Linda had once been.

Linda dropped her gaze and smoothed an invisible crease in her dress. 'You know what it was like for me.' She laughed again, but this time the sound was bitter. 'Hell, for both of us, growing up.'

When she finally met Rachel's gaze, Linda's eyes were clouded with the past, and Rachel knew her friend was remembering the black eyes she'd suffered, the bruises that had adorned her body like jewelry, bruises her father had put there. 'We didn't deserve to live like that.'

'No, we didn't.'

'Nothing can screw this up for me, Rachel.' Linda managed a faltering smile. 'I love David.'

'Your secret is safe, Monica.'

'I know it is. But . . . I just had to make sure.'

'Then stop worrying and tell me about your fiancé.'

Linda gently pressed her fingers to the corners of her eyes before any tears could fall and ruin her flawless make-up. A hesitant, almost guilty smile curved her mouth. 'I'll admit, while I adore David, I love his money, too. That sounds terrible, doesn't it?' She held out her hand, tilting her engagement ring. 'But it's more than that. He's a wonderful man.'

'You don't have to explain anything to me. I understand.'

313

Sobering, Linda said, 'I knew you would. You always did.'

Rachel had to swallow the urge to give advice. Linda didn't want to hear what she undoubtedly already knew: that as long as Linda continued hiding behind lies, she'd live each day in fear that her secret would be discovered. 'I hope everything works out the way you want it to.'

Nodding, Linda trailed her French-manicured nails over her necklace. 'I didn't think I'd see you here tonight.'

'Why not?' Rachel set the cards in the center of the table and laced her fingers together in front of her. 'I've been raising money for charity at events like this for the past two years.'

'Yes, I know. You always were the good one of the bunch.' She laughed, her eyes warming. 'Who would've thought we'd turn out like this? You an entrepreneur, me the future wife of a senator. It just goes to show what can happen when you want something badly enough.'

'Yes,' Rachel responded, unsure if a response had even been warranted.

'But I'm sure your shop keeps you busy.'

Normally, Rachel would have taken the opening to promote her store, but at the moment she only wanted to do her job so the time would pass quickly and the night would end. She glanced past Linda, hoping to catch a glimpse of Jackson. She wanted to find him, ask him if he'd discovered anything. But milling about would only hurt her case if something were stolen, so she remained glued to her seat. 'Would you like me to read your cards?'

Linda glanced down at the deck, her mouth thinning with distaste. 'I'm surprised you're still toying with those things.'

'They're not a game,' Rachel said calmly, though every defensive nerve in her body clamped tight. 'You should remember that from the times I read yours when we were kids.'

'Keep your voice down,' Linda snapped under her breath. Drawing a trembling breath, she glanced over her shoulder, then rose to her feet in a graceful move. 'Thank you, but no. I already know what my future holds for me.'

Rachel watched the demonstrative sway of Linda's hips as she walked away, her self-assured smile as she turned to greet an elderly couple. Linda exuded the confidence of a woman born to wealth. But Rachel understood the skill and determination it took to hide the troubled girl lurking inside.

Though it went against her rule about invading another person's life, Rachel silently asked the cards if Linda would succeed in keeping her dream.

She laid the deck on the table, then chose three cards at random. The cards' sign didn't matter, only whether they were reversed or right side up. If they were reversed, the answer would be no; if right-side up, then the answer would be yes, Linda would live her dream.

She turned the cards over. All three were reversed.

* * *

315

Leaning over Rachel's chair, Jackson braced his hands on the wooden arms and whispered against her ear, 'You look troubled. Is there anything I can do to help?'

Her soft intake of air told him he'd startled her. He hadn't meant to sneak up on her, but she'd been so absorbed in the three cards on the table, he could have entered the room yelling and she wouldn't have noticed.

She turned her head, bringing her lush mouth within inches of his. Too close for him not to do something about it.

Before he could kiss her, she said, 'Troubled? Whatever would give you that idea?'

'You're frowning.'

She forced her brow to smooth. 'If I were in trouble, Jackson, what would you do to help me?'

With the need to touch her spreading to every part of his body, he tightened his hold on the chair before he did something that would embarrass them both. He'd known better than to get to close to her. How often had her rich, addictive scent reduced him to a state where nothing mattered except loving her with his hands and body and mouth? The way she looked tonight, so elegant and soft, yet off limits in her wine-tinted backless gown, made him want to drag her from the room. The image appealed to him so much, he considered it for a second longer.

'First I'd kiss you.'

Her gaze immediately dropped to his mouth. A breath shook out of her. 'Then what?'

'I'd make love to you until you couldn't think about anything except what I was doing to you.' Everything inside him demanded he act on his promise and ease the need that pounded from his groin to his heart to his brain.

'If you keep looking at me as if I'm the main entrée on the buffet table, neither one of us will be able to think straight.'

'But we'd be feeling pretty damn good.'

'You'd better watch it, Jackson. I see smoke coming out of your ears.'

Returning her grin, he straightened and buttoned his coat to hide the bulge in his slacks. When her gaze slid down past his waist, she studied him with an absorbed look that made his heart strike his ribs. He sucked a breath through clenched teeth as desire flashed hot and swift through his veins. 'Woman, unless you want me to . . .'

'All right. All right, I'll behave.' Her cheeks flushing to a peachy rose, she laughed softly and looked away. 'I just didn't want to be the only one suffering.'

Rounding the table, he took the seat the slender brunette had vacated only moments before. Meeting Rachel's daring gaze, he realized that over the past two days she'd changed from elusive to evocative. A change he welcomed, though at the moment it was wreaking havoc on his system.

With a reluctant sigh, he decided it was time to get back to business and the reason he'd come looking for Rachel.

'Who was the woman you were speaking to earlier?' He knew Monica Beaumont was Senator

Hastings' fiancée, but the conversation he'd over-head between Rachel and Monica – or was it Linda? – through the mini receiver in his ear had put his instincts on alert. Rachel would be furious if she learned he'd bugged her table, but he wondered if he'd made a mistake not doing so before now.

'Monica . . .' Rachel paused, her brow dipping slightly. 'Beaumont I believe is her last name.'

He watched her collect her cards with meticulous care then set them aside. Each movement shifted her red velvet dress, warming the color until it glowed like soft fire. 'Do you know Miss Beaumont?'

She hesitated for an instant as if considering the question. 'Not really.'

Don't lie to me, Rachel! Resisting the impulse to demand the truth from her made his gut tighten. The two women had known each other as kids – a fact he'd gathered Miss Beaumont didn't want known. Rachel was the rarity who would respect the woman's wishes, regardless of how it might look. It wasn't against the law to change your name, but her keeping it a secret alerted every suspicious nerve in his body. He'd have Andy check out the woman first thing in the morning. Until then, there wasn't any reason to confront Rachel about her withholding information from him. Besides, he didn't have it in him to add more tension to the battle.

'I like your hair up like that,' he said, surprised that he'd said what had been in the back of his mind since first seeing her earlier that evening. She'd twisted the black length into a satin rope at the crown of her head, leaving wisps curling around her face.

Her eyes widened slightly, curving up as she smiled. 'Thank you.'

'But I prefer it down.'

A dark brow arched. 'Do you?'

'As soon as this party is over, I'm going to remove those pins.'

When her breathing slowed to a tremble, he knew the idea affected her, but that was nothing compared to what the image was doing to him. It still shook him, almost violently, the depth of his need for her. He leaned closer. 'If I kissed you right now, do you think anyone would notice?'

'Your spies might. I am being watched, aren't I?'

'They don't count.'

Her lips quirked, bringing laughter to her silver eyes. 'Don't you have work to do, Mr Dermont?'

'Unfortunately, I do. A little longer, Rachel, and all this will be over.' And then what? he wanted to ask. But now wasn't the time to talk about their future.

He rose to his feet, then, because he couldn't stand the temptation any longer, he positioned himself so he could run the back of his fingers across her cheek without anyone seeing. 'You're not wearing your amulet.'

Her hand instinctively fluttered to her chest where the disk usually lay. He'd never seen her without it.

She tilted her head back, her gaze searching his. 'I decided I didn't need it.'

He watched her, trying to discern the look in her eyes. Hope? Resignation? He couldn't be certain which. Then he realized what he saw was trust. She trusted him with her body, and, he suspected, her heart, though she hadn't mentioned love yet. It was too soon, he conceded, their relationship too volatile for her to consider loving him.

He grazed his fingers over her skin once more. But what about *his* heart? She'd certainly touched it, making him care about her more than he'd thought possible, more than he had Sandra, or all other women combined. His feelings for Rachel weren't just about sex, though he craved that from her. His need bordered on possessive, driving his male single-mindedness to claim her as his own. He wanted to mark his territory, brand her off-limits to all other men. His feelings for her were sincere at best, barbaric at worst, but he couldn't change how he felt.

He wanted her to be his, exclusively. And not for the short term.

The path and the strength of his thoughts caught him so off guard, he took a step back. Not in retreat, but in amazement that he had it in him to feel anything so powerful at all.

'I'll see you later,' he said, despite his need to stay and kiss her.

He turned away, intending to make another sweep of the house. The woman standing directly behind him brought him to an abrupt halt.

'Penny,' he said, glancing past her shoulder to her boyfriend. Standing a few feet from Mark was one of his men, Eric, who'd apparently spotted the couple and had followed them inside. He nodded, and Eric backed a discreet distance away.

'Oh, my God, Penny!' Rachel shot to her feet and embraced her sister. Closing her eyes, Rachel clung to the younger woman, her relieved expression that of a mother who'd found a lost child. 'Why did you leave without telling anyone? We were scared to death that something had happened to you.'

Before Penny could answer, Rachel's eyes opened, widening with alarm. She took her sister by the shoulders and held her at arm's length. 'You're not supposed to be here.' Pressing her fingers to her mouth, she glanced frantically at Jackson then looked back to her sister. 'What are you doing here?'

The younger woman frowned at the panic in Rachel's voice. 'We just got back in town. I called Mom, and she said you've both been worried, so I thought I'd stop by and let you know I'm fine.'

'You . . . No, this isn't happening.' Rachel gripped Jackson's arm, her desperate tremors spreading where she touched him. 'You've got to get her out of here.'

Jackson agreed, but he couldn't help but be suspicious. After her mysterious disappearance, what were the odds of Penny's unwittingly choosing tonight to return?

Penny crossed her arms over her chest and propped out her hip in a rebellious stance. 'We don't mind staying to help out. Besides, I want to tell you where we went. You'll never believe what I've done.' A secretive smile split her pixieish face.

'Tell me later.' Rachel caught her sister's arm, but stopped short of dragging Penny from the room. After a brief glance at the crowd who were watching with mild interest, Rachel said, 'You can't stay here. You've got to leave.'

'I don't "got" to do anything.'

Rachel spun around to face Jackson. 'Take her home, please.'

'What's going on here?'

Ignoring her sister, Rachel clasped her hands together and brought them to her lips. She whispered urgently, 'You have to take her away.'

'Stop trying to boss me around.' Penny snorted. 'I'm not going anywhere.'

'Jackson, please!' Rachel insisted in an urgent whisper.

He clenched his jaw, his mind racing with the twist of events. He'd taken so many precautions for this party even he thought some of them had been extreme. He'd bugged Rachel's table, hired more guards, added additional cameras and had a van with surveillance equipment stationed outside. But he'd never once considered that Penny would show up. He was tempted to give in to the urge to shake Penny and Mark for throwing a major wrench in his plans. His only consolation, and it was a minute one, was that if the couple had been spotted before entering, they wouldn't have had a chance to survey the house. He hoped.

322

Turning to Penny, he said, 'I'll have one of my men drive both of you home. He'll stay there until Rachel and I can join you.'

Penny cocked a brow. 'And just who do you think you are? Sending me home with one of your employees to babysit me? I don't think so. It's my job to stay and help. And that's what I intend to do.'

'Penny,' Rachel pleaded, 'you don't know what's been going on here.'

Jackson gave her a disbelieving look, which she ignored.

'Jackson's only trying to protect you. Please, do as he says.'

'Penny's right,' Mark said, speaking around the toothpick protruding from his mouth. He draped his arm around Penny and hugged her to him. He winked at an affluent couple who was staring at him, gape-mouthed. 'We'd rather hang out here. This place isn't too shabby.'

'We need the money, Rachel,' Penny explained.

'Staying is out of the question.' Jackson felt the muscles in his back twist with tension. 'You'll leave or I'll call the police.'

'That's not necessary,' Rachel hissed, though she forced a smile as several people walked by. To Penny, she said, 'I'll loan you whatever money you need in the morning.'

'You know,' Penny said, glaring at Jackson, 'I take back every nice thing I ever said about this guy. He's a jerk.'

'No, he isn't. He's trying to help you.' Rachel reached for the amulet that wasn't there. Jackson curbed the instinctive urge to put his arm around her to lend her support. Watching her now with her silver eyes flashing, her shoulders straight with determination, he doubted she needed any from him. The depth of her reserve amazed him.

Rachel said, 'If you never listen to me again, *please* listen now. Do what Jackson says, and let his man take you home. I promise I'll come over as soon as I can to explain everything.'

'This has to do with the burglaries, doesn't it?' Penny asked insolently.

Rachel sucked in a breath and stared disbelievingly at her sister. Grabbing Penny's hands, she pulled her closer. 'What do you know about them?'

'Mom told me.' An angry, defiant light entered the young woman's powder-blue eyes. 'You think I did it, don't you?'

'No!'

'Yes, you do.' Penny worked her hands free, then stepped back. Her mouth thinned into a stubborn line. 'Fine, I'll leave. On my way out, I'll see what I can pocket.'

'Don't . . .' Rachel started after her sister, but Jackson caught her arm and pulled her back. He nodded to Eric, who followed the couple to the front door. Taking a two-way radio from his pocket, he arranged to have Penny and Mark escorted home and guarded until he arrived.

Feeling her tremors, he forced Rachel into her chair and knelt beside her. She clenched his hands with icy fingers.

'She wasn't here long enough to take anything,' Rachel said, the words rushed and fearful. 'She wasn't.'

'I know, baby,' he said with a calmness he certainly didn't feel. 'It was just bad timing.' Or was it? Penny had known about the Women's Fair, and had been scheduled to work it according to Rachel. Had Penny flown home from her quick trip to Mexico intent on resuming her stealing spree?

But she knows we suspect her. Why would she risk coming back unless she was innocent? Or, he mused, maybe she thought she'd remove herself as a suspect if she confronted them?

Jackson ran his hand over his mouth. He was no closer to finding any answers; he was simply adding more questions. If nothing was stolen, it wouldn't prove anything, and it wouldn't clear Rachel or Penny. If something was taken, with Penny and Mark under constant guard, the pendulum would swing back to Rachel. As the owner of the store where the stolen merchandise had been found, the police would zero in on her.

Penny's return had accomplished only one thing that Jackson could see: it had destroyed his last chance to prove to the police and, he admitted, to himself, that Rachel was innocent.

CHAPTER 19

Rachel gathered her cards and stored them in their box. Securing them in her purse, she vaguely registered the clink and rattle of dishes and the hurried steps of servants carting away trays of uneaten food. The hushed conversation among the musicians as they packed their equipment replaced the earlier sounds of music and laughter. It was nearly one in the morning, and she felt the effects of every minute she'd spent smiling, reading cards, and assuring people who had everything that they would have more.

She couldn't precisely recall what she'd told her clients. She hadn't been able to focus after her sister's sudden reappearance. Jackson's comment about its being bad timing was like calling a hurricane a passing shower. If her sister had the bad judgement to leave without word, *why* had she chosen tonight to return? Rachel didn't want to believe Penny had anything to do with the thefts, but her return seemed too perfect to be a coincidence.

She'd also hinted that she'd done something Rachel wouldn't believe. Lord only knew what that would entail. Rachel closed her eyes to relieve their dryness, then rubbed the back of her neck. She wished she'd listened to what her sister had to say before she'd left. Maybe that would have relieved the almost superstitious dread building inside her.

'Are you ready?'

She opened her eyes to find Jackson bent over her, his hands braced on the arms of her chair, his whisky-brown eyes inches from hers, intense and probing. Suddenly alert, she asked, 'Has anything happened?'

He straightened and took her hand, helping her up. 'Nothing's been stolen, if that's what you mean.'

She leaned into him as his arm came around her waist and he guided her into the front hall. 'Thank God,' she said, though she knew it proved nothing. 'I want to go home and change before going to Penny's. It's on the way, and will only take a minute.'

On the front landing, he stopped. 'It's late. Are you sure you don't want to wait until morning? I still have her under surveillance, so she won't go anywhere without my knowing about it.'

She shook her head. 'I won't be able to rest until I talk with her.'

Pressing a kiss to her temple, he said, 'All right. I'll follow you home, then we'll take my car.'

The discreet clearing of someone's throat brought their attention to the front door, where Mrs Gibbons stood with her hands clasped at her waist. Senator Hastings, with his confident politician's stance, waited beside her.

'I'd like to have a word with you, Jackson,' Mrs Gibbons said. 'Before you go.'

'Yes, ma'am.' Turning to Rachel, he said, 'I'll meet you at your house as soon as I can.' He turned and nodded to a four-foot hedge. A man wearing black from head to toe emerged. It took Rachel only a moment to realize that the camouflaged linebacker would be her escort home. Aware that her future was at stake, she didn't consider arguing.

Waving, she called good night to the party's host and the senator and made her way to her car.

Conscious of the set of headlights trailing her at a discreet distance, she drove through the city that never shut down entirely. Cars bulleted down the interstate, well over the speed limit, disappearing ahead of her as if swallowed by concrete. Early morning darkness pressed over the town, heavy and oppressive, despite towering street lamps and colorful neon signs that held the night at bay. Or perhaps it was her own nervous exhaustion that made her feel as if the world were closing in. She drove automatically, her mind unable to think beyond the coming confrontation with her sister. She could still see the cold, wounded look in Penny's eyes. A look that would haunt her forever.

Arriving at her house, Rachel unlocked the front door. She checked the street, but saw no sign of her guard. Maybe she wasn't supposed to see him?

Miss Bastet's meow from the dark hall startled her. Feeling for the light switch, she turned it on and stepped inside, closing the door behind her.

'What are you doing awake, sweetheart?' Setting her purse on the hall table, Rachel lifted the cat and received an answering purr. Not wanting the distraction, she hadn't taken Miss Bastet to the party. At this late hour, she'd expected to find that the cat had reclaimed her usual spot, curled into a ball on the pillow beside Rachel's.

She grinned, thinking about the stubborn battle between cat and man over who got to sleep next her. Neither Miss Bastet nor Jackson wanted to share. Rachel still wasn't sure who would win in the long run. They'd better work through their differences, she mused, because she wanted to keep them both. The admission made her stomach flutter with hope.

There was no use denying the intense feelings she had for Jackson, though their time together seemed more dream than reality. Probably because it had taken her twenty-eight years to meet a man who could affect her the way he did. She cautioned herself to move slowly; Jackson was as guarded and distrustful as he was gentle and caring, and after coming to know him, she felt certain that he wasn't looking for anything permanent. Which put her heart at risk of being hurt.

Passing through the living room, she switched on a lamp and set the cat on the sofa, giving her one last scratch beneath the chin before she went to change. Jackson should arrive at any minute, and she wanted to be ready to leave as soon as he did. Something caught her attention from the corner of her vision, a shape and color that was out of place. She glanced at the coffee table and froze, a chill spreading down her spine. Her breath turned cold in her lungs. The sudden lurch of her heart struck her breastbone.

'No.' The word shook out of her. She turned her head, searching the room. She expected the shadows in the corners to separate and give her nightmare a body and face. Dread prickled her skin like needles. Everything remained quiet, eerily so, as if something were watching from the dark, waiting. Or someone. The same someone who had broken into her home, not to steal from her, but to leave something behind.

Even as logic told her not to, that she might destroy any fingerprints, she picked up the statue sitting in the center of her table, arranged among the scented candles and silk flowers as if she'd chosen it for that exact spot. Only she'd never seen the statue before except in pictures. The museum-quality bronze sculpture of a man holding a sword was David with the head of Goliath at his feet. Rachel thought it fitting that whoever was trying to frame her had chosen this particular piece. At the moment she felt as small and defenseless as David had, only her enemy was so large, she couldn't see it. David had survived by using his wits. Somehow she had to do the same. But how, when she didn't know what she was fighting, or why.

She heard a bang from outside. An instant later her front door burst open. She spun around just as Jackson rushed inside. He come to an abrupt halt, his expression of disbelief matching the shock that left her dazed. He held still, not speaking, his gaze flickering from hers to the bronze statue in her hands. Then his eyes went carefully blank, guarding his thoughts.

He thinks I stole it. Only he couldn't figure out how, she realized, since he'd had her watched the entire evening. She could feel his withdrawal, sense his doubts. The soul-deep distrust he'd harbored for so many years resurfaced, closing him off, pulling him farther and farther away from her. Unable to stop it, or even believe it could happen so quickly, she felt the bond they'd begun to build shatter as if their last few days together had never happened.

'Jackson . . .' She paused as sirens punctured the tense silence, a confirmation that everything was coming to an end. 'You know I didn't take this.'

He clenched his jaw, flexing the muscle. He didn't move closer, didn't gather her to him the way she needed and tell her he believed her. Sirens echoed through her neighborhood, blasting louder as if they originated from inside her home.

'The reason Mrs Gibbons asked me to stay was to report the theft of a statue.' His voice was so hard and cold and devoid of emotion that she shuddered. 'That one.'

'It wasn't me,' she insisted. 'And it wasn't Penny, either.' Though whether she believed it or said it out of habit, she wasn't certain any longer.

'How can you be so sure?'

'You . . . you've had her watched since she showed up at the party.'

'She could have taken it before tonight. We don't know how long she's been back in town. She could

331

have been staying at a hotel. And she has a key to your house.'

'She wouldn't set me up like this.'

'That's just one theory.' He scanned the room, his gaze lingering on various pieces of furniture.

A theory she wouldn't consider. Penny had been hurt when she'd thought Rachel had suspected her. Her sister could be moody and temperamental, and she might resent Rachel at times, but she wasn't evil. Whoever had planted the statue wanted to *hurt* Rachel.

Hearing a commotion outside, Jackson stiffened. Two men in wrinkled suits and loosely knotted ties entered through the open door. The first one pulled out a wallet and flashed his badge at her.

'Jackson, tell me you believe me.'

'Keep quiet,' he ordered, and stepped aside to face the detectives, nodding to them.

'Dermont,' the first man said. 'I'm surprised to find you here.'

'Hutchins. Rawlins.' Jackson shoved his hands deep into his pockets and fixed his hooded gaze on the two men. 'What's all this about?'

'You know these men?' Rachel wasn't sure why it alarmed her that Jackson was associated with the officers, but his distance and the fact that she couldn't sense any of his thoughts frightened her. He didn't glance at her or answer.

'Miss Gold, I'm Detective Hutchins. This is my partner, Detective Rawlins. We have a warrant to search the premises.' Hutchins held out a set of folded papers. His gaze slipped down to her hands. 'But it looks as if a search won't be necessary.'

'I didn't steal it,' she said, disregarding Jackson's warning to keep quiet. She wasn't a thief, and she intended to make that fact clear to everyone.

The two men exchanged a questionable look. 'This statue was reported stolen less than an hour ago. If you didn't take it, Miss Gold, how did it come to be in your possession?'

Gripping the cold sculpture in her hands, she said, 'It was on my table when I got home.' Jackson tilted his head, finally meeting her gaze. His brown eyes were sharp and hot, angry and empty, all at once.

He wasn't going to defend her, she realized, though her mind couldn't completely accept that fact. He stood close enough for her to touch, yet miles away, cut off from her emotionally. She knew she should insist that someone had set her up, but she knew it would be useless. If he didn't believe her by now, nothing she said would change his mind.

Something inside her clicked off, stopping the avalanche of emotion sweeping down on her. The fragile bond between them had snapped, she thought dully as her will to fight drained out of her. All she could do was focus on Jackson's disbelieving face, the stark acceptance in his eyes, and feel the deep, searing pain it brought.

Refusing to look away, wanting to catch the slightest shift in Jackson's expression, she asked the detective, 'How did you get a warrant so fast? And why was I suspected?'

In her heart she was afraid, so deathly afraid she knew the answer. After learning about the theft, had Jackson turned her in without even waiting to verify if she'd taken the work of art? His distance, his very silence spoke for itself. Despite the times they'd made love and the bond she'd *thought* they'd forged, his distrust of her hadn't begun to fade. He'd thought her guilty from the very beginning . . . and had stayed close to her until he'd proven himself right. He'd used her. That fact hurt more than the certainty that someone had set her up.

But she *had* been framed.

Somehow, she had to find out who had done it and why before she was convicted and sent to prison. But she'd been caught with stolen merchandise three times. If Jackson had told the authorities about the necklace and the vase, who would believe she hadn't taken the statue?

'We had an anonymous tip that you were seen putting the statue in your bag,' Detective Hutchins said. 'When we checked, Mrs Gibbons confirmed you were at her party tonight.'

'A tip that *I* took the vase?' She glared at Jackson. He'd had her watched every moment. He'd left the house with her, had sent a bodyguard to follow her home. He had to know she hadn't taken it, but the flinty bronze of his eyes conveyed nothing but doubt.

She wanted to ask if he was the anonymous caller but the words stuck like bitter mud in her throat. She couldn't believe he'd have done something so devious. He might doubt her, but he wouldn't hide

334

behind a phone call while accusing her of the burglaries.

'Rachel,' Jackson warned, 'don't say anything else.'

Ignoring him, she asked, 'So you immediately obtained a search warrant because of an anonymous call? How did you manage to get a warrant in the middle of the night?' Fierce, burning anger turned her breathing shallow and harsh. Whoever was trying to ruin her life had all but succeeded. Now that Mrs Gibbons knew Rachel was a suspect, every one of her clients would know about it by morning. Even if she proved herself innocent, the damage was done.

'The senator,' Jackson said, though to whom, she wasn't sure.

'Why would he do that to me?' she demanded. Jackson's empty gaze fixed on her. Then it dawned on her. The senator thought she'd stolen the vase from him. But why would he come to such a conclusion unless someone had told him she was involved? Rachel wanted to close her eyes and sink into the couch. Had Jackson told the senator about his suspicions?

Another man wearing white cotton gloves came forward and took the statue from her.

Detective Rawlins said, 'Anything's possible when you're dealing with money, Miss Gold. You might keep that in mind and listen to Dermont and not say anything else.' Taking out a pair of handcuffs from his coat pocket, he fastened one around her wrist before she realized they were intended for her.

Jackson's hand clamped over her free wrist. 'Is that necessary, Hutchins?'

'You know it is.' The two men exchanged challenging glares. 'If you have a problem with it, Dermont, you can wait outside.'

Releasing her, taking a step back, Jackson gave her an unreadable look as Hutchins read her her rights.

Rachel closed her eyes, locking back the swell of tears. She barely heard the words the detective recited, but knew he was telling her how anything she said would be used against her in a court of law, how an attorney would be appointed for her if she couldn't afford one. Words she'd heard before while watching television. Words she'd never thought would be applied to her.

Now, the statement was not only implied; someone had gone to a lot of trouble to make sure it would stick.

Jackson shoved the door to the control room open and crossed directly to Richie Collins, one of seven night technicians who manned a select group of accounts. Jackson had phoned from his car, instructing Richie on what he wanted done before he reached the office. If the younger man had thought it odd that the boss was coming in at four in the morning, he hadn't let on.

Rounding the half-circle desk that contained a fleet of monitors, Jackson said, 'Tell me what you found. And it better be good.'

'We picked up something, but I don't know how much it'll help.' Richie tapped on his keyboard, bringing up one window after another. Then, one monitor blanked to gray snow. The screen rolled and displayed a hazy black and white image of Rachel's living room.

'What's wrong with the picture?' Jackson ran a hand through his hair, then leaned over the technician to use the keyboard to try and sharpen the picture. Nothing worked. 'Shit.'

'My guess is that the RF signal from the camera needs adjusting. I talked to Will, who installed the unit. He said it was a rush job and he didn't have a chance to test it.'

'I know. Dammit, I know.' Drawing back, Jackson pushed the lapels of his tux aside and rested his hands on his hips. He was going to catch hell from Rachel if she ever discovered what he'd done, but it would have been worth it, if only the video had been clearer. Breaking his promise had been his one chance to prove her innocent, and he'd blown it.

'This would have been perfect, too.' Richie pointed to the screen as shadowed images began to change and a person appeared. 'But it's so blurry, I can't tell if it's a man or a woman.'

'It's a woman,' Jackson said caustically. But whether Rachel or Penny, he couldn't say for sure. He noted the time on the lower right-hand corner of the screen. He'd already verified that Penny was still in her apartment with Mark. Rachel could have made it home by the time indicated on the screen if she'd hustled. Which meant . . . that she'd stolen the statue? He couldn't believe that. Not yet.

Aware of the risk he was taking, and that he might hurt Rachel in his attempt to help her, he picked up the phone and dialed Detective Hutchins, who answered, sounding overworked, harassed and sleep-deprived.

'Hutchins, it's Jackson Dermont.'

'You know we had to book her, Jackson, so . . .'

'That's not why I'm calling. I have something you might be interested in seeing,' he said, praying for all he was worth that he wasn't making a mistake. He heard the creaking of a chair as if the detective had leaned forward to listen. 'Can you arrange for someone at I-Systems to meet us at their lab to digitize a video?' If anyone could bring the picture into focus it would be I-Systems, which specialized in photo recovery, usually for government agencies, the FBI, CIA, and occasionally the local police.

'You got something on tape?'

Jackson hit the pause button. The screen filled with black hair framing a pale, slender face and dark fathomless eyes. Praying his gut instincts weren't wrong, he said, 'Yeah, I got something.'

'All right, give me half an hour.'

Jackson hung up. 'Copy the video, Richie. I'll take the original.'

As the technician went to work, Jackson closed his eyes and tried not to think about what would happen to Rachel if he was wrong. Because he couldn't lose her. Not ever, and certainly not by his own doing.

Water dripped from the dull silver faucet into a sink thick with rust stains and deposits of lime. One fat, wet drop after another clung to the rim in an attempt to hold on before it lost the fight. *Drip, drip, drip.* Never-ending, like the memories of finding the statue, of seeing Jackson's disbelief, of being hand-cuffed and driven to the police station in the back of a patrol car.

Rachel had no idea how long she'd watched the incessant trickle, but she thought several hours had passed. People were beginning to stir in the jail cells nearby. The woman in the bunk above her had stopped snoring and was breathing deep and regular. There were no windows, so she had no idea if the sun had risen. During the time she'd been sitting on the thin mattress with a coarse blanket wrapped around her shoulders, the lights had never been turned off, obscuring the distinction between night and day.

There had to be a reason for that, she thought with detachment. Maybe to keep the inmates from realizing how much time had passed – how much time they'd lost.

The tight, burning aches in her body told her to lie down and rest, but her mind refused. After being booked as the only suspect behind the burglaries, she'd made her one phone call to her mother, telling her what had happened. Hearing the strength in Emily's reassuring words had nearly rendered Rachel to a child-like state. She'd wanted to sink to the floor and pull her knees to her chest, but her mother's optimism that she'd take care of every-thing had renewed Rachel's faith that she would find the answers. Somehow.

She needed an attorney, but the only ones she knew were members of her clientele. She didn't think any of them would represent her, so she'd agreed to a court-appointed lawyer for her hearing to set bail. She could find another attorney later, if necessary.

Details that needed to be handled circled her mind in an endless trail. Images of Jackson tried to sneak in, but she refused to think about him. Thoughts of him were too painful. She had to stay focused, work through the facts. Only the facts continued to jumble together, all ending with the question of why anyone would want to frame her.

When she'd first arrived at the station, she'd expected to see Jackson. Despite his earlier distance, she'd needed him by her side while she'd suffered the humiliation of being fingerprinted and photographed. But he'd never come. Numb and disillusioned, she'd endured the process alone. She pulled the blanket tighter around her as the chill in her heart cut deeper.

Hearing the muffled tap of footsteps on the slate-gray tile floor, she held her breath. A female officer appeared and unlocked the cell.

'Gold, you have a visitor.'

The woman sleeping above Rachel snorted and rolled over. Rising from her cot, Rachel ran her sweaty palms down her prison-issue pants. They'd taken her dress, her purse, everything after they'd booked her. The rough, matching blue shirt she wore grated against her bare skin. She followed the prison guard through several corridors, then

340

into a small, dismal room with a battered table and two chairs. A five-foot-long mirror filled one wall. She wondered who watched from the other side. Was Jackson there, congratulating himself on solving the case? She briefly closed her eyes to shut out the thought, then took a seat facing the mirror.

She stared straight ahead as if she could see past the silver layer, see the shadowed bodies hiding behind the protective glass. It was easier than trying to study her own haggard reflection. Her eyes were sunken, the skin beneath bruised purple from fatigue. Her hair had been pinned into an elegant French twist. They'd taken the pins, so now it fell in a black tangle down her back.

The door opened and a heavyset man wearing a dove-gray pin-striped suit and carrying a scarred briefcase entered with a harassed sigh. Setting the case on the table, he pressed his mouth into a grim line. He could have been anywhere between thirty and fifty; his thinning hair and round, tired eyes were so ordinary, he exemplified the average man who rarely received special notice. From his uncivil disposition, she suspected he knew it. 'Miss Gold, I'm Larry Morrison, your attorney.'

'Thank you for coming.' Her throat tight from strain, the words broke.

He didn't bother to answer or look at her, but withdrew a folder from his briefcase and opened it. He didn't even sit down. 'Since you've already been formally charged, we'll be going before the judge at eight o'clock to request bail.' He finally glanced at her over the top of the folder. 'Will you be able to pay it?'

She had money in savings, her nest egg to protect her against difficult times. Money stashed away so she'd never be caught helpless again. If she didn't have enough for bail, she could use the store as collateral and borrow it. But how much would that cost her? She closed her eyes, refusing to give in to the sting of tears.

Everything she'd worked for might all be gone before the day ended, senselessly lost. 'That depends on how high the bail is set, I suppose.'

'Hmmm.' The sound made her think he didn't care whether she got out of jail or not. He went back to studying his papers, making her feel more alone than ever. She shook off the sensation. He was here as her legal counsel, not as a shoulder to cry on. She didn't need his comfort anyway; she needed his knowledge to get her out of jail.

'You have no previous record, but being caught with the merchandise isn't good. I'll ask for leniency since this is your first offense . . .'

'I didn't steal the anything.'

He regarded her again over the folder's edge. '. . . but considering the statue belonged to Mrs Gibbons, who happens to be tight with the judge, I wouldn't count on it. There has been some mention about a vase being stolen from Senator Hastings. Would you know anything about that?'

She pushed to her feet and turned away to pace. She wanted to scream over and over until someone listened, *I'm innocent! I am innocent!* No matter how many times she said the words, no one seemed to hear her. She leaned against the wall, the cold from the stone seeping through her shirt and beneath her skin. Tears she'd been too shocked to shed up until now pushed against her eyes. She tilted her head back and blinked. She couldn't fall apart yet.

Needing something to hold on to, she reached for her amulet, but they'd taken that from her as well. She shook her head, remembering that she hadn't worn the amulet, believing she hadn't needed it. She'd had Jackson.

'Try to fix yourself up before the hearing. It might help,' she heard her attorney say, his voice muted as if he were speaking from a tunnel. She heard movement, then the door opened. 'I had expected Detective Hutchins to be here to question you, but since he's out I'll send the guard in to take you to your cell.'

The door shut with a click so empty, so heartbreakingly final, that tears slipped down her face. Not even her attorney, the one person who was required by law to defend her, believed in her. How would she ever hope to convince a judge? Or a jury if it went to trial?

Hearing someone enter, prepared to be returned to her cell, she forced a deep breath into her lungs. Opening her eyes, she dimly thought it fortunate that she'd taken that breath, because she didn't think she'd be able to draw another for some time. Jackson stood in the open doorway. The top three buttons of his starched white shirt were undone, the tie missing altogether. Though his tux was creased with wrinkles, he still managed to look devastatingly . . . handsome . . . and out of her reach.

There were shadows beneath his eyes, with deep lines fanning out from their corners. His hair fell in waves across his brow, the way it did when he raked his hands through it. He looked tired, drawn, as if he'd fought a battle and had lost. She wanted to ask if he still believed she was guilty; the question burned in her heart to be asked, but the words wouldn't come, not yet anyway; she felt too raw, too torn, too *betrayed* to confront him now. She doubted she'd ever ask him the question. She wanted, needed his belief in her now more than she needed air, but she wouldn't beg for it.

'How are you holding up?' he asked.

Aware of the tears on her cheeks, certain that she looked small and vulnerable and frightened huddled against the wall, she tilted her chin up and managed a grim smile in answer to the comical question.

He glanced at the mirror then crossed to her, stopping a foot away. He raised his hand to touch her, but stayed the act and rested his hand on his hip. Despite everything he'd done to hurt her, she still loved him. As crazy and insane and hopeless as it might be, she loved him. But the love bordered on pain.

She knew it was lunacy for her to care for him at all, but she couldn't change what she felt. Right or wrong, she needed him. She wanted to feel his thumb grazing her cheek, inhale his special scent.

If only he'd hold her, the relentless tremors in her body might cease. She hugged her waist and looked away, afraid the tears would break loose and drown her in grief.

But there were issues that had to be dealt with. So far no one had mentioned Penny. Rachel had to know if he intended to go after her sister as well. 'You're not looking so hot, Jackson.'

'I think we've both had better nights.'

The quietly spoken words induced memories of the past two nights she'd made love to him, falling asleep in his arms, waking with his body wrapped around hers. She'd thought she'd found the man she could love for the rest of her life. She wanted to believe it still. Fool that she was, she wanted . . . Clenching her hands, she reminded herself that he didn't love her. He never had. He hadn't made her any promises except to solve the case. Why couldn't she remember that?

'They're going to set bail in a couple of hours,' she said, needing to steer her mind away from him.

'Try not to worry about it.'

She smiled, though it felt brittle on her lips. 'Why would I worry about being arrested for something I didn't do?'

He started to say something, then hesitated, casting an annoyed glance at the mirror. He looked back at her, his brown eyes clear and focused, yet she couldn't read them. But she'd never been able to read Jackson, sense what he thought or felt. That had been her downfall, she realized.

'I'll be in the courtroom with you.'

'You'll excuse me if that piece of news doesn't make me feel better.'

'I didn't want this to happen.' His jaw clenched, and before she could register his intent, he reached out and lightly brushed his thumb over her cheek, lingering for an instant. Though her mind told her to pull away, she couldn't. 'Trust me, Rachel.'

Her vision blurred and a tear escaped. She'd trusted him to help her, believed he'd find the person behind the thefts. She'd trusted him so much, she'd made love to him, giving him her heart in the process. 'Trust you, Jackson?' she whispered. 'How can I possibly when you don't trust *me* enough to believe I'm innocent?'

His fingers flexed against her skin, then he withdrew, stepping further away. A muscle pulsed in his jaw as his face turned dark with anger. He shot a glaring look at the mirror and exhaled a breath through his nostrils. She tensed, wanting to know who was watching them, listening in and keeping Jackson from saying more.

Running a hand through his hair, he gave her one last look she couldn't interpret, then he turned to leave. At the door, she asked, 'What about Penny?'

At the threshold, he paused, but didn't look back. 'I've taken care of everything.'

Of course he had, she thought as helpless fury squeezed the air from her lungs. Jackson had taken care of everything; that was why she was in jail.

CHAPTER 20

Rachel came to an abrupt halt by the door reserved for prisoners and stared in horror at the crowded courtroom. Behind the table where her attorney sat, leaning back in his chair with a bored expression on his plain face, her mother, Penny and Mark sat together, hands linked in the first row of wooden benches.

Excited murmurs rose, then were cut off as if a dozen invisible hands had simultaneously clamped over everyone's mouths. She felt a dozen pairs of eyes turn to her. People she recognized. Mrs Gibbons, the Donaldsons, Senator Hastings, all watched her with silent condemnation. They were clients who'd shopped in her store, women whose cards she'd read, civic leaders whom she'd helped raise money for charity. Everyone present had been a victim in the crimes. Was that why they'd jammed into the courtroom? To ensure justice was served?

Linda sat beside the senator, her hands clenched in her lap, a frown pulling at her full mouth. Biting down on her lip, she looked about the room and gripped the edge of her seat as if she wanted to come to Rachel's defense, but was too afraid to move. Rachel didn't blame her. How did a person fight the wealthy? She wished she knew. But she thanked God that, besides her family, there was at least one person who hadn't condemned her already.

Jackson entered the room, hurrying forward and passing through the swinging gate. Stopping beside Larry Morrison, he bent to whisper something to her attorney, who tensed, then shook his head. Whatever Jackson said next had Mr Morrison running his hand over his receding brow and nodding.

Apparently satisfied, Jackson returned to the back of the room, where he stood with his arms folded across his chest. With disarming accuracy, his fixed stare landed on her.

Rachel's knees buckled, but the guard's grip on her arm kept her from sinking to the floor. What had Jackson told her lawyer? Surely nothing that would help her, but would he go out of his way to see that the charges held? Her heart hammered against her chest. She took small, gulping breaths. Her vision dimmed as shivery pulses of light exploded before her eyes. Someone wanted her in jail and it was going to happen. No matter what she did or said, no one would listen. Not the judge, her attorney. And most importantly, not Jackson.

The guard led her to her seat. Judge Reiman, an elderly man with a horseshoe of snow-white hair and a face lined by years of witnessing the sins of his fellow man, entered through a side door. The bailiff announced for everyone to rise.

After the formality, Rachel remained standing beside Mr Morrison.

'Miss Gold,' Judge Reiman said in a voice that boomed with authority and intimidation. 'You have been formally charged on one count of theft. Do you have anything you would care to add before I determine bail?'

'Your Honor,' Mr Morrison said, 'before we proceed any further, I'd like to move that all charges against my client be dismissed.'

Rachel's attention snapped to her attorney, who continued looking straight ahead as if she weren't there. A series of gasps and the stirring of bodies disturbed the austere quiet.

Judge Reiman didn't pound his gavel, but gave the audience a warning glare that had the same silencing effect. 'That's a highly unusual request, Mr Morrison. Would you care to expand on the reasoning behind it?'

'Evidence has recently been discovered by the police that will prove my client innocent.'

What evidence? she wanted to demand, but the prosecutor, Ms Kent, a woman in her late forties whose harsh, battled features gave her the look of a hound dog on the hunt, interrupted, 'I object, Your Honor. The accused was found with the stolen merchandise in her possession not an hour after it was reported missing. Obviously the defense is trying to create doubt so you will be lenient and reduce the amount of bail.'

'Judge Reiman, if you'll give me a . . .' Rachel's attorney glanced uneasily at the back door '. . . a few minutes, I'll prove that this hearing isn't necessary.'

'I'll listen to what the defense has to say.' The judge waived his hand dismissively at Ms Kent. 'Overruled.'

Rachel faced the back of the room and met Jackson's gaze. Her chest constricted painfully as she tried to sort out what was happening. Had he found the person responsible? If he had, that meant he'd continued his search. But he hadn't believed her, she'd been certain of it. When he'd managed to look at her, silent reproach had chilled his brown eyes. He'd refused to speak to her. But if evidence had been found, no one would have known to look for it except Jackson. She pressed her fingers to her mouth, too afraid to even hope she was right.

Senator Hastings rose from his seat and moved to the front to whisper something to the prosecutor. Tension pulsed from him in a dark aura, spreading out to electrify the room. Both the prosecutor and the senator tilted their heads to look at her. Rachel held their gazes, clenching her hands until her nails dug into her skin. The senator had orchestrated her immediate arrest; what was he trying to do to her now?

The normally congenial man finally straightened and returned to his seat, but not before sending Rachel a brief warning glare.

'If we could bring a television and VCR into the court,' Mr Morrison said, 'I'll prove the legal system has made a grave error in arresting this woman.'

A tape? From the corner of her eye Rachel saw her sister pale. She gripped her mother and Mark's hands, looking as if she wanted to flee. What kind of film could Jackson have found? And did it involve Penny? Had the tape been in her apartment? Or had Jackson, with all of his sophisticated equipment, recorded her doing something illegal? Rachel pressed her palms to the table to keep from collapsing into her seat. But if her sister was on the tape, why hadn't Penny been arrested yet? Why drag the hearing out?

'Your Honor, I must object,' Ms Kent demanded. 'This is a bail hearing. *If* Mr Morrison has discovered evidence that will vindicate Miss Gold, why wasn't it brought to my attention before now?'

Mr Morrison spread out his hands in a practised show for appeal. 'As I stated, I received the information only a few moments ago. Had Miss Gold not already been booked and her bail hearing set, I have no doubt the charges would have been dropped and she would have been released.'

'Reviewing evidence at this stage is highly unusual, Mr Morrison,' Judge Reiman said.

'I'm aware of that, Your Honor. However, if you'll allow me to proceed, you'll understand why I've made the request.'

'Very well . . .'

'Your Honor,' the prosecutor interrupted, her voice thinning with annoyance. 'This so-called evidence that Mr Morrison says he has should be introduced during trial, not at this hearing. We have no idea where this tape came from, or if it's been doctored. I must object to the defense's blatant attempt to undermine the rules that govern this court.'

'By breaking the rules Ms Kent is so concerned about,' Rachel's attorney returned, 'I believe we'll save time and taxpayers' dollars by preventing a trial that should never take place. As for where the tape came from, it was acquired by Dermont Technology, who has had Miss Gold under surveillance.'

'Though it goes against precedence,' the judge said, then nodded, 'you may continue.'

With an angry straightening of her shoulders, Ms Kent resumed her seat. Certain that her legs were liquefying, Rachel sat as well. She gripped her hands in her lap, afraid of what the next few minutes would reveal.

During the time it took for a maintenance man to roll in a four-foot-tall metal stand with a TV mounted on the top and a VCR on the shelf below, Rachel watched her attorney repeatedly pull a handkerchief from his pocket and wipe sweat from his brow. His hands visibly shook. Why was he so nervous? He'd been confident earlier. Why the change?

Leaning forward, she demanded in a whisper, 'What have you found?'

Folding the white cloth into a neat square, he stuffed it into the top pocket of his coat. 'There's no time to explain.'

'But . . .'

'Not now, Ms Gold.'

Positioning the TV so the judge and the audience

could see, the man plugged both units into the wall outlet, then left.

'Whenever you're ready, Mr Morrison,' Judge Reiman said.

'Um, Your Honor,' Rachel's attorney said, blowing out a breath, 'the um, evidence . . .'

'Mr Morrison, what is it?'

'If the court could grant the defense a few additional moments, there seems to have been a delay in bringing the tape.'

Ms Kent popped up from her seat. 'It's obvious there is no tape, Judge Reiman. The defense is merely trying to confuse matters so his client will receive a lesser bail.'

Rachel glanced around, as confused as everyone else in the room as to what was going on.

'There is a tape,' Mr Morrison said. 'Detective Hutchins took the video to I-Systems to have the footage enhanced. He should . . .'

There was a commotion at the back of the room as the detective pushed through the double doors, waving a cassette in the air. 'Your Honor, if I may?'

The reality and the consequences of what was happening suddenly clarified in Rachel's mind. Once the tape was played, she might be set free, but if the tape revealed what she feared most, her sister would be arrested instead. Rachel grabbed her attorney's coat sleeve and forced him to face her. Under her breath, she asked, 'What's on that tape?'

'I don't know.'

'*What?*'

353

'Mr Dermont asked that I request a delay. He said he had proof that would clear you and unveil the real thief.'

Rachel leaned back in her chair, sure she was going to vomit. She recalled Jackson's departing words, *'I've taken care of everything.'* He'd warned her that he would turn Penny in if he learned she was guilty. Had he found the evidence and intended to follow through with his threat? After spending half her life taking care of her family, she couldn't stop now. She had to prevent the tape from being viewed until she knew for certain that it wouldn't implicate her sister.

Mr Morrison gave her an annoyed look, then pulled away. She turned to Jackson with a silent plea. Her suspicions had to be wrong, but he merely watched her, his brow creased with a frown.

Her attorney took the tape from the detective, slipped the cassette into the player and reached for the play button.

'Stop!' Rachel cried, surprising herself and the rest of the room. 'There's no need to watch the tape. I confess. I . . . I stole from my customers.'

'Rachel!' Jackson's shout reverberated from the back of the room. The explosion of conversation and the pounding gavel joined the paralysing buzz in her mind. She heard her mother crying behind her, and Penny's urgent, disbelieving whispers, but Rachel couldn't face them. She couldn't bear to see the anguish on Emily's face, because she wouldn't be able to ease it.

Jackson jerked her around to face him. 'Damn it, Rachel, what the hell do you think you're doing?'

354

The rage in his eyes threw her off balance. 'Confessing.'

'You didn't do it.'

'Yes, I did.'

The gavel pounded once more, hammering the noise to silence. 'One more outburst and I'll clear the court,' Judge Reiman ordered. 'Young man, return to your seat, or I'll have you removed.'

Jackson gently shook her. 'Tell him the truth.'

From the corner of her vision, she saw her sister visibly shaking, watching them, her eyes widening with fear. 'I can't,' Rachel whispered.

The crack of the gavel made Rachel jump. 'Whoever you are, young man, return to your seat,' the judge demanded.

'Rachel,' Jackson pleaded, ignoring Judge Reiman, 'you made me believe in you.'

'But my sister . . .' The look he gave her forced her to stop.

'Trust me.'

'Miss Gold, what is going on here?' the judged asked in a barely tolerant voice. 'Are you pleading guilty to the charges?'

She wanted to trust Jackson, she loved him, but could she risk putting her sister's life in his hands? She felt as if she were balancing on a cliff, teetering on the edge. It didn't matter if she clung to the solid wall or took the plunging step off, her life would never be the same after today. She might lose her sister, her store, even Jackson – possibly all three, and there was nothing she could do to stop it from happening. She'd never been a gambler, but she knew there were times when you had to roll the dice in order to win. She'd given that advice to her clients countless times. If the man who didn't believe in trust needed hers, she had no choice but to give it to him.

She faced the judge. 'No, Your Honor. I'm not guilty.'

'This is absurd!' Senator Hastings rose to his feet.

'Darling, please.' Linda gripped his arm and tried to urge him back down beside her.

He pulled free and pointed at Rachel. 'This woman is a criminal who doesn't deserve bail!'

'May I remind you, Senator,' the judge said, his eyes narrowing, 'that you're not an officer of this court and have no say here.'

'Your Honor, Rachel Gold was invited into our homes to provide a service. Instead she helped herself to priceless antiques, one of which she was found holding. She just admitted to stealing it, only to change her mind. Don't you think that's a bit strange?'

'Yes, I do.'

The senator waved a hand to the TV. 'And you're going to waste everyone's time by watching a video?'

'That's correct.' Judge Reiman leaned back in his chair and focused a warning scowl at Senator Hastings. 'You may watch, Senator, or you may leave. Whichever you decide, you will do so without saying another word.'

The judge nodded to Mr Morrison. 'Proceed.'

As the tape began, Rachel didn't recognize anything in the grainy, black and white picture. The room seemed back-lit, as if the light-colored sofa, chair and coffee-table glowed in the dark. Nothing stirred for a full minute.

Jackson eased her into her chair. Quiet settled over the room, as if everyone held their breath along with her, waiting for her worst fears to materialize and she'd see her sister on the small screen.

A light changed, brightened to reveal the room in more detail. A movement on the couch caught her attention: a dark form slowly expanding. *Miss Bastet.* Rachel suddenly realized she was watching her own living room.

'You put your equipment in my house,' she whispered in disbelief. The detective's voice became background noise as he explained to everyone in the room what they were watching. Her mind grappled with denial and anger, but she was too stunned for either to form completely.

Jackson looked at her, his eyes lacking any trace of remorse. He'd promised he'd never invade her house with his surveillance equipment, and he'd gone back on his word. Her stomach roiled with nausea. She felt invaded, impotent with a surge of helpless fury. How long had the camera been installed? Before their first kiss? Or after they'd made love? Was there more than one?

'Watch,' Jackson said.

She linked her fingers together in her lap and focused on the screen. After stretching, Miss Bastet began licking her paw and cleaning her face. Over and over again. Rachel knew the cat's routine. Miss Bastet would groom one side of her face, then the

357

other until her coat gleamed. The cat paused, sitting up and meowing to something off screen. A shadow passed over the carpet.

'What was that?' Rachel asked, sitting up straight.

The flash of an arm appeared on the right side of the TV as someone walked past. Miss Bastet turned her head, watching whoever was moving through Rachel's house. Then the person entered the camera's range, bending over the table. The fuzzy image revealed dark hair, and a gray, loose-fitting coat. When he straightened, Rachel's gaze went to the table – where the statue of David now sat.

'Oh, my God.'

The person turned, moving directly into the camera's lens, catching the thief full in the face. The ensuing gasps echoed like the resounding whoosh of a trap door falling open. Mr Morrison hit the pause button, freezing the pale eyes, the features that were too hazy to be discounted as Rachel's.

'As you can see, the face on the video is blurred,' Detective Hutchins said. 'After Mr Dermont informed me he'd had Miss Gold under surveillance and that his company had a tape that might clarify matters, we took the video to I-Systems to have it digitized.' Hutchins produced a large manila envelope and withdrew several pictures. He handed one to the prosecutor, the judge, her attorney, and finally one to Rachel. 'They were able to enhance the resolution and reveal the real thief.'

The photo trembled in Rachel's hands as she stared at the desperate face of a woman. It was the face of a childhood friend, a senator's fiancée, a ghostly image of a stranger who had tried to send her to jail.

It was the beautiful face of Linda Monroe.

CHAPTER 21

Rachel lurched to her feet, looking to where Linda was seated with the senator. Her chair was empty. Detective Hutchins noticed her absence at the same time as Rachel. He pulled a cellphone from his coat pocket and dialed a number, issuing orders to whomever he'd called.

He hurried to Senator Hastings side and urged him up from his seat. 'Sir, I'll need you to come with me.'

'What's going on here?' Jerking free, the senator brushed a hand down his suit.

The detective withdrew another photo from the envelope and handed it to the senator. 'Your fiancée was the one who stole the statue and planted it in Miss Gold's house. Now, if you'll come with me.' As they reached the door, Rachel could hear the detective ask, 'Do you know where she might have gone?'

Looking confused, his face flushing with distress, the senator stammered, 'She . . . she said she was going to the ladies' room.'

'It doesn't matter. We'll find her.'

Judge Reiman cracked his gavel against the desk. 'I suppose the evidence is satisfactory enough for the prosecution to drop all charges against Miss Gold.'

Ms Kent rose while gathering her papers into a neat stack. 'Yes, Your Honor. The prosecution will dismiss the charges immediately.'

Pandemonium erupted around Rachel. Everything happened so fast and loud she couldn't absorb it all. She heard her sister squeal and her mother thanking God. A handful of reporters swarmed the room, each one shouting questions over the others. There were outcries, the banging of the gavel, and repeated warnings from the judge. People surged against the wood partition behind her, but she couldn't register who they were.

Slowly, she sank to her chair and lowered her face to her hands. *She'd been cleared. Penny hadn't been arrested.* The phrases repeated over and over, filling her mind until she couldn't hear anything else. She thought she should cry with relief, or at least laugh, but she couldn't feel anything past the numbness swimming in her mind.

'It's over, Rachel.'

She sensed Jackson kneeling in front of her, felt his hands on her arms. She straightened and met his steadfast, unrelenting stare. He'd known neither she nor Penny had stolen the statue, yet he'd kept the information to himself. He'd let her agonize over her family's fate when a few simple words would have ended her frightening ordeal. 'Why didn't you tell me?'

361

He glanced at her fingers clenched in her lap. He wrapped one hand around both of hers, enveloping her in his heat. She realized with a start that she was cold, achingly cold. The brittle feeling went clear to her bones, cutting into her soul.

When he met her gaze, there was pain in his eyes, pain and guilt and regret. Emotions he'd always kept hidden. She didn't want to see them now.

'We weren't certain who was on the video until an hour ago. Detective Hutchins didn't want to reveal the evidence until we knew for sure.'

'So you left me sitting in a jail cell, terrified that I might go to prison?' She pulled free of his hold. 'You let me doubt my sister when you knew she wasn't involved in any of this!'

'I had no choice, damn it!' He glanced up when Emily and Penny crowded in to hug her. He helped Rachel to her feet and stepped back to give her family room.

'Oh, Rachel, I'm not sure what just happened,' Emily said, cupping Rachel's face in her hands. 'But I knew you didn't steal anything.'

'No kidding,' Penny said, scowling at Jackson. 'How did you get mixed up in this thing, anyway?'

Jackson wedged between the two women and took Rachel's arm, steering her away. 'She'll tell you about it later; right now we have something to straighten out.'

Before Rachel could protest, he ushered her past the judge's bench to a side room. The female guard who'd brought her to the courtroom stepped forward, took Rachel's other arm and pulled both her and Jackson to a halt.

'You aren't allowed to pass through here, sir. Once she's released you can pick her up in the jail lobby.'

Grinding his jaw into an inflexible line, he glared at the officer before finally relenting. 'All right.' He faced Rachel, his stance resolute and stubborn, and possessing more strength than she could withstand. 'I'm taking you home and I won't be leaving until you listen to what I have to say.'

The guard didn't give Rachel the chance to reply, for which she was grateful. She'd been given a reprieve from jail, but her freedom felt like a boulder strapped to her back. Not knowing what to think or believe, she turned and left the frenzied room.

Standing in the middle of her sunroom, afternoon light beamed through the windows, warming her like a welcoming quilt, enfolding her in familiar scents and sounds. She needed this, the normality and comfort that being surrounded by her things gave her. After arriving home, she'd showered, washing away the last twenty-four hours, reluctant to leave until the pipes had emptied of hot water. Slipping into a linen shift dress, she'd retrieved her amulet from her jewelry box.

Now, cradling the pendant in her palm, she traced the symbols with the tips of her fingers and sat on the rattan loveseat, rearranging her dress beneath her legs. She stared out of the window to the stand of oaks lining her yard. She'd always thought of them as her cocoon, keeping her world protected and hidden away.

Now that she was back, she thought it might be some time before she left again.

Her release from jail had been a delayed, confusing process. Linda had been found and arrested before she'd managed to escape the courthouse. The senator had demanded she be released until he'd learned that Monica Beaumont was really Linda Monroe, then he'd had his hands full explaining her duplicity to the hungry press.

Though Linda hadn't been forthcoming with her reasons for framing Rachel, Detective Hutchins surmised that Linda had been afraid Rachel would reveal her secret past, ruining her chance to marry the senator.

Except Rachel had had the stolen necklace in her store long before she'd known about Linda's deceit. The detective had contacted Mr Weatherby, the auctioneer, and had confirmed that Penny had bought the necklace from him . . . after he'd purchased it from Linda. An unfortunate coincidence, but Weatherby's was known for dealing with extravagant pieces. Evidently the rise up the social ladder must have been an expensive one, and by stealing from her new, rich friends Linda had found a way to fund the trip.

The only happy news of the day was learning that Penny and Mark hadn't flown to Mexico to evade being arrested – they'd gotten married. Penny had blurted the news the moment Jackson had ushered Rachel out of jail. Penny had smugly informed her older sister that she didn't need Rachel to worry about her any more, she had a husband to do that now. Her young, headstrong and impressionable Penny was now a married woman. Rachel still wasn't sure how to react to that.

Propping her elbow on the back of the couch, she rested her head on her bent forearm and listened to the hesitant fall of Jackson's footsteps behind her.

They hadn't spoken a word since leaving the police station, or, more correctly, she hadn't spoken to him. He'd cajoled, pleaded, even threatened her to get her to talk, but she couldn't, not yet. There were so many troubling issues to deal with, she didn't know where to start, or even if she wanted to. She'd known from the beginning that she risked being hurt if she became involved with him; she'd just never realized how deep the hurt would go.

He stepped past her and sat so she was forced to look at him instead of the trees blooming with spring. He'd shed his coat and held Miss Bastet in his arms as if they were the best of friends. As much as she wanted to, she couldn't look away and she couldn't stop her heart from beating painfully against her chest. Wrapping her free hand around her amulet, she wondered if feeling this kind of heart-wrenching loss was the reason some people were afraid to love. Maybe they were right, she thought, feeling tears well in her eyes. The pain you risked wasn't worth it.

Blinking rapidly and looking away, she admitted that was a lie. If she could erase the last day and go back to the first night Jackson had made love to her, she would. If given the chance to recapture the pure joy, the feeling of completion she felt with him, she wouldn't have to think twice, she'd grab the opportunity with both hands and run. Despite his doubts and her common sense, she'd fallen in love with him. But she would survive. Survival was what she did best.

'Are you hungry?'

She shook her head, unable to answer.

'I could make some tea.'

She closed her eyes, wanting to weep at the quiet persistence in his voice.

He took her hand and held on when she pulled against him. 'Don't shut me out, Rachel. I can't stand this silent treatment.'

Opening her eyes, she gave him a look that said *tough*. She pushed away from the couch, intending to go to her room, lock her door and stay there until he decided to give up and leave. She made it as far as the threshold before Jackson caught her around the waist and hauled her back against him. His other arm came across her chest, his hand clamping her shoulder, effectively pinning her body to his.

'Do you know what I went through while you were in jail, knowing I might not be able to find the evidence to clear you?' he asked, his voice a low strangle of emotion. 'I was out of my mind, Rachel, afraid that I'd fail. All I could think about was you being convicted and imprisoned, and there wasn't a damn thing I could do about it.'

Feeling a crack in the dam that held her emotions, she said, 'You could have told me that you believed I was innocent. I thought you were working with the police to prove I was guilty. Do *you* have any idea how much that hurt me?'

'I know, baby, I know.' He kissed her temple, bending to press his face into the curve of her neck. 'I wanted to tell you.'

'I cared about you, Jackson. I wanted . . . God help me,' she whispered as her throat constricted with the need to cry, 'I thought . . . I was stupid enough to believe you cared about me.'

'I don't *care* about you, Rachel.'

Jerking as if he'd slapped her instead of murmuring against her ear, she pulled away and pressed a hand to her stomach, certain she was about to be ill. She gripped the door jamb to steady herself and forced air into her lungs. Her mind swam dizzily, and she had the insane urge to laugh at herself for being a fool.

Jackson took her by the arms and turned her to face him. She was too numb with disbelief to stop him. 'Caring is too small a word to describe how I feel about you,' he said with such uncharacteristic tenderness that she shook her head.

'I love you, Rachel.'

'No, you don't.'

'Yes, I do.' He threaded his fingers up through her hair, holding her so she couldn't turn away. He signed and clenched his jaw, looking determined and resolved all at once. 'Saying I love you doesn't begin to describe how much you mean to me.'

'What? What are you saying?'

The brown of his eyes softened, intensifying with a hunger she'd never seen before. Something inside

367

him had changed, and she knew it wasn't her imagination or wishful thinking. Nor was it a trick caused by the light flooding the room. The emotions he felt were real, and he was going to let her see them.

'I trust you.' The torn, heartfelt honesty in his eyes crumbled the resistance she'd been clinging to. 'Long before I knew for certain that you weren't responsible for the thefts, I trusted you.'

He shook her slightly. 'Do you understand what I'm saying?'

She understood. His lack of faith in her had been their greatest barrier. Had he really changed so much in such a short time? She wanted to believe he had, but it was almost too much to hope for. And the strength of her hope, the need to believe him, frightened her.

She needed time to understand what was happening. Grasping the other reason she'd been furious with him, she said, 'I want that camera, and anything else you've put in my home, taken out immediately.'

He clenched his jaw as he smoothed his palms down her neck to her shoulders. 'You understand why I wired your house, don't you?'

'You went back on your word is what I understand.'

A stubborn fire smoldered in his eyes. 'And I'd do it again if it meant clearing you and Penny.'

'But you weren't sure that was what would happen.'

'No,' he admitted. 'But I had to do something. And security is what I do best.'

Since she couldn't argue with the outcome and its benefits, she crossed her arms beneath her breasts, and said sullenly, 'I want that equipment gone.'

'Will tomorrow be soon enough?'

She nodded.

'Good, because I don't want company right now.'

'You're not staying, Jackson. I'm tired, and I'd like you to leave.'

Ignoring her, he drew her close until her crossed arms butted his chest. 'I've been thinking about how empty my townhouse is, and how much I like being here with you.'

She tilted her chin in defense against the heat rising from his body, from the sheer need to be engulfed by his presence. 'Hire a decorator, Dermont.'

He shook his head and placed a kiss at her temple, then another beneath her ear. 'I have something else in mind.'

'Stop that.' She turned her head, but it only gave him better access to the sensitive spots along her throat.

'Don't you want to know what I've been thinking about?'

Holding back a moan as he nipped her skin with his teeth, she swallowed and managed to say, 'All right. Tell me.'

'I could move in here.'

'And live in sin?' She tried to twist away, she really did, but the attempt failed miserably. 'I don't think so.'

'It didn't bother you when we spent the last two days together.' He slid his hands around her back, his palms molding to the curves of her spine. He trailed his fingers down the indention to her lower back, where he drew small circles.

Rachel's breath caught. 'A temporary lapse of sanity.'

He chuckled, pulling away to meet her gaze. 'Actually, what I have in mind is something a bit more permanent.'

'What are you hinting at? You want to buy my house?'

'No, I want you to marry me.'

Her mouth dropped open, and the abrupt buzzing in her ears became so loud, she was certain she hadn't heard him right. 'Excuse me?'

'And if you don't say yes, I'll be forced to drag you to the floor right here and make love to you until you change your mind.'

'Marry you?' Marry Jackson? The need to believe he wasn't teasing burned in her like a ferocious, hungry fire. She'd never let herself hope, even dream that he would want her this much.

'I'm not leaving until you agree to be my wife.'

'Well, when you put it like that . . .' Tears brimmed her eyes. 'My answer is no.'

'No?' The corner of his mouth curved with an endearing grin.

'Absolutely not,' she said, wondering where she found the strength to deny him.

His gaze skimmed down her face to her breasts and crossed arms. 'That sounds like a challenge, Ms Gold.'

Her nipples pebbled and her breasts filled with

heat as his stare lingered on her. She knew it would only be a matter of seconds before her resistance crumbled to ash. 'Take it however you like. I'm not marrying you.'

'Yes, you are,' he whispered. 'I know you're mad at me, but I'm hoping you'll forgive me.'

His fingers slipped the straps of her tank dress from her shoulders.

'What are you doing?'

'Carrying out my promise.'

'Jackson . . .' Unable to resist, Rachel lowered her arms, letting the fabric slide over her skin. In a soft swoosh, the dress pooled at her feet. Except for the amulet that hung between her breasts, she stood naked before him, her body tense and sensitive, anticipating the moment that he'd touch her.

Lifting the amulet, he pulled it off over her head and held it in his palm, staring down at it for a moment. 'You don't need this any more.'

She reached for it automatically. 'I . . .'

He held it out of her reach. 'We have passion, Rachel.'

He cleared his throat. 'This isn't easy for me to say, because I've never said it before. I love you. No one has ever made me as happy as you do. And I can't help but trust you. So you see?' he said, dropping the necklace on to her dress. 'We don't need a symbol for love, because we have each other.'

Her entire body trembling with relief and joy and yearning, she cupped his face between her hands. 'Have I mentioned how much I love you?'

Burrowing his face against her palms, he said, 'As a matter of fact, you haven't.'

'I'll tell you how much,' she promised, tilting her head so her lips almost brushed his. 'While you're trying to convince me to marry you.'

He gathered her close, grazing his palms over her back, touching her, cupping her body against his where she belonged. 'You've got a deal.'

The falling sun dipped behind aged and gnarled oaks, casting lacy shadows into the warm, flower-scented room. A baby squirrel sat upright on the window ledge, his head cocked, listening to the brush of wind, the distant laughter of children several yards away. The old house creaked with familiar, comfortable sounds, acknowledging another day of settling in.

Surrounded by whispers and tender, murmuring sighs, a cat curled into the loveseat's cushion. Closing her eye, she purred softly, having found contentment.

THE EXCITING NEW NAME
IN WOMEN'S FICTION!

PLEASE HELP ME TO HELP YOU!

Dear *Scarlet* Reader,

As Editor of *Scarlet* Books I want to make sure that the books I offer you every month are up to the high standards *Scarlet* readers expect. And to do that I need to know a little more about you and your reading likes and dislikes. So please spare a few minutes to fill in the short questionnaire on the following pages and send it to me.

Looking forward to hearing from you,

Sally Cooper

Editor-in-Chief, *Scarlet*

QUESTIONNAIRE

Please tick the appropriate boxes to indicate your answers

1 Where did you get this Scarlet title?
Bought in supermarket ☐
Bought at my local bookstore ☐ Bought at chain bookstore ☐
Bought at book exchange or used bookstore ☐
Borrowed from a friend ☐
Other (please indicate) _____

2 Did you enjoy reading it?
A lot ☐   A little ☐   Not at all ☐

3 What did you particularly like about this book?
Believable characters ☐   Easy to read ☐
Good value for money ☐   Enjoyable locations ☐
Interesting story ☐   Modern setting ☐
Other _____

4 What did you particularly dislike about this book?
_____

5 Would you buy another Scarlet book?
Yes ☐   No ☐

6 What other kinds of book do you enjoy reading?
Horror ☐   Puzzle books ☐   Historical fiction ☐
General fiction ☐ Crime/Detective ☐ Cookery ☐
Other (please indicate) _____

7 Which magazines do you enjoy reading?
1. _____
2. _____
3. _____

And now a little about you –
8 How old are you?
Under 25 ☐   25–34 ☐   35–44 ☐
45–54 ☐   55–64 ☐   over 65 ☐

cont.

9 What is your marital status?

Single ☐   Married/living with partner   ☐

Widowed ☐   Separated/divorced   ☐

10 What is your current occupation?

Employed full-time ☐   Employed part-time ☐

Student ☐   Housewife full-time ☐

Unemployed ☐   Retired ☐

11 Do you have children? If so, how many and how old are they?

_____

_____

12 What is your annual household income?

under $15,000	☐	or	£10,000	☐
$15–25,000	☐	or	£10–20,000	☐
$25–35,000	☐	or	£20–30,000	☐
$35–50,000	☐	or	£30–40,000	☐
over $50,000	☐	or	£40,000	☐

Miss/Mrs/Ms _____

Address _____

_____

_____

Thank you for completing this questionnaire. Now tear it out – put it in an envelope and send it, before 31 March 1999, to:

Sally Cooper, Editor-in-Chief

USA/Can. address
SCARLET c/o London Bridge
85 River Rock Drive
Suite 202
Buffalo
NY 14207
USA

UK address/No stamp required
SCARLET
FREEPOST LON 3335
LONDON W8 4BR
Please use block capitals for address

FIGOL/9/98

Scarlet titles coming next month:

FIND HER, KEEP HER   Judy Jackson

Daniel St Clair is everything Jess Phillips should avoid. She's a career woman – fighting to make a living in a man's world. Daniel, she tries to convince herself, is a pompous university intellect with a pretty face and a nice body! When Jess accepts Daniel's help, she gives in to the physical attraction between them. Why not? They're both unattached, intelligent adults . . . but Jess should have remembered that romance plays by its own rules and it plays to win!

THE TROUBLE WITH TAMSIN   Julie Garratt

Tamsin runs away from love but soon discovers that 'out of sight' doesn't necessarily mean 'out of mind.' She likes men – she might even be in love with one of them: cheating Patric Faulkner, lost love Vaughn Herrick, and the attractively menacing Craig Andrews. Then there is Mark Langham - the one person Tam can always rely on to be there for her. But Mark's patience is wearing thin, and it is only when she begins to lose him that Tam realizes just where her true happiness lies. But is she too late for love?

JOIN THE CLUB!

Why not join the *Scarlet* Readers' Club – you can have four exciting new reads delivered to your door every other month for only £9.99, plus TWO FREE BOOKS WITH YOUR FIRST MONTH'S ORDER!

Fill in the form below and tick your two first books from those listed:

1. *Never Say Never* by Tina Leonard ☐
2. *The Sins of Sarah* by Anne Styles ☐
3. *Wicked in Silk* by Andrea Young ☐
4. *Wild Lady* by Liz Fielding ☐
5. *Starstruck* by Lianne Conway ☐
6. *This Time Forever* by Vickie Moore ☐
7. *It Takes Two* by Tina Leonard ☐
8. *The Mistress* by Angela Drake ☐
9. *Come Home Forever* by Jan McDaniel ☐
10. *Deception* by Sophie Weston ☐
11. *Fire and Ice* by Maxine Barry ☐
12. *Caribbean Flame* by Maxine Barry ☐

ORDER FORM

SEND NO MONEY NOW. Just complete and send to **SCARLET READERS' CLUB, FREEPOST, LON 3335, Salisbury SP5 5YW**

Yes, I want to join the *SCARLET* READERS' CLUB* and have the convenience of 4 exciting new novels delivered directly to my door every other month! Please send me my first shipment now for the unbelievable price of £9.99, plus my TWO special offer books absolutely free. I understand that I will be invoiced for this shipment and FOUR further *Scarlet* titles at £9.99 (including postage and packing) every other month unless I cancel my order in writing. I am over 18.

Signed ....

Name (IN BLOCK CAPITALS)...

Address (IN BLOCK CAPITALS)..

....

Town.. **Post Code**...............................

Phone Number ....

As a result of this offer your name and address may be passed on to other carefully selected companies. If you do not wish this, please tick this box ☐.